About the Author

Maria is a minister's wife living in north-west England and is actively involved in her local church and wider Christian organisations. She has always loved writing and also enjoys swimming, walking, spending time with friends and a good cup of coffee.

The Boy from the Snow

Maria Johnson

The Boy from the Snow

Olympia Publishers

London

www.olympiapublishers.com

OLYMPIA PAPERBACK EDITION

A CIP catalogue record for this title is
available from the British Library.

ISBN: 978-1-84897-952-9

First Published in 2018

Olympia Publishers
60 Cannon Street
London
EC4N 6NP

Printed in Great Britain

Dedication

"For my husband, my parents and my brother, for all the love and support they have always shown."

"To God, be the glory, great things He hath done!
So loved He the world that He gave us His Son!"

Part One

Chapter One

I awoke with a sudden start, panting and drenched in cold sweat. My eyes flew open into complete darkness, for it was still the dead of night. The vivid dream that had woken me was still present, so I closed my eyes tight and tried hard not to let the images fade. Catching the dream, however, remained ever elusive as my mind returned to reality – it was like trying to catch one's own shadow. Eventually I gave up trying to recall the lost fragments of it and simply turned to ponder what my conscious mind could remember.

This dream was no stranger to me; on the contrary, I had had it countless times throughout my life. Each time, despite its unpleasant nature, I had felt an urgent instinct to know its meaning – and each time I had failed. The dream comes from the first moments of my life I can remember; a time when, as a boy, I was lost in the snow. I was not long three, so it was far too young for me to now recall any specific details, but my parents had often related the account to me. They searched for me for two whole days, during one of the worst blizzards our kingdom had ever known. They have always said the fact they were able to find me was nothing less than a miracle. My parents fed me warm milk mixed with herbs, honey and spices, as a tonic to aid my recovery. My parents told me I slept a deep slumber for four days, but I could vividly remember flittering moments of weakness – of high fever, delusion and confusion. Whenever I woke, my mother would feed me yet more of the milk tonic. It took me three weeks before I regained normal strength and could leave the house.

The frequency of the dream had decreased since childhood and now as an adult, I only have it rarely – indeed, this was only the second dream I had experienced in almost a year. The contents of the dream did not seem so strange at a surface level, but what compelled me most was that I always woke from this dream as from a nightmare, as I had done tonight, in shivers and a sweat, even in the heat of summer. I always felt as though something hidden had eluded me.

That was why my mind tried to catch the images as they faded away, as I was desperate to learn this last part that forever remained hidden and seemed to perturb me so. The last image I could ever hold on to was of the thick snow of the storm falling swiftly to the ground, with a combination of deep despair, presumably at being so lost and alone. In the dream, I looked skyward to see the swirling blizzard and the frozen flakes landing on my face – and this was always the point at which I woke so abruptly.

As of every previous occasion, the dreams fully left me as I awoke further still. I opened my eyes again, peering into the darkness that surrounded me. Though I could not see it, I knew well the stone slabs that sloped above me, and I could hear my brothers sleeping in their beds. Some were sleeping quietly whilst others were snoring loudly – but over the years I had grown used to the noises of slumber. I was a soldier here in the Kingdom of Gaeson and had spent much of my enlisted time sleeping here.

Each of these chambers was vast, holding up to fifty soldiers in each – and this was repeated in the other three chambers, positioned on each corner of the castle walls. Two of the chambers, one in this tower and one in another, were inhabited by our female warriors. We all also had abodes within the castle town itself, for when we were recuperating from battle or were on leave.

A chill bit deeper into me now, and I shifted on the thin bed and shivered. It was not yet the season of spring, and there were still furious squalls and the dreadful cold that seeped into your bones; indeed, presently my muscles had grown stiff from the cold and I could barely feel my fingers. I gathered my blanket closer about me, but it was thin and ragged and so did little to keep me warm. In the end there was nothing for it; I was wide awake. I sat up and stretched my neck gently. One of the men began snoring loudly; to my surprise my brothers remained asleep, despite the noise stretching across the length of the chamber.

I ignored my brothers' snoring, running my hands through my hair distractedly to find it was now matted and damp with sweat. I was thankful for the length of my hair that stretched ran untidily to the start of my neck and around my ears, protecting them for the most part against the fierce elements. My hair was a dark brown yet had a tinge of red, not unlike a leaf's colour during the autumn. I then moved to clench and unclench my numb hands into fists, attempting to circulate warmth back into them. This done, I now felt my eyes were itchy from dust and rubbed them. I was never sure if I liked the colour of my eyes; they were dark blue with flecks of grey, giving the appearance of a storm. My eyes often made me seem severe, even when I was jovial.

Now I was fully awake, I realised how acutely thirsty I was. I gave a sigh and flopped back down, hoping to be able to ignore my parched throat. I turned over and over again, but the thirst would not desist. On the contrary, it grew stronger and stronger until I could think of nothing else, and the mysterious contents of my dream seemed a distant, irrelevant past. I forced myself to still and closed my eyes, but that only made my throat stand out all the more. Eventually I sighed in annoyance and stood slowly, soon flinching as my bare feet touched the icy stone floor.

I sneaked past the bunks to the window where the water jug sat, as silently as possible so as not to disturb my brothers. As I inched my way forwards, I then reflected on how perhaps I did not need to be so stealthy with the loud snoring of one particular neighbour. I continued quietly regardless until I reached the window. I poured myself a generous goblet of water from the jug; as I did I perceived it was cold – nigh, frozen. Still, my thirst was great and so I drank, each swallow causing a small gasp as my body reacted to the freezing temperature. As my thirst was quenched, I grew idly curious to see the view outside.

Bracing myself, I slowly pushed the wooden window frame open. There was no fierce wind or storm, but even though the night was all stillness, the cold still bit deep into me. Due to the disorienting dark, it took me a few seconds to register the landscape before me. In the next moment, I dropped my cup from my hand in shock; it crashed to the floor, causing the water to pool across the stone.

"We're trying to sleep, be silent," an irritated voice complained.

"Be silent, pray," another brother called, but I was too transfixed by the scene the window afforded me to pay these men any heed. For in the distance was a sea of golden lights, all headed in our direction, the bearers of which looked to be a mass of an army. In short, an army was heading right for me.

"Close that window!" a third man shouted.

"Awake!" I shouted, as I raced to the corner of the room. I was met with further groans and curses as my brothers sat up, shaking their heads. My hands groped for the rope of the alarm bell. "Wake up! Wake up!" I shouted repeatedly, as I tugged on the rope with all my strength. "Enemy at the gates!"

As soon as I sounded the bell, the complaints ceased and all were rapidly rousing from their beds. We had been trained to respond to the alarm and as such dressed noiselessly in our haste. I ran back to my own bed and gathered my clothes, throwing on my tunic.

"What is happening, Daniel?" It was John, my oldest friend, who spoke a minute later, already mostly dressed and crossing the room towards me.

"I do not know," I answered quickly. "It is strange that the watchmen did not sound their horns," I commented with a frown. "They are faithful and sharp; something must have prevented them."

John nodded in agreement as I pulled on my leather boots. This done, we headed for the chamber door and rapidly began to descend the stone spiral steps in the direction of the armoury. We had long been trained for an attack, responding to feigned horns, and so we marched as one. The soldiers from the other regimental chambers in our tower were filing out behind us, and soon all I could hear was the thudding uniformity of our steps upon the stone. Within a minute or two we had reached our destination, and each soldier began putting on armour.

"My parched throat was very fortunate," I realised aloud, as I placed my loose chain mail over my tunic and then fitted my breastplate into place. Otherwise we would still be slumbering unawares, and the attack would be a terrible surprise. But by now the whole castle was alerted to the danger, for the alarm bell I had rung had triggered the horns, which were continually sounding across the whole castle. The men and women who were not in our army, but chose to fight, would soon be called upon to fight in reserve if we could not hold the castle. The evacuation to the caves of the elderly, children, and women who chose not to fight but to protect and aid, would already be underway. The caves were located beyond the north end of our castle, built deep into the hill upon which our kingdom was based.

"Yes," a voice said next to me, "we can all praise God that you were thirsty."

I glanced up and smirked, already knowing who the voice belonged to. It was Aife, an archer I knew well, who was picking up her weapons. Aife was fairly tall, with pale blue eyes and hair the colour of oak, which was tied in her usual various braids and tethered in an intricate bun around her head. Apart from her bow, her weapon of choice was a spear, rather than a blade, which she executed with seemingly effortless ability and will. She was as fiercely loyal a friend as she was as fiercely able, one of the best female warriors in our army. She also had a warm heart and a sardonic sense of humour, which she had just demonstrated – and her wryness always served to lighten our spirits. Aife was one year younger than I, and as such I had known her almost as long as the eight years I had served in His Majesty's army.

I was now prepared for battle, as I placed my sword in its sheath and picked up my shield. As I turned to join the line of soldiers filing out of the armoury, I caught a glimpse of dark curls and knew at once they belonged to Her Highness Princess Evelyn, who was picking up her shield and a small dagger. I joined the other soldiers in bowing my head as we walked past. Princess Evelyn would be on her way to aid the people in the caves and defend it, along with twenty or so others, should the walls be breached. The caves continued from our castle to a secret entrance by the great lake, so Princess Evelyn and her warriors would hinder the enemy while the people escaped.

We were marching again in continued haste, now from the armoury to a medium-sized hall, where we often gathered for briefings or to discuss training or strategy. We already had our assigned positions, but we would meet briefly here to be instructed by the captain of the guard. As we filed in, I saw the captain was there before us and was duly impressed, as I had been the one to raise the alarm and we had dressed in such haste – but then it was his duty to be here first in order to lead us. We came to form our ranks before him, and I was greatly encouraged at our number – we totalled almost six hundred soldiers. But then I remembered the view from the window of the sea of lit torches that never seemed to end. I prayed earnestly that my mind had manipulated the view, that my imaginings had far exaggerated their forces.

The captain was a man of tall, sturdy build. He looked like he could be as much as well into his forties, for his charcoal hair was flecked all over with grey, and his face, though sharp, was weary after years of battle. His eyes were a deep, vast blue which could reassure and speak comfort in one moment, but could just as well spark fear in the next. His armour befitted his rank; it gleamed as though it was pure silver, like when the moonlight shone on the great lake. The captain waited a few seconds, until our movements had fully ceased and we stood together before him, waiting to be addressed.

"Good evening," the captain greeted us, "although I am unsure how good our evening is." He placed his arms behind his back, surveying us for a moment. "I have orders from His Majesty King Reghan that we and the other regiments are to advance upon the army." He paused here, and I could feel the tension in the room grow, becoming almost as tangible as the blade of my sword. The fact we would soon be fighting with those marching upon us was obvious, but we had all still prayed it would not come to this. We had not had an enemy at our door in three years, and as such were no doubt accustomed to a life of comfortable peace. We had several new recruits joining our ranks, some of them barely out of boyhood. No matter how much training we did, nothing could truly prepare us for the horrors of the first real taste of battle.

"Do not be afraid," the captain continued, speaking into the dismay and fear that threatened to steal into all our hearts. "We do not know who they are yet, as they have not yet raised their standard. Nor do we know how vast their numbers are, though they do appear to be many." Some of the more nervous among the men shifted their stance slightly; by and large, we remained motionless while the captain talked into the uncertainty of the night.

"We know they meant to take us by surprise, but now we know of them," the captain assured us. "Perhaps they felt they needed to come secretly into the night, in order to have an advantage. Well, now secret they are not. We do not know them, but we know ourselves – we know our strengths, our courage, and our loyalty to all that is good. That may be all we need to defend our people from this enemy at our door."

The captain concluded his speech and drew his sword, raising it into the air. As he did, a ray of moonlight glinted off his blade and gleamed at us. A series of clunks of metal followed as we followed suit and drew our own swords.

"For the king!" the captain declared.

"For the king," we echoed, raising our own swords high. The same metal clunks were repeated as we replaced our swords once again, for now. We turned and moved silently to our positions that we had practiced since I first joined the army. Tonight, however, we were all aware that this was not training. This battle, this night, was real. I kept my hand on the hilt of my sword, clutching it tightly. The feel of it beneath my hand comforted me.

I was an archer as well as a soldier, so I joined the other archers, with their strong bows and their arrows swift and true. Aife came to take her usual position beside me; John was placed on a lower castle wall elsewhere. She held her spear firmly in her hand, her bow and sheath of arrows still strapped to her back – as was mine; we need not ready them yet. I sensed her mood was grim yet determined, matching my own mood, and no doubt it was the same for every other soldier as we waited for war to begin.

I looked out from where we were perched, high as we were on the castle wall, to the mass of men still approaching, much nearer now. The beacons that lit them were still too far away to help us identify individual men; at the moment they seemed a blur, a mass of shapes, so many that I could not even begin to count them. I turned my gaze downwards to see the captain giving signals above us to other men and women. My sight shifted back out to the fields beyond our castle to the vast mass of men lit by many beacons, so many I could not even begin to count them. I tried to imagine the dismay on their faces, as by our own beacons they would see us ready and prepared for them rather than a castle that slumbered on unawares. This encouraged me further, but I still sensed a mixture of anxiety and disappointment, that the peace we had enjoyed was so abruptly ended.

Soon the captain stopped his calls for orders and we then simply stood, tense and ready, for the enemy to advance, as there was nothing to do now but wait until they stopped. We had already faintly heard the enemy's boots stamping upon the ground, and that crunching upon the grass and soil was increasing in volume with each passing moment. I had only been in two battles before myself, and already I felt fear rising up my throat, but I stood firm, swallowing my anxiety back down. The marching grew louder and louder until suddenly it stopped, and the enemy stood united before us. I now witnessed three men on horseback step out a few paces and then stop, still lit by beacons. At this distance, the men could be recognised, as could the standard he bore; it was the seal of our enemy, King Cedric. I heard sharp intakes of breath around me as others also now recognised him.

"This was not so unexpected," Aife murmured now under her breath. She had spoken true, as I suspected many of our brothers and sisters had assumed King Cedric had been behind this attack. We had not spoken of it, however, apart from Aife's comment, as talking of the enemy did nothing more than breed more fear, either through words of despair or false boasting and reassurances. King Cedric reigned in the Kingdom of Klumeck, to the northeast of here, near the very tall hills that were situated

18

along the middle of the island. The distance from our kingdom to Klumeck could be made in two days, as the terrain of further north made it much harder to travel. King Cedric also happened to be a distant cousin of King Reghan, whom we served. This seemed to bring even greater tension, as the bitterness and resentment resulting from their royal feud then hung in the air for the rest of us.

"That is not expected, however," Aife commented presently in a still grim but now confused tone.

I glanced out again and, to my own surprise, saw that another soldier bore a second standard, which hung atop our own castle walls. The standard they bore was the seal of Rheged, which was the greater kingdom we served. The flag showed two thick diagonal lines that met pointing upwards in the shape of an arrow. There were three ravens also on the flag: two either side of the tip of the arrow, with another placed beneath the tip where the lines met. The mystery was why King Cedric was donning Rheged's seal.

Rheged encompassed the whole of the northwest of this island. The capital Kingdom of Rheged was Caer Ligualid, where His Supreme Majesty King Urien reigned. This was greatly surprising, because although Klumeck was within Rheged's borders, it was a rogue kingdom that continued to rebel against His Majesty King Urien. It therefore seemed a matter of confusion and hypocrisy that King Cedric would don King Urien's seal, since he was currently not at peace with Rheged.

"Stand guard," the captain called out in a shout, and we looked down to where he stood on the lower castle wall again. "Do not it be fooled by Klumeck's standard; it must be deception of some kind. He is still our foe!" Here he loudly ended his speech and then we saw him depart in haste.

We continued drinking in the tense silence for a few minutes, and then heard the creaking of the large wooden door being unbolted, and the portcullis raising. But a moment later, we saw His Majesty King Reghan, the king whom we served, exiting the castle and gallop out into the field, accompanied by the captain and the personal guard, one of whom carried our own standard into the night, and another carried King Urien's seal-the seal that, for some unknown reason, Klumeck was also bearing.

The moment His Majesty King Reghan had set off into the battlefield, so had King Cedric and his escort and they now galloped towards each other hard, meeting across the hill in order to negotiate – though I did not deem a peaceful outcome likely, since Klumeck had marched all the way to us. There was surely one purpose on his mind – and that purpose was battle. As King Cedric came uphill, and King Reghan rode down, and the two met together, so did the guards escorting them with their torches and seals. Now, by the flickering light, we had chance to examine King Cedric closer than ever before.

I myself was studying him for the first time, as the last battle my people had had with him was three years before I had joined the army. I perceived him to be speaking fast, whilst his countenance was contorted in anger and his eyes hardened in rageful ferocity. King Cedric had a thick beard, though his hair itself had waned a little, showing his years – for his age I guessed late forties or even early fifties. As I pondered, the meeting ended abruptly; His Majesty King Reghan abruptly turned back around and rode back to the castle, the captain and personal guard on his heels. Sadly, then, I was to be proven right about my earlier prediction of war. We watched now as the door and portcullis opened once more, admitting them passage into the castle before it was slammed shut again.

Then there was silence. Moments passed tensely at an infinitely slow pace. I happened to glance down to where John stood as he looked back; we caught each other's eye before our gaze returned to straight ahead of us. Presently the captain gave a signal, and the other archers and I readied our arrows upon our bows. Then there was nothing but to wait for King Cedric's men to advance. Each breath we took seemed like a passing of a day as we waited. We drank in the ever tense air. It was the calm before the squall. Finally, I saw King Cedric and his men raise their swords. The archers raised their bows higher and pulled back their arrows tighter, my movements copying theirs.

"Charge!" All erupted into action as King Cedric shouted the order, his voice reaching out to us from down the hill across the still night. But the night was still no longer – now all was noise as King Cedric's army ran out to meet us, shouting as they ran. We held our arrows tautly in place.

"Fire!" the captain shouted. We all in unison released our arrows, letting them fly out into the night. We saw them pierce men's flesh, heard their cries as they fell down, but it barely made a dent in their forces. Quickly I retrieved another arrow, placed it on my bow.

"Fire!" the captain shouted again, and we obeyed, sending arrows into the night once more. "Fire at will!"

They were almost at our walls. I could see their large ladders; they would be climbing up within moments. My arrows pierced a few more men as the tall ladders emerged at the top of our wall. I swiftly dropped my bow and drew my sword in time to cut down the first man who had managed to climb all the way up his ladder. He fell to the ground, and I promptly moved on to the second.

My second parried my blow with more ability than the last; he now struck out and I dodged him. He lunged forth and I dodged again; he slashed out and this time I parried him. We did a dance of blade upon blade, metal hitting metal, each aiming for flesh. After a minute or so, I managed to dodge to the side, and as I avoided his blow, I pivoted and slashed out at his side, my blade finding home at a point underneath his chain mail. He staggered but still twirled and brought his blade towards me, but here I easily dodged him and put him to the sword also.

After four or five such confrontations, an enemy soldier attempted to strike me, lunging at me with force. I dropped to the floor to avoid it. Hastily I rolled across the ground, and as I did, my face touched the stone of the wall, already slick with blood. The soldier dived towards me and I thrust my sword up, sliding my blade into his stomach. With some effort, I pulled my sword clean and took a moment to catch my breath and wipe my face. I turned to see a man running towards me. I held out my blade, ready and awaiting him. Then at the last moment I dodged to the side, and in the brief spell where he continued running, he lost his footing and toppled over the castle wall. I then heard a growl behind me and instinctively raised up my sword; my senses served me well, for even though I could not see him, I thrust my sword up in the air behind me, just stopping his blade from falling upon my back.

This done, I swiftly pivoted on the spot to strike another blow. I perceived his eyes to be hardened in a particular frenzy; his face was particularly enraged. I pondered I might have just killed a close friend of his – but there was no time for remorse, and besides, were not they the ones who had marched upon us? What option did we have other to defend ourselves and our people? This soldier brought his sword down on me again and again with unquestionable force, and I knew I would not overpower him. I therefore timed my opportunity, and as he raised his sword high again, I ducked to the side and sliced his knee. The man staggered, dropping his sword. I saw I had the rare chance to spare him and butted him hard with the hilt of my sword; he fell to the floor unconscious. I stooped towards him briefly, praying for his safety and thanking God I had been given the chance to spare a foe.

It was the first few soldiers I remembered the most; after that they became a blur of shapes, a series of men I had to fight. I often felt like a piece of my soul was struck with each man I killed, but there was no time to stop and dwell upon it. It was either kill and save our people, or be killed and risk our loved ones seeing harm. As we fought on, the night paled and the dawn neared, with the sky growing greyer as the numbers of the fallen grew, both foe and enemy alike. We heard nothing apart from the groans of the wounded and the fighting, but that was more than enough to deafen us. As we continued to strike the enemy down, we began to see that victory was plausible and then even likely, for King Cedric's men had not yet been able to enter our castle town; we were holding them on our walls. The night and their torches had made them seem a far stronger force than they were, much to our relief.

The battle was severe, even if their numbers were less than originally supposed. I had only experienced two battles since I joined His Majesty's army nine years ago, such was our time of peace. The blades of my men danced with the blades of theirs, slicing and crashing into one another's flesh and drawing blood.

I struck another man down and saw there was no one to fight with at the present moment, so quickly I took out my bow and cast a few arrows into the night. I had let my fourth arrow fly when I heard footsteps. In another moment I had turned, dropping my bow and drawing my sword, to parry his blow. Such was his force at running that he did not stop, and instead fell over the castle wall, descending to his death.

Suddenly, out of nowhere, an enemy sword sliced into my arm with precision. The force of the blow caused me to drop my sword as I cried aloud in pain and collapsed to my knees. I dodged a strike from him, jumping to the left with all my might. As he approached again, I saw there was nowhere else to dive; I had become trapped. I began to pray, preparing for my death. He raised his sword high in the air and brought it down in an arc before me, but then I saw the blade of a sword strike him in the neck, cutting into his flesh. My foe cried out in pain and fell to the ground dead, his blood spurting all over me. It took a second for me to realise, disorientated, that I was going to survive. My left hand then rapidly moved to my right arm in an attempt to stem the bleeding.

"Daniel," John muttered. It was he who had saved my life! A faint smile traced my face in gratitude, despite the pain in my arm. Blood was still pouring forth, streaming over my fingers and down past my wrist.

"Hold on, brother," he murmured, dropping to my side. He examined my arm. "The wound is not too deep," he told me.

The surgeon arrived and dropped to his knees also while John made way for him. The surgeon took a sack of wine and opened it.

"This will hurt."

I wanted to point out I was already in pain, but my words turned to a groan when the wine stung me as he poured it over my wound. I noticed, through gritted teeth, the lighter colour of the wine – he had mixed it with marigold to speed the recovery. He now took a cloth and wrapped it tight.

"Here," he said, handing me some juniper leaves to aid my pain. I stuffed them into my mouth and chewed. He handed me the bottle of wine and I took a few large gulps. By the time I had finished, the dizziness and pain had subsided a little and I now stood.

"You were fortunate. The wound is not too great."

I stretched my arm – it hurt to move, but it would do.

"I have other patients to attend to," he informed me. "I will see you shortly to fix a better dressing." With that he left swiftly, heading to the next wounded man who I suspected would be in much worse condition than me.

I bent to pick up my sword with my other hand, which was a strange feeling. As I straightened again and placed my sword back in my sheath, I saw the battle was over. Hardly anybody was still fighting. I turned and suddenly saw the man I had spared staggering in the distance on his wounded knee upon the grass, limping through the dead bodies. I was about to wonder how he got down to the field from the wall with his injured knee, but then I saw three others beside him; perhaps they had carried him down and out of the castle, having earlier moved him from the wall without my noticing. Indeed, I had been so focused on the battle I had not had time to think about the man I had rendered unconscious. I realised now that the knee I had struck had been hastily bound with some dirty rags of cloth.

These four enemy soldiers were retreating along with those others of Klumeck who had survived, along with King Cedric, who was on his horse at the front of the line, one of them raising the high standard which bore his seal and the other, still confusingly, bearing the seal of King Urien and Rheged.

"How fares Aife, brother?" I questioned, my eyes still on the escaping Klumeck soldiers and their king as John came to stand next to me.

"She is well; our sister has survived the night. She is already in the armoury," John expounded, adjusting his leather gloves as he spoke. "It is curious that our enemy should use King Urien's seal," he murmured, voicing the irregularity that we all had noticed.

"The captain seemed to think it was some kind of trickery," I ventured at length, and then turned to him. "Why were we not forewarned?" I wondered aloud. "Why did the watchmen not sound the alarm?"

"We have already solved that mystery." John's reply was grim. "Some of our archers found the guards when they went to their positions. They had been dragged into a store cupboard and were sound asleep. There were cups in their hands, which had traces of a sleeping elixir to cause their slumbering."

My eyes widened at this discovery.

"A spy within our ranks?" I wondered, and then groaned as I moved my arm. The pain was still there, but it was endurable. I had escaped lightly compared to some of my brothers and sisters who still lay among the castle walls, having given their lives to defend our people.

"Yes," John replied, "we believe a spy is among us. Somebody put the elixir into their drinks – some sort of spice added to the herbs to cause them to slumber. It's a good job you were thirsty," he added with a smile. I managed to smile back. "The captain has ordered all those wounded to go back and rest."

I nodded and we trudged across the castle wall. As we did, the view changed from the sloping hills to our castle town.

The Kingdom of Gaeson was surrounded by hills and peaks and it overlooked the great lake. The kingdom was based upon a hill, with the castle at the highest point and the castle town beneath on the other side, facing west. At the foot of the hill was grass and forest. To the south and east was the majority of Rheged, and to the west lay the ocean, easily viewable from the castle's towers and balconies on a fine day.

The kingdom had been founded just over a hundred and eighty years before – it now being the year of our Lord 590 AD – as a stronghold of independence in the aftermath of those who said they came from Rome, an empire across the sea. Gaeson's hill became a point of resistance, and later therefore became a kingdom in its own right. These "Romans" eventually conquered the vast majority of our island over the next forty years or so, but also kept departing our shores as long as we would pay tribute to them. This situation remained until AD 410 when the Romans were forced to leave, as the grand empire they had governing their own lands became unstable.

However, the Romans departing did not give us peace – by this point us Britons had simply exchanged one group of invaders with another. The Saxons had come to us, also from across the sea – and we had been warring with them ever since. This was the enemy that the heroic and legendary leader His Majesty King Arthur Pendragon, one of the most famous Briton kings, had fought and defeated several times, and had led the way against the Saxon scourge. It was His Majesty King Arthur who had had so many noble knights serving at a round table, so that all discussions were equal. The tales of his heroism and courage were known by all.

During his life and after he died, however, many things about him passed into folklore and legend (him being born around 495 AD and dying at the age of fifty two in AD 547, after one of his sons killed him). Some of these myths were clearly falsehoods – such as that his wisest advisor Merlin was really a wizard, or that his kingship had been determined by pulling a sword out of a certain stone no other man could. Some said that King Urien had known King Arthur personally and had spent much of his time in Caer Ligualid, Rheged's capital city, where our Lord King Urien reigned. Interestingly, it was a myth that King Urien had apparently married King Arthur's half-sister Morgan Le Fay, who was about twenty-five years younger, when she was a young teenager.

Our capital was a legendary city; all the children of Gaeson had been told tales about its three spires and its pool of pure water, purer even than the great lake. All of Rheged was to be subject to King Urien's supreme rule. King Urien's eldest son and heir was His Highness Prince Owain. This was why we were so surprised to see that King Cedric had chosen to bear King Urien's seal, given King Cedric's betrayal and treason. King Cedric's lands, Klumeck, was vastly smaller – more akin to a fortress than a bustling town of trade.

Klumeck and Gaeson had long been allies in a time of peace, but when I was around three, not long after I was lost in the snow, there was an epic battle between our kingdoms. Since then, peace was fragile and could be easily disturbed – there had been three other attacks in my lifetime, this being the third – and the battles were always initated by King Cedric. We had never been enlightened as to the reason for this feud, but I knew it was fierce, for King Reghan never wished to hear King Cedric's name spoken aloud.

There was an interesting legend, recorded in the accounts of Rheged, which spoke of the ancestors of King Reghan and King Cedric. The legend went that forty and a hundred years ago – just a few decades after Gaeson was founded – King Reghan and King Cedric's direct ancestors were brothers, the only two sons of the first king of Gaeson. King Reghan's ancestor, the elder brother, was due to inherit Gaeson, whilst King Cedric's ancestor, the younger brother, also had the noble desire to become a king. The account tells of how the younger brother, being of a kind and compassionate nature, chose not to attempt to usurp his brother's inheritance, but rather to build a fortress, a minor kingdom the other side of the forest, where the long tall hills were. The younger brother saw this was a weak side of Rheged, where enemies could come. He saw this as the chance to become a king in his own right, and yet aid Rheged and ally himself to his brother. Together, the brothers would rule and serve their father in their different positions.

Their father had agreed to this, as he saw the military advantages and was relieved there would be no warring between his sons. The brothers remained close, loyal allies to one another, the older serving Gaeson with nobility and love, while the younger ruled the Klumeck kingdom with justice and courage. It was only twenty-one years ago that this alliance fractured. The battle occurred when I was three, when King Cedric suddenly attacked Gaeson not three weeks after the night I had been found in the snow. My mother took me into the caves whilst my father fought in the army to defend us.

That night in the caves, in my mother's arms, is my next clearest memory. I could still recall vividly, even now, the muffled shouts and cries of the battle above, and the noise, much closer, of water trickling and dripping in the caves. I was too young to understand the mortal danger we were in, as my mother held me tight and comforted me in the dark. I was rather anxious of the fear that everyone else had, and the grim faces of the soldiers assigned to protect us, as we all sat and waited to see if we would survive the night.

"It looks as though our peace with King Cedric is over," John spoke now. I almost started at his voice, dragging my thoughts from the history of my kingdom and the darkness of those caves to the present day. I glanced at my friend now, that I had known since we were eight – we had even enlisted in the army on the same day together. John was one year older than me, and his eyes were a strong deep blue and his hair black in colour. Upon a closer inspection, I noticed his hair was not just matted with sweat, but also with blood.

"You are injured, brother," I told him. "You have hurt your head."

"It is nothing," John replied, touching his head almost absent-mindedly. "I think it happened early on in the battle when I was knocked to the ground. I hardly feel it now," he assured me. "It's you we need to think about, with that arm."

"I am fine," I stated, even though that was clearly not the truth. John smiled sarcastically but made no further comment.

Presently, we stopped in our journey down the castle walls. We had made it clear of the fallen corpses strewn across the towers and balconies. John and I had been situated on the highest point and so had to descend the steps where many dead still lay. We stood at the bottom of the steps and glanced back up at where the fallen would still lie, and then panned our gazes round to the field – that same field where King Cedric and his surviving warriors had retreated – to where the bodies of our enemy lay strewn about. Their violent blood pierced my mind, the images of the dead burning onto my mind, but I looked all the same. To reflect on the fallen had always been our way of respecting the dead, both friend and foe.

John now pressed a clenched first to his chest and brought his knuckles to his mouth before pointing in the direction of the dead. This was our custom of marking the fallen. I did the same with my good arm. We maintained a few more moments of silence before I shifted balance, sending an ache into my arm. I swallowed the pain, but John noticed; he always did. He turned now to glance at my wound.

"Come, the infirmary beckons," he said, a faint smirk on his face – for he knew how much I disliked infirmary visits.

Together we trooped into the armoury, and the place was bustling with soldiers. From the number I saw, I estimated that most of us had survived the battle – and that made my heart glad. The castle servants would be here soon to clean the armour, upon returning from the caves. We removed all armour except our swords, which we were obliged to wear at all times to be ready for service. Aife, and others like her who used spears instead, donned a small dagger. I was now dressed in a simple outfit of a tunic, trousers and boots. I saw the blood had stained the long sleeve of my undergarment.

Thus changed, we again departed. As much as I wanted to avoid my appointment, I knew my arm needed seeing to. As I followed John's footsteps, I prayed my arm looked far worse than it was, thanking God that I had survived the night. For though I was in a substantial amount of pain, I knew there were many others – dead, dying and wounded – that were in far worse shape than I was.

When we came to the infirmary, I noticed there were several patients, ranging from those with minor wounds to those who were fighting for their lives. A few women were in here, running from bed to bed, trying to keep these poor men alive. I suspected these women may not have gone to the caves at all, such was their courage and sacrifice.

"Ah, Daniel," the surgeon greeted me. He came through, his hands stained with blood. "I can attend to you now," he added as he rinsed his hands in a small bowl already scarlet in colour, and then dried them with a towel. "Come here, please," he instructed. The surgeon made me sit while he applied a proper dressing and tied off the bandage. "You were lucky – a slight change in the angle of his blade and this could have been your whole arm."

"Will I be able to fight?" I questioned.

The physician smiled. "I think so," he assured me. "But you will need to rest it for a week."

"A week?" I objected immediately. "But I…"

"If you do not rest," the doctor informed me, cutting me short, "the wound will not heal properly. You have the choice between letting the wound heal, or damaging your arm further so you may not fight at all."

At this, I reluctantly agreed.

"You have been on active duty for many weeks; it is time you had a few days to recover. I am sending you home until the wound is healed."

"Thank you, doctor," John pre-emptively answered for me, in case I protested further. I stretched my arm gently, feeling its stiffness. "Don't be disheartened, Daniel. You have earned your rest."

"John is right, Daniel." I looked up to see the captain and we immediately stood, clasping a fist against our chests in salute. He saluted likewise and nodded at us. "You need to allow your wound to heal, Daniel. You're one of the best soldiers in our regiment," he added with a smirk. "You're no good to me if you can't even hold a sword."

"Yes, sire," I answered. John clapped me on the shoulder of my uninjured arm and I saw he meant to escort me. I opened my mouth to protest but closed it again, knowing John would not pay the slightest bit of attention to my objections. John grinned, taking my silence as agreement.

"We live another day, my brother," John said as we left the infirmary. "We can be thankful our town of Gaeson is safe."

"Of course," I agreed. "But at what cost?" I added thoughtfully, as we walked out of the castle on the other side of the hill in the direction of the town. This entrance opened almost immediately on to the courtyard, stepping on to the pristine stone floor. Indeed, this courtyard was probably the cleanest thing in all of Gaeson, as we often had festivals here, and the castle balcony that overlooked the square was where all the royal announcements of the king were made. Around to the left, following the curve of the hill, were the stables where I had worked as a child.

"So many dead," I reflected now with a sigh, as we left the courtyard behind us and went instead on the wide dirt path that connected the castle to the town itself.

"Aye," John agreed, "so many have given their lives to protect our fair city. But it is worth fighting for, is it not?" he murmured, as we surveyed the town from this view.

"Daniel, John," Aife called, and we turned to see her running along the path. Now without her armour, she was dressed in a brown tunic and a long white skirt that came down to her ankles. "I heard you were injured, brother," Aife murmured as she came to a stop, looking at my arm concernedly.

"Do not worry yourself, sister. It is just a scratch," I replied, and John smirked.

"Just a scratch indeed," he repeated. "The surgeon said it could have been your whole arm. You need to be more careful, brother," he added, playfully tapping the back of my head.

"It was not my will that this would happen," I returned quickly. "The enemy blade came out of nowhere; I did not even see him. I am to be confined in my house for an entire week to rest it," I added now to Aife.

"Good," Aife replied, and grinned and folded her arms. "John and I will make sure you keep to that arrangement with the good doctor."

I grinned in resignation, and the three of us made our way down the steep path together. We came to the town, with its large, tall buildings of houses and places of trade alike. We walked the rest of the way in silence, contemplating the battle of the previous night. The city was by and large deserted – all the citizens would have returned to their homes by now. Now was the time of relief and yet caution; people would be thanking God behind the safety of a locked door. In a few hours, no doubt the place would be alive with activity again – things must go on as they always had. We turned onto a steep side street – the street of my house.

My home was a simple place, modest enough. It was by now early morning, and a little shade stretched over the cobbled street, cast by the tall houses either side. We came to my house, which, due to my father's provision of us when I was a child, was more than enough than our needs. It was not one of the most grand, but it was still among the more spacious dwellings within Gaeson.

Presently we came to the doorstep, and here I bid goodbye to John and Aife, with them both saying they would visit soon. I watched them walking for a moment, until they reached the top of the street and disappeared from view. I then turned back to my door, suddenly aware of how weary I was. With a grateful sigh I unlocked the door, already relaxing at the familiar sights of home as I walked into the house.

Chapter Two

As I entered my house, I noticed it was as spotless as it always was, and relaxed as I took in the sights of home. Though it was now early morning, a fire was already roaring; I was glad of this, for the night had been as cold as it had been long and I was in need of warmth and comfort.

"My lord," my oldest friend and manager of my house, Sarah, came forwards quickly and bowed to me as she entered. As she was still bent, she took my good hand and quickly kissed it. "It is good to see you, Daniel. I am so glad you have come back safely. But you are injured!" she added, spotting my arm in the first instance, concern and anxiety in her eyes.

"It is but a scratch, Sarah. The wound is not too deep," I replied, waving away her concern with my good hand. I had decided not to impart to her what the surgeon had said about my losing my arm. "It is good to see you safe also," I told her with a smile.

Sarah was two years younger than I, and had dark brown hair and eyes; her hair colour always seemed to me to be the colour of chestnut. Sarah lived in my dwelling, taking care of the affairs of my house; she also tended to my frail mother, who lived here also. Sarah and I had grown up together, as from when I was six my parents and I had moved to live next door to her. Sarah's parents had run the bakery shop, and my memories of playing with Sarah in each other's houses are also combined with the smell of fresh bread.

Five years ago – in the last advancement against our kingdom – her father had died in a fierce battle, having been conscripted to the war effort. Her mother had already died three years before from fever. Sarah's parents had run into debts with the bakery and so had been forced to sell the shop and the house. I had not been able to bear the thought of one of my dearest friends without a place to stay or on the streets of the castle town, so I had employed her to manage the affairs of my home and tend to my mother.

"The water for your bath is ready," Sarah informed me now. I smiled – she had predicted rightly I should wish to wash away the grime of the battle. "Everyone has returned from the caves," she continued, "so I reasoned your return would be soon. I bid you go and rest; I will prepare you something to eat."

I thanked her and took the water carefully from the fire. As I crossed to the bathroom, she departed to the kitchen. Soon I could her humming a tune of our childhood as she began to chop vegetables. As I poured my bath, childhood images came to mind: Sarah and I running through the streets, chasing each other with wooden swords, nibbling the less than perfect loaves her mother had pulled a face at and given to us. My father had taught both of us how to use a sword, and we used to practice with each other daily. Sarah was one of the women who went to the caves always armed with a sword, ready to join Princess Evelyn to defend against the enemy whilst the townspeople fled. After I had met John, the three of us spent most of our childhoods practising sword fighting, running through Gaeson's hills and woods and riding.

That portion of our childhood was before either of our fathers had died. My own father died four years before Sarah's when I was fifteen, only a little before John and I signed up in the army together as soon as we had become conscription age. Both Sarah and I had been left fatherless in the aftermaths of battles, as was the way of war – but somehow I felt Sarah's loss was more shocking. My father had been a soldier all his life, so he was prepared for battle and the risk of death. Sarah's father had been a baker who had been conscripted. Sometime after his death, Sarah informed me her father had not even been trained with a blade, but still he had not let fear overtake him. Not for the first time, I reflected on how Sarah's father and other volunteers like him had showed the most courage. Aye, I could feel fear keenly – but at least I knew how to fight, how to hold a sword. It took true bravery to remain standing with your brothers and sisters on the eve of war when you knew you had learnt no ability.

Alone in the bathroom, I removed my boots and clothes that were covered with dirt and grime, sweat and blood all mixed together – some blood mine, some of the men I had killed. A lot of the blood stained on me had belonged to that last man, where John had pierced his neck. Often men tried to deny the blood they had spilled on the field, but I knew our Lord saw all and so it was futile to try to hide anything from Him. Instead I chose to relive their deaths, difficult as it was, because their lives were just as equal in the Lord's sight as ours. As I removed my clothes, I murmured a quick prayer for each of the families that would have lost a brother, a son, a cousin, a friend.

As I did, I thought again of the man I had spared who I had last seen staggering across the field after King Cedric. I wondered once more if he had known the man who had toppled over the castle wall, whether the man I had spared had become so enraged at me because his friend or relative had just died. I uttered a quick prayer for him, that God would grant him safe journey home. I prayed now that God would comfort all those in Klumeck who would have lost loved ones and friends, as grief was a heavy burden I wished on no one.

I added cold water so it would not scald and gently slid into the bath. My muscles relaxed the instant they were submerged and I basked in the warmth. The once sparkling water was already dirty – I was glad my soldier's salary was enough so that my mother and Sarah could have clean, hot water of their own, and not have to follow my bathwater too often. I grabbed the soap and began to wipe the dirt off me, careful not to dip my bandage into the water. When I was done bathing, I dressed once more in fresh tunics Sarah must have warmed by the fire that morning, knowing I would be battle-weary.

Now I was refreshed, I went upstairs while Sarah continued to prepare my meal. There were five bedrooms in this house – my father had been fortunate enough to provide for us well in this home. Sarah lived in one of these rooms, my mother in another, and I took the room I had grown up in whenever I was home. The other two rooms we often let out; there had often been strangers staying here when I was a child, some of them travelling tradespeople who needed a warm bed for a few days. There was no one lodging here presently, however. I came to my mother's chamber at the top of the stairs now and knocked on it gently – I did not want to wake her, although she was probably awake still from the evacuation this morning. My poor mother slept most of the time, so weak she mostly stayed in her bed.

"Come in," came her strong voice – though her body was weak, her mind and tongue were sharp, able and full of wisdom – and I entered. "Daniel," she said, relief plain. "It is good to see you, my son. But you have been wounded!" she added with worry.

"Only a minor wound, it is nothing," I assured her, slipping into the chair next to her and taking her hand. Her hair was thick and long; though it had been dark scarlet like mine, it was now peppered with grey. Her eyes were a sharp, unwavering green that spoke of her wisdom and wry humour. Though her body was frail, her face always appeared strong and full of life. "How fare you, Mother?"

"I feel a little stronger this morning. Although I feel my folly and weakness keenly," she said with a sigh. "Sarah had to get two other women to help carry me. They must not lift me up again; I only slow others down. Next time I shall stay here," she added resolutely.

"Not at all, Mother," I countered rapidly. "We are all in this town together; we would not want to leave anybody behind. Especially somebody as wise as you." She gave a wry laugh. I put a hand to her forehead. "You do not feel so warm this morning," I affirmed after a moment, lowering my hand. This encouraged me greatly – often she had great fevers and Sarah had to apply a wet cloth regularly in an attempt to cool her. "Sarah is preparing a meal. Would you like some food?"

"I would love some," she replied, a smile on her face. This too encouraged me further – at times she had no appetite at all, often when she was struck with a fever. Despite having to be evacuated to the caves, she seemed today to be the most well I had seen her the last few months; perhaps she was at last recovering.

I left the room to prepare a tray for her. I thought she coped well indeed with her condition. The good doctor had been to see her several times over the years, but nobody was really sure what was wrong with her. She could move all her limbs; it was not like paralysis – the surgeon had described it simply as 'weak'. It had happened a few months after my father had died – and that was nine years ago. I often wondered if somehow the grief of losing my father had caused her energy to leave her. Sarah said my mother was always more joyful whenever I was home – it would be good to spend a few days with her.

Our house was near the top of Gaeson, not far from the castle itself. As such, it was close to the top of the town's hill, and so made travelling even more difficult for her. However, the view from her bedroom window, when it was open, provided solace to the steep streets. If she felt strong enough, occasionally Sarah or I would help her to partake of the view. One could see much of the rest of the castle town; if she stretched her neck, she could even see a glimmer of the fields and mountains beyond.

Even though it was a luxury to simply rest and spend time with my mother and Sarah, I grew increasingly restless as each day passed. I kept on the alert, in case there was word of another attack. I was ever anxious to join my brothers again. The hours stretched into endless paths of time, and it seemed nothing would fully occupy me until I was healed and back with my brothers and sisters.

"Are you sure you're ready?" John asked me, as I stretched my aching arm. I was attempting to practise my sword fighting – I longed to return as soon as I could to the castle, even though it was only the third day that had passed since the surgeon said I should rest.

"I have to practise my sword," I replied, a little impatiently, "or what use will I be to anyone?" We were stood in the little yard behind my house, using wooden swords for practice. Aife and Sarah stood in the yard also, watching and chatting with one another.

"Very well," John answered with a shrug. "Just do not go beyond your limits, or you will do yourself further injury."

I nodded as we began circling one another around the yard. Holding the wooden blade ached but a little; I found I could easily bear it. John advanced at me and I parried; the sudden lunge of my arm brought with it a jolt of pain, but not more than I could stand. He came forwards, and I parried him another three times in quick succession. The fourth time, I twirled away instead and attempted to bring the wooden blade down onto John, but he now parried me.

"Good," John commented, and I smiled.

"That was the easy part," Aife stated now, and we glanced at her. She nodded at the sword about my waist. "I doubt our foes will use wood when we fight them again," she added wryly. "You need to practice with a proper blade."

I nodded and reached for it.

"Take care, Daniel," Sarah cautioned, as I held my blade in my good arm. "It will be far heavier than the wood."

I braced myself for the extra weight as I took the blade in my wounded arm. A tug of agony rocked through my arm, but I managed to hold my blade upright. I gritted my teeth against the pain and managed to parry John's blade as he advanced upon me again. To my encouragement although it brought me much pain, my ability was almost good as normal until, after a few minutes of fighting, John knocked my sword and the angle with which he hit it caused my arm to wrench to the right, making me cry aloud in pain and drop my sword.

"I think that is enough for one day," Sarah declared. "You must not overdo yourself." A stubborn part of me wished to continue, but my better judgment won, and I reluctantly replaced my sword.

"You've done well today," John stated now, patting me on the back, while I raised my good arm to wipe my forehead, where a bead of sweat had gathered due to my exertion. I was warm, despite the cold weather. "You are almost at your normal strength," he affirmed. "By the end of the week, you should have recovered fully."

"Mind you rest, though," Aife warned, stepping forwards from where she had been leaning against the wall. "We should not really have practised today, so you're not to do any more practising until that arm is recovered. We insist," she added, as I opened my mouth to object. "John and I are going back to the castle. We shall visit again soon."

"Rest, Daniel," John said, as Sarah and Aife left. "You need to relax; you have earned it, brother," he added, repeating his earlier sentiments.

I sighed as I watched them leave, longing to go back with them to the castle, but knowing I had to rest it four more days.

As it happened, though, I only had time to rest two more days, as on the fifth day that passed there was word of another legion from King Cedric, and soon the horns began to sound. I had practised a little that morning, and my arm was somewhat sore and stiff when holding Sarah's sword, but there was nothing preventing the use of my limb. I took off the bandage, instead placing a thinner cloth around it for protection. I headed out of the front door.

"No, my lord," Sarah murmured, coming out of the house behind me. I turned around to face her, already having taken a few steps away on the street. "You must let it heal; you know what the doctor said. You could damage your arm further."

"I must go back, Sarah," I emphasised. "While I remain here, our brothers and sisters will be fighting and dying. I cannot simply stand by; I must help where I can."

"Daniel," Sarah tried again, "I insist that you cannot! You are not fit."

"I am fit enough," I replied. "I must go. I require your horse. Besides, what would you do to stop me?" I questioned, in a moment of annoyance. I picked up my helmet and turned to her, repeating, "I require your horse."

"You cannot have him," Sarah muttered, but I mounted her horse anyway and gathered the reins in my hands. "So is this how you march off to battle?" she challenged me, and I turned back to see she had folded her arms. "Is this how you would converse with me? You are as a brother to me." I could see how upset she was, but there was nothing I could do.

"And you a sister to me," I told her. "Look at the sky, dear sister," I said, pointing at where the sun sat. She followed my gaze. "It is nearly nightfall. That is when the battle is to take place, I am sure of it. I must do my duty. I pray all here will be kept safe."

Finally Sarah relented and nodded, crossing the street to where I was sitting upon her horse. "Then ride well, brother – I will tend to your mother. She will not be left behind."

I smiled and nodded – I already knew this to be the case.

She took my hand and bent to kiss it briefly. "May God be with you, Daniel."

"May He also be with you, Sarah," I replied. I squeezed her hand tightly for a moment before quickly letting go and hurriedly made my way back for the castle.

It only took me a few minutes upon horseback to reach the castle. I dismounted Sarah's horse and tied him up in the stables. I had worked here as a stable boy, before enlisting in His Majesty's army as my career, so I was able to be swifter than most in securing him. Some soldiers, who had grown up in other occupations, had never even ridden a horse before enlisting. I had loved the work; the pay helped contribute to my house and I loved to be among the horses. I ran up the steps to the armoury and threw on my armour; this done, I ran along the corridor to the small hall where my brothers and sisters would already be gathered. It was the same hall where we had been briefed by the captain six days before – was it only six? I wondered now. Not even a week since the enemy had advanced upon our door and here they were again – it had taken them some skill to amass their army so speedily.

"Daniel," John greeted me, his voice a mixture of surprise. He was standing in the corner with a few other men and the captain. I perceived his countenance to be pleasure to see me, and also disdainful that I was not at home recovering – this proved an interesting combination.

"Well, you were right, John," the captain stated, looking up from his battle plans and folding his arms as he saw me. "You said he would come."

"Yes, sire, that is what I suspected," John replied, and sighed at me. "You are two days early, brother. You should not be here."

"I am ready, sire," I returned quickly to the captain. "I heard the horns and knew battle would be soon upon us. I could not do nothing and I am recovered enough."

"John is right, Daniel," the captain told me, looking up now from the battle plans. "You should be resting."

"I have been resting, my lord," I emphasised. "My arm feels fine now." Well, it was a little stiff – but that was nothing. I stretched it out so they could see my ease of movement. "I couldn't sit by and do nothing while my brothers and sisters fought," I finished quietly.

"I hope your arm is as good as you say," the captain remarked. "Go join your ranks, all of you," he added, in a raised voice. We immediately did as he said. "Soon they will appear again."

As we moved out to our positions – the same places as six days before – I noticed how the stones were sparkling again. They had been washed clean from the blood that had been stained and pooled upon the castle walls. With a grim heart, I knew they would not be clean for much longer – soon blood would be spilled upon this stone once more.

"I thought you might be here," Aife muttered. She had come to stand next to me in her usual position, and I noticed now her eyes were narrowed as she stood next to me, idly changing her spear from one hand to another. "You are supposed to be resting. How do you hold your blade now?"

I drew it, holding it out. I even sliced through the air from side to side. I felt a low ache but found it was easily bearable. Without warning, Aife jerked her spear towards me and I parried her swiftly – it caused a tug of pain, but nothing like what it had been two days previous.

"Very well," she said with a shrug. I realised we were then being watched by the other soldiers, and replaced my sword in its sheath.

"Do we know why King Cedric is attacking?" I asked Aife now in a low voice, while our captain issued orders to specific men.

"Why do kingdoms fight?" Aife answered with a shrug of her shoulders, grimly staring straight ahead. "To increase their power and influence. The war between King Cedric and King Reghan has been long known. Our kingdom is blessed with good land. He would take it for his own if he won this war. The legend goes King Cedric's ancestor had long dreamt of returning in power to take the place he believed God had really given him."

"That is but a myth," I replied swiftly. "The tales say the two brothers remained allies and our peoples could be allies this day. We could be brothers, rather than foes. Why must he possess this land?"

"Why must all men take and have greed?" she responded faintly. "It is because they can. It is in our nature to love ourselves more than others. It is natural for us to take too much of what is a gift, to take what does not belong to us."

I frowned and eventually nodded. I knew all of Aife's speech was true, but I still wondered at why King Cedric had broken peace so suddenly. Why now, after such a time without fighting?

"Be ready, people," the captain called to us now. "We will fight for our king till the end of all things. We have pledged allegiance to him and we will not falter now. We will stand strong. For our king!" he shouted.

"For our king," we echoed, as we had done seven nights before. We did not know the reason for the attacks then and we were no closer to knowing the reason now – but we would still fight till there was no more breath in us. At the back of my mind though – no matter how much my loyalty and determination to serve the king tried to push the thought away – the question of why we were doing this was close to my lips. I could sense my brothers and sisters had this feeling too. We waited tensely as the portcullis was raised, as it had done a few days previous. We marched into the cold night air, but nobody was around – the enemy forces had not yet reached the top of the hill in front of us.

"This is ridiculous." A strangled whisper went out from us and we turned to see who spoke. "We did this before and people died. Why are we fighting again, when we do not know why? Why are we fighting when we have had peace?"

It was a young man who spoke – nay, he was still a boy. He had straw blonde hair and small blue eyes. We all wished he could take back his words, rather than feel the rebuke of the captain – even though an element of his speech had resonated with each one of us.

"That is not your concern." In the piercingly still night, with all of us silent, a whisper had not gone unnoticed. Our captain marched towards us, parting the men until he found the boy. His face was stern, his eyes as cold and angry as the night. "The horrors of battle are nothing compared with what I will do if you flee," the captain hissed. Each word, each syllable, punctuated the crisp air, spoken with menace and disgust. "If you question His Majesty's orders again, I will slay you myself. You will stand firm and you will do your duty." The captain paused, staring at the boy with his angry eyes. "Is there anything I have said you do not understand?"

"No, captain. Sorry, sire," the boy managed to rasp out. I thought the captain's treatment of the boy had been harsh – but the captain could not afford to have disobedient soldiers, or we could all be dead.

The captain moved away, and once I was sure he was far enough, I took another glance – the boy was almost next to me in line. His eyes were so young; I wondered what age he must be. His eyes were filled with tears but he was blinking rapidly, his pride refusing to let them fall. I reached out to put my hand on his shoulder and he jumped. If a hand on his shoulder made startled him so, I wondered how he would fare in battle, how he would even live this night.

"Take heart, friend," I whispered, seeking to encourage him. Aife and a few other soldiers turned their heads, but I carried on speaking quickly. "It is folly to question orders – but fear not. God is with you and I know he is watching over us." The boy's eyes, still struck with fear, turned to me and hardened. The tears in his eyes receded, so at least I had distracted him momentarily from his turmoil.

"God?" he questioned with bitterness. "What God is this? A God that does nothing to prevent our absurd demise?"

"Hush," I rebuked him swiftly – the captain was not so far away and the boy had unwittingly increased his volume, "or your demise will happen before the fight has even started. That would be the absurdity." I paused again, taking a glance at the captain, as I did not want to be caught speaking – but the captain had moved down the line, and I felt I had to encourage this boy. "God is not responsible for the folly of human hearts," I whispered to him. The boy did not respond. I looked at him a moment longer. "How old are you?"

He turned to look at me again with his fearful countenance. "I am fourteen next month," he whispered back. My eyes flew wide in surprise – fifteen was the age of signing up. "I was told I had to volunteer, because so many men were killed or injured in the last battle."

I nodded – but still, so young!

"I live in one of the poorer areas of the town, with my mother and two sisters who are not yet ten," he continued.

"You are good to be fighting for them here," I replied, intending to reassure this poor, frightened boy. "You need not fear their fate; they will be heading for the caves as we speak."

"No," he whispered back. "No, my lord, you do not understand." His eyes darted left and right with fear, but the captain was still at a good distance and so had not yet returned. "My mother has a bed sickness. It is I who works to care for our family. My father died in battle three years ago, the last time King Cedric attacked." The boy paused and swallowed here. "My mother was forced to work so we could eat. She became ill two years ago. If I die tonight, my family will starve."

My eyes widened in recognition; he was not so terrified of his own fate. No, his fear was for the fate of his family should he die here tonight, in the midst of battle. It was perfectly understandable to be afraid for one's life, but that was not why the boy had such fear. This was fear for his family, which was far more honourable.

"What is your name, boy?" I asked him urgently; the captain had turned around and would soon be walking along our line again.

"Joshua, son of Rachel, who is a seamstress," he replied. His eyes grew even more fearful as the captain neared.

"Joshua, look at me," I told him, but he was nervously darting his eyes still. "Look at me," I repeated, and this time he met my gaze. "Joshua, God is with you. He is watching us and with us, even now as we stand in this hour of darkness, as we stand on the brink of the abyss. I swear, though," I added, "that if you are slain, I will do everything in my power to ensure your family are provided for."

His eyes widened in disbelief. "You… you would do that, my lord?"

The captain was nearing; there was not much time now. I nodded. "I swear."

"My lord," he repeated. His eyes welled and he seized my hand quickly and bent to kiss it. "Thank you," he rasped. "Thank you, my lord. Thank you."

"Do not fear. Remember God is with you, Joshua. Now face the front," I ordered, and he nodded and turned.

I also turned, just as the captain walked past us. Because I had been so absorbed in the task of comforting this poor boy before battle started, I had missed His Majesty King Reghan riding out – for whatever reason, the captain had obviously not been a member of his personal escort. Through the lighted beacons, much like the previous battle, I saw King Cedric's angry eyes and hardened countenance, and I gripped the hilt of my sword for comfort. Again, I saw King Cedric bore the seal of King Urien and frowned; perhaps it was meant to distract us. I watched, tense, as King Reghan now turned and headed back to the castle, heard the metal sounds of the portcullis being raised. We were on the cusp of battle again, and I ever tightened the grip of my blade.

The captain came to stand in front of us again and drew his blade, raising it above his head. We all followed suit, raising our own swords with him, and Aife and those others of us who bore spears raised them towards our foes accordingly.

"For our king!" the captain shouted.

"For our king!" we repeated, and the spear-bearers lowered theirs so they rested upon the ground, whilst the rest of us replaced our swords.

"Ready your arrows!" the captain shouted. The other archers and I readied our bows, Aife placing an arrow upon her bow the same time I did. The night was as cold as it had been earlier, but it was much cloudier; without the light of the moon or stars it would be much harder to see one another's movements.

In those last fleeting seconds before battle began, I stole another glance at Joshua. He stood behind, ready to fight those who breached our walls. I saw his eyes were no longer darting nervously around, but rather stared straight ahead; I also noticed his face did not look so afraid. I hoped I had been able to comfort him and that God would help me keep the vow I had just made to him, should the worst happen.

My eyes snapped back to the front, and in the next moment we heard King Cedric shout from down the hill. The enemy charged forwards.

"Let fly!" the captain roared, and we fired our arrows, unleashing them into the night sky. I saw my arrow pierce a man's flesh. "Fire at will!" the captain shouted, as a second later I had prepared another arrow and let it free.

Soon our enemies were once again crossing over the wall, and the screams of the wounded rang in my ears. Our swords danced with theirs into the night, the metal of our blades slicing and plunging into flesh. Like in the last battle, after the first few men I cut down they blurred into one another. I twirled my blade from man to man. I knocked a woman to the ground but praised God I was able to spare her, as I did the next man after her.

Just then I spied young Joshua on the floor. Another soldier was advancing slowly towards him. I rushed forwards, but out of the corner of my eye I saw a blade flash out at me. I skidded backwards, almost losing my balance along the castle wall, and it sliced down through thin air. He slashed again and I parried him. I cut his sword out of the way, pivoted on the spot and brought it down upon his shoulder. My foe fell to the ground and I struck him again, giving him a clean death.

My eyes roved frantically but there was no sign of Joshua. Two men were fighting before me and as they moved past, I saw him. He was still alive, managing to use his sword to weakly defend himself from his attacker – but I saw the boy would die at any moment. I sprinted the few metres. The huge man from Klumeck knocked Joshua's sword from his hand. The man raised his sword. Joshua closed his eyes, preparing for death. The man brought his blade down through the air…

I got to him just before his blade connected with Joshua's flesh and impaled him in the side. The man grunted in pain and surprise and fell down dead. As he collapsed, I put my feet onto the man's chest and used him to lever my sword out. Joshua's eyes had been closed and now they opened, realising the blow had never come. His eyes were filled with relief.

"My lord," he rasped, trying to even his breathing, "thank you." His heart was filled with fear; so was mine if I admitted it. I had been a soldier long enough to know how to use my fear lest it should overwhelm me, but this was clearly Joshua's first battle; he was so young and this was clearly his first battle. I had still been a stable boy at his age. Possibly this boy had never even seen death before – but then his father, like mine, had died in battle.

I was by his side now and pulled him up. He wiped blood from his face, which trickled down from a gash in his cheek.

"Come, Joshua. For our king," I told him, trying to encourage him.

He nodded; his eyes were grim and determined. "For our king," he replied.

In the next moment, I turned to fight another foe and then another – by the time I moved back, Joshua had gone. I uttered a quick prayer for his safety and protection before continuing in the fight. As I turned, I had a quick glimpse of the field over the castle wall – the enemy was still running towards us strong, but they had not yet breached the courtyard and the town.

"How have they amassed so quickly?" I asked quietly as I surveyed the scene. Then the question fled from my mind as I dodged a blade to my right. A brutish man grinned savagely and slashed again. I stepped back, knowing I would have to be careful in this fight. As I did so, I glanced down and saw a cloth, stained with blood, bound tight to his knee. My gaze jerked back to his face as I realised he was the Klumeck soldier I had spared in the last battle, as I had been the one to wound his knee so. The man's eyes hardened as he recognised me and he grinned coldly.

"You. You spared my life. Why? It is no matter," he added before I could reply. "You should not expect to receive mercy from me in return. I will have my vengeance," he concluded, as be began to advance upon me.

"That man who fell," I deducted, as he began to advance. "Who was he?" I asked, taking a few steps backwards – and his glare hardened further still.

"He was my brother," this Klumeck soldier replied, advancing still further – my heart did feel remorse as I circled around him, still yards apart.

"Then I apologise," I began, and he sniggered with scorn. "It was not my blade that killed him. I dodged his sword as he ran towards me and, as you saw, he kept running and fell over the castle wall. You have come to invade us," I continued. "You would have done no different if I were coming to Klumeck's fortress. Indeed, each time I come to face Klumeck I do so knowing one of your army killed my father in a battle such as this one. But I do apologise to have caused you such grief," I added.

The man sneered. "Your words mean nothing!" he snarled. "Let's fight, you and I!" He charged then, lashing forwards. I parried his blow, causing him to stagger back – but only slightly. I began to circle again. Instinctively, I knew if I were to win this, I needed to wait for him to attack first. This man wanted to shed my blood; he sought revenge for his brother, and also to prove his pride and not suffer the humiliation of being defeated by me a second time. These motives, therefore, made him desperate and overeager, and I suspected this would be his downfall.

I was right. I had only circled for a few seconds more when, with a cry choked with anger, he lashed forwards, charging me. I waited until the last moment before I jumped to the right, bringing my sword down. It only connected with his armour, but it was still a blow to him and he gasped in pain. Then he was around again, and I was forced to leap once more. The man grinned, despite the blood running from his temple. He wiped where the blood fell into his eye, pausing a moment to survey his scarlet fingertips. Then his grin was gone.

"Say your prayers, boy," the man barked.

My hand tightened on the hilt of my sword, waiting, silently obeying his request and asking God for aid. Then this frenzied soldier charged again. Once more, I waited until he was nearly upon me before evading him. Then, at the last moment, I dodged him, bringing my sword down. He had anticipated this move, however, and parried me, and then I felt his fist hit my head with all his might. Stunned, I stumbled backwards, and my dulled senses only just made me divert from the course of his blade, which only seemed to enrage him further.

"Now you die!" the man growled, and as I ducked to avoid another blow, I brought my sword around to slice his knee where I had cut him the last time, and quickly followed this with hitting him with my leather gloves full in the face. The man collapsed to the floor, dazed, his eyes still upon me as I approached him. "Kill me, as you did my brother," he snarled.

"I apologise for your brother's death," I told him solemnly. "I shall not kill you this night." I just glimpsed the surprise in his features before I swiftly swung my shield and it batted into his head, rendering him unconscious at once. I then took a moment to stoop down – yes, he was still alive; God had granted me the chance to spare him a second time. Unconscious as he was, he would appear dead, which would prevent further harm to him. Alive and writhing, someone with the desire to spill blood would surely kill him. I murmured a swift prayer for his safety, and then I was embroiled in a fight once more.

Eventually, the last of Klumeck's forces began to fall. No doubt it was because so many had volunteered – men and women like young Joshua – that we had been able to ward them off again. As I glanced out across the field, I saw King Cedric departing again. I knew not why he had attacked again so suddenly, or the reason behind his violent campaign. It looked as though even more of us had fallen this time, as those of Gaeson killed or captured the last few of Klumeck fighting. I caught a glimpse of the man I had spared for the second time being carried in on a stretcher – this time he had not been able to escape into the distance, following in the trail of his king.

As I watched the rest of Klumeck descend the hill, I reflected on how I was not sure how well we would defend our people should King Cedric gather his troops again. Twice he had attacked and twice we had defended – could this happen a third time? Perhaps King Reghan would be forced to recruit warriors from smaller trading settlements nearby. Either way, the outcome did not look too positive at present.

I turned to walk down the castle wall, careful to avoid the bodies and to not slip on the stones now slick with blood. The castle servants would soon be at work again, gathering the dead bodies to be burnt, and wiping clean the castle once more. It was a dreadful business, but such was the way of war. I exhaled in relief, seeing that the battle was over. I tried to clean the worst off my sword upon the stones before replacing it. I wondered if that boy, Joshua, would still be alive. I wiped the sweat from my forehead with the back of my hand, and then turned back in the direction of the armoury.

As I came to the end of the length of the wall, absently massaging the spot where the Klumeck man had hit me on the head, the sun was just beginning to rise. I turned to descend the castle steps, but then a clump of long blond hair caught my eye and instantly filled me with dread. The blond soldier had a Klumeck soldier on top of him, but I could tell that the soldier with blond hair was from Gaeson by the armour on his breastplate. I walked over towards the two bodies, feeling as though time had stopped and that my legs had gone numb. I sank to my knees next to them and, fearing what I might discover, I pushed the soldier on top to the side – and as I did, my worst suspicions were confirmed.

For it was Joshua who lay there, pale and lifeless, his eyes and mouth open wide in horror. His face was flecked with blood, but it was not just the cut to his cheek. Deep, crimson blood pooled at his neck where somebody had struck him. His skin was as pale as white stone underneath the blood and gore. With my rough, dirty hands, I attempted to close his eyelids, but they would not remain shut.

"Daniel." John's face startled me and I looked up at him. "There you are. I'm glad to see you alive, brother..." His smile faded as he saw my expression, and I saw his gaze turn to see the poor boy who was on the ground next to me, his head still in my lap. I looked away from John, glancing down to Joshua once more.

"Who lies here?" John asked me quietly.

"His name was Joshua," I answered after a moment, my voice rasp and hoarse and sounding strange to my ears. "Not yet fourteen." I saw surprise register on his features that a boy so young had been fighting. "He was terrified." I said wanly.

"The boy the captain rebuked last night," I heard Aife say from behind us. She came to sink to her knees beside me, putting a hand on my shoulder. "You did your best for him, brother. You spoke comfort to him and encouraged him greatly with the promise you made to care for his kin."

I made no response as a tear slowly slid down my cheek.

"Give him here, Daniel," Aife said softly, and ever so gently laid him down so that his head rested upon a rock. She then arranged his arms so that they crossed over his chest. This done, she then picked up a couple of loose stones from where the castle wall had been struck and placed them over Joshua's eyelids so his eyes remained closed. "Now he could be sleeping."

"Thank you, sister," I muttered as I wiped another tear, though I wasn't sure if I agreed with her. For no amount of stones on Joshua's eyes could remove the horror that was forever struck upon his features. "He should not have fought," I protested aloud, suddenly not caring who heard. "There was no reason for him to die. No reason for us to be here."

"Watch your words, Daniel," John's voice warned me, still standing a little apart from us – I noted his tone had hardened slightly, but I did not pay him heed.

"Come, John, you know I speak the truth!" I hissed. "Not yet fourteen!" I repeated angrily, looking from John to Aife now. Another tear had fallen in my distress, and I wiped it, further smearing my face. Another tear joined it, my eyes blurring. "He should have been in the caves, not here among the dead. We still do not know why we are fighting," I continued. "We don't know why King Cedric is attacking. This night and the night five days ago – so many are dead and wounded and we do not know why!"

I finished my speech, and for a moment all was silent. Aife stood now and stepped back, but I barely noticed her movements, so lost was I in Joshua's horrified pale skin beneath his thick coat of blood.

"We fight because we have to," John replied now, and I heard the rebuke in his voice. "We fight because to not do so would be to give up our children, our homes and our way of life. We fight to serve our king, who is good and true in his protection over us. Is that not enough?" he challenged me.

I paused, wiping my face again with the back of my hand. "Of course it is," I agreed at length, though my assent sounded rather mechanical. I was still kneeling on the ground and then felt so lost and helpless, for I knew there was nothing more I could do for him. Slowly, I got to my feet also, wiping sweat from my brow.

"Take care, Daniel," Aife warned. "What you have said could be construed as treason. Technically we could report you." I looked up at them – would they do that? She smiled suddenly as if she had read my mind. "We will not, of course. Take care, that is all we mean. We know you did not mean those words, but a stranger…"

"I understand. Thank you, both of you." I stood slowly, turning to look at Joshua one last time – though I knew the sharp horror in his countenance would remain forever ingrained in my mind. "Seeing him die when he was so young and afraid was difficult," I concluded.

"We'll speak no more about it," John replied, patting me on the shoulder.

The three of us stepped away from Joshua now and peered over the castle wall. I took in the scene of bodies, as we had done only a week ago. With John and Aife beside me, we then – in complete unison and without any speech said between us – performed the same action John and I had done last time. The three of us clenched our firsts, beat them against our chests, and pointed them out towards all in Gaeson who had been slaughtered. Out of my peripheral vision, I could see many other Gaeson soldiers who had survived doing the same. We stood there for a further moment before, with heavy hearts, we walked away from the stains of battle in the direction of the armoury.

"How is your arm?" John asked now, as we left the castle wall and descended the stone tower steps, falling in with the footsteps of other soldiers.

"Fine," I lied. In truth it hurt like the blazes, but it was good enough to use – the last thing I wanted was more days of sitting around and resting while there was work to be done. He nodded, although from his face it looked as though he did not fully believe me.

Presently we entered the armoury, which was by now crowded with Gaeson soldiers taking off their items of war. Soon the castle servants would be here to begin the arduous task of cleaning it.

"Do you think the captain would mind if I take this day's leave?" I asked them as I unbuckled the belt which held my sword, and began removing my breastplate.

"Considering you returned earlier than you should have done, I doubt the captain would have a problem." Aife smirked. "We'll be sure to inform him. Take care," she added, repeating her earlier words – but this time they were without rebuke.

I nodded and managed a faint smile. I nodded at them and then departed from their company, leaving the armoury and walking down the corridor.

"You." I turned at the voice to see, through an open door, a long room where Klumeck prisoners were currently being held whilst they awaited medical attention. I perceived the voice to have come from the brutish soldier sat by the door, with a fresh cloth banded around his knee. It was the man I had been able to spare for the second time; the man, I realised again, whose brother had toppled from the castle wall a week ago. "It is the second time you have spared me," he stated. "Why?" His voice was rasped and gravelly.

"We are told to love our enemies," I answered simply. "I have no wish to kill if I can help it. That is why," I expounded as he regarded me. "I am truly sorry I was not able to spare your brother from falling from the wall – even though he was my foe."

His face hardened at the mention of his brother, and he now looked away.

I glanced down briefly at the clean bandage on his knee. "I pray you recover quickly," I told him, but the man still turned away. "May God be with you," I stated, and left him.

I crossed the courtyard, but this time, instead of heading down the path to the town on foot, I took a higher path that wound a little way around the hill to come to the stables where I had worked as a young boy. I reasoned that I might well need my horse, should Joshua's family come to reside in my house along with my mother and Sarah.

Soon I came to the threshold of the stables and was greeted with that sweet, musty aroma of horses and hay. I normally found this environment calming and peaceful, in sharp contrast to the pace of a soldier – but today I found it stifling. I suddenly found I had to stagger a few steps and lean against a wooden fence for support.

Without warning, the image of Joshua jolted me afresh, quickly followed by the sight of the brother of the Klumeck man I had spared, his wild countenance and his flailing arms as he fell to his death. The brutality of these images bore into my soul with such ferocity that I had the sudden urge to vomit. I had a few seconds to run around the corner of the stables – and then fell to my knees, spilling the contents of my stomach upon the grass. I retched until there was nothing left, and then sat back upon the grass, breathless and panting.

I remained there a little while, wiping my mouth roughly with the back of my hand. I had experienced countless deaths since becoming a soldier – but never before had I experienced it so cruelly and without reason. I had also never before been forced to confront the relative of a man I had killed. It had not been my blade that had killed him, but I had not stopped him from falling off the castle wall to his doom either – on the contrary, I had leapt out of the way as the means of defeating him.

After a few seconds, my breathing eased and I sensed my health return to normal. As I retrieved the skin of water from my belt and took a drink, my dizziness that had also overcome me subsided and my vision focused. I looked towards the sky and saw the day was dawning fine, with the bright orb of the sun rising slowly higher in a cloudless, azure expanse. It was still bitterly cold, and as I got to my feet again, the air I expelled briefly formed a sphere of mist before vanishing. By the time I had walked back round to the stables I was much recovered, and the warm smell was its usual comfort. The stables were large and split into three compartments, each housing fifty or so horses in long cubicles. I went to the far left compartment and journeyed down the cubicles. On the left I came to my horse, who darted her head and neighed softly at my approach.

My horse was a twelve-year-old mare named Epos. I had known her all my life, having assisted my father in the birth when I was twelve. Her coat was a colour akin to parchment, with dark grey for her hooves and mane. I led her out of her stall, stroking her neck as I did so – indeed, I found solace in her presence, which was as comforting as always. I readied her as quickly as possible, and was soon riding out with her in the direction of the town.

As Epos galloped along the path, I soon caught up with the line of citizens that were heading from the caves, and slowed my mare to a walk and made a few enquiries. By the time we had journeyed back to the town, I had discovered where Rachel the seamstress lived. As I changed Epos' direction, I caught Sarah's eye.

"My lord," Sarah said, moving through the line to greet me. "It is good to see you alive. How is your arm? You look ill," she added, frowning.

"I am well and my arm is fine. My mother?" I questioned, but as Sarah opened her mouth to answer, I saw she was being partially carried further back. "I see she is well-tended," I added, my observation bringing a little warmth to my heart. "I shall be back at the house later, but I have urgent business to attend to."

"Very good," Sarah answered briefly, as I kicked Epos into a canter, leading her down to the far end of town where I now knew Joshua had lived. The sun had risen further and now the morning light was harsh against my weary eyes. The sharpness of the sun had made for a beautiful day – but the good weather proved a stark contrast to the pain and tragedy that permeated the air. Everything around me was illuminated by the strong daylight; all around me the stone of the castle town gleamed, and it seemed wrong, as if the very town was mocking its inhabitants.

I felt that my appearance also was in keen disparity from the weather; I was all too aware of my ragged impression, and I probably still had signs of the dried blood on my face. I had paused to wash my face and hands as best I could, but some of the grime would only be removed with a hot bath. How could I have such luxury, when there was a mother who did not know her son was dead?

As I journeyed through the town, I perceived it to be slow and heavy – many would be dead and wounded, others laden with sorrow and grief. Fortunately, the Klumeck army had not invaded the castle town as they had done in the past, so there was no physical damage that needed repair. As I rode Epos through the town, I saw many people sobbing. I knew Joshua's family would suffer a similar grief, so though my horse moved with pace and urgency, I was somewhat tempted to slow her and therefore deter relaying the dreadful news I had to tell. I prayed for God's strength as I went about this dreadful task, as I knew with each step Epos took, I was one step closer to telling Joshua's mother that her thirteen-year-old boy was dead.

Chapter Three

Presently, I led Epos down a certain street and recognised Rachel's house from the description I had been given earlier. I dismounted my horse and tied her up next to the house before knocking on the door.

"Greetings, my lord," she said, curtseying as she answered the door. I took in her appearance – the dirt in her clothes, a little filth her hair. What most struck me was her eyes – they appeared so old and tired, the kind of weariness normally found in adults. "My mother bids you welcome into her home, and…" She trailed off then and frowned slightly; I had to smile as she paused, obviously trying to remember what her mother had instructed her to tell visitors. "Oh, she is sorry she could not be here herself to greet you, my lord."

"May I speak with your mother, child?"

She nodded and gestured the way. Inside I saw another girl, older – in a similar state to her older sister. The elder daughter was making a dress, and as I entered the room she pierced herself with a needle, screwing up her face in irritation and placing the bleeding finger in her mouth.

"Is the fighting over now?" she asked me, in between sucking her finger.

I nodded.

"We got the signal that we could go home," she explained. She paused then. The question of her brother's fate was clearly on her face, but she did not ask. "My mother is teaching us our trade," she said instead. "We make dresses, my lord. My sister and I try to do the trade in her place, but we lack the skill and the speed of our mother."

"Your mother is a good teacher, for I see you sew well," I commented, as I watched how intricate her needlework was.

The girl smiled as she stood, laying the dress carefully upon the table. "If you would follow me, my lord, I will take you to see my mother." She gave a curtsey.

I inclined my head in assent, as was the polite custom. I followed her through the house and up some stairs till we came to her mother's chamber, and the elder child knocked on the door and opened it.

"Mother, there is a noble gentleman to see you," she called, and then turned back to me. "Please excuse me, my lord. I shall continue with our trade." She gave another curtsey. I inclined my head a second time, and the girl walked back through to the main living area. She had left the door open.

"My lord," Rachel the seamstress greeted me as I stepped over the threshold into her chamber. I noticed that although she only looked about ten or so years older than me, she was frail and confined to the bed, in a much similar state to my own mother. "Please excuse my state…" she said, and winced as she tried to sit up further.

"Please, my lady, do not try to get up on my account," I said swiftly. I longed to spare her as much pain as possible, though I knew my next words would deliver harsher a blow than her illness ever could. "My name is Daniel. I am a soldier…"

"This is about Joshua," she cut across. I could see from her eyes she already knew what I was about to say.

Words failed me, and all I could do was nod, despising myself for my weakness.

"No…" she murmured, her face crumpling. "Oh, my boy is dead – part of my very flesh!" She put a hand to her mouth as she began to weep. "Oh, my boy," she murmured again, "how are we to live? How…" She broke off as a wave of coughing overtook her.

I quickly grabbed the jug of water from the table next to her bed and poured her a cup. "Please drink, my lady."

She took a few sips and her breathing eased, but her tears still fell.

"I am sorry for your loss," I told her in earnest.

She swallowed. "Thank you for coming to see me, my lord. You must be hungry." Again she swallowed and reached for the bell next to her. "I will get my daughters to prepare you something."

"Please do not bother," I said, my hand gently stilling hers. She looked away, hiding her tears. "There is no shame in grieving, my lady…"

"Please, my lord," she cut across bitterly, "please do not call me that. I am anything but a lady. What a mother I am to have my children grow up in this condition. Oh, my boy…" she said again, her grief overwhelming her. I held her hands quietly for a few moments in the initial outpouring of her grief before I spoke again.

"I knew your son only briefly," I told her at length, "but I saw enough to know he had been brought up well. He knew compassion and decency, and he had much love for you and his sisters. He fought bravely and well."

She managed a small smile at this.

"My…" I paused, knowing she did not like this term. "Rachel," I decided, and she nodded. "Joshua told me about your illness. He was distraught at the thought of death, because he thought you might starve without him being able to put bread on the table."

Her eyes filled again with tears.

"I promised him that if he died, I would provide for you all."

Her eyes opened wide, stunned.

"It is a promise I intend to keep, Rachel," I told her earnestly.

"What, my lord? But why…" The question trailed.

I hesitated – dare I tell her the truth? In an instant I decided I would.

"I am about to tell you something you must never repeat," I whispered.

She nodded, her eyes watching mine.

"I do not think your son should have been in the war. He was too young for conscription age and died no more than a boy."

She nodded again, tears falling out of her eyes. She squeezed my hand. "Thank you, my lord; I knew the risk you took to say that. But we are not related by blood or by marriage. How could you be responsible? I must alleviate you of your promise – although I sincerely thank you for it."

"I intend to keep my promise," I replied, repeating my earlier words. "God put it on my heart to help you. My wage is not the most grand, but it enabled me to keep my father's home. I have my housekeeper, Sarah, to run my affairs. There are more than enough rooms for all of us. I bid you come live with me there."

Her eyes widened – I could tell she could not believe it. Then disbelief gave way to grief once more, and she wiped her mouth. "If you would excuse me, my lord, for a moment. I need to tell my daughters… could you perhaps call them for me?"

"Of course," I agreed gently, and stood. "Take all the time you need."

I left her chamber and descended the stairs. "Your mother wishes to see you both," I told the two girls, who at once went up there. The elder sister had a pained countenance, and I wondered whether she might already suspect the truth. I remained downstairs, wanting to give them as much privacy as possible – but I could not help imagining the scene. What sorrow Rachel must be having in her heart while explaining to her daughters that their brother was dead.

I pondered now how unnatural it was to lose a child. A child was meant to outlive a parent and inherit what was left to them; that surely was the way of things. Surely a parent was meant to watch their child grow into adulthood, marry and live. If Joshua had been a fully grown man, it would be different – though it still would be desperately sad. My mother knew I could die in battle, and the five times I had been in one and come back alive I had seen the relief in her face. But this – a boy who should not have been fighting – this was unbearable.

That Klumeck soldier God had granted me to spare twice now come into my mind, fresh and sharp. I remembered how I had beheld his brother toppling off the tower wall, the terror and panic etched into his face in a silent scream as he realised what was happening. I could not help but dwell on how I was responsible for the grief of the soldier I had spared; I imagined now that the man who had fallen would have had a mother grieving, as would every other soldier I had ever killed – but such was the way of war. All those other ponderings gave way now to divert to Joshua, laying on that stone wall again. The horror on his face that had pierced through to my soul, beyond any armour I could use. I closed my eyes to attempt to still my mind, shook my head to rid myself of the memories.

I heard the girls come downstairs again, and opened my eyes as they entered the main living area. Their eyes were filled with grief not yet expressed to full measure, but tears were already falling fast. They sat down at their little table together, all thought of sewing lost – and both turned to look at me with such despair and hopelessness that I fought to breathe.

"I am so sorry," I whispered, my words feeling trite and sorrowful. The girls did not respond. "Does your mother wish for me to come upstairs?"

After a moment, the older sister nodded – and then they became still once more. It seemed as though nothing in the world was moving at all except the fast, hot pace of their weeping.

"I bid you excuse me," I said roughly – it was all I could do to walk back up the stairs to Rachel's chamber.

"I could not accept your kindness, my lord," Rachel said, as soon as I entered her chamber again. I walked over to her, not hindered from this course of action in the slightest.

"Joshua was fearful of what would happen to you should he die," I replied. "I bid you come live with me and I will provide for you and your daughters. You can restart your business."

She wrapped her shawl around herself as she thought. "You can see my condition for yourself, my lord. If I was to agree to your generosity, how could I move all the way across town?"

"I have brought my horse," I answered, thankful there was something helpful I felt I at last could contribute. "She is faithful and strong and will not let you fall. So," I added, as Rachel had voiced no further objection, and therefore assumed the matter had been decided, "I suggest we start packing your things." Had the house been in better condition, I would have waited a few days till they had adjusted to their initial grief, but because they had so little food and clean clothes, and their house seemed so cold, I wanted them to come now so they could have a good meal and a warm bed as soon as possible.

Within the hour, Rachel and her two daughters – by this point I had discovered the older sister was called Alena and the younger Ruth – had packed all the things they could need, including their mother's things. When the time came for us to leave, I picked up Rachel from the bed as gently as I could and slowly carried her outside. The girls followed, and whilst they stood on the street, locking up their old home, I placed Rachel upon Epos, who neighed softly. The two girls turned back to me.

"Let me take that," I murmured, quickly taking the biggest bag from Alena. The sisters now only carried a small bag each, which I assumed contained all the things on earth they owned. I took hold of Epos' reins in my hand. "It is this way," I stated, and led Epos on in a slow walk, going slowly because of Rachel's condition and the slow pace of the children. I was partially thankful now that the streets were deserted, for I was sure we would have received strange looks from all directions.

It took twenty minutes for us to walk across the town, up the steep incline of Gaeson's hill. As we walked, we passed the church building where we met each Sunday, situated halfway between the castle and the town, and the three of them stopped for a moment. I reasoned it was not just to catch their breath, but also to lift up all that had happened this dreadful day to God.

By the time we arrived at my home, they were all exhausted. I took Rachel into my house and carried her across the threshold into the living area, where I was pleased to see a roaring fire. I settled Rachel down into the nearest chair to the flames. Alena and Ruth ran over also, clinging to the chair and slowly outstretching their cautious hands to the fire, as if they had not sat next to one for years.

"My lord," Sarah greeted me, coming down the stairs. Then, as she spotted the newcomers, she curtseyed and said, "Good day to you."

I felt a stab of guilt that I had not come here to warn Sarah of the new guests, as surely they would add much to her workload – but my heart had compelled me to go straight to tell Rachel of Joshua's death as soon as physically able.

"Hello, Sarah. Rachel, this is Sarah," I said, introducing them.

Sarah smiled warmly at Rachel, and I glimpsed a faint smile upon Rachel's tired, pained countenance.

"Sarah is my oldest friend. She manages the affairs of my house and helps care for my mother; they both live here with me," I explained. "Sarah, this is Rachel and her children, Alena and Ruth."

"A pleasure to meet you, I am sure," Sarah replied politely.

Rachel managed to nod, but the children only clung deeper to their mother.

"Sarah, I need you to prepare the two spare rooms," I instructed. "Rachel is to have one, the children to share the other. They will all live here from now on."

Sarah's features turned to surprise momentarily, but then she nodded. "Of course, my lord." She left at once to prepare.

I heated some water onto the fire, wondering when it was they had last been able to bathe – bathing could be expensive in the poorer areas of our town. Rachel remained quiet, staring into the fire. This I could understand – she had just lost her son. The two children sat at a bench, looking sombre and anxious. This I could just as easily understand – in the last hour they had been informed of their brother's death and promptly been removed from everything they had ever known. I hoped I was making the right decision to move them so quickly, but I had feared they would starve should I leave it any longer.

As I stood again, the younger daughter shivered, and I realised the front door was still wide open. I went outside again to where I had left Epos tied up next to the house and guided her down the narrow alley that led to our yard – I would take her back to the stables later. For the time being, I removed all the riding gear from her and forked out some fresh hay. When I came back inside, I saw Rachel and the children in the same position, not having moved. Just then I heard Sarah coming downstairs to enter the living area also.

"Sarah," I greeted her, "I wonder if you could show Alena and Ruth to their new room?"

The two girls were reluctant so I crouched down to their level. "Your very own room is upstairs. I wonder if you would like to unpack your things. We can hang up drawings like in your old home to make it your own. You can see most of the castle out of the window." I saw a little interest spark in their eyes.

Sarah now stepped forwards. "Come along," she encouraged them warmly, as she picked up their few meagre possessions. "Let us not wait until breakfast."

With a nod from their mother, the children stood and cautiously followed Sarah upstairs. Rachel glanced at me and managed another faint smile at me in thanks, but her gaze was soon back on the fire.

I left her and headed for the kitchen. There were a few of Sarah's rolls that had been baked yesterday, and a cooked chicken in the larder. I cut up the chicken and bread, put it with a few root vegetables, and divided it up into six portions. I also retrieved some wine and measured some out from Rachel. This done, I headed back to the living area.

"Here," I stated simply, as I handed Rachel the food and the wine.

For a moment, the sadness in her face lessened as she looked at it with full and open astonishment, as if the portion was too much for her. I wondered when her last good meal had been – not that what I was offering was particularly grand. I pondered if she might be bedridden simply because she was starving. Another moment later and Rachel dived into the meal. I heard footsteps and saw the two children appear, still withdrawn from me. I handed them their food.

"I know this is new and difficult," I told them, "but I swear I will not harm you. You are safe here. I promised your brother I would take care of you. I want you to consider this as much your house as it is mine. Please eat," I encouraged them – they were staring at the food as if they had never seen food before. "You must be hungry."

At this, the children began to eat with almost wild enthusiasm. "I will go and aid Sarah," I added as I stood – I knew Rachel and her children would wish to adjust to their surroundings and have some time on their own to grieve Joshua. I also wished to explain things to Sarah, as she did not yet know why this family had come to live with us. I headed upstairs, taking three plates for my mother, Sarah and myself. I entered my mother's room first and saw Sarah in there also.

"My son," my mother smiled. "I was relieved indeed to see you in the square. Sarah tells me we have visitors who are coming to live with us?"

"That is right, Enid," Sarah affirmed, plumping up fresh pillows as I gave my mother her plate. "Thank you," Sarah said, smiling as she took the other plate from me. "I am sorry I did not prepare the meal…"

"It's quite alright, Sarah; you were busy up here. Besides, I know how to cut a chicken," I added. I sat on one chair in the room, Sarah took the other and the three of us began to eat. "I'm sorry I couldn't warn you about Rachel joining us. I hope you do not mind that they live here. If you do not wish it, I could try to find them somewhere else…"

"Your father left you this house when he died," my mother interrupted, "it is yours to do with as you wish. But who are they, Daniel?"

I swallowed a mouthful of chicken. "I fought alongside Rachel's son last night," I explained. "He was still a boy – only thirteen. He was conscripted after so many died in the last battle. He protested at our fighting last night when the captain spoke to us, before the fighting broke out. Joshua was terrified, but not for his own life – he was fearful for Rachel and the children's survival. His words almost cost him his life before the battle started. I tried to reassure him and promised him that should anything happen, I would take care of them and ensure they would not starve."

"Joshua died," Sarah guessed now quietly, "in the battle."

I nodded, feeling the tightness of my throat.

"That is why they have come to live here. That was a very good thing you did, Daniel," she said gently.

"Indeed," my mother agreed, "they are of course welcome here, but do we have enough money to provide for them? I know you have your soldier's salary, but…"

"I think we should be fine," I affirmed. "We will manage with them here." My voice still sounded tight and I now cleared my throat. "If it pleases Rachel, we could restore their old house and let it out; enough people come to trade here, and someone will want to reside in it. The money from the house will allow Rachel and her children to restart their business; in time, they could even start paying for board here."

Presently we finished our meals, and I took our empty plates back downstairs, leaving Sarah to finish preparing Rachel's room. By this time the water had been prepared, and I helped Rachel to the bathroom. By the time Rachel and her children had been bathed, Sarah had fetched clothing for them from out of her wardrobe. For the children, she gave them the clothes she had worn when she was a child that she had kept from when she moved from her old house to live with my mother and me. At the time I wasn't sure how practical this had been, but was now grateful for her sentimentality. Besides, I knew the market would be open again tomorrow, so we would be able to buy any extra clothing that was necessary.

Later, after the water was again heated, I stepped into the bath myself, as I had not yet washed off the grime of the battle. As I sank into the water, the faces of the men I had killed overcame me, and this time I let them, no longer distracted by the urgency of finding Rachel. This battle had been fierce, perhaps fiercer than the last one. I thought again of that Klumeck soldier I had spared, who was now imprisoned here at Gaeson. But it was perhaps the sight of Joshua, dead and bloodied, that was disturbing me the most. I wondered at the man who had killed such a young boy – but then the enemy would not have known Joshua's age. Joshua was a terrified boy, but I could recognise his determination underneath that. I was sure Joshua would have fought bravely, and therefore would have presented himself to the enemy like any other soldier. It was like that in battle – every soldier was either for you or against you. You either maimed or killed, or you were maimed or killed yourself.

After I had finished bathing, I told Sarah I was going to rest, and at once succumbed to sleep, so fatigued I was from the battle. When I woke, I saw it was night. It was another cloudless night, for I could see the large cream of the moon; the clear nights only seemed to make things colder. I crossed the room and splashed cold water on my face. I attempted to sleep again, but since I had been sleeping since early afternoon I was now wide awake. I stood and dressed, buckling on the belt that carried my sword. I left my chamber and went downstairs as silently as I could, for the rest of the house was now quiet. I paused in the hall to scribble a note for Sarah informing her of my departure, then pulled on my boots at the door and exited into the yard.

"Hush, girl," I murmured, as Epos neighed softly. I saddled her up and led her out of the yard and down the alley. Once back onto the street, I swung up to mount her and set her off into a quick trot back to the castle. I knew I was technically still meant to be resting, but my mind was giving me anything but rest. I wished to speak to the captain – I was determined to find out more about why King Cedric was suddenly attacking. In the aftermath of this violent battle and what had happened to Joshua, I found I shared the boy's sentiment all the more. I felt we had a right to know why war had suddenly come upon us.

Upon reaching the castle, I was informed my captain was keeping watch on one of the higher balconies. Intending to volunteer to keep watch, I dressed in my armour and slung my sheath on my back. As I journeyed through the castle, I perceived the castle servants to be hard at work and were still cleaning the stones now; I was careful where I trod, picking my way past the mopping and the buckets of water. The walls and floors that were now newly cleaned still seemed to cry out with the blood of the fallen.

As I proceeded higher up the castle, I saw the field beyond the castle walls where Klumeck had advanced upon us; there were many embers still going from the fires where bodies had been collected and burnt. Eventually I stepped out onto the balcony and perceived the captain to be at the other end, but I found myself distracted momentarily by the sight of the stars, which lit up the sky from one end to the other. I had not seen stars as vivid as this for years, not since I was a child.

"Hello, Daniel." I turned from the sky to glance at my commander. The captain was not facing me, but had clearly sensed I was there. "Come and join me," he offered, moving a hand from where he held it behind his back to beckon me forwards.

"My lord," I greeted him as I walked over. He was facing out towards the battlefield where I had seen the embers glowing a few minutes earlier. I followed his stare to where many carcasses of the dead must lay.

"I thought you were supposed to be resting," he muttered, turning now to look at me. "Why are here in your armour and not at home?"

"I wish to be here, in case we are needed, sire," I stated simply. "In fact, I was wondering whether I could help keep watch tonight. I have slumbered all afternoon and am now restless. Perhaps there is another I could relieve who could rest in my place?"

The captain regarded me a moment, and then gave a short nod.

"Sire?" I asked ere long and he did now turn to look at me. "I was wondering if you could tell me anything more…"

"About the attacks?" he finished for me, as his gaze went out to the field. His voice sounded detached, as if his mind was elsewhere. "It has been a dark few days indeed." The captain sighed wearily. He glanced at me again, quicker this time. "Ah, I may as well tell you. The way gossip goes through this town so quickly… all will know soon enough." He paused here as we both stared out into the night; a quiet breeze rifled past us.

"King Cedric believes Our Sovereign has something that belongs to him," my captain explained now. "He is attacking because, according to his words, His Majesty King Reghan is refusing to oblige. King Cedric will continue to fight until it is returned to him. In truth, King Reghan knows not what King Cedric speaks of."

"What is the item, my lord?"

The captain glanced at me again, fixing his deep, heavy blue eyes upon me. "Not what, Daniel, but who." He paused again, and I frowned. "King Cedric believes that twenty-one years ago, his heir was kidnapped and taken into our kingdom."

My eyes widened in surprise. "But how can that be, sir? His Majesty does not have any male heirs," I pointed out. "There is only Princess Evelyn."

"His Majesty has tried to explain that, but King Cedric refuses to listen." The captain exhaled slowly. "King Cedric insists the same is true of his niece."

"He believes there is a female heir also?"

The captain nodded, pinching the bridge of his nose.

"So King Cedric is instigating this war in order to discover his lost heirs," I concluded. "Twenty-one years... that's when war first broke out," I added suddenly, with an abrupt jolt in my memory of sitting in my mother's arms in the caves.

The captain nodded wearily.

"So every time King Cedric has attacked..."

"Apparently, it has been to secure his heirs," the captain surmised. "His Majesty King Reghan has only just discovered this, after interrogating one of the enemy we captured alive."

I nodded as I took in this new information.

"Twenty-one years ago there was a rumour that King Cedric's nephew and niece had come to Gaeson," the captain admitted, and now it was my turn to glance at him. "But when His Majesty launched an investigation to the missing heirs, he discovered from his spies that the heirs had in fact died in Klumeck."

"I imagine His Majesty has tried to tell this to King Cedric," I supplied and the captain nodded, "but I suppose King Cedric does not believe him."

"You suspect right. King Cedric is adamant, despite His Majesty King Reghan's insistence, that the heirs did come to Gaeson, and that they are still alive somewhere. His Majesty told me all this himself this morning and said that King Cedric will not rest until he sees his heirs, either alive or in their graves," the captain concluded.

"So that is why King Cedric marches upon us." Both of us, at the sound of this new voice, turned on the spot and fell to bended knee in perfect synchronisation – as both of us already knew the identity of the voice. Princess Evelyn now stepped out of the shadows, turning down the hood of her cloak. "Good evening, captain of the guard," she addressed the captain formally.

"Your Highness," he greeted her, whilst I lowered my head further to stare at the ground. I did not greet her myself, but instead remained silent, for it was our custom that only the highest rank of the soldiers present could dare speak to the royal family. She did not speak for a moment, and I dared to raise my head just a little. I saw now her cloak was open; underneath it she was wearing a pale blue gown, with fabric that hung down from her sleeves. Her long dark curls currently hung loose. I risked glancing higher to survey what I could of her countenance; I perceived her mouth to be drawn in a thin line. I was curious to her expression, but did not dare raise my eyes higher.

"Soldier, raise your head," she ordered, after another few moments of silence.

I raised my head, assuming she was addressing me since there was no one else present.

She was frowning at me with a certain scrutiny. "Have we met before?" she questioned.

I opened my mouth to speak, but the captain answered for me:

"It is unlikely, Your Highness. He has never been personally assigned to you."

Her eyes lingered over to me for but a moment longer. "No, I suppose not," she replied at length, and turned back to the captain.

I kept my face impassive, though secretly I harboured disappointment. I had hoped... but there was no reason why she would recognise me. After all, we had been but children.

"With respect, Your Highness," the captain said after another moment's silence, "it is not safe for you to be here."

"You sound like my father," she said. She sounded almost bored as she wandered to the edge of the balcony. My face remained impassive, but her speech was surprising. She was the only person in the kingdom to be able to speak of the king in that manner. "So many dead," Princess Evelyn murmured now. "Do you agree with the blood that has been spilt this night, captain?"

I kept my face to the ground as she turned around to us, again remaining expressionless despite her outrageous question.

"I live to serve His Majesty, Your Highness," the captain replied calmly, "though battle is a terrible thing, I trust in my lord the king's judgment."

She smirked. "Spoken like a truly faithful servant. Your loyalty does you great credit, captain of the guard." She had folded her arms now, the fingers of one hand tapping her elbow before she turned to us once more. "I am sure my father knows best. I know he is trying to protect me," she added with a sigh. "But I could no longer lead the defence of the caves, watching my people fear for their lives and the lives of their loved ones fighting above. I know he's trying to protect me," the princess said with another sigh, as if trying to pacify her earlier statement. "But I need to know why our kingdom is being attacked and he refused to tell me. Presumably for my own protection. Our people are dying, and I think we should know why." She turned back towards us. "Goodnight, gentlemen. I will be sure not to get you into trouble."

"Your Highness," the captain answered promptly, bowing his head quickly. We watched Princess Evelyn raise the hood of her cloak and draw it more closely about her as she descended the steps, the opposite exit to the one I had used. The captain raised his eyebrows at me but said nothing. There ensued another bout of silence; I wondered whether I should bid my leave.

"What happened to that boy?" the captain asked suddenly, in a somewhat hoarse tone. "The young boy, the one who spoke out last night," he expounded, as if I had not immediately known what he had been speaking of.

"The boy is dead, my lord." My voice sounded so hallow, so mechanical.

The captain took a sharp intake of breath and then exhaled it slowly out again. "I had no choice, Daniel," he declared roughly, his voice just as abrupt and hoarse as before. "Did I want to have to order him to fight, barely out of his childhood? What soldier would wish that?" he asked; I perceived his question to be rhetorical and so did not reply. "I had to speak with him so harshly, otherwise others could have spoken out also," the captain stated. I detected he was speaking to himself rather than me. "I could not have afforded such anarchy at the best of times, let alone on the brink of battle." He paused here and sighed. "Orders are orders," he said flatly.

"Of course, sire. You did all you could," I added, seeking to give him affirmation, though he had asked for none. He nodded, and I sensed the shift in his demeanour; I suspected he now wanted to be left alone. "Goodnight, sire," I bade him.

"Goodnight, Daniel," he said, that weary sigh in his voice.

I inclined my head in a short bow and turned to leave.

"Wait," he ordered, and he turned back to me. "What was his name, that boy?"

I tried to swallow the emptiness I felt. "His name was Joshua, sire," I replied, my voice sounding as hoarse as he had been.

The captain nodded.

"Captain," I said again, and there left his company, my conversation with him still ringing in my ears. In my almost nine years of serving under him as captain, I had never known him to be anything but strong, resilient, and ready to both encourage and rebuke. I had never before heard the roughness in his voice; indeed, he had sounded almost emotional. As I travelled higher to the main castle wall, I pondered that I had glimpsed the man behind the armour and position, which was a rare privilege.

"You've been relieved," I stated to the first man I saw; I noticed he was a newer, younger recruit. "I am to take your place. You can go and rest."

The man bowed with a thankful smile. "Thank you, sire," he answered gratefully as he handed me the horn. He now left, heading, I presumed, for the regimental chambers.

I, in turn, was grateful to have something to do, as I was completely alert. Also, although they would probably not express it, I wondered whether they would find it difficult living in the same house as a soldier, seeing as how their son and brother had just died in battle. Before I could stop myself, I imagined his body now, surely a carcass that had long been burnt upon the fire. I shook my head mentally of the image of Joshua's remains as I entered the chambers, focusing instead on the night sky.

As I looked out on the castle wall, I saw all was quiet and still. It was strange to think that it was only a week previous when I had discovered the enemy through the window due to my thirst; that night seemed so long ago. Whilst my eyes remained trained on the still scene before me, my mind drifted further back than recent events, to another far more pleasant memory. My memories took me back to when I was a boy, nine years old, to the only other time the princess and I had met, as children in the snow.

***

It was deep in the month of winter. There was thick snow encased everywhere, but I felt safe and warm here in the stables. This was not the kind of terrifying blizzard I had nightmares about, from when I was lost as an infant, but soft, fresh layers upon the ground that I crunched with my thick boots wherever I trod. I loved snow during the day, when the world was crisp and pure and everything seemed so still. I stopped shovelling in new hay to pause to look at the fields once more, each one clothed in a vast, white blanket.

I loved it here in the stables, with its musky smell, and the snorts and neighs from the horses. Currently we housed about eighty of them, as many had been lost in the last battle. It made me sad to think of those beautiful creatures lying on the ground, dead or dying. Before I could stop myself, my thoughts became even sadder when I envisaged the one time I had seen a horse die.

The leaves were just falling from the trees; I had been clearing out the old hay when it happened. The horse in question had become more and more distressed; Father had noticed this about her earlier in the day. Without warning, the horse had fallen to her knees and started pawing the ground distractedly. My father had touched her; the horse's mane had been hot and damp. Father had told me then he was not sure whether the horse would live; I was to carry on with my chores, and we would have to see whether she made it through the night.

Later on, when I had finished the day's work, I sat with the horse with my hand on her beautiful copper neck. My father saw me like that and told me it was time to leave; he would return later to see how the horse was doing.

"Don't make me leave, Father," I had whispered to him, my eyes filled with tears. "I want to stay with her and comfort her until she gets better again."

"No, my son, come away," my father told me gently, getting down onto his knees beside me. "The horse might not get better, Daniel."

I looked up at him fearfully.

"The horse might well die."

"Then she might die while you are returning me home," I murmured back. "Please, Father. Let her not die alone – I wish to be with her."

My father regarded me.

"Please," I begged.

Finally my father nodded.

"Very well," he said. "Let us stay here together and we will see how she fares." He unlatched the pin that attached his cloak and, upon removing it, placed it around my shoulders. He then sat down next to me and gathered me in his arms; thus entwined, with my hand still on the horse's neck, we sat there together to wait in the dark.

I could not remember what happened next; I think I may have slept, for the next thing I knew, my father woke me to tell me the horse was dead. Tears streamed down my face and my father had to carry me away, for I did not want to leave her, cold and alone in the stables. When we returned the next morning, the horse was gone. For weeks her stall remained empty, before new horses arrived and one took her place. Now I imagined many horses like that, hundreds of them as in a battle, all lying like she had been. Tears slowly slid down my face.

"What are you crying about, boy?" It was a voice that spoke softly through the air, and all at once I knew this was the sweetest voice I had ever heard. I turned to see a girl wearing a small, brown cloak, fashioned together by a large blue pin. Her voice had been sincere and her face was not mocking; instead, she spoke with much concern for a boy she'd never met. With her white dress and thick dark curls, I thought she was an angel.

Self-conscious of the emotion I had expressed, I wiped my eyes. "Nothing," I replied, moving towards her, and then stopped with a frown. "Have we met before?" I knew I recognised this girl from somewhere, but I didn't know where.

"No," she replied, "we do not know each other." She said it a little too quickly, as if she had something to hide. "Here," she added, handing me a small cloth. I took it swiftly and wiped my eyes, trying to erase the truth of my tears. "Do you work here?"

"Yes. I tend the horses," I said, a little proudly. "Somebody has to look after them during the winter. Father helps me when he's at home. He's a soldier. I'm going to be too, one day, when I'm older. Do you have a job?" Most children had work, not like men, who work all day to bring food home, but a task they have for a small portion of the day. The work was paid if you did a good job. I did not mind this work – I liked the fact that I was working with my people, all serving each other. Besides, I loved being with the horses.

"In a way," she said.

I frowned at her again when she didn't give me any more information. I glanced down at the cloth and noticed the luxury of the material. White and soft, with lace trimmed round the edges. I did not know this material, but it was far softer than anything I had ever felt before.

"Princess Evelyn, are you out here?" a new voice called out, agitated and distressed. The girl started at the voice and looked a little panicked – and my eyes flew open wide in recognition, my mouth also agape. All this time, I had been talking to the princess!

"Your Highness," I said hastily, as I stepped back, trying to give her the proper respect. Flustered, I began to bow.

"Don't!" she hissed. "Please, don't give me away. Say you haven't seen me." With that, she darted into the stables.

I followed her with my eyes, frowning further. Why would the princess want to hide? I wondered. Was she in some sort of trouble?

"You there," the royal guard came over to me, looking both anxious and angered. "I can't find a little girl. Has she come out here?" Out of the corner of my eye, I saw the princess poking

75

through a sack, her head shaking no, her eyes pleading to me. "Well, boy?"

"No, sorry, sire. I haven't seen her." I knew this was a lie – but how could I give her away, when she had asked me with those beautiful eyes and sweet, sweet voice? Besides, she was the princess – it was my duty to follow her orders.

The guard scrutinised me a moment longer, and then broke into a gallop in another direction. Once I was sure the man had gone, I ran into the stables. She edged out and smiled in relief when she saw he had gone.

"Your Highness…" I began, attempting to bow again.

"Stop that silly bowing," she hissed. "Can't you tell I don't want to be found out?" She went outside the stables now and looked around cautiously as I followed.

"Why are you hiding?" I asked, so confused I was forgetting to address her properly. She turned to me, smiling radiantly.

"I just wanted to see the snow," she replied, bending down and stretching out her hands into it. "I'm never allowed out onto the snow, apart from one hour a day under supervision, and then I'm not allowed to do anything. Yesterday I threw a ball of snow and it hit him in the face." She giggled. "He wasn't going to let me go out today; he said it was too cold, but probably it was because of the snow in his face." She pulled a face then and, despite my sad thoughts, I giggled. "So he shut me in the library, but I went out of the window. It's not that far to the ground," she added. She bent down and picked up the snow with her bare hands. "Isn't it beautiful?"

"Yes," I replied instantly – but I wasn't talking about the snow.

She raised an arm and threw the handful of snow at me. It hit me full on the face, a sheet of cold and wet that took my breath away. The princess laughed and a moment later, I broke into laughter too. For the next few minutes, we threw balls of snow at each other. She had just began to form another ball in the snow when we heard the sound of galloping.

"It's the guard!" she hissed, and darted into the stables.

This time, I ran back inside also. I had just grabbed a tool, beginning to shovel the hay again, when the horse galloped past and I straightened, the tool still in my hand, whilst Princess Evelyn came out again.

"You have to help me get back," she whispered. "If I can crawl back into the library, I can hide in there and pretend I was there the whole time, hiding. I jammed the window ajar with a stone – I can get back in there if it's still there, but not on my own. Will you help me?"

"Yes." I answered without hesitation. I did not think of the consequences as, after all, this was the princess – this was my first royal order. I went out of the stable first to check the coast was clear, but the guard had gone.

"Come on – I mean, Your Highness," I added nervously, and she giggled. Together we ran across the short distance from the stables to the library. The snow was falling thick and fast, so our footprints would be easily covered. We soon came to the library window.

"Wait, your cloth," I told her, holding it out.

She looked at it, and giggled, seeing it was sodden from my tears and the snow. "You keep it," she said. "I have hundreds just like it. Hold out your hands then," she added.

I outstretched them as instructed them. I felt her dainty feet as she put them in my hands and the softness of her hand that she put on my neck. With such proximity to her, I noticed she had some kind of perfume on – despite it being the cold depths of winter, I was suddenly reminded of berries ripening in the warm sunshine.

"Lift me up then," she instructed and I swallowed rapidly.

"Uh, sorry." I flustered and raised my arms. She gripped the wooden window ledge and pulled herself up. I realised what she was doing was a risk, as obviously in this weather the window was closed, so she would not be able to look inside.

"Good, the stone is still here," she giggled. With that, she opened the wooden board of the window with a flourish. "No one's here," she called, and climbed inside before turning to me. "Thank you. I think you would make a fine soldier," she added. "You have just proven yourself an excellent knight."

I smiled widely.

"What is your name, boy?" she asked me. I opened my mouth to tell her, but then her head jerked to the side. "The guard is returning, I must go. Goodbye, my boy from the snow."

Before I could bid her farewell, the window was shut and she had disappeared behind the wooden board. I turned and ran too, all the way back to the stables, and darted back inside. I saw the sack was in a mess from where the princess had hidden. I tidied it up, ensuring it did not look like she had been there.

Once done, I looked out at the sky and saw from the sun it was about half an hour later; my father would be here soon. Hurriedly, I picked up the tool to get on with my chores, but I found myself too distracted – all I could think of was the encounter I had just had with the princess. I smiled at the thought of her sweet voice and her dainty hands, her concerned eyes and dark curls. I reached into my pocket to look again at the cloth, and now noticed her initials were etched into one corner, with delicate flowers sewn around it. I realised I was holding it carefully, as if it was my most prized possession in all the world.

With a sudden rush, I realised that even though I was only nine years old, I loved her. Right then and there in the stables, I vowed to serve and fight for her, with all the strength God would give me.

***

I smiled now at the memory, still staring out as I walked up and down my position upon the castle wall, the horn on a rope hung loosely around my neck. With my eyes still out on the distance, I opened the top of my breastplate and reached in to the inside of my tunic to the inside pocket I had sewn in myself, which I had done in all of my tunics. Carefully, as to me it was still my most prized possession, I removed the cloth I kept there – that same cloth the princess had given me when I was nine. I roved a finger against the soft lace of the fabric. By now, the flowers and initials had faded, but they were still visible. I knew it was folly of me to have kept it for so long, but its presence had comforted me much over the years. I carried it with me everywhere, even in battle – not as a kind of superstitious charm, but because it helped me remember the vow I had made in the snow that day, and why I was fighting. I had never told my parents, nor Aife, nor John or Sarah about that meeting with her that day in the snow and the cloth she had given me.

After my encounter with Princess Evelyn, I had begun to see her at public events, in the courtyard where the king made his announcements. I had grown up going to this courtyard, but for some reason I had never noticed the princess before. In truth, I used to find royal events and announcements rather boring; it just meant waiting around while speeches were said, and men and women were rewarded for whatever they had done. To me, simply it meant time away from my parents or the horses. My father and mother had scolded me when I had once, much earlier, voiced that opinion – and after that I was silent, although I secretly remained bored nonetheless.

After my meeting the princess that day, however, I watched the royal proceedings with enthusiasm. This had greatly pleased my parents, who must have thought that finally I was taking an interest in the monarchy and becoming patriotic for my king. They did not know I was so enthusiastic because I was hoping to glimpse the princess I had met in the snow. Glimpse her I did – and I was able to watch her age with grace and wisdom, becoming a noble woman. She retained her small, warm eyes and her thick dark curls. Her voice, though deepened, was still sweeter than the sweetest honey. Each year she had grown, I had also grown in a fierce love to serve and fight for her. It turned out I had made a true prediction that day in the stables, when I had vowed I would always love her – for even up to this day I loved her still.

Alas, I had not told anyone else this – John and Sarah, Aife, the captain, not even my mother knew. They knew of my fierce passion for my kingdom and for protecting my king, but they did not know of my secret vow to fight for the woman I love. I knew I could never hope to express my love to her, or to have that love returned, but it was enough to fight for her in this way. I knew I would probably never marry, unable to marry the one I love the most – but for some reason, this rarely bothered me. I was strangely content to remain as I was, fighting with all I had in me to protect her.

I knew other fighting warriors felt this way; although many soldiers married, there were quite a few who chose to remain unattached due to the risks of a soldier's life. There was something safe about loving one I knew I would never be able to marry, as I had seen so many wives and husbands grieving. I myself had experienced it first hand, having lost my father at his sudden death in battle not long before I enlisted. For a few weeks before the enrolment, I was not even sure I would still join the army, as I did not wish my mother to have the pain of a lost son as well as a lost husband. The anguish that my mother would have was a risk enough to endure, let alone having a possible wife as well who may mourn me; I certainly did not wish that pain on anyone else.

Not even that dreadful thought, however, had deterred me from fulfilling my vow to the princess. As I stood there on the castle wall, turning the old cloth with her faded initials over in my hands, I felt an affirmation of my desire to fight for my king and to protect Princess Evelyn. I pledged myself to serve her once again as I stared out at Gaeson, knowing without hesitation that I would give my all to serve her, no matter what the cost to myself. To ensure her wellbeing, I would gladly give my last breath.

Chapter Four

The horn suddenly sounded, but it was not me that had blown it. Surely not again! I looked wildly around from where I was upon the wall, stuffing the cloth hurriedly back into my tunic and closing the gap in my armour. My eyes scanned the darkness for a moment, but there was nothing. In all my wonderings, I had not stopped scanning the landscape beyond the walls. Where was the enemy? I saw the other watchmen had begun descending from the wall, and here I quickly joined them – nobody sounded a false horn, so the enemy must be somewhere. Could it be King Cedric once again? I wondered now. Could Klumeck have rallied their forces so quickly?

I was already dressed for battle, so there was no need to visit the armoury. I instead ran straight towards the small hall where we gathered for the captain to brief us – perhaps the captain had more information about why the horn had been sounded.

"Help!"

I stopped dead at the sound of the scream. I felt a lurch of dread, for I knew exactly who the scream belonged to.

"The princess," I whispered – I would know her voice anywhere, even halfway across the kingdom. The scream came again and I broke into a sprint in the way I had come, in her direction. "You three, with me," I shouted to three other soldiers as I passed them – with me being in the higher rank, they followed me without question.

We had not run far when the scream came again. "The courtyard!" I called rapidly, and the four of us burst out into the night air once more, wielding our swords. I scanned the darkness, and just in the corner of my eye, at the opposite corner of the courtyard, I spied some men wearing Klumeck armour.

"There!" I shouted. A moment later and we were running through the courtyard. More of Klumeck's army had appeared and we engaged them. We left the courtyard now, running down a cobbled alley to the south parts of the castle. With every step,

I prayed for Princess Evelyn's safety. We turned a corner and saw Princess Evelyn bound and carried by two men.

"Halt!" I shouted, pointing my sword at them, but they refused to stop. One of the men had a knife to her throat, and I knew without them telling me what would happen if I advanced any further. I edged cautiously, assessing my options, when suddenly an arrow appeared as if from nowhere, lodging itself into the head of the man wielding the knife.

I glanced up to see Aife, who smirked at me as she prepared her next arrow. Another arrow came from the archer next to her. My eyes rapidly followed it as it flew down to impale another foe's neck. The man screamed and fell to the floor. I saw my opportunity and launched myself forwards to slash my sword in the chest of the first enemy I came to.

To my relief, the other men I had called now ran forwards to engage the remaining Klumeck soldiers in battle. Princess Evelyn was now only held by one man, and she was beginning to succeed in wrenching herself free. Eventually she brought up her knee between his legs, and as he stumbled she escaped his grip. Her hands were still bound, but she was free and began to run – but had only taken a few steps when another man from Klumeck made to grab her.

"Your Highness!" I shouted, darting forwards. The man, seeing my advance, roughly released her. I raised my hand and brought it down; he parried and moved to the left to strike again, but I blocked him. I raised my blade, preparing my next move, when an arrow whistled past my hair to pierce his skull. I glanced up to see it, then leapt over the man to reach the princess.

"Hold still, Your Highness," I murmured. I carefully sliced her bonds with my blade.

"You," she said – I presumed she recognised me from meeting the captain and me on that balcony only a few hours ago. "You have my thanks," she replied in relief.

I turned to face the rest of the Klumeck men. The princess stooped to the man who had been pierced with an arrow in the neck and picked up the enemy blade. Another foe came forwards, and before I could even move she had cut him down, wielding her blade with skill and ease.

Princess Evelyn and I now faced the enemy – there were six men opposing us, but more and more of our own forces were spilling through into the courtyard, led by the captain and John. But then another group of Klumeck soldiers suddenly ran into the courtyard also, pursued by more of Gaeson's army. I cut another man down, deducing that there were no more than two or three scout teams of spies; their stealth meant they had somehow managed to enter our gates undetected. Still, I was encouraged by our number, and soon most of them had been cut down.

"Daniel!"

I turned at the captain's voice, and that was when I spotted him. He was lying on his back on the cobbled stone floor, with blood spurting from his chest. I dropped to my knees next to him, my hands at once trying to stem the bleeding, but he pushed me away. Moments later, another soldier was at his knees, doing the same thing.

"Daniel," he panted, his bloody hand grabbing the metal of my armour, "You need to get the princess out of here. They clearly intended to capture her; she must not fall into enemy hands. The way to the castle is blocked," he rasped.

I looked up and saw he was right; there was now a bloody skirmish at all the entrances from the courtyard to the castle.

"The king will no doubt be safe," the captain murmured. "You cannot get her to the castle, nor the caves, lest you are followed. We must follow the protocols."

"Caer Ligualid," I murmured – it was the protocol to escort the royals to safety in our capital kingdom should our own castle be overrun.

The captain nodded, breathing heavily.

"Yes, sire," I assented immediately. "I will protect her all I can, upon pain of death." I reached and grasped his hand as blood began to dribble out of his mouth.

I lifted my eyes and saw the captain was right; by now, all entrances to higher up the castle were blocked. The only exit I could see was east of us, away from into the town. The only exit not blocked by those who would slay us.

"Get the princess out of here," the captain ordered. "Head to the forest, head to Caer Ligualid. I will tell the king; he would want her to be safe."

"Yes, sire. Take care, captain," I replied, grasping his hand with mine. I stood swiftly and looked at John. "I'll see you soon, brother," I told him. He could only give me a nod before I had turned away.

Through the dim light, I saw the princess in the midst of battle. At any moment, as with any of us, she could be struck. I sprinted over and put to the sword the enemy in front of her. "Come this way, Your Highness. I have orders to take you to safety."

She ignored me for a moment to strike down another foe, and then turned back to me.

"You doubt my blade, boy?" she questioned me angrily, her eyes narrowing as she wiped blood from her temple from where she already had a small cut.

"Not at all, Your Highness. But even the most skilled may fall. I bid you come with me to safety, Your Highness, on the captain's instruction. Your people need you alive," I pleaded.

She raised her head and our eyes met.

"Please, Your Highness. It is the protocol."

"Very well," she relented.

We turned and ran to the exit, but before we could leave, another Klumeck man blocked our path. I raised my blade, but before I could do anything else, he opened his mouth in a silent scream and fell to the floor, dead, to reveal Aife's knife sunk deep into his back.

"Hurry!" Aife shouted, removing her weapon. Before she could say anything else, all three of us were embroiled in another fight – but soon all three opponents had been cut down.

"Thank you, sister. Your Highness, I bid we leave right away," I added, and the princess nodded. The two of us broke into a run again, leaving the courtyard behind as we exited through the portcullis undetected.

We ran not down the hill towards the town, but around to the stables, as I had deduced that if we should have any chance of escaping, we needed to go on horseback. I wondered as we ran if going to the stables might trigger a memory of our meeting, but I realised this wouldn't necessarily be a connection with the boy she met in the snow. From her perspective, she had first seen me a couple of hours ago when she surprised us on the balcony. Was this really the same night? I wondered; the scene had changed from stillness to chaos so swiftly.

We came to the stables, running past the same fence where I had gotten faint at the memory of Joshua early this morning. We headed in and I hurried to Epos' stall, readying her as soon as possible. Princess Evelyn was silent for the most part – until, when I was preparing her own horse, she suddenly gave a loud gasp and stepped backwards.

My hand on the hilt of my sword, I went over to investigate, and at once saw why she had shuddered – a hand was protruding out of the hay. I bent and moved away some of the straw to reveal a dead Gaeson soldier, with an arrow coming out of his stomach. Princess Evelyn stepped back, half drawing the Klumeck sword as she looked around. I bent to examine the body further.

"This wound is old, Your Highness," I assured her quickly. "The archer is no doubt long gone from here. But we shall be swift nonetheless." I looked more closely at the man. He wore a large cloak, only a little stained with blood. I removed it carefully from his corpse and held it out to the princess.

She took it and put it on, understanding hastily. If it was discovered she was the princess, we would be pursued instantly. Without his cloak, we saw he also carried a sword. The princess now stepped towards the dead archer, stooping down towards him to exchange the sword she held for his.

"I would rather wield a blade of ours than theirs," she murmured, as she placed her sword in its sheath. We jerked our heads up at the loud cries piercing through the night. "We should be fighting with our people," she hissed bitterly.

"My orders are to take you to safety, Your Highness. It is better for your people that you are spared."

Her eyes met mine and I saw the anger in them, the longing to go back.

"Please, Your Highness. It is the protocol, and the horses are prepared."

"Very well, soldier," she muttered. "Let us depart, if that is what duty requires." There was anger still in her eyes.

"My lady," I said, holding out my hand. She put her foot in it, and suddenly I was nine years old, with her placing her feet in my hand while I pushed her up to the library window – surely only fifty metres or so from where we currently stood. But this time it wasn't a day in the snow while I helped her enter a window unseen; this time it was escaping into the middle of the night, whilst our people were being attacked.

I hurriedly placed my foot into the stirrup and swung myself up, glancing over to check that the princess was ready. Seeing that she was, I gathered the reins in my hands.

"Ride as quick as lightening, Epos," I called to my horse, and kicked her into a gallop. We rode at once, Princess Evelyn following me close behind with her cloak positioned over her head. Our horses' hooves thundered loudly as we rode through the town long deserted by its people; they would now be huddled in the caves. I felt a keen sense of wrong, as the princess did. I should be with my brothers and sisters in arms, not running away in the middle of the night – and I could tell Princess Evelyn felt the same way. As keenly as the sense of wrong was, however, I knew the princess' life lay in my hands, and my duty would always be to her, without mentioning the vow I had made as a child – therefore how could I not have Epos gallop us away to safety?

The minutes passed tensely; neither of us spoke. We had by now descended the bottom of the hill down through the town – the enemy did not come down the western side, as it was the opposite direction to where Klumeck hailed. We rode through the simple wooden barricade, built when our forefathers had first settled in Gaeson, and kept riding down. Just before the treeline I paused and looked back, but I could see nothing except glimpses of fire from the tip of the castle that was visible, where firing arrows were surely reigning down from both sides. I swallowed and gripped my reins again; as far as I could tell, we had escaped undetected.

I moved Epos into the forest, now at a gentle canter. Princess Evelyn travelled on her horse alongside me, matching me pace for pace. Soon we were in the thick of densely packed trees. Above me, beyond the intermingling branches, sat the vast canopy of the sky. I was thankful now for the clearness of the night, as though it made things colder, I was better able to get my bearings from the position of the stars and the moon.

In time, I turned Epos' trajectory further north, so we were travelling parallel to the great lake rather than towards it. The shouts and cries of the battle faded with every move, until all we could hear was the sounds of the forest: the whistling of the leaves with the breeze, the humming of the insects and other wildlife. Though the noise of the woodland was altogether making quite a din, it seemed to me peaceful in contrast to the screams of the wounded and dying.

"I think this is far enough," the princess presently called to me from atop her horse. "They may be waiting for us tonight, as soon as we leave the forest." Her tone was tired yet commanding; I agreed with her instincts. "We must hope by the time we leave the forest tomorrow, they will have stopped their search."

"Yes, my lady," I answered. I dismounted Epos; the princess swung down off her own horse to stand next to me, not using the hand I had offered. I took both reins and tied up the horses to a nearby tree. "Would you like some refreshment? I have only water, I'm afraid," I added, holding out the skin to her.

"Thank you, soldier." Her hand touched mine briefly as she took the water from me; though my heart jumped inside at the contact, my expression remained impassive. Princess Evelyn seemed to look right through me as she took it from me; it felt odd that she would see me as a stranger.

She moved to sit down on a stump of a tree; I remained standing at attention. "Please sit, if you wish," she offered, gesturing her hand around the small clearing we found ourselves in.

I went the short distance across the clearing to the tree where Epos and the other horse were tethered. Epos nudged her head so that it rested upon my shoulder.

"That horse seems to know you well," she commented.

"Aye, my lady. I have known her since she was a foal. I used to work at the stables, before enlisting," I ventured. I had hoped she would have recognised me at this new information, but she only nodded. I knew I had only been one of several stable boys at one time, however, so from her perspective I might not be the boy she had met that day.

There was a pause here, in which I realised how cold it was. Since we had stopped riding, our sweat had cooled to make us doubly cold. I was even more thankful the princess had taken the cloak; hopefully that would be enough to keep her warm.

"I think it is safe to sleep now, Your Highness," I said, when she had drunk her fill and handed the skin back to me. "I will remain awake all night to keep watch."

"Very well," she replied, and gave a nod. She rose from the log and slept instead on the floor. The ground was soft and springy with moss, so I hoped it would provide my lady with enough comfort.

Princess Evelyn now bundled up the excess of her cloak's hood, turning it into a pillow of sorts. I stood and removed the large portion of water I had strapped to the horses, allowing them to poke their heads in and guzzle some of it down. In another small container I had placed some carrots and oats, and held it out to them.

"You both did well today," I murmured to them quietly, for I knew we would not have been able to escape so easily without them. Whilst they ate their fill, I scanned the edges of the clearing in order to keep watch. When they were content, they neighed softly and lay down next to each other, with Epos lying closest to me.

I sat back against the trunk of the tree. I took a drink of water myself and then prepared to keep watch, slinging the bow from my shoulder and loosely placing an arrow from my quiver behind it. I continued to look all around, but there was still no sign of anyone. When a few minutes had passed, I stole a glance at Princess Evelyn. Her eyes were closed, but I noted a frown of apprehension upon her countenance that told me she was probably still awake. I wondered whether she was as alert as I was in our current circumstances, even without the slumber I'd had all of this afternoon.

This afternoon, I recalled slowly. Was it really the same day as when I had bid Rachel and the girls to come and live with me? Could it have only been around twenty hours ago when I had spared that Klumeck soldier for the second time? This time yesterday, Joshua had still been alive, living and breathing and fighting. An uncertain lump rose in my throat and I swallowed hard. Two battles on two consecutive nights... I could not understand it. How had they been able to face us after one day when we had defeated them? It had been only two scout teams, but still... how had they been able to send them out so quickly, when it took a day to reach Klumeck? Unless...

My eyes widened at the possibility that they could have left some of their number behind when they retreated, in order to infiltrate the castle in secret. Thinking further, I speculated as to whether this could be the same group as those who had caused the watchmen to slumber in their last battle.

"You're thinking it could be connected, aren't you?" I turned to see Princess Evelyn propped up on an elbow, looking at me. "That the Klumeck soldiers who put the elixirs in the watchmen's teas are the same as those who tried to kidnap me. The same thought had crossed my mind."

"I'm still keeping watch, Your Highness," I replied, trying to comfort her. "If there is anybody out there, I will warn you. I advise you to sleep, Your Highness."

"I cannot sleep." Princess Evelyn had given up all pretence of slumber and was now sitting up, pulling the cloak round her and sitting up against the bark of the tree. "I cannot help but think of my father and of the battle."

"I have those same thoughts, my lady," I admitted. In truth, our people were constantly at the forefront of my mind.

The princess frowned then; she was looking at me with the same curiosity as she had done this afternoon. "You know, I am sure we have met before," she said to me suddenly. "I recognise you somehow, but your captain said you had never been personally assigned to me. "But," she added suddenly, "it was your captain who said we had not met, not you. You did not say anything at all. Well, soldier – have we met before?"

"Yes, Your Highness," I admitted. Her eyes widened, waiting for me to continue. "It was a long time ago. We were but children."

She frowned, puzzled, before her eyes suddenly opened wide in realisation. "You said you worked in the stables," she stated, and I nodded. "You're the boy I met in the snow, in the stables that day! You're the boy from the snow," she remarked in realisation. "You're the one who cried and I gave you my cloth. You said you were going to be a soldier like your father before you. We threw snow at each other, and then you helped me through the window."

"Yes, your highness," I repeated. Despite our current predicament, my heart lightened a little that she had remembered me.

There was a pause. "What is your name?" she asked, as she adjusted her cloak again. "I often wondered who you were."

"I am Daniel, son of Kellen, my lady," I responded, inclining my head to her. There was another pause here while I relaxed my hand on my bow. "Forgive me, Your Highness, but were you successful in your plan that day? I have always wondered whether the guard caught you or not."

A ghost of a smile traced her features. "Yes," she told me faintly. "I hid myself into the corner of the room, where there were thick shadows. When the guard rushed in, I came forwards and asked where he had gone. I explained I was present there the whole time, so I could better escape into my book. He looked like he might faint with relief. He could not scold me, for what had I done in his eyes except wish to better concentrate on my reading? The boy from the snow..." she murmured. "You became a soldier, just like you said you would. I know I am in good hands," she added suddenly, her smile growing.

I smiled in return, but then her smile faded, and I felt my own diminish as we imagined the battle at Gaeson, my brothers and sisters fighting and falling all at once. My head tilted upward as I looked towards the heavens; the night sky was just as vivid as it had been.

"Your Highness, the stars," I murmured.

She followed my gaze as she glanced up at them; a wisp of a smile glimpsed her features. "Aye, they are beautiful indeed," she agreed. "My father used to tell me about stars." Then her countenance hardened, but she said nothing more. I did not reply either, lost in thought about how our people, how her own father the king might be dead.

"It is such folly," she burst out fiercely, "that so many could be dead or dying and we sit here in perfect peace, where I can do nothing to aid my people! I should be in the caves, ready to defend them to the last," she concluded, deep bitterness in her tone. "What folly those protocols are," she hissed.

"It gives my heart comfort to know you are out of danger, my lady," I ventured. She turned, the anger still in her expression. "It will give the king hope, to know that you are safe. Once we reach Caer Ligualid, His Majesty King Urien might well give us reinforcements. They were only two scout teams, Your Highness; my prayer is that we would have easily overcome them."

Princess Evelyn's eyes remained hard, but she said nothing more. My heart yearned to comfort her, but I knew not what to say. I could assure her of her safety with me, but she already knew that – and that was not her worry. Princess Evelyn was not concerned about herself, but the fate of her father, the king, and our people. For that, I could offer her no guarantees. I swallowed a lump of helplessness as I looked towards the stars again.

As I did, I was reminded of the One watching over us, who was the greatest king of all and sovereign over all of us. I trusted He would not let a hair fall from King Reghan's head unless He wished it to be so. The same God who had once made a promise to an old, childless man that he would have a people with more than the stars in the sky and the sand on the shore. Looking up at the endless stars, I knew that same God was watching over us. He was still with us, even now, as we hid in this forest, watching over Sarah, my mother, John, Aife, Rachel and her two daughters and the captain – if indeed he was still alive.

"Your Highness," I murmured, and she looked up at me. "I do not know if our brothers and sisters are still fighting; I myself do not know if our people will survive this night. But I do know that God is watching over us; that He has not abandoned us. We can trust in Him even when our own strength fails us. If we put our hope in God, He will not put us to shame, my lady."

A faint smile appeared on her face again and she nodded; I prayed my words had given her solace. "You speak well, Daniel son of Kellen. Does your father still live?" she questioned me, and I paused, lowering my eyes slightly.

"No, Your Highness. He died in the service of the king, nine years ago – only a little before I enlisted in the army myself."

"I am sorry," she responded, picking up tufts of grass and scattering them about as she spoke. "I often wondered whether I would meet you again, after I saw you that day," she added, offering a whimsical smile, which I returned. "I think I might be able to slumber a while," she added now with a sigh, throwing the remainder of the grass away.

"I will be here, my lady," I assured her.

That small smile played at the corner of her mouth again as she moved back into a lying position. "I know," was all she said, before she turned away from me and closed her eyes.

Still completely alert, I leaned back against the tree trunk and had a drink of water from my own skin. It was cool and refreshing on my tongue. The two horses were still lying next to me; I deduced from his change in breathing that whilst the other horse had fallen asleep, Epos was still awake. As I sat there, Epos stretched her neck over so that her head just rested upon my shoulder. Presently she neighed softly, though not loud enough to wake Princess Evelyn – if indeed she could have fallen asleep so quickly after our last conversation. With my eyes still trained on the trees all around the clearing, I reached up a hand to stroke her, and with that I readied my bow again and settled down to keep watch for the night.

The next time Princess Evelyn opened her eyes, it was morning, but the dawn had not long broken. She had tossed and turned at various points, but she seemed to have slumbered for the most part. She sat up now and turned to me.

"Morning, Daniel," she said, running her hand through her hair, which was a little tousled from her night's sleep. I did not dare look at her, for with her curls loose and her eyes still full of slumber, she seemed to look more beautiful than ever.

"Good morning, Your Highness," I returned. My words sounded sudden, awkward even to my ears, and I hoped this was my imaginings. "There was not a movement out of turn throughout the night, my lady," I told her, as I handed her some water.

"I am pleased to hear it," she answered, before taking a long drink. "I am sure I will survive without breakfast," she commented, standing up still dressed in her cloak. She handed the water back to me. "Let's away to Caer Ligualid."

"My lady," I assented, and helped her upon her horse before swinging up onto Epos. I looked up at the early sky to get my bearings and set Epos off at a canter, facing north. Princess Evelyn rode parallel to me, and together, after an hour or so, we had broken free of the forest. Though it was a relief to be out of woodland, I knew the greater risk of riding in plain sight, and so we took as much caution as we possibly could.

From what I could tell this early in the morning, the day looked like it would be fine. The great lake lay beside us and we journeyed alongside it; the sun sparkled upon the surface of the water and gleamed upon the fields. My eyes scanned the landscape furtively as we rode, but there was no sign we were being hunted. The best outcome I could hope for was that either we had escaped entirely undetected, or that any foes who may have spied us had assumed we were simply refugees escaping Gaeson and not worth bothering with.

We paused as little as possible. It was fortunate my father had oft described his sojourns to Caer Ligualid – enough to have my bearings and look out for landmarks. We continued north along the great lake until we had left it behind, and soon afterwards, to my relief, we came to the narrow path through the large mountains that my father had told me about, and I knew Caer Ligualid and safety lay on the other side. Soon peaks towered above us on either side, and the imposing range seemed to press in on us. I tightened my hands on the reins, anxious at how quiet it was, and how narrow a view the mountains afforded us.

"Daniel," Princess Evelyn called suddenly, and I jerked my head round. "Look!" She pointed behind us, but I had already seen them. Five men were riding swiftly upon us, bearing Klumeck armour.

"Hurry!" I called back, not addressing her by her title lest the enemy should identify her. I kicked Epos into a gallop a second or so after Princess Evelyn crossed past me; her being in front, I would be able to better protect her. Epos neighed loudly, clearly getting agitated. I reached down to stroke her parchment coat. "Easy girl," I murmured. "Just keep going."

The narrow, winding path kept us out of range of their arrows. Blood pounded in my ears, while Epos' hooves thundered upon the ground as we rode past. Then, all at once and without warning, an arrow flew past my ear. I looked up to see three or four men hiding behind large rocks on the mountainside, firing arrows down upon us. "Watch out!" I warned the princess.

"Take the road to the right!" Princess Evelyn shouted, the same time as I saw the sharp, rocky path she was referring to. I took it also, following close behind. I was sure they had planned us to divert off here and so this could well be a trap, but what other choice did we have? To stay on that narrow path, with enemy archers down on us, would surely have meant death.

"The treeline," my lady called to me, as a sparse wood came into view. We plunged into the wood, and I could hear the enemy riders closing in on us. We were now riding on a steep incline as we rode around the tall trees, which were so few they gave us no opportunity to lose the Klumeck soldiers chasing us. We then came out of the woods as abruptly as we had started, and we found ourselves on a grassy knoll.

That was when we saw the cliff. A great ravine, with only darkness below. My attention had been on escaping our enemies, and in the confusion of the forest I hadn't noticed how high up our path had taken us. We put as much distance as we could between ourselves and the Klumeck soldiers before Princess Evelyn and I pulled up our horses short. We swung ourselves down, and I knew we only had a few seconds. I glanced at the princess.

"I will do all I can in my power to protect you," I swore to her, as I readied my bow.

Princess Evelyn drew her sword. "I know, boy from the snow," she murmured. She held my eyes for a moment, as if trying to convey some silent message, but I could not guess her meaning.

The first few riders emerged, and I held taut my bow. I released the arrow and it impaled the first soldier's chest. I plucked another from my quiver, and in the next few moments had shot down another three in quick succession – but there were too many of them. A few feet away from us, they launched themselves off their horses and ran forwards, wielding their blades. I dropped by bow and drew my sword, just in time to strike my first enemy. My blade lodged itself deep into his side and he fell down dead. I pulled my sword out, kicking his body away, to see another advancing.

The enemy soldier and I circled around one another. The extra moments I used to assess our situation – the princess still had her hood up, so she had remained undiscovered. I counted twelve men, including this one in front of me. It would be difficult to overcome them, but not impossible. Princess Evelyn remained by the horse, sword ready to pierce. The other men had by now stopped; some were even jeering. I could see why – my opponent was well-built and extremely tall. Defeating him would be no easy task. I continued with bated breath, holding back, waiting for him to strike.

Suddenly, he lunged forth with an angered cry. I saw his movements and jumped to the side, easily avoiding him. He turned as I did and thrust out his sword, slicing the air inches away from my ear as I ducked. I twirled around and brought my blade crashing down, but he brought his shield forwards to block me. He raised his shield now, slamming it into my face.

I staggered backwards, but he hadn't broken anything. I heard cheers from the crowd of Klumeck soldiers. He leapt forwards again and I again dodged it; as I did, I brought my sword up, slicing underneath his arm and across his chest. He fell to his knees and began to cough up blood. The other soldiers had stopped jeering.

"Please…" he spat. I knew what he was asking; every soldier did. If a soldier was not able to escape death, we prayed at least for a quick end.

I nodded at him. "God be with your spirit," I replied, and brought my sword against his neck, cutting his head clean from his shoulders.

The twelve men roared together in outrage and ran forwards. I quickly readied my blade, clashing it against the first sword that attempted to slay me. Princess Evelyn had now jumped into the fray, in the midst of our own battle. Where had they come from? I wondered. I fought as swiftly as I could, and Princess Evelyn was more skilled with a blade than most, but there were too many of them. I began to worry the princess would not survive this fight.

Just then, I saw a different company of soldiers crest the hill. My heart sighed in relief as I immediately recognised the seal of Gaeson. It gave my soul great joy when I saw John and Aife were with them. Surely we would be saved! The men and women from Gaeson rode through the enemy soldiers slashing and cutting as they went and easing the battle greatly.

As we continued to fight, I presently became aware of one Klumeck soldier who was continuing to advance upon Princess Evelyn. She was being successful in warding him off, but the Klumeck soldier was forcing her to jump back to evade him, and as such, she was getting nearer and nearer to the cliff. I began to make my away over to her. She took another step back and was now stood next to Epos – next to the cliff's edge.

I started to run over, after my delay of having slashed a man's throat with my sword, and then twirled around and stabbed another man in the chest. I hurried onwards to her, just in time to see the Klumeck soldier ram Epos' rear with his shield. As I sprinted to Princess Evelyn, Epos cried out and rose onto her hind legs, kicking out with her front hooves. My lady darted aside to evade her, and far too late I realised what was going to happen. I leapt up into the air and thrust out with both arms – one found Princess Evelyn's wrist, the other Epos' reins – just as both of us toppled over the cliff.

"My lady!" I shouted, as we hung over the edge. She grabbed hold of my wrist tightly. I glanced up to see Epos hunched over towards us, her poor neck straining with the weight. "Hold on, girl. Step back!" I called to Epos, but she was too frightened and pained to obey this instruction. Then the Klumeck soldier Princess Evelyn had been fighting with appeared at the edge of the cliff, sword drawn, ready to cut the reins.

"Have mercy!" I called out. "I carry Princess Evelyn!"

With her free hand, the Princess removed her hood. Murmurs of her name rang through the crowd. The soldier lowered his sword, and I breathed out slowly in relief. He now unstrapped the reins from Epos, and held them himself, with the aid of two other Klumeck soldiers who had come to help. I knew we would be in King Cedric's captivity, but what other choice did we have? The reins were now untied from their loop and lengthened, and the other end was lowered down to us.

"Your Highness," I called down to the princess, and she glanced up at me. "I am going to lift you up. I bid you take hold of the rope," I instructed her – for my arm was growing tired, and I did not know how much longer I could hold on to both her and the rope from Epos' reins.

Princess Evelyn nodded, and with a last strain of strength I pulled her up. With her free hand, she grabbed hold of the bottom of the reins that now dangled beside her. I still had hold of her wrist, and as I brought her hand near to the rope, she instinctively gripped hold of the rope with this hand, so now she held the rope with both hands.

"I am secure," she called.

With this, I let go of her wrist and gripped the rope with this hand also – so now both of us held onto the rope with both hands, which was much easier. She was now dangling only a few inches below me.

"All will be well now, Your Highness," I murmured, as we began to be pulled up. But then something shifted, and the rope jerked. "Hold on, my lady!" I called down to her, as we were pushed against the rock, loose stones falling down around us.

I fell down past her, but I still had hold of the rope and gripped it tight; she was now a few metres above me. I looked up and all at once I knew something was wrong – disastrously wrong. The rope from Epos' reins was old and far too thin, and it was beginning to strain under our weight.

"Hurry!" That was John's voice! He appeared over the top of the cliff. "The rope will not hold!"

Already I knew it was too late. It was too late for us both to get over the cliff; the rope was already breaking. I quickly scanned the rock, but the surface was smooth. There was no time to find a proper foothold; I knew what I had to do.

"Daniel." Princess Evelyn looked down, tears in her eyes; I knew she had understood well what I had decided to do. "Don't do it," she pleaded, having predicted, shaking her head fiercely. "That's an order, Daniel," she stated more clearly. It was with a bittersweet irony that in order to save her life, my last act would be to disobey her – but there was no other way to keep my vow and spare her the pain of death.

"All will be well, your highness," I answered quickly, "just hold on tight."

She was shaking her head, tears falling down her face. The rope gave another tug.

"I regret to disobey you, but it is the only way you will be safe." I began to ready myself for death, committing my life to God. "My lady," I murmured, and she looked at me. I took in her features once more, for surely this was the last time I beheld her face – her small, warm eyes, that sweet, round mouth, and her beautiful curls. "I love you," I declared, and saw surprise register there briefly. Then I let go of the rope.

"No!" Her sharp cry echoed and faded from my ears as air rushed past me, and she soon disappeared from view. Then I was falling through the abyss until black overcame me and I knew no more.

Part Two

Chapter Five

I opened my eyes and at once felt immense surprise that I was still alive. Immediately I felt severe pain, as if I had been stabbed with several swords at once. I blinked and raised my head to look down at my body, which caused another bout of pain to slam into my head. I was expecting limbs to no longer work or to have been amputated, but nothing seemed to be too out of place – I did not even have broken bones. Apart from my head, which felt like a cannonball had struck it over and over again, I seem to have survived reasonably well. I found I was restrained by ropes; from this I deducted I was probably imprisoned in Klumeck.

Next, I looked around the chamber and perceived the room I was in to be extremely grand. The walls were a cream colour with a scarlet trim, with landscape paintings hung on them; on the ceiling, I saw intricate patterns and swirls in gold lace. A large goblet of water, full, sat on the table beside my bed. I found I could just about reach it. After taking a long drink, I felt much refreshed. I tried to untie my bonds, but the cords were thick and seemed unmovable. Just as I was striving to set myself free, I heard a key move in the lock, and the large oak door opened.

"You were fortunate to survive, Bryce." I turned swiftly to see His Majesty King Cedric himself enter the room, escorted by two guards who followed behind him.

"Your Majesty," I greeted him in return, my voice hoarse and strange to my ears. Who was Bryce? I wondered. He must be mistaken in my identity. I was still restrained, which saved me from making the difficult decision of whether I should bow; instead I simply inclined my head. I wanted to respect him as a king, but he was also the enemy of the king I served.

"The current of the water spared you and you drifted to the river bank," King Cedric continued. "That was where my men recovered you. You have been unconscious for twelve days," he informed me.

My eyes flew wide in surprise. "My life is in your debt, my lord the king," I answered quickly. "But where is Princess Evelyn?" I was desperate to know where she was. Was she safe? Was I a prisoner? Would I have to try to rescue her from the clutches of King Cedric's forces?

"I don't know," King Cedric said now. "Presumably she got safely back to Gaeson after the battle."

I surmised from this that Gaeson's forces must have overcome Klumeck's – I still did not know why Caer Ligualid's forces were there, seeing as they had only surveyed the scene and not actually come to our aid.

"Then I must plead on her behalf, Your Majesty," I stated quickly. "I beg of you to not attempt to kidnap her again."

King Cedric nodded. "I well understand your sentiment, my boy. Your loyalty does you credit." He crossed the small room to open the window. A breeze blew in, but it was nowhere near as cold as it had been. He stayed in his position by the window. "However, there is something you should know. I have never attempted to kidnap Princess Evelyn, nor would I. The order for her kidnap did not come from me."

I frowned in confusion. "I do not understand, sire," I responded. "I fought off your men myself when they breached our courtyard. They were dressed in Klumeck armour, bearing your seal."

"They may have been wearing my armour; that does not necessarily make them my men." King Cedric sighed and then turned to me. "To clarify, these forces were intruders in disguise. Almost a month ago," he expounded, "I sent a small number of men to a nearby village under our protection that had become under threat. The men never returned, and when I sent more to the village, none were discovered.

"According to my men, there were two scout teams that had infiltrated your kingdom," King Cedric continued. I nodded, for this fitted with what I knew, then stopped as the pain in my skull hit me again. "Only one of these groups was working for me. Their mission was to gather information. Not to engage any soldiers in combat, and certainly not to attempt to kidnap Princess Evelyn. The second group were not my men. I reason they wished to stir further hatred between our two kingdoms. I have my suspicions as to who these men were," he added, pre-empting my next question, "but have no proof as yet." He moved now to sit down on the wooden chair next to the bed. The other guards remained standing at attention, either side of the wooden door.

"Then the group of Klumeck soldiers that had been pursuing the princess and myself," I stated now, as I was keen to hear his account further, "were they also your men, sire?"

"I believe not. I have deduced that the men pursuing you along the mountain path, who engaged you on the cliff, were more of those disguised as my men. It was a sizable regiment that I sent to the village – about thirty men in all. But where were you headed with the princess?" he questioned me, and I frowned further.

"To Caer Ligualid, Your Majesty," I answered him. "That is the protocol that exists, should any members of the royal family be in immediate danger and cut off from the castle."

King Cedric's eyebrows rose in surprise. "That is the path you seemed to take," he agreed, "but I am shocked such protocols still exist, given our state of affairs."

It was my turn to be surprised now.

"His Majesty King Urien, of course, has always welcomed me in his kingdom," he added, gesturing around the chamber with his hands. "But King Urien's relationship with King Reghan has been rather strained at late." From the way King Cedric moved his hands, he seemed to be saying that we were in Caer Ligualid – which would make no sense.

"I assume I am in Klumeck, of course, having been captured by your men, my lord the king," I answered him.

King Cedric said nothing at this for a moment; he simply seemed to stroke his chin in thought, and then finally he leant forwards to speak. "We are not in Klumeck, but in Caer Ligualid," he declared.

My eyes flew wide in shock. Instinctively, I turned to the window, but was immediately held back by the cords still tightly wound about my wrists and ankles.

"Of course, you may survey the view for yourself. I apologise for your restraints," he added, as he gestured his hand and one of the guards by the door came forwards to release me, "but you are a soldier of war, after all."

"Of course, Your Majesty. I find your generosity quite overwhelming, my lord the king," I replied, rubbing my wrists where the cords had been. I slowly got to my feet, using a hand against the wall for support, and made my way to the window. I pushed the wooden covering further out and took a glance. Immediately I knew we were in the beautiful city – I had a good view, and the landscapes entirely matched the legendary accounts I had grown up with. To my right was a good view of the castle; the silver walls were renowned among all the kingdoms of the northwest. I could almost hear my father telling me stories about Caer Ligualid, whispering because I should be slumbering, and my mother would surely rebuke both of us if we were caught.

I snapped myself to the present and turned back to King Cedric, who seemed to smile at my confused expression.

"I can see a long talk is to be had between us – but now is not the time. You require sustenance." He waved a hand, and one of the guards stepped out of the room. A few moments later he returned, bearing a tray. On it was a plate bearing grapes, figs, bread, hunks of beef and a large glass of wine.

"Please eat," he insisted. "It will help your recovery."

I did not understand. This was fine food, and I was in fine clothes, in a fine room overlooking Caer Ligualid. If I was King Cedric's captive, I should be torn to pieces in the interrogation cell of a hidden prison in Klumeck. That was what happened to those imprisoned at Gaeson, though nobody spoke of it.

My eyes flickered back to the window, which was still open. From the view I had seen, I reasoned we were presently quite high within the castle. If I jumped, I could well be killed from the fall. I had only just survived a fall off a cliff, and there would be no river to save me this time – surely I would not live if I dared try it again. I glanced back to my captor, who I saw watching me with amusement in his eyes. Behind that amusement, I perceived his eyes to be full of emotion – an odd thing to observe in a king. I glanced at the food – could it be poisoned? I reasoned quickly – if I did not eat, the king may well kill me anyway for daring to refuse his hospitality. If his purpose was to interrogate me, then I would need my strength – and I prayed that if the food was poisoned then I would die quickly. I tasted the beef – it was good. Indeed, the moment the meat touched my mouth, I was struck with ravenous hunger and began to eat rapidly, forgetting all sense of manner or decorum.

"I see that my alliance to Rheged and His Majesty King Urien is a surprise to you. King Urien has always been more than accommodating to the people of Klumeck. What does King Reghan say? You are free to speak; you will come to no harm here."

My eyes widened in further confusion – no harm? How could that be the case? He had already confirmed I was a prisoner of war. Perhaps King Cedric was trying to lull me into a false sense of security – therefore I had best be on my guard. In all these thoughts, I realised I had not answered King Cedric's question, and I swallowed; my mind was taking longer than normal to produce speech.

"His Majesty King Reghan has always informed us that you are at war with King Urien and the Kingdom of Rheged," I answered at last. "That Klumeck has always been at war, a rogue kingdom that is not allied with anyone."

King Cedric's eyes flew open in shock, and his hand went to slam the arm of his chair. "That is not true!" he exclaimed. "King Reghan is the rogue that wages war against us. But that is not the most pressing matter," he added, silencing my protest with his hand. "As I said, you have been unconscious for twelve days. The spies that I had secretly placed in Gaeson had followed those infiltrators who were not my men and came to meet you on the cliff top. The leader of those spies informed me that after you fell from the cliff and Princess Evelyn was lifted up, the infiltrators scattered.

"The soldiers of Gaeson also retreated with Princess Evelyn," King Cedric went on. "The leader of the spies ordered that your body be retrieved, as there might be some valuable information on your person that might help us in the war against

Gaeson. Upon finding you, they discovered you were alive, so they brought you here as a prisoner of war. I happened to be here in the service of His Majesty King Urien – and as soon as I saw you, I knew." He stopped there, his voice cracking. I waited, but he spoke no more; he simply stared at me with such intensity, as if he was looking upon my very soul.

"I do not understand your meaning, sire," I told him finally.

"How did you get that scar?" King Cedric asked, urgently and rather abruptly.

I frowned; I had several scars since my time in the battle.

"The scar on your left side, shaped like a mushroom," he prompted.

"I do not know, Your Majesty," I answered. "I have had it for as long as I can remember."

"What do you remember?" His voice now took on an even more earnest tone. "What is your earliest memory?" His question only furthered my confusion. "Please answer. You will not be endangering your people with your response, surely."

"It was when I was about three," I replied, knowing the answer right away. My earliest memory was of that time when I was lost in the snow. It was what I had always dreamed about – the dream that had always turned into a nightmare. "It was snowing," I continued. "I was lost and had managed to get outside the kingdom borders. All I remember is…" I paused, recalling it vividly. "I remember cold and fear. I was so scared I would never find my mother and father again."

My eyes had cast downward while I spoke, and now I looked back up at him. He did not speak, but his whole face seemed locked in intensity.

"My boy…" he whispered finally. "I've found you at last." The moment he spoke those words, the world seemed to go still – for his words sank deep into my bones, and suddenly I knew what his next words would be. "You are Bryce, my nephew and heir," he declared slowly. He was claiming me to be the lost heir of Klumeck.

"No, that cannot be true," I muttered, at once forgetting how dangerous it was to disagree with a king. "I'm sorry, my lord the king," I amended, "but you must be mistaken. I am Daniel, son of Kellen," I emphasised. "I am a soldier of Gaeson."

"You think I would not recognise my own kin? You are Bryce, son of Adair," he refuted me. "I long suspected that my heir was still alive, living somewhere in Gaeson," King Cedric said, seemingly ignoring my interruptions. "King Reghan's men tried to capture you and your sister, Lynette, when you were a child, but I knew they had not succeeded. Your parents must have adopted you the day they found you in the snow."

"A sister?" I questioned. "No, I'm an only child. My apologies, my lord the king, but I do not know of what you speak."

"You must know her," he insisted, "for you were not alone in the snow."

I shook my head. I did not remember anybody else.

"A girl two years younger than you. Her hair and eyes always seemed to me the colour of chestnut." My eyes widened at his description – I knew then exactly who he was referring to.

"Sarah," I wondered aloud. "She is my oldest friend. She manages my affairs in my home." Could it be true? Sarah was my sister? She was King Cedric's long-lost niece? Surely it was impossible.

"You received that scar while your mother was preparing your bath," he added, changing the subject. He pointed to the spot underneath my clothes, where my mushroom-shaped scar lay. "The water was too hot, and it flicked onto your side and it burnt."

"My parents..." I enunciated slowly. My father was a soldier. My father was not a soldier. My mother was an invalid at home, sick in bed. My mother was not my mother; she was not in my home. I did not know what this meant...

"I am sure you were brought up honesty and with love," King Cedric assured me. "From the age of three, you would have been brought up with these parents. But before that was a whole life you cannot remember. A life of being in the Kingdom of Klumeck."

"No," I whispered, shaking my head. "I was born in Gaeson. This cannot be true."

King Cedric turned to me. "Gaeson and Klumeck were once allies," King Cedric said, with no regard for my objections. "I'm sure you have heard the legend of my ancestor and how he left Gaeson."

I nodded mutely, my throat too tight to speak. This revelation was too much. Could it be true? How could it be true? Surely it was not true!

"The two descendant kingdoms had always been at peace, until King Reghan came to the throne." He chuckled softly in sarcasm. "He is a foolish man, Bryce, corrupted by greed and power. He does not serve the Kingdom of Rheged. He is a king merely for his own gain."

"Watch your words," I said sharply, again briefly forgetting this man was a powerful and dangerous king. "My name is Daniel, not this strange Bryce," I began. "King Reghan is a true king, faithful and just," I affirmed. "He has always told us it is you who is corrupted by power and greed."

At this, one of the guards stepped forwards and drew his sword a little.

"Back to your position," King Cedric ordered loudly, turning to him. The guard immediately stepped back, bowing in full submission. "I admire your loyalty, but is that how you would honour your future king?" King Cedric turned back to me now, standing to full height – and I saw, for the first time, anger in his countenance as he glowered down upon me. "It is you who should watch your words, boy," King Cedric said, folding his arms. "You might be my nephew and heir, but I am still a king. I would have been tempted to have your head for speaking to his king like that, let alone a prisoner of war. I tell you that you are my heir, and Bryce is who you really are," he finished.

"No, who I am is the life I have lived till now," I retorted, seemingly unaffected by his severe warning. King Cedric's temper grew further at my speech, but I would not let him take away my identity. "You are a powerful king, sire, and I mean you no dishonour," I continued at once, attempting to pacify him. "You may even be my uncle," I conceded. "But, my lord the king, you will not take away what God has made me and give me a strange name. The parents who raised me gave me the name Daniel, and I will stay by this name."

He remained facing me, considering this for a moment, before nodding. "That is your right. From now on, you shall be Daniel. But your king is not as you claim," he declared now. I found myself clenching my fists in anger, for his bitterness and scorn was more than I could stand. "If he is as faithful and just as you say, why then does he wage war against Rheged for no reason? Why then did he never tell you that you were my heir? Oh yes, my boy," he told me, nodding. "He would have known of your existence. It was he who tried to take you both from me all those years ago, when he killed your parents. One night, twenty-one years ago, he sprung up and struck us, secretly. He has never admitted to what he did that night, but all of Klumeck and Rheged know of his treachery."

"You attacked us twenty-one years ago," I protested slowly. I was so confused, and I could feel doubt against King Reghan beginning to seep into me like a poison. "His Majesty has always told us you attacked us and broke peace," I continued now. "King Reghan told us how that was when you took your army and invaded our kingdom without reason, slaughtering all who stood in your way."

King Cedric regarded me for a moment before giving a weary sigh. He sat back in the chair and shook his head. "You are correct that we attacked Gaeson on that night," he admitted. "But that was two weeks after King Reghan had sent his small, secret force to steal you and Lynette, and to murder your parents in their bed."

He paused in the telling of this account for a moment and pinched the bridge of his nose, closing his eyes briefly. A servant handed him a goblet of water and he took a long drink. As he drank, the sunlight reflected off his silver cup, casting light onto his face. I was struck by how weak and old he appeared, though of course I would not vocalise my thoughts. I thought again that even with all the pomp, power and gold, beneath the façade of wealth and prosperity, a king is still a mere man, mortal and corruptible. Was it possible King Reghan had succumbed to corruption?

"King Reghan had long wanted to rule both kingdoms," he resumed, wiping his mouth with the back of his hand. "His plan was to slaughter us and claim Bernicia, our enemy across the lands, had done it. King Reghan would then rule both kingdoms – presumably he would choose someone in his personal guard, or some noble official or other to be ward of Klumeck until one of his own offspring could become king under him. You must understand that I broke peace and attacked that night to try to get you and your sister back," he emphasised now. "That is why I keep attacking, because I wanted to find my heirs. Again and again I pleaded with him, but he refused to tell me anything, even if you still lived. I have only managed five attempts on Gaeson, because King Urien has only consented but a few times. He sees it as nothing more as a family feud, when in fact King Reghan was hiding my own blood from me. I succeeded only recently in persuading His Majesty King Urien to aid me, finally seeing King Reghan as the threat that he was."

Here King Cedric finished. I put down the long empty and forgotten tray onto the bed beside me as I tried to think, trying to ascertain if there was any honesty in King Cedric's account.

"You still attacked us," I said now, shaking my head. This man would not be absolved of blame for the innocent blood he had shed. "Twice in one night, while our wounded fell!" I protested. "A young boy died, leaving his family in danger of starvation. His name was Joshua. A boy who was not yet fourteen, a year younger than our conscription age, and he died because you brought your men to our gates. We had no choice but to defend ourselves."

"I am sorry for his loss, but that was not my doing," King Cedric replied heavily. "I am sorry so many lives were lost, but King Reghan's evil is a fire that had to be quenched. I assumed that all of Gaeson were aware of King Reghan's evil. I am sorrier to learn that you have all been blinded by his folly. Perhaps Gaeson is a good kingdom still, with peace and prosperity, with his evil war carried out in secret." King Cedric shook his head. "His evil is more than I had believed possible, if you would so easily give your lives for him."

I shook my head, unable to believe what I was hearing. My king evil? It could not be possible.

"This cannot be true," I whispered a third time. King Cedric said nothing, and there was silence for a moment before I remembered something else. "You caused our watchmen to fall into a deep sleep! You gave them some elixir so we did not even know you were coming."

King Cedric frowned and shook his head. "That was not on my command. It must have come from your own people. Unless it was those who disguised themselves as my men," he added.

My eyes widened in realisation – for that was the conversation I'd had with Princess Evelyn in the forest, that those who had attempted to kidnap her, who had infiltrated the castle walls, had also been those who had caused our watchmen to slumber. I put a hand to my head, feeling suddenly faint.

"You are still weak," he told me," his voice suddenly calm and gentle. "You must rest. When you are better recovered, I bid you visit King Urien, the King of Rheged himself. He will confirm everything I have said. Rest," he said. "I swear, you will come to no harm here." He turned to leave, his guards with him. He turned back to me. I stood up again, but felt my strength leave me; I was forced to grip hold of the top of the chair next to the bed.

"This cannot be real," I whispered. "I am a soldier from Gaeson. You are my enemy. These are simply lies. You are trying to turn me against my people, against my king."

He shook his head and before I could move, he had crossed to me and gripped my shoulders hard. Without the support of the wall, I had no choice but to cling to him before I fell.

"I am not your foe, Daniel. I am your uncle, and everything I have is yours. You are my long-lost heir, and one day you will inherit my throne."

I shook my head, but this increased my dizziness. The room began to swirl.

"Here." He guided me so I was sitting on the bed. "I shall leave you to recover – you need your rest." He turned to leave, and the man who claimed to be my uncle paused on the threshold. "I speak the truth, Daniel. I pray you will come to believe my words." With that, he left, shutting the door gently behind him. My confused soul barely had time to think before my strength left me, and I fell at once into a deep slumber.

***

The dream I found myself entering upon beginning sleep seemed as detailed and vivid as reality ever could be. I found myself in a medium rectangular room with a large table next to me. The table seemed particularly giant, well beyond the normal span of furniture. My first thought was that this was simply because of the strangeness of my dream, but then vast hands bent down to pick me up, and I realised it was because, in my dream, I was a child. I felt warm, comforting hands close around me, and suddenly a man was before me – a man full of smiles with his eyes showing great wisdom.

At once I knew this man, with his smile and wise eyes, was familiar to me. The man held me with arms outstretched, lifting me up and down, while my infant self clapped and giggled. As he continued to beam down upon my toddler self, with a jolt I realised how alike this man was to me. I noted his dark, storm-like eyes, and the angle of his jawline, which was in likeness to mine. If King Cedric's account could be believed, could this man be my real father?

Another woman came into view now, with long, sleek red hair and deep eyes akin to the colour of chestnut. She held a much younger infant – not much older than a baby – enclosed in her arms. The baby was partially covered by cloths and too far away to see in any detail. As the man lowered me to the floor, I saw the warmth of her eyes and the love in her smile. Like with the man who had held me, I had recognised this woman immediately.

I saw now that the man took the younger child, and suddenly the woman was bending down to me and her arms enveloped me. Emotion rapidly surged through me and overwhelmed me as this woman held me. An untapped memory of feeling was pouring into my brain as this woman, with her auburn hair, held me close. I felt elated at the love this woman felt, and increasingly sorrowful to know this dream, this forgotten memory – this could be all I would ever have of this woman.

The infant form of myself was now holding onto her, grinning happily. This young boy that was me buried his head into the nape of her neck; she laughed softly, her voice as sweet as honey.

New people had entered the room now – another man and another woman. As my toddler self turned to look, I recognised the man immediately as King Cedric, but far younger, with none of the solemnity that seemed always behind his eyes. Holding onto his arm was a woman with dark hair and a kind smile. She seemed a little familiar, but I could not place her. As I surveyed them walk to where I was still being held by the other woman, I realised the woman's stomach was full – she was with child. Was this family mine? I wondered. Had they been stolen away from me? Was King Cedric right about all that he had said – did I truly belong in Klumeck, in a life I could no longer remember?

King Cedric and the woman who was next to him were almost next to the first man and woman I had seen. As they came closer and stopped, I felt the dream begin to disintegrate. The images began to fade. I was desperate for another look, but my toddler self was not turning around, and I had no control over his functions. At the last moment, however, he twisted around to smile once more at the people I now knew could be my parents... I had one last fleeting glimpse of the woman's smile, and one more gaze into the man's storm-like eyes, before the images were gone forever.

***

"Mother! Mother, where are you?"

The other dream had gone, but I realised I had not yet woken. Instead my dream had appeared somewhere else – I was walking in a blanket of snow. With a lurch of my heart, I realised it was the dream I had had throughout my life; the dream where I was walking lost in the snow. The dream that always turned into a nightmare.

The images were the sharpest and clearest that they had ever been. I was able to see myself clearly, not just a blur in the distance. To my shock, now I could focus in further on my infant self, I saw I was not traipsing through the snow alone. I held on to a little girl by the hand. She was a tiny thing; I estimated not

113

much older than fourteen months. I saw it was the same girl I had seen in the previous dream, and now that she was much closer and not covered with cloths, I saw her hair and eyes were the colour of chestnut. It panged at my heart to see she looked so familiar and similar to Sarah. Could this little girl be my sister? Could she be Sarah?

"Look, Enid! A boy."

The girl was gone from my hand, and although I was watching this dream at a distance, I felt keenly the loss of contact. I started at the fact that one of these woman had the same name as my mother. The two women approached me, and I saw that one of them was indeed my mother – younger, but definitely her. The woman who had raised me, clothed me, fed me. Was this woman not my natural mother?

She picked me up, and I sensed a strange combination in the dream – whilst I acutely felt the familiar, comforting embrace of my mother, I also felt a distress and confusion I had never felt this before, as if this woman was a stranger to me. My infant self looked about wildly whilst this other woman now came closer, and I saw she was Sarah's mother, Bridget. She was now picking the little girl up.

"Mother! Mother, where are you?" I was crying out for her. Looking up at her, I sensed this was back in familiar dream territory – I had always dreamt of her sympathetic face as she held me tight. Up till now, I had simply assumed this was when she found me in the snow, but as my three-year-old self sensed, I now felt doubt and fear in my eyes – knowing rather plainly that this woman holding me was not my mother.

"Hush, child." The woman who had raised me cradled me in her arms. The events that were unfolding resonated within me, and I was filled with a certainty that what I was watching was the past, that this was real and not simply imaginings. I was feeling things so deeply – the frozen blizzard, the distress, my tears which appeared like ice on my cheeks, and my completely numb feet.

"Lynny!" my three-year-old self cried. "Lynny!" The instant that word tumbled anxiously from my infant mouth, I recognised it – another long suppressed memory awakened. Indeed, as certain as I was this was dream was in fact remembering my real personal history, I now instinctively recognised this infant was indeed my sister.

"This Lynny must be the girl," Sarah's mother murmured, as the two women busied themselves in covering us with their shawls to protect us from the bitter cold. "It is a miracle they have been found, the poor things. They look half dead," she went on. As the two women spoke for a few more moments, the blizzard stopped abruptly and the clouds shifted, allowing the strong moonlight to shine upon the snow.

"Look, Bridget!" The woman who I had always believed as my mother pointed at the snow before us. "What is that in the distance?" The dream changed to focus on the looming object in the distance. The two women peered closer, and suddenly a large wooden object was revealed, and I recognised its shape immediately.

"It is a carriage," said Bridget, Sarah's mother. "This must be where the little children have come from. I wonder where the horses went." She stepped forwards.

"Ah!" My mother hurried forwards as Bridget shrank back from the driver's seat.

"The driver is a Gaeson soldier," Bridget called to my mother, having to speak loudly over the noise of the snow. "He is dead – an arrow has pierced his chest."

My mother's eyes went wide as she stepped up to look closer. She gasped and then frowned further. "I do not recognise him as a friend of my husband's," my mother said. "But I do recognise the arrow that kills him. It bears the seal of Klumeck," she continued. She stepped back from the carriage, whilst the woman who had raised Sarah looked towards the ground.

"The carriage marks are just visible in the snow. Their trail comes from Klumeck!"

Shock filled me. If these images were real and we had come from the direction of Klumeck, could King Cedric be telling the truth with his account?

"These tracks come from Klumeck!" Bridget announced again. "Was perhaps this soldier escaping from Klumeck with these two children? Where would they have come from?"

My mother frowned suddenly. "We cannot tell anyone else in Gaeson about this," she whispered. Bridget turned to her in surprise. "My husband told me an account he had heard today," my mother continued. "Something he should not even have told me, but I believe he was compelled to, as it was so strange to his ears. There were three soldiers on a scout team near Klumeck last night, who arrived back early this morning. My lord Kellen heard their conversation – Kellen said the soldiers had heard rumours that the royal family had been attacked; none but King Cedric and Princess Imogen's children had survived – but the two children had gone missing! A boy of three and a girl of one."

Shock now showed on Bridget's countenance as she continued to hold the little girl. "Are you suggesting," she asked, a little breathlessly, "that these two children are Klumeck's missing heirs? The king's niece and nephew?"

"They must be!" my mother exclaimed. "Think of the timing. We hear that two royal children of their gender and age have disappeared, and we come to find them not far from Gaeson's borders and their path has taken from Klumeck."

"Then you are correct, Enid – we must never tell anyone, except our husbands," Bridget agreed. "His Majesty King Reghan would never allow them to return; you know how things are tense between King Reghan and King Cedric. All know war is looming."

"Yes," my mother affirmed, nodding. "It is too dangerous to attempt a reunion. We should at least wait until their strength has returned. We must separate them for now," she added, "lest people guess their true identity. We shall simply tell them that they are children of our relatives visiting us. Come, let's get out of this snow before the cold kills them."

With this, my mother held me more tightly, and the four of us made our way back up to their horses.

"Do not fear, little one. I will keep you safe," she whispered to me, bundling me tight in her cloak so I did not fall. "Hold on tight to the reins," she murmured, and I did as I was bidden. I saw Bridget mount her own horse, with the little girl securely tied to her in cloths. The two woman bade each other goodbye, and the other woman, who carried the small child, disappeared from view. I felt my toddler self suddenly realise he had been separated from his tiny sister, and hysterical panic overcame me. As we rode towards Gaeson, as my mother rode me away and the storm brewed up again, I began to scream, my sobs lost in the fierce wind and ever swirling snow.

***

I jolted awake, the same way I always did from the dream about the snow, breathing heavily and covered in cold sweat. Right then I knew why I always woke up from this dream as from a nightmare, though all I could remember was the snow. I had now relived that missing piece that had always eluded me. My mother had told me it was a nightmare because of being lost, but it was because I had been so hopelessly torn from my sister. The dream resonated deep within my soul, and at once I knew the woman and man were my parents, and that the tiny child was Sarah.

As I sat up in bed, I felt tears begin to roll down my face at the knowledge that I had been stolen away from the parents who had borne me – for surely the dream had been so real, and matched King Cedric's speech so entirely, that it had to be the genuine account of things. I was enraged at my parents' deception – that is, the parents who had raised me. As grateful as I was that had raised me in love, clothed me, fed me and kept me safe, I could not withhold my anger at their lies. I despaired more to think that the father who had raised me had gone to the grave knowing I was not his true kin. I had known Kellen, soldier of Gaeson, as a man of honour, integrity, decency and truth. Indeed, it was because of him that I too had become a soldier. Could he have lied to me the whole of my life, up till his death, about who I really was? Was it possible a man of such integrity could have deceived me so?

My mind still warred that my dreams could have been my imaginings after all – that because of my fall off the cliff, King Cedric's words had mingled with my weakened brain to create such a fantasy. Even as I suspected this, however, my heart told me it was true all the more – despite the fact that, in many ways, I was desperate to cling to the idea the dreams had been invented. Never before had I felt such conflict, as my mind clung to the faded images of the man and woman from the dream. As much as part of me wanted to dismiss them as pure ridicule, an equally large part of me wanted to know more about them. I was haunted by the comforting embrace they had given me, the feel of their arms enclosing me – it was giving me such joy, and almost suffocating me at the same time.

Abruptly, I pulled the covers from me and tried to stand, but the dizziness overcame me, and I was forced once again to grab the wall for support before I fell. In my weakened state, I crossed the wall to the window and opened it fully. Fresh air flew in, and I was afforded the view of Caer Ligualid once more. The moon was a thin crescent slither, and though there were more clouds the stars were clearly visible. I reasoned from the clouds that it must have rained once or twice while I slumbered. The legendary spires were still visible, lit by beacons that must never go out – they made the spires take on an amber, flickering glow.

The sight of it brought me a little peace and comfort, as did the knowledge that I knew I was safe, as long as King Cedric was convinced I was his nephew. This was a claim I was finding harder and harder to disprove, especially given my recent dreams and the certainty in my heart I had felt upon waking. That conviction that the dreams I had dreamt this night were in actuality episodes of the past kept growing stronger and stronger. As I stared out into the night, I wondered how long I could resist what my heart seemed sure was truth.

Before I could help it, I was examining the contents of my dreams once more. If they were simply my imaginings, how had I been able to recognise the man and woman in that first dream so completely? The other man in the dream had definitely been King Cedric – an image of him from years past, before time and war had fatigued him. The heaviness I had seen in his eyes upon meeting him had also not been present in the dream – and sadness filled me, because I was now sure I knew the reason for the form of his eyes now.

Indeed, in all my enquiries into the claims made on my past and my identity, I had given no thought into King Cedric's past, and what it would mean for him if all he had said was true. If my dreams were as true as my heart told me they were, then the woman with her belly full of a child must have been his wife.

The King Cedric I had dreamed of had also shown true joy and contentment in his countenance. A nameless dread filled me and I knew, before my mind could ask the question, what had happened to the woman who had held his arm, his wife that was carrying their child. My cousin, I realised suddenly, if the claims were all true. I could only guess that his wife and child had also been murdered the same night as my parents – the same night Sarah and I had been separated.

As I gazed at the slither of the moon, at the glowing stars and the slow, lazy movements of the clouds, I wondered how I had not before heard of the account King Cedric had told me, of how the man and woman he claimed were my parents had died in their beds, or how King Cedric's heirs had been lost. But then King Reghan hated any mention of King Cedric, and when the subject would have been talked about most was right after it happened – when I was a simple toddler struggling with fever. Then any rumours of King Cedric's royal family would surely have been overshadowed by the battle that occurred three weeks after I was found – when I had my first lucid memory of sitting in that cave in my mother's embrace, feeling the almost tangible fear strong around me.

I supposed that by the time I would have been old enough to be curious, the rumours would have passed into dubious legend and would probably no longer be mentioned. Indeed, it showed how it had been forgotten, for the most part, on account of gossip. That when the captain had told me it all, on the balcony of Gaeson's castle, it was the first time I had ever heard the account.

As I thought of Gaeson, my thoughts roamed back to my mother (if she still was), to Sarah, John and Aife, to the captain, to Rachel and Alena and Ruth. Lastly, my thoughts turned to the princess. I prayed all were safe and well – I did not even know whether the captain was still alive, for his wounds had seemed severe indeed when I had last bid my farewell to him. Presently, my mind conjured up that last image of him, when he was lying on the square with his chest pierced open, and coughing up blood as he breathed. His last order to me had been to escape with the princess, but I had been captured en route – or had I been rescued? I was no longer able to tell. Whatever the method, I had been separated from the one I had vowed to protect. I clung on to the hope that I had not failed my captain, that the princess was safe back in Gaeson.

A shiver started through me as a sudden breeze blew in. My body was much weaker now, and I knew I should probably go back to bed and rest, much as I felt compelled to lean against the window and wrestle with all King Cedric had told me and all the questions that came to my mind. Sensibility won over my questions, and I shut the window, the breeze whistling past and causing it to thud louder than I intended. I staggered back to bed and collapsed onto it. It frustrated me greatly that a few steps would cause me to be so weak. I prayed my strength would return by morning and that I would recover quickly – and that was my last thought before my weak self succumbed to a fitful slumber once again.

Chapter Six

When I next awoke, I felt immediately my prayer had been answered – I felt much stronger, though I still had some weakness. I got out of bed, more cautiously this time. Though the chamber spun ever so slightly, I found I did not need to grasp the wall, and was greatly relieved at my renewed balance. I went to the window and opened it once more, seeing from the light monochrome sky that it was not long after dawn. A bird I had startled upon opening the window so abruptly flew off into the grey canvas and across to the horizon. I leaned against the wooden window ledge as I attempted to calm my breathing. My thoughts immediately took me back once more to the man and the woman who I was now sure were my biological parents. If that was true, who were the parents I had always believed in? Who was the woman living in my house in Gaeson?

I stretched my hands and arms out of the window for good measure, testing the ease of movement; to my encouragement, my limbs felt far less stiff. I was still wearing the fine clothes I had been in the last time I had been conscious, so I hoped it really was the next morning since my conversation with King Cedric, and that I had not slept through another twelve days. At length, I turned from the window and saw a fresh goblet of water on my bedside table, and took a long drink. After splashing a little of it on my face, I went to my chamber door and found it unlocked.

The door revealed a grand corridor with polished grey stone, furnished with scarlet red carpet and ornate paintings which hung from the walls. It was far greater adorned than the corridors back at Gaeson, and so I felt quite out of place as I journeyed through the castle.

"Your Highness." I heard a guard's voice, and turned to see a Klumeck soldier looking at me. But rather than being about to confront me in battle, I realised he saw me as his prince. "King Cedric asked that you meet with him after you had awoken, my lord prince. Permit me to escort you."

I swallowed and composed myself.

"Very good," I replied, trying to sound as regal and dignified as possible. "Lead the way." I gestured with a wave of my hand.

The guard bowed his head in assent, and I followed his footsteps. As we walked I felt increasingly uneasy, and longed to hold the hilt of my sword in comfort to rid me of my apprehension, but alas, I was still unarmed. I consoled myself with the knowledge that if my dreams were reality and I really was the heir of Klumeck, then my newly discovered uncle would surely wish no harm to come to me.

The guard from Klumeck presently led me to a wide, white-washed balcony with stairs extending from it either side. Indeed, it was not unlike the balcony where the captain and I had conversed with Princess Evelyn nigh two days ago, when we had attempted to escape to Caer Ligualid and slumbered in the forest. No, it was two weeks further, I reminded myself, if what King Cedric had said was true. All had changed since then.

"Ah, Bryce. Or Daniel, of course, if you would prefer it," King Cedric corrected himself. He was speaking to me from the balcony – I was still at the bottom of one of the staircases. "I bid you come and join me," he gestured.

"Your Majesty," I greeted him as I obeyed, walking up the staircase to stand beside him. "Is Princess Evelyn really safe?" I questioned him now – despite the recent revelations I would have to investigate, her safety was still my greatest priority.

"To the best of my knowledge," he replied rather neutrally. "As I told you yesterday, she returned with the soldiers from Gaeson sent to her aid. Contrary to what you may believe, it was not my orders to kidnap Princess Evelyn. I have long known the pain of losing one's heirs," King Cedric added poignantly. "I would not wish that agony on any other, not even my enemies. How do you fare this morning?" he added, a little abruptly.

"I am much improved, sire," I answered. "I am ever grateful to your generosity and to the hospitality of Caer Ligualid."

King Cedric acknowledged this with a nod, but made no further comment.

"Where is my armour?" I asked after a pause, and he turned to face me with surprise on his features. "I am a poor soldier without my sword," I expounded.

"You do not need one here, Daniel. You are among friends, whether you believe it or not. The Kingdom of Rheged already recognises you as my nephew and heir," he continued. "You are the only one who doubts this."

"I do not know what to think," I admitted. We again fell into a natural silence, and the image of him from my dream came back to me, with his arm held by the woman with child. Without warning, a ball seemed to knot in my throat, and I pushed it down with difficulty. "You said that if I am your heir, then I have this Lynette as my sister," I began neutrally – for I wished to test the accuracy of my dreams. "Did I shorten her name?"

"Yes," King Cedric smiled. "Due to your young age, you found her whole name rather difficult to pronounce. You used to call her 'Lynny'."

My eyes widened in shock – this matched up exactly with what I had been calling her in the dream.

"You're beginning to remember, aren't you?" King Cedric asked with passion, taking a step further towards me. "I can see it in your eyes. Do you now accept the truth?"

I searched King Cedric's face – this man who could be my uncle. I could see none of the evil I had always heard of. King Reghan had dismissed King Cedric as an evil, tyrannous dictator, and I had never before seen reason to doubt my king.

"Well?" King Cedric prompted, for I still had not answered him.

"I do not know," I told him. My mind and my heart were at odds with one another, and I did not like it. For my mind told me this was folly and deception, as it went against all I had ever known to be true about myself. Simultaneously, however, my heart was confirming deep within me that these things were true, and part of me still longed to know the woman in the dream with that soft, sweet laugh who had held me so close.

"If I were to become your nephew and heir, then my whole life would change. I would be forced to leave everything I know and vowed to protect," I stated at last. The king nodded beside me, and now I turned to him to voice one of the many questions that had come to mind. "Just before I fled with Princess Evelyn, my lord king, I had a conversation where he told about your missing heirs. The captain told me His Majesty King Reghan had only just discovered your claim that you had living heirs in Gaeson."

"A despicable lie!" he exclaimed, his hand slamming the stone of the balcony wall. "Nay, Daniel, he knew since the day he sent men to slay you all in your beds." He paused to take a deep breath. "I apologise for my anger," he added ruefully. "The injustice that your king," he said, spitting the words, rife with sarcasm and disdain, "would deny his actions and lie to his people only worsens his atrocities. I miss your parents sorely, especially your mother my sister. I had no one on the whole earth of whom I was fonder, except..." He trailed off, and suddenly I knew of whom he had been about to speak – the woman who had held his arm, with her kind smile and belly full with a child. His hands gripped the cold stone of the balcony wall until his breathing evened and the anger left him.

"Except your wife," I finished for him, my voice strangely emotional. King Cedric raised his head to stare at me, and I saw the agony in his countenance that I had guessed correctly. "Your wife that was pregnant, wasn't she?" I continued quietly.

"How could you know that?" he asked hoarsely, his expression turning to further shock. "You only discovered the truth yesterday, how could you know?"

I shook my head, unable to reply.

"You do remember," he muttered, "don't you?"

Again, I could not answer him. I stared out onto Caer Ligualid; the clouds had lightened considerably now, revealing the sun as it slowly rose. This balcony afforded me the view of the city of Caer Ligualid itself, gleaming interconnecting streets securely encompassed by its stone walls. It was a truly beautiful place and gave some comfort to my confused soul.

"Yes," King Cedric murmured ere long, and I turned to look at him. "My wife was pregnant. She had only a month or so before our first child would be born when she died, the same night your parents did. I loved her dearly." He smiled whimsically. "We were so happy together, and I was so excited about becoming a father. But it was not to be," he ended sadly.

"I am so sorry, my lord the king," I managed, for this account was tragic indeed. Again there was a pause in our conversation. "The man and woman you claim as my parents," I said now, "what were they like?"

"Your mother, Imogen, was my sister. She was but one year younger than I," he added with a wistful, reminiscent smile. "She had long, sleek red hair and beautiful chestnut eyes; that is where Lynette's eye colour comes from," he added with another smile. Again, I noticed he used "chestnut" to describe her – was it coincidence that was the term I used to describe Sarah? "She had laughter that was warmer than a lit fire," he continued, and this panged at my heart, for this what I had remembered from the dream.

"Your father Adair was a fine and strong man," King Cedric began his account, "three years older than her. Adair served under my father as the hand of the king, and then under me when I inherited my father's throne. I had been on the throne three years before you were born – six years when Imogen, Adair, my wife and child all died, and when you and Lynette were lost. I was working late in my study, which was a little way down the corridor to where my wife had retired early – it being so close to the baby being born, she needed her rest." King Cedric broke his account to wipe his mouth with the back of his hand.

"A group from Gaeson had secretly entered our castle," he continued. "I deducted later that they first killed my wife, killing her with such swiftness before she could wake and scream. Had I but been with her…" He stopped abruptly here. Never before had I seen a king so emotional, so fragile and human – and this surprised me deeply. King Cedric clearly believed me to be his nephew and heir, or he would not be revealing such misery.

"The only thought that comforts me," he murmured, "is that Angharad was asleep when the blade cut her throat, and that it happened so swiftly that she did not feel any pain. The last time I spoke with my wife was a happy one; I pray that her happiness was her last thought, not pain and fear. After they cut her throat, they moved further down to the corridor to deal with Imogen and Adair. They killed Adair first and this then woke Imogen, who managed to scream before her throat was also slit."

I closed my eyes briefly at his speech – was this how my true parents had died? Was it true that my genuine father had not died in battle as I had believed, but had died in the middle of the night, by order of King Reghan?

"I fear we elevate kings too much," he told me now, sounding extremely weary. "We hold them as higher beings, not as mere mortals." King Cedric was still in his discourse; I listened intently, despite what disdain I might still have had for him. "My subjects think I can do no wrong, but I know I can. I have made many mistakes. I could wage a war against Rheged herself, and I would still have loyal people willing to die for me. It is a great power to be a king, Daniel. King Reghan has long abused that power. Do you believe that kings are perfect, divine beings? Or are they capable of falling? Nay, Reghan must be stopped. He wages war against Rheged, for no reason other than his own greed and power. We must stop him before it is too late. There is a bigger war coming, Daniel. A bigger war which may well defeat us when the time comes."

"Bernicia," I murmured, glancing to the east, where it lay far beyond my own eyes could see, far beyond the majestic plains of Caer Ligualid. "You really think they will attack?"

King Cedric turned to me, shock clearly on his face. "What do mean? They have already been attacking, my boy. That is also why His Majesty King Urien has recently aided my attacks, because King Reghan has refused again and again to help us in our war against them. There have been two battles already; both times he has refused to obey King Urien and help."

My eyes had flown wide in shock at his speech. "No one knows this in Gaeson," I said, my voice so hoarse it was barely above a whisper. "We believed Bernicia was still gathering her forces for an attack in the near future. If what you say is true…"

"What reason would I have to lie about it? You know I am giving you a genuine account of things," King Cedric added. "You have said you had a nickname for your sister and that my wife was pregnant when she died," he continued. "You know nobody had told you that information – you only know it because you are beginning to remember."

I opened my mouth and closed it again, not knowing what to say in response. "I bid you take me to see His Supreme Majesty King Urien," I replied ere long. "I need to hear this from his lips."

"Of course, but the king is presently away on other business. He will be back tomorrow. His Majesty will certainly confirm what I have said then. You should know, nephew, that His Supreme Majesty will not stop his attack on Gaeson just because you have been discovered. We mean to attack Gaeson again," he expanded, "after His Majesty King Urien has explained the strategy to us upon his return."

"You cannot!" I protested loudly. "Forgive me, your majesty," I apologised immediately, as King Cedric motioned to stop a guard who had stepped forwards at my outburst. "But they know nothing of what you speak. If what you say is true, then all of Gaeson is unaware of his corruption and greed."

"Be that as it may," the man who seemed all the more likely to be my kin conceded, "King Reghan must be stopped. Duty will oblige us to obey King Urien's orders, my nephew, however difficult that might be."

"Whether I am your heir or not, my lord the king, I shall never go against Gaeson," I objected now. "I will not wage war against my own people."

"I am not asking you to, Daniel," he replied, no longer sounding hard, simply weary. "I have long prayed for peace between our two peoples. Our ancestors were close brothers to the end of their days; our peace was only broken the night King Reghan ended it."

I shook my head vehemently and the movement made me dizzy; I reached out and to touch the balcony wall for support.

"You must rest, Daniel. You are not yet recovered," he told me, his voice becoming gentle again. "We shall speak again later, my boy. In time, you will come to see the truth of these things."

I did not reply but simply stared at him. "This cannot be real," I whispered hoarsely. "Before yesterday, I was simply a soldier from Gaeson, and you were my enemy. You are now expecting me to accept that I am really your long-lost nephew,

Prince of Klumeck and heir to the throne – and that the king I have served all my life is really an evil tyrant who murdered my parents."

"Yes," King Cedric replied evenly. "As well as my wife and unborn child." He took a deep breath. "I realise this must be difficult to believe."

I smiled a little sarcastically, for this seemed the understatement of a lifetime. "Your wife and child died, and your heirs went missing twenty-one years ago, my lord the king," I stated now. "Why did you not remarry and produce another heir to secure your throne?"

A small smile now played on the king's face. "My advisors have oft asked me the same question over the years. It is purely because I believed you and your sister were still alive. It was I who put you on that carriage, to take you away from your home. There were three other guards with you to take you to Caer Ligualid. The road from Klumeck to here is oft dangerous, particularly with the conditions as it was – but it was the safest place to take you."

"You sent us to Caer Ligualid?" I asked, forgetting in my surprise to address him properly. I had had many surprises in the last twenty-four hours. "Then how was it we came to be in Gaeson?"

King Cedric nodded, his face back on the view. "I have asked myself the same question countless times. The day after the attack, after I had discovered who was behind the attack and made safe the kingdom, I sent men to return you both back to Klumeck. However, not far into the journey, they came across the three Klumeck soldiers I had sent to escort you the previous night. All of them were dead, along with two Gaeson soldiers – evidently there had been some kind of fight. There was no sign of you or your sister, or the carriage that bore you. The blizzard had been so severe that there were no tracks left… the only conclusion I had was that the Gaeson soldiers had stolen you away."

"I was found in the snow alone," I stated. "Something must have happened to the guards from Gaeson." My head started to spin again, and I put my hands out to the balcony to steady myself.

"You still need rest," King Cedric told me. "You have heard quite a lot of difficult truths today. I am sure you still have many questions, but we have had enough conversation of the past for today. Guard," he ordered, before I could add anything else. The guard stepped forwards. "Please escort Prince Bryce back to his chambers. You are welcome here, my boy," he continued. "If, when your strength returns, you wish to explore this fair city, you would be more than safe to do so."

"Thank you, Your Majesty," I managed, inclining my head to him. "You have given me a great deal to think about."

He gave me a brief nod and then swept away with the swish of his cloak. How sure and strong were his footsteps, and with such purpose. It was the mark of a king who knew who he was and where he was going. In contrast to me, who no longer, it seemed, knew either of those two things. With that, I left his company and followed the guard back through Caer Ligualid's castle.

As we walked, my brain continued to swirl and pace with teems of unanswered questions. With every second that passed, I found myself more and more convinced of all that King Cedric had said. The look on his face when I had mentioned his wife and child... I saw no possible way that his reaction had been fabricated. Surely that meant I really was his heir, since no one had told me about his pregnant wife. Plus, I had remembered the nickname for Sarah.

"Your Highness," the guard said as I opened the door, and I turned back to him. "One of the castle servants recovered this from your clothes yesterday; it seemed to be inside an extra pocket. They wondered if you might wish it back," he added, and offered me the white cloth Princess Evelyn had given me when we were children.

"Thank you," I added, barely able to keep the desperate relief out of my voice as I almost snatched it out of his hands. "The castle servant is to be congratulated. Farewell," I added abruptly and closed the door behind him.

Almost dizzy with relief – and probably also from my weakened state – I made my way to the bed, noting impassively that the bedclothes had been changed, as had the water in the goblet. There was also a bowl of boiled wheat, but as I was currently not hungry I ignored it. I held the cloth in my hands, chiding myself that in everything that had happened, it had been completely forgotten. I knew such sentimentality was folly, but this remained the most precious possession I owned.

I sat on the bed now and drew my knees up to my chest, placing my head in my hands whilst I tried to think, trying to sort out fact from fantasy. I closed my eyes and concentrated, visualising that woman from the dream I had instantly recognised. Was this woman my true mother?

All I had seen had seemed so real that surely it was not purely my imaginings. Sarah and I both had similar coloured hair – a fact I had first seen as coincidence. Was it purely coincidence, or was it because we were both that woman's offspring? I had the facial features of the man in the dream and also his storm-like eyes... but the dark red of my hair would be from the woman. Whereas Sarah had the woman's lighter complexion and features, but the brown hair of the man. Was Sarah truly my sister?

The more I thought about Sarah, the more this could be true... the bond we had had from childhood, the affinity we had shared for each other. I could remember the first day we met, when they had moved into the house next to ours. She ran over with a shy smile and took my hand, as if it was the most natural thing to do in the world. The look on our mothers' faces, I wondered now. Was that joy appropriate for two strangers who had just met? Or was it at the reuniting of two long-lost siblings?

Indeed, the more I pondered these things, the more they seemed to resonate deeply in my heart. The images of the man and the woman... I knew those faces! I was sure of it. As I pondered more, a faint sound passed through my mind; it was the laughter of the woman from the dream. I smiled, unbidden. Why should a stranger's laugh cause my happiness? I wondered now. The woman's laughter was so warm and utterly contagious.

What would it mean if I became King Cedric's heir? I wondered now. The whole of my life would have to change. I would presumably live in Klumeck rather than residing in Gaeson. I would no longer serve King Reghan. King Reghan... the mere mention of his name in my mind had caused rage to well up within me. The emotion was intense as well as strange. So recently I had been ready to give my life in King Reghan's service, and now I was battling not to hate him. For if King Cedric was true in his account, then King Reghan had murdered my parents in cold blood, as well as my aunt and the unborn cousin I would never know. I felt my hands clench – people have hated for a lot less.

"Could it be true?" I whispered aloud. King Cedric had said King Urien would be back tomorrow. I got up from my bed now and went again to the window. This window afforded me the view of Caer Ligualid's sloping hills, and the three spires that made the city legendary. My father – or the man I had believed to be my father until yesterday – had often travelled here as a soldier, and he used to whisper the stories to me at night, sometimes long after I was supposed to be asleep. I could still remember the thrill and suspense I felt at hearing such tales of beauty, honour and courage.

I felt weak again, and clambered back to my bed. As reluctant as I was to remain in bed, King Cedric was right that I needed more rest. I lay back onto the pillows and found myself thinking of Princess Evelyn. I prayed she was safe, as I did for John and Aife and the captain, if he was still alive. I frowned as I thought of Princess Evelyn – things seemed to have become complicated, as now the father of the woman I loved could be the man who had murdered my parents and torn me away from my family. I consoled myself with the knowledge that Princess Evelyn could have no idea of the atrocities her father may have committed... even if he was corrupted, surely there was no way for her to have become so. I still held the cloth in my hands. Her face slipped from my mind as the last of my consciousness faded away – but not before the woman from the dream appeared, along with the sweet notes of her laughter.

When I next awoke, I could see from the sun shining in through the open window that it was now afternoon. I had forgotten to close it after examining Caer Ligualid's view once more, and now shivered from the extra chill that had fallen in the room. My stomach now rumbled with hunger, and I wolfed down the boiled wheat that had long grown cold. I changed into the fresh clothes, taking care to secure Princess Evelyn's cloth within my tunic. As I finished dressing, I remembered King Cedric's words about exploring. My limbs felt as though they needed exercising, so I left my chamber to see this fine city for myself.

"So, here is the long-lost prince of Klumeck. Greetings, Prince Bryce."

I turned abruptly at the new voice to see a man, rather small in stature, sitting atop a table, with his legs swinging free. I had come to the main entrance of the castle, where across the long chamber stood the currently raised portcullis. The man seemed to be in his forties, with thick black hair and beard and a quill behind his ear.

"Though you seem to doubt this truth for yourself, soldier of Gaeson." He smiled broadly – was he mocking me? In truth, I found his strange manner unsettling.

"I await to hear the truth confirmed from His Majesty King Urien, when he returns from his business tomorrow," I replied, still watchful of his countenance.

"A wise reply, but King Urien will certainly agree with King Cedric. I have often wondered whether King Cedric would finally find you. That was a night of tragedy indeed," this stranger concluded.

"And who might you be?" I asked him, feeling a little defensive for no apparent reason.

The man smiled even broader. "I am Taliesin," the stranger replied, "friend and royal bard to His Majesty King Urien. I have written many odes about his life and wars, his deeds and his wisdom. I have also written odes to King Cedric. Perhaps your discovery will be my new inspiration," he concluded.

"I would prefer it if you did not," I responded. "I would prefer for you to not make poetry out of the recent struggles with my identity. Perhaps you would be kind enough to draw your inspiration from another source. Good day," I added abruptly.

"Good day, Prince Bryce," he answered from behind me, for I had already turned away. I had wished to get away speedily from his speech, from his broad grin and his tone which I had not been able to discern. As I left the castle gates, however, I was soon fully absorbed in the beauty of the city and was able to forget the bard and his probing words.

Caer Ligualid seemed far fuller of beauty and wonder than even my greatest boyhood imaginings. The grass even seemed greener, the blades softer when I reached my hand out to touch them – such thoughts were folly, but this place indeed seemed magical. It was as if I had stepped into the world of one of the stories my father used to tell me as a child. But which father? I asked myself suddenly. I paused on the cobbled street, ignoring the people moving past me on their daily lives, and thought. Which father would have read me these stories, if I now had two? Which mother did I truly belong to – the one who had borne me, or the one who had raised me? This dose of truth was a hard one to swallow, if it really was truth. I had grown up secure and safe in the knowledge of my parents – good people who loved me and had brought me up to know the Lord.

There was a bucket of water reserved for the horses to drink, but currently it was deserted. I edged to it cautiously and gazed at my own reflection. My face was bruised more than I had realised, and there was a large cut just underneath my right eye, extending so it even crawled a little up my nose. If this was how I looked after sixteen days, I must have looked a sight when I was first found.

But even if it was disfigured, there it was: my face. Whose was that face? Had I been living a lie up until now? I rubbed my chin gingerly. My chin had always been rounder than I had liked, and my nose was shorter than some. I glanced at my storm-like eyes and they blinked back at me strangely, as if my reflection was unknown to them. Stooping, I peered closer. Was it my imagination, or did my features have some likeness to this man who claimed to be my uncle? Or did it just seem that way, after finding out his story?

Surely now too, I saw Sarah! Yes, her likeness lay somewhere around my cheeks and the roundness of my chin. I had long before noticed we looked alike; this prospect had thrilled us as children. We used to even play pretending we were brother and sister. Our respective mothers had encouraged and laughed us along especially in this game. Maybe it gave them joy to see us glimpsing the truth they could never tell us.

I stood now and continued on my stroll round the city with a restless sigh. Street after street I continued, determined to see the other legend my father had told me about which I had dreamed of as a child – the crystal pools. It was at the base of a river that flowed through the middle of this ancient city. The terrain of the city was fairly flat, but at this point the pools became slightly lower. My breathing was getting heavy but I pressed on forwards, determined to reach these pools that I had dreamt of. Eventually I came to the stone wall that had been built around the pools and went through the small gap.

It was even more glorious than I ever could have imagined. The stone wall was tall and curved at the top, so there was not much light. People had thrown their coins into the water for luck, and the silver gleamed. Different pebbles from all over Rheged, including ones from the coast shore, which could be visible atop Gaeson, sparkled too in the bottom of the water. It was custom for travellers to place pebbles they may have picked up on the way and throw them in the pool, but alas, I had none about my person. A couple of others were there, sitting and looking into the pool, but by and large the place was deserted.

The shape of the wall caused dim light to enter, so that the pools almost glowed and the light from the pebbles and coins danced and sparkled. I watched, entranced by how the spectacular show of colours had been created from both shadow and light. Then the clouds shifted, and I could see again my reflection staring back at me, both familiar as it always had been but, at the same time, I appeared almost a stranger. Who was I? Where did I belong? I was staring intently at the water still, but I knew it would hold no answers.

I bowed my head and prayed, asking God to calm my heart that was warring within me. I thought too of the men I had left behind and prayed all would be safe. I prayed too for Princess Evelyn and those I cared for the most – including the mother who had raised me, even if she was not the one who had given birth to me. Even if she had deceived me for most of her life. I prayed for Princess Evelyn once more, and knew then that my heart's regard for her had not changed, even though loving her had perhaps become more complicated.

Eventually I left the pool and headed back through the city, not knowing any more answers than when I had arrived there. By the time I returned to the castle, I felt very weak – though I had recovered much since yesterday, the whole of my body now ached. My arm was still a little stiff from how it had been pierced in the first battle, the battle that seemed to have been the start of everything. I reached my temporary chambers and collapsed back onto the bed, feeling the last of my strength leave me. I sank to my knees and prayed for the wisdom to know who I was, and whether I could trust the man who I had believed my whole life was my enemy. I had barely spoken my last "amen" before I sank into a deep, restless slumber once again.

***

"His Majesty King Urien is ready to see you," a guard informed me, after knocking on my chamber door. It was the next morning, after I had spent a fitful night and finished a small breakfast. "This way, if you would follow me." He led me down the stone staircase. My hand longed to reach for the handle of my blade, if nothing else but to reassure me – but if it was true I was among friends, then I need not fear. I had to be content with my hand hanging limply by my side as I walked.

Presently we walked down a whitewashed corridor, where red, soft carpet lay beneath my feet. Huge wooden doors revealed the king's hall. It reassured me that this was a kingdom of peace, and I knew I was safe here in these walls, particularly if I was viewed as King Cedric's heir. I also knew I could trust in King Urien, since he was the greatest king in our entire kingdom. He was the one that King Reghan was meant to serve, so I knew I would abide by King Urien's authority. Even if he spoke against King Reghan, I would submit to his rule.

We entered into the palace hall, much larger and grander than that of Gaeson – but that was no surprise. I walked behind King Cedric to bow before King Urien – and as I saw his face, I fought not to react. I had seen this man before, though I was also sure I had never met him in my lifetime. But sharp recognition had hit me, so fierce it almost taken my breath away. I could remember clearly having a fear of this man. I took him in, with his sharp jaw, grey gristle beard, and his hardened, icy, pale blue eyes. I could understand from his expression what King Cedric had said, about him being a man without mercy. I could understand why men would tremble under this king's wrath.

"Your Majesty," I greeted him, bowing low.

"Ah, at last," he added, leaning forwards to further survey me, his icy eyes gazing down upon me. "You have the scar?"

I bowed again and lifted my tunic up to reveal the scar I had been given as a child – the one that had enabled King Cedric to recognise me. King Urien nodded and I lowered my tunic again.

"Yes," he said gruffly, at length. "It is indeed you. I recognise your scar, boy, seeing as I was there when you received it."

My eyes widened at this, but King Urien made no further comment.

"Welcome Bryce, prince of Rheged and soldier of Gaeson," the king addressed me, as I approached his throne further. "Although I hear you now go by the name of Daniel."

"Your Majesty," I answered again, bowing low once more. That was it, then. He had himself addressed me as the Prince of Rheged and identified me as King Cedric's lost heir. I rose to standing, wondering where I should begin – there were so many things I could say, but I was not sure how to say them. "I have many questions, Your Majesty."

"I am sure that is true, but now is not the time to ask them. You can rest assured that everything King Cedric has said is true. You are indeed his nephew, the lost heir of Klumeck that was stolen from him in a moment of King Reghan's treachery." He descended the steps from his throne now. "How ready are the men?" he questioned another soldier.

"We are ready, sire, awaiting your orders," he replied, bowing. The king nodded, walking through to outside the hall, his hand on his sword. Since everything King Cedric had said was true, I could already guess what these orders would be.

"Your Majesty means to attack Gaeson," I murmured. The King turned to me, yet his eyes remained impassive upon seeing my anguished expression. "Sire, please do not. They do not know of King Reghan's betrayal. My people believe they are allied to you."

King Urien frowned, as if pondering this for a moment. "So you are King Cedric's heir," King Urien said. "What are you to inherit exactly, boy? Klumeck is nigh but destroyed by King Reghan's soldiers. You and your brothers have waged war against the defenceless Kingdom of Klumeck for long enough." It was true; I had battled against Klumeck in the past.

"That was always in retaliation, Your Majesty," I replied, but I didn't know now whether that was the truth. What if we were blind soldiers, always being the ones to strike against Klumeck? What if Gaeson had attacked first, against what we had always believed? "That is what we all believe," I confirmed. Throughout my life, I had heard legends that spoke of Klumeck as a tyrannical monster, under the evil King Cedric. But now I wondered whether those legends were meant to describe Gaeson.

"The people do not know," I murmured. "We always believed Klumeck was against you, that we were the ones allied to you. Please, Your Majesty. Allow me to go back to warn them. If I return, we may yet resolve this peacefully."

"No," he replied at once. "Do you think I would allow that, when King Cedric has found you at last? Besides, if what you say is true, King Reghan will know you have discovered him the moment you walk back into Gaeson. You will be tortured and killed. Here you will be safe. Your orders are to assist your uncle in the impending attack."

"Against Gaeson, sire?" I questioned. He turned to me. "Your Majesty, please do not ask me to do that. I now know who I am… but do not ask me to wage war against my own people. The people whom I have served all my life. Not when there are innocent people still there," I pleaded. His face was still impassive. "Your Supreme Majesty, I beg…"

"King Cedric," King Urien cut me off loudly and coldly, "I suggest you teach your nephew to hold his tongue. You have your orders, boy," King Urien continued, his hard stare once again feeling like it was boring into me. "I had hoped you would be willing to follow orders, as you are a soldier, are you not? That is all."

"Forgive me, Your Majesty," I managed, before King Urien had exited the room with the swish of his cloak. I straightened again and turned to the man I now knew was my uncle. "You told me I would not have to fight my own people," I said now.

"I told you I would not ask you to," King Cedric replied heavily. "I did not know what King Urien would request of you, though I had hoped he would spare you this task. I know this is difficult, but we have our orders. Come, my nephew." We began to walk across the hall, following the direction of King Urien. Presently, however, three soldiers came up to King Cedric wishing to speak with him. "You go on ahead, Daniel, this will take a moment."

"As you wish," I replied, still unsure what to call him. I left the king's hall and stood outside in the corridor for a few seconds. I was searching my heart, but I knew beyond doubt what I had to do. I ran out in a different direction, to prepare myself for my task that would defy my uncle, King Urien and the whole of Rheged – for I was going back to Gaeson.

I knew I could easily die, either by King Urien's hand for disobeying his orders, or by King Reghan's hand once he discovered I had learned the truth. King Urien, too would see me as a traitor, disobeying his orders. But I had no choice; I had to warn my brothers and sisters. I had to stop King Urien's force from killing so many who did not know the truth about whom they served. Even though my decision surely meant my death, I felt more peace than in the last few days since I woke up here. I had found peace in simply knowing what I had to do.

I snuck into the armoury. After searching, I was relieved to find my own armour – at least I could go back dressed as a soldier from Gaeson. If I had showed up as a soldier from

Klumeck, surely I would be cut down on sight. I found my old sword and placed it in my sheath before heading to the nearby stables.

As I entered the stables, ready to prepare the first horse I saw, a familiar happy neighing reached my ears, which brought me much joy.

"Epos," I said happily, stroking her mane between her ears. "It's good to see you, old friend," I murmured, leading her out of the stall and readying her as speedily as I was able to. "Come on, girl, let's go home," I muttered, and swung up to mount her, gathering the reins in my hands.

"Don't do this, Daniel." My head jerked up at the new voice to see King Cedric walk out of the shadows. "I have only just found you, my nephew. Please don't go."

I took in this man, this man who was my uncle – but I knew I had no choice. "I now know you are my uncle and my kin," I declared, "and that makes it all the harder to leave you. But I must go back. I cannot leave my people to their fate when they do not know the truth."

"King Urien has expressly forbidden it, Bryce!" King Cedric objected passionately. "If you are discovered, King Urien would not hesitate to kill you."

"That is why I know you will not tell him," I replied. "Let me go, and this war between our peoples could end tonight. If I am alive after tomorrow, then I will accept the consequences for my disobedience. If my life is forfeit, then so be it." I turned Epos around to face towards the exit of the stables.

"You are all I have left." I heard his agony, the difficult emotions in his speech, as I glanced up at him a final time. "You are all I have left of my sister. Do not risk your life so easily, not just after I have found you. Do not do this, Bryce. I beg you."

"My heart is full of sorrow to leave you, but I cannot stay. I pray that God goes with you, uncle. I pray that He keeps you safe and grants that we meet again." With that, I kicked Epos into a gallop.

"Bryce!" King Cedric shouted, but I fought not to look back. Instead I sped on, the thought of my brothers and sisters pulling me forwards to home. I had to warn them; I could not let them harm John, Aife, or the captain – nor could I let harm come to Sarah, Rachel, Alena or Ruth. My heart grew further in anguish as I imagined the harm that might befall Princess Evelyn. With every beat of Epos' hooves upon the ground, however, sorrow increased in my heart that I was leaving the identity I had just found, and I was going further and further away from the man I had just discovered was my uncle and my kin.

Chapter Seven

As soon as I caught sight of the top of the stone walls visible atop Gaeson's hill, I smiled. Every bone in my body seemed to sigh in relief at the familiar sights of home. My time at the Kingdom of Rheged and travelling back had been exhausting. I knew there would be no battle until tomorrow – it would be safe to return, but not for me. My smile faded and my body tensed again as I thought of the reaction my arrival would bring. I was surely considered dead – I had not seen anyone from Gaeson since I had cut the rope. I had thought that would be the time for Jesus to call me home – but obviously the Lord had better plans when I opened my eyes in Rheged twelve days later. Was it really only three weeks since I had woken up with my parched throat to see King Cedric's army marching against us?

But now I was to return and knowing the truth – that I suspected none knew in Gaeson, apart from King Reghan himself and his closest advisors. Anxiety filled me as I imagined the kind of welcome I was sure to receive from the king, once he discovered what I knew. I now knew it was true – His Majesty King Urien had confirmed it with his own mouth and he had no reason to lie, as far as I could tell. King Urien was supreme over all of Rheged, so I was obliged to accept his word, as I had once done with King Reghan. That man who, three weeks ago, I was vowing to fight for with every fibre of my being, I now knew had been corrupted by power and greed. The moment I opened my mouth to share this news with my brethren, I would be considered a traitor.

Oh, what King Reghan had done! I gripped the reins tighter in anger and felt keenly some of the rage I had witnessed from King Cedric. All the time as I had been fighting against King Cedric – the man who was my uncle – he had been the one to be allied with Rheged! Gaeson, not Klumeck, was the rogue kingdom who had instigated senseless war! All the time we thought we were fighting alongside Rheged, we were actually its foes. King Reghan's deception twisted my stomach just thinking about it. Not only that, King Reghan was the man who had murdered my parents. The man and woman from the dream who had held my infant self with such goodness and love, with his warm eyes and her sweet laugh – King Reghan had sent his men to murder them in cold blood. I felt such intense rage now that I prayed God would give me the self-control not to slaughter him as soon as I saw him.

I was now riding Epos up Gaeson's hill; I was almost there. As I journeyed the last mile or so, I felt my thoughts growing calmer. For as corrupted as he was, I would not kill him for the sake of his daughter. I strongly reminded myself that I had not returned to seek vengeance, but to warn my brothers and sisters, even though I would be considered a foe and I would be risking torture and death. But what choice did I have? I still loved my people and my home. I had to warn them, even though I was defying the might of King Urien and turning my back on Rheged herself. My conscience would never have let me sit by and see Gaeson needlessly slaughtered, when there need be no bloodshed at all. When peace could still be made and war could still be avoided.

"Daniel!" The watchtower guards greeted me from a distance, and I saw a soldier break into a run – no doubt to inform the others that I was back. I had hoped to greet my mother and Sarah before I was escorted into the castle, but I knew there was only a remote possibility for that. Presently the portcullis was raised and the wooden doors were opened.

"Captain!" I greeted him in pleasant surprise. I had wondered whether I would see him alive, for the last time I saw him his chest was full of blood. I was truly glad to see him safe.

"Daniel," the captain returned warmly. He reached out and our arms clasped one another; I inclined my head in a swift bow. "It's good to see you," he smiled. "The surgeon managed to restore my health and I am much recovered – but you have been away for many days! I am surprised to see you, my friend."

"There was a river at the bottom of the cliff," I explained. "I have been unconscious until two days ago. I returned as soon as I could." I had given as casual and vague account as possible, as

I wanted to extend these few moments where I would still be regarded as friend rather than foe.

The captain opened his mouth with a slight frown on his face, no doubt to ask more questions – but then two guards came to stand beside him. The captain bent his head to listen and nodded.

"The king has learnt of your return," the captain stated now. "He bids you go and report. I'm sorry there's no time for you to go home and greet your family or rest, but it seems His Majesty is as anxious to discover where you have been as I am," he added.

For no apparent reason, King Reghan's request to see me filled me with anxiety. But surely to him I was just an ordinary soldier who had gone missing. Perhaps he had already suspected I had been a prisoner at Caer Ligualid or Klumeck and had learnt the truth and was then able to escape my captivity and return home.

"I have discovered many things," I replied at length, "I am anxious to see His Majesty also." He clapped a hand on my shoulder, obviously glad I was back alive and well. I relished in the fact he still saw me as "friend", for I knew that could soon no longer be the case. I found myself remembering that night on the balcony when he had been so honest in speaking with me. Would he now believe he had simply shown weakness to a traitor? Soon I would be seen as the worst kind of liar. I was particularly sorrowful that I might not be able to see John and Aife, to inform them I was alive and ask after them while they still considered me a brother in arms.

We travelled along the short path from the portcullis to the castle. I regretted I might not even be able to see the town of Gaeson, for it rested further down the hill and so was currently out of sight. Still I took in the scenery, knowing this was how Gaeson looked when I last belonged here; before I was revealed to be a prince of Klumeck and foe of King Reghan.

As we continued on the path, I found I could just spy the stables I had tended as child. It was there I had first met Princess Evelyn, and it was there that I had fled with Princess Evelyn to Caer Ligualid just two weeks ago. It was probably folly to be so sentimental – but I could not help but wonder how long this castle would hold me in her arms.

We had now entered the courtyard with its stone that shone silver, where the king had made all his public announcements. It was here two weeks ago that Princess Evelyn had been almost kidnapped by Bernician spies, and the captain had almost died. We passed the fountain in the middle which seemed to hold nothing but the purest water. We came now to the other side of the courtyard to the vast oaken doors of the king's hall. These doors were opened wide by the guards escorting me. I walked up to him and bowed low.

"You." He stood as soon as he saw me, his face expressing rage.

I raised my head up slightly to see his countenance and blinked, confused. His reaction did not seem to make sense. I had expected his anger when he had discovered the truth, not as soon as I walked in this hall.

"Your Majesty," I greeted him as sincerely as I could, bowing low, knowing I was bowing to the man who had murdered my parents, my aunt and my unborn cousin. As I bowed, I tried to suppress my anger and discern his. Perhaps he had reasoned that since I had not died, King Cedric or one of his people had told me the truth. But why would they bother to converse with a prisoner? I wondered. Unless King Reghan had sent spies to Caer Ligualid, and they had discovered the truth about my identity? Currently I could not see the reason for his rage.

"How dare you stroll in here as if you are to be honoured? You are not!" King Reghan growled, further enraged. His glare was awful, staring violently down upon me. I knew in that instant he would not allow me to even speak before he had me thrown out of his presence – I would not be able to warn Gaeson about the attack after all.

"Daniel!" Princess Evelyn greeted me as she entered the room, no doubt at the sound of her father's outburst. As good as it was to see her alive, I had hoped the princess would not be present for my humiliation, and sighed inwardly. "Father? What has happened? This man saved my life."

My head was bowed low, so I was unable to express the gratitude of her defending me. It gave me hope that even if all others cast me aside, she might believe me.

"Mind your tongue, daughter," the king replied, his words venomous. "This boy is no more than a traitor and a liar. He now serves the Kingdom of Klumeck. This is true, is it not? Answer me!" he shouted – I had not even the time to fathom the accusations put to me.

"My whole life, I have strived to make myself worthy of you, my lord the king," I responded quickly. I was evading the question and we both knew it. "If His Majesty would let me speak, I bear grave news…"

"Silence!" the king roared, having practically screamed. "What about now?" he asked, his voice suddenly quieter. "Have you returned to serve me, or have you now joined that fool King Cedric?" the king spat.

I took a moment to glance Princess Evelyn, who had confusion and concern on her face. I wanted one last look at the woman I loved, before she could condemn me.

"Well?" King Reghan growled.

I swallowed and looked him in the eye. "I regret, my lord the king, that recent events have made my allegiance to you no longer possible. I have uncovered truths about you, Your Majesty, which means I must protest your ruling."

"Lies!" he shouted in a further growl. "My spies have uncovered a great deal about you, Daniel. I knew you woke up in Klumeck's kingdom. It didn't take long for him to convince you to betray me!"

"As God is your witness, you know that is not true, Your Majesty," I told him, as calmly as possible – but anger was boiling up within me. In the next moment, a sword was against my neck. It did not strike me, but I instinctively staggered.

"You are lucky I do not strike you down now," the captain hissed, with the blade against my throat. "You will speak no more against His Majesty."

I looked at my captain with sadness in my heart. I had expected anger, but not hatred such as this – and not so strong from the man that I would still serve, gladly, if not for the king whom he put his allegiance to. The man who had regarded me as a brother three weeks ago, when I had last seen him on a stone floor with blood spurting from his chest.

"Take him to the dungeons, captain! He is to be executed at dawn tomorrow," the king growled, and I felt the captain drag me away. I glanced at Princess Evelyn, but her face was cast to the ground. I knew now she would never call me a faithful servant again after how it appeared that I had betrayed her.

"Captain," the king called, and he made me stop. "Gag him, so he cannot spread more of his lies." The king sat back down in his seat.

"Your Majesty," the captain assented, and marched me out of the room.

I felt numb. Executed? My captain waved a hand. Another soldier stepped forwards with a piece of cloth that he rammed into my mouth, with such force I almost choked.

"You two, with me. The rest of you, about your duties," the captain ordered.

Two soldiers grabbed hold of me and began to march me down one corridor after another, in the direction of the dungeons. I saw other men and women, soldiers and castle servants alike, recognise me and then stop to stare as they saw me bandied about like a common criminal. I kept my head down, wishing to minimalize my shame as much as possible.

"I'll take it from here," the captain stated. The other guards inclined their heads and walked away. The captain shoved me hard down the spiral staircase we had reached. I fell and rolled down, striking my head against the stone cold of the steps. The captain drew his sword and crouched down to me, holding his blade up close against my throat. "How could you betray us like this, Daniel?" he hissed at me. "We all trusted you and I…" He paused. "I called you friend, though I was above you in rank. Well, no longer; I see now that was my folly. On your feet."

I stood slowly, wishing to speak to him, but I was still gagged. The captain gave me a push, and I made my way down the dank, narrow corridor of the dungeons. I soon came to face the dungeon guard, who grinned at me coldly, and I could see the gaps where his teeth had been; the ones that remained were black and rotten.

"So, fresh meat, eh?" the guard asked me, as the captain tied me up. He gave me a look of such disappointment that I had to turn my face away. "We shall have some fun together, you and I."

The captain reached up and pulled the cloth out of my mouth, which was a relief. I swallowed and seized this opportunity to speak.

"Captain, I beg you to listen…"

"Do not speak to me," he cut across me loudly. "Guard." The captain nodded to my new captor, and the guard bowed as the captain turned to leave. That was it, then, I reflected. I had been renounced as a traitor and liar, and not even worthy to speak. I stared after him, watching his footsteps, before turning back to the mad, toothy grin of my captor.

I would never be able to tell how much time had passed in that cell with the dungeon guard. Had it been an hour? Two? Could it already be dawn? All I knew for certain was the pain the dungeon guard had inflicted upon me. My whole face writhed in agony, but I prayed for the strength to look him in the eye and not look down, despite the blows he was dealing out. I did not know the guard's name; I had never seen him before – but I knew I would remember his face for the rest of my life. His eyes were cold and hard; it looked as though there had never been any warmth in them. But they were shrewd; I could sense this man's intelligence. His eyes were also dark, so dark they appeared to be coal. This caused him to appear even more irate. At the moment his eyes also seemed to be hazed with wine. His face was thin, his features narrow, and his mouth looked like it had rarely smiled.

My torturer's hard fist came flying out at me again from the right. It hit me with a force that took my breath away. Not for the first time, I tasted blood. He turned to pour himself some more wine, and while his back was turned, I gingerly moved my mouth. I was astonished that none of my bones were broken yet. The blows were hard, but I could tell from his frustrated expressions (the ones he thought were unseen by me) that they

147

were not as menacing as he wished. Maybe it was the wine, dulling his senses and therefore softening his blows. It gave me some small comfort to know he couldn't torture me as ably as he wished – but soon that comfort would disappear, for the more he grew frustrated, the more he hit me. I got the impression that were he sober, he would have impressive precision; one simple touch to break my jaw, another to dislocate my shoulder.

When he turned back, he held up a cup of water to me, taunting me. My lips were dry and cracked. How long had I been without water? I wondered again how much time had passed. It felt like days, though I knew it could only be hours; surely I would know if King Urien's men had already arrived. Oh, for that clear liquid to wash away the taste of my own blood – I had been forced to swallow several mouthfuls of it, thick and salty and warm that made me want to vomit. However, I did not ask him – I did not want to give him the satisfaction, and I knew he would not give it to me regardless.

"You can stop this any time you like." He spoke, one of the rare times he had done this so far. One could hardly call this an interrogation; he had barely asked me a question. He was just battering me for sport. His words came out rough and slurred – he was definitely intoxicated. "It's your own doing, this." He gestured with his goblet as he spoke, and wine dripped onto my battered face. My tongue was out before I could help it, lapping it up – anything to take the taste of the blood away. It was refreshing and sweet, but increased my thirst further.

The man laughed, almost to the point of hysterics. "You like that, eh? Maybe I'll give you some more if you talk. Maybe it's this you want, and not water, eh?" he added, his voice hardening – and before I could say any more, he had thrown that precious cup to the ground, the water spilling out in a pool on the floor.

"I want to speak to my king," I rasped. It was the twelfth time I had said this, but thus far to no avail. I had even attempted to tell the guard of King Urien's army, but he had simply laughed and punched me to stop my words. Here he laughed again, but this time there was no manic hysteria about it. This laugh was hollow, empty and sadistic.

"You actually think he'll come down to see a piece of filth like you? Why would he?" he questioned me, at last giving me another chance to speak.

"Because you have it wrong," I said – and I was so exhausted and weak I couldn't keep the exasperation out of my voice. I had no idea "interrogation" would be this brutal – but I supposed that one is meant to be able to pry the deepest, darkest secrets out of your enemies. Except when they mistakenly treat a friend as a foe. I spat more blood out of my mouth so I could talk better. "Princess Evelyn, then, if His Majesty refuses to see me. Please. I've done nothing wrong."

His cruel eyes examined me, and then he grinned. I sensed he felt he had won some sort of battle over me, as if my plea showed my weakness. Then he raised his fist. It came crashing into my right temple, and the room started to swirl into oblivion.

When I woke, my eyelids were heavy and sore. I opened my mouth slowly – it wasn't broken, but I sensed how close the bones were to fracturing. I opened and shut it gently a few times, trying to ease away the stiffness – but it was too painful to move it. I lifted my head and looked around, as far as my swollen eyelids would let me. I saw I was alone, in darkness. I knew it had to be the same day, but it felt like many days since I had been taken to this cell. All time seemed blurred into one.

I licked my parched lips and tasted blood. Now I was alone, I could not help the tears that began to fall. I was glad it was darkness; I was glad nobody could see me in my weakest hour. I prayed the Lord would deliver me from my distress, but I knew not if He would. The tears stung as they rolled quickly down my bruised face, my bleeding lips. I winced as they opened cuts anew, made not three weeks previous when I fell from that cliff. I wept as silently as I could muster.

Suddenly, the door opened and a lamp filled the room. The torturer was back. I swallowed and blinked, trying to remove signs of weeping – but their trails would be plain across my face and I had no way of wiping my tears, no way of erasing my weakness and shame.

"So here you are." My spirits lifted at the voice, only to sink again. It was not the torturer, but Princess Evelyn – her speech had started off sweeter than honey and had quickly evaporated into bitter malice. She came to stand before me, and I heard her gasp as she took in what my awful appearance must be; I had not seen a mirror since the captain tied me up down here.

Her Highness quickly regained composure, and instead she glared at me coldly, far from the face that gave out such easy love and care to all her people. In that instant, I knew she did not believe me. "Well, this is the price to be paid to you. My father must be just, especially to traitors." The bitterness of that one word hit me harder than all of the combined blows I had received from my interrogator.

"I haven't betrayed you, Your Highness. I am a traitor to no one." My swollen mouth made it difficult to speak. Her face hardened in a sarcastic grimace. "I'd never hurt you, my lady." My voice was hoarse and barely above a whisper; I did not have the strength for much more – but it still echoed around the empty room. "I'd die first," I whispered to her.

I sensed there was an internal battle within her. Was there a part of her that wanted to believe me?

"I almost did, when I fell from the cliff. I'd gladly cut that rope again, right now," I emphasised. I saw her face flicker again, still deciding whether to trust me. "I would fall upon my own sword in an instant if it meant you were safe. That is why I have returned, knowing I would endure these blows. Knowing I would be hated. I had to come back, to warn you of what was coming."

"Oh? What is coming, Daniel?" she asked me. There was a sarcastic quality to her tone, but at least she had asked me.

"King Urien is coming to attack Gaeson at dawn," I whispered frantically, the first time I had been given opportunity to express the truth. I saw her expression change to confusion and disbelief. "You think Gaeson is allied to Rheged, but this is not the truth. King Cedric is aligned to Rheged, and we are the rogue kingdom. That is why Klumeck's forces have always appeared stronger, even though we are the bigger kingdom. King Cedric is fighting with the aid of King Urien himself, and he will be here tomorrow at dawn," I finished. I saw her frown, her features harden. "I would not lie to you, Your Highness. I would never harm you."

"I used to believe that," she told me – and this hit me hard. I fought not to flinch – such a physical reaction would cause my face further pain. "But you have hurt me, Daniel. How dare you accuse my father of such things? That he deliberately would war against King Urien. You will pay for such treachery." She raised a hand suddenly, and I braced myself for further pain. To my astonishment, she simply gingerly felt my face, smoothing my hair out of my eyes and erasing the tear marks. My heart yearned at her touch, despite her fingers pressing against my wounds.

Then, in the next instant, her hand dropped and her hard exterior was back. "Goodbye, Daniel." She walked across the cell floor. "I doubt we shall meet again before you die tomorrow."

"Wait, Your Highness!" I cried out. She paused in the doorway. "Please believe me. I am only wishing to protect you and Gaeson." She had not stopped. "I only woke up from falling off that cliff two days ago," I told her now. "Do you really believe my heart could change so easily?"

She did stop then at this last speech, turning back to me in the doorway.

"I am still your boy from the snow, Your Highness," I murmured.

Through the dimness lighted by the lamps outside, I saw her shake her head, her eyes filled with tears. "No," she whispered, "I do not believe you are. The soldier who fell off that cliff – he was the boy I knew. I see now that the boy I met as a child died from that fall and a traitor now stands in his place."

I shook my head, though the pain hurt me so. "No," I whispered, as I watched her exit the dungeon chamber and leave me alone in my dark, endless prison. Without hope and awaiting execution. I watched her leave, and more tears fell down my face, stinging my cuts and bruises anew. That look of pain on her face… that had hurt me more than all of the pain the guard had inflicted upon me, more than all the blows he had dealt me. Then my head shot up before I could stop it as the door opened again. Was this the torturer back? Was it time for me to die?

"Hello, Daniel."

My eyes widened in surprise to see John and Aife standing at the doorway; my heart was made a little gladder to see my friends were well. They walked up to me, their faces hardened.

"So," John said quietly, "quite a situation we're in."

I could not tell from his speech whether he believed me. John and I had a strong friendship, a bond closer than many who are linked by blood – but was that enough for him to think I was telling the truth? Or even if he still believed in me?

"What you've said is treason," he told me at length.

"I know," I admitted. I saw something resolve in their eyes. I realised they had both been hoping I would deny what I had said, that if I did so then the situation would not be as irreversible as it appeared. Then John sighed, as if my fate was sealed. "How long have you known me, John?"

He shook his head, staring at the floor. He was seeking to avoid the question – but I couldn't afford him to.

"How long, John?" I begged desperately.

He looked up at me now, staring at me straight in the eye. "We were eight. I was boasting about my skill with a sword. I saw you walk past and I challenged you... and you beat me." John gave a small smile at the memory. What he said was accurate – I could remember it vividly, for he was the first person I could call a friend apart from Sarah. This young, plucky boy was saying how many other boys he had beaten. I was walking home and tried to avoid them. I kept myself to myself, but John had challenged me. I surprised even myself by beating him – but then, my father had taught me with a wooden sword. My father... I shook my head mentally, dragging myself back to the present.

"In that time, have I ever given you a reason to doubt me?" I was relying on my character – these two friends knew me like no other did. If I could not convince them I could still be trusted, who else would I turn to? "Aife? Have I?" I persisted.

"No," Aife answered at length; John still had not commented, but his expression remained pained. "Until now," she added, whilst John was still searching my face. "To speak against the king is treason," Aife concluded.

The door opened suddenly and the captain walked in.

"Sir," John greeted him. "We had to come and see for ourselves."

"I understand, John," the captain murmured. "By now you will have seen how deep his treachery runs. How he has spoken against the king whom we serve."

"What if the king is wrong?" I asked frantically. The captain drew his sword, holding it to my neck for the third time. "Even if the king is lying?"

The blade drew nearer, the captain's livid face before me. "Hold your tongue, Daniel, before I cut it out," he hissed.

"Sire," I begin weakly. "King Urien is coming with his army at dawn."

The captain stared in disbelief and then sniggered. "A likely story," he answered sarcastically. "You only want to delay your execution. Come, John, Aife. Let's away from this traitor," he added. The captain began to leave.

"I am the long-lost heir of Klumeck, captain," I called out to him.

The captain turned around slowly, as if he could not have heard right. John and Aife also looked upon me in shock.

"I did not wake in Klumeck, my lord, but in Caer Ligualid. King Cedric was there and told me I am his nephew. King Urien then confirmed this with his own lips. He ordered me to turn against Gaeson and be in the attack against her," I finished.

The three of them exchanged glances, but said nothing more.

"How could I do that?" I rasped now. "Captain, King Cedric had recognised me as his heir. I am to inherit Klumeck's throne, but I chose to come back here against King Urien's orders so as to warn you of the attack. I came back, risking my life, because of what might happen to you all. I had to warn you," I repeated desperately.

"Oh, that is too much!" he scorned me. "A young soldier just happens to be a long-lost prince!" He snorted in sarcasm. "Pray tell me, Your Highness," he added mockingly, "how do you know this to be true? How can you trust in him?"

"I began to remember him," I replied now hurriedly, before this one opportunity for truth sped me by. "I remembered my true mother and father, and my sister. My sister, who is the other lost heir. Her name is Sarah."

"Sarah!" Aife exclaimed, still more shocked.

I nodded, despite the pain to my head – I could not speak for much at a time. The captain looked deep in thought. John still had not said anything, but was clearly thinking fast.

"My lord." I addressed the captain, "Not so long ago, you said I was one of your most loyal soldiers. That has not changed. I had to do this – I had to warn you of what His Majesty King Urien was planning. How would I be a true brother, if I did not do anything else?" I paused. "I'm not expecting you to believe me. If I didn't know it was true, I would want to stop someone else for saying such heresy. But knowing it is true… knowing it would cost the lives of those who are most dear to me… how could I do anything but come back?" I looked from one to the other and back again. "I don't expect you to believe me," I repeated, "but I would hope you believe in me."

"The order has been said for your execution," the captain stated, a frown still upon his face. "To go against His Majesty's orders is treason."

"To go against His Majesty King Urien's orders is treason, and King Reghan has done this countless times," I answered him.

The captain's eyes hardened.

"I went against King Urien's orders, in order to come back to warn you. Listen to me, I beg," I implored, looking between the three of them. "Think on this – what if I am right?"

"Maybe we should listen to him," John spoke at last.

The captain turned his glowering face to John.

"Sire, Daniel has never caused me to doubt in him," John expanded quickly. "I may not believe him yet… but I do believe in him." My heart was full of thankfulness at his kind speech. "What if he is speaking the truth?"

"Watch your words," the captain snapped to John, "You speak too much."

"Do I?" John challenged him. "How can we be so sure the king could not turn to corruption and greed? He is only a mortal man, after all."

"Enough of this!" the captain bellowed, and drew his sword. "I will not hear any more of this treacherous heresy, unless you want to die alongside him. Daniel is lying," he concluded, but I saw what looked to be doubt in his eyes.

"I have known Daniel since I was a child," John answered simply. "We saw with our own eyes how he fell to save the life of the princess. He almost died in service to the king. He then comes back, risking torture and pain and death. What reason would he have to lie, apart from to save his people? If what he says is true, then he came back at the risk of his own life to warn us."

"Yes," I answered, feeling almost faint with relief. "I snuck away to warn you. There is an attack coming at dawn," I repeated desperately. "King Urien will send wave after wave of his army. He has no shortage of soldiers – he could well send the whole might of Rheged against us. If we can make King Reghan see the error of his ways, if he could somehow surrender…"

"Surrender?" the captain barked. He came within inches of my face, so that his breath and spit moistened my bruised cheeks. "I have never surrendered. Gaeson's army does not surrender."

"Even if the fight is for no reason? Even if we fight for folly and deceit?" I questioned him. "Also, something even bigger is happening. This is the time for Klumeck and Gaeson to unite under Rheged once more, for Rheged is already at war with Bernicia." The three of them took a step back at my speech, shock clearly written on their faces. "King Urien has asked King Reghan to aid him in the battles, but King Reghan continues to disobey. This is despite the fact that Bernicia may have already breached our gates," I concluded.

"What are you speaking of, Daniel?" Aife asked sharply.

I turned my head to look at her, despite the pain to my head. "King Cedric told me that it was not one of his men who caused our watchmen to fall asleep that night, when all of this began," I explained, "nor was it his men who attempted to kidnap the princess."

"Don't be ridiculous," the captain snapped. "Those were Klumeck soldiers – one of them speared my chest, remember? You were there, fighting with them alongside me," he added.

I shook my head and immediately regretted it as the pain hit me again. "King Cedric told me that he sent a small escort of his soldiers to a nearby town. The escort never came back, and when he sent more men to investigate, they discovered the bodies but not their armour. King Cedric suspects his armour was stolen by Bernician spies who then infiltrated our kingdom, probably to stir up hatred between us and weaken our armies."

"What folly," the captain concluded, taking a step closer. "I should slay you where you stand," he said, and drew his sword, but I held his gaze.

"Then why don't you?" I challenged him. I saw him press closer and feared he would actually strike. "This is the fourth time you have threatened me, sire. This is the fourth time you have almost slain me. I believe there is doubt in you of the king, and that is why you are so angry at the thought of rising against him."

He drew his sword closer to my heart, so that it pierced my flesh. I grimaced in pain.

"Sire, it is not our place to kill him," Aife protested. "Those are not the king's orders."

The captain drew back his sword. The cut was not too deep; only a little blood came. "Neither is it for us to release him," he hissed back. "Why should I believe you over my king?"

"Could we not visit Caer Ligualid herself?" John suggested, as the captain replaced his sword. "To see for ourselves if what Daniel says is true."

"You could be killed on sight, seen as enemies of Rheged," I warned them. "If nothing else, you would be held captive. Besides, war will have raged since then. It would be too late; the forces are arriving at dawn. Please, sire," I implored the captain again. "We must attempt to persuade the king."

"What would you have me do, Prince of Rheged?" he challenged me now. "Walk up to the king and confront him? He would not let you speak earlier. He would not let us talk him down."

"Then he must be taken down forcibly, before many lives are cost," I replied. Their eyes widened. "Though I would hate for that possibility."

"That would be betrayal indeed," the captain hissed. "I have heard enough folly. John, Aife," he said, "let us bid hence and forget this conversation."

"With all loyalty to you, sire, I cannot," John answered, "for I believe him."

The captain turned, anger in his face for his orders being questioned. Aife had not spoken.

"If Daniel is right, sire, then we have to act. Otherwise there will be needless bloodshed fighting all of Rheged. It would not be simply King Cedric we are warding off. That would explain why King Cedric's forces are always stronger, quicker, much more than ours, even though our kingdom is much larger. He is fighting with the force of Rheged herself," John declared. "She will mean to take this land, by force if not by our wilful surrender. Should we not declare ourselves friends of Rheged? It is what we always thought we were. Will we now betray her?"

I could see a flurry of activity inside the captain's mind, as if he were torn in indecision.

"What say you, Aife?" John asked her quickly.

"I say we trust him," Aife replied. "Why not go and visit Daniel's mother? She would tell us the truth about these things. Sire," she said, turning to the captain, "if King Cedric is attacking on King Urien's authority, then we need to follow him. Gaeson has always praised King Urien; King Urien is the supreme king over all of Rheged. Would we now go against our master?"

This seemed to resolve something in the captain, and he turned to cut me loose. I fell to the floor, weak.

"You will hold your tongue, boy, for the fifth time I will strike you."

I nodded as John helped me stand. Aife retrieved a skin of water from her belt and handed it to me. I gratefully accepted it, and after taking a long drink, I splashed some of it on my face to cool my cuts and wipe some of the blood.

"Put this on," the captain instructed, handing me a helmet. "I would rather you not be spotted. We are going to pay a visit to your mother," he added, "for she will tell us the truth of these things."

"Yes, sire," I responded, and followed the captain's lead, feeling as I did a mixture of joy and anxiety at the prospect of seeing the woman who had both raised and deceived me.

It did not take us long to reach my home. The captain knocked immediately, and the noise of the knock was sharp and loud, inconsiderate to those who lived here – particularly Rachel and the children, who would still be recovering after Joshua's death. The door opened quickly to reveal Sarah.

"Daniel!" I barely had time to blink before she had come forwards fast to embrace me. I embraced her back tightly, feeling a sudden rush of affection in knowing the woman I held truly was my sister. "We all feared you dead," she murmured. "Then we heard word you were back, but that you had been arrested as traitor and were awaiting execution!"

"Do not fear, for all is well, dear sister," I reassured her, joyous to reflect that this was no longer just a word to describe our close friendship, but that we truly were siblings "I'm sorry I could not return sooner, but I was recovering."

The captain cleared his throat, and Sarah jumped back as though burnt. I knew then there was no time to even begin to utter the truth to her.

"Forgive me, my lord," she added quickly, bowing swiftly. I sighed inwardly at the captain's reproachful gaze. I preferred it when she called me by my name, but in the captain's eyes it was not the proper term, as officially I was her employer. "It is good to see you alive, sire. But...what is going on, my lord?" Sarah asked me, as the captain, Aife and John traipsed in behind me, the captain still giving no regard for the lateness of the hour. "I bid you please be discreet, my lord," Sarah requested him, "for the children slumber."

"Children?" the captain asked, not bothering to lower his voice. "What children are these, Daniel?"

I hid a sigh- the captain was not one for being discreet. "It's alright, Sarah," I continued, ignoring the captain briefly. "This is the captain of the guard. And you know John and Aife." They both nodded back in greeting. I glanced at the captain now. "Rachel the seamstress and her children live here with me now. They are the family of Joshua."

The captain met my gaze and nodded, my explanation enough.

"Sarah, we came here to talk to my mother."

"Now, my lord?" Her sleepy eyes squinted in confusion. "It is the dead of night..."

"I know," I replied, "but this cannot wait." The captain was already heading for the stairs. "Sire," I called sharply, and he turned, affronted by my tone. "I would bid you let me go first in my own home, in order to wake my mother. It would not do her well in her condition to be wakened by someone she does not know."

"If she is your mother," he said sarcastically, but he let me pass first. I saw Sarah, now slightly more awake, darting her eyes between me and the captain, her confusion evident.

"It is a long tale, Sarah, which I will explain to you later," I told her as I passed her in the hall. "Much has happened of late."

We carried on upstairs, and I knocked on my mother's door. As she bid me entrance, I saw the same look of love she had on her face whenever I saw her, for as long as I had known her. This love was multiplied by joy, no doubt at seeing me alive.

"Oh, Daniel, my boy! I had thought you dead – and then Sarah told us you were to be executed..."

I crossed the room and clasped her outstretched hand tightly in mine. "Do not worry yourself. All will be set right," I added, as the captain raised his eyebrows slightly in scepticism.

As I held onto my mother's hand, I prayed justice would be done regarding my fate. Looking in to the eyes of the woman who had raised me, I knew that even though she had not given birth to me and she had deceived me about it, she had saved me from the blizzard, and raised me with her husband in love as one of their own. Whatever became of me, I had experienced a happy childhood, secure in their love. I would strive not to forget this, whatever the truth was.

"But what has happened to your face? Are you well, my son?" she asked me now anxiously. "Oh, my lords and lady," she added before I could reply, as John, Aife and the Captain also entered the chamber. She pulled up the covers closer to her, a blush entering her cheeks. I had rarely seen my mother – if she was my mother – look so flustered. "I am sorry I cannot get up to greet you properly."

"Nonsense, you are ill." My tone was slightly sharper than I had intended, and she noticed, too, for she glanced my way in confusion. "This is the captain of the guard," I explained, making my voice gentler. The captain inclined his head in her direction. "You already know John and Aife. I am sorry to wake you in the middle of the night, but I must ask you something."

"But...your face, Daniel! You are wounded; you must rest," she murmured, gesturing a chair. The captain shut the door behind him, so we would be undisturbed.

"It is nothing," I protested, but I sat all the same, still feeling weak. "I want you to tell me the truth," I continued evenly. "Is it true that you adopted me, and that Sarah is really my sister?"

She gasped in surprise, and then, after a moment, she nodded.

"Yes," she replied now in a quiet voice. "Oh, I have long awaited this day, when you would find out the truth." Her gaze had turned from me to stare at the bed. "I did not know whether I should dread or speed its coming... but it is here now." Her head lifted; her eyes once more met mine. "My son, ever have I loved you," she murmured earnestly.

Instead of this bringing me comfort, I felt lost and isolated, separated by her deceit. I let go of her hand.

"Oh, do not be angry with me, my son," she pleaded. "Yes," she affirmed adamantly, nodding her head almost defiantly. "You are my son. We raised you from three, when I found you and Sarah in the snow. Bridget and I found you half naked and cold and close to death. In my eyes, you were meant to be there, my son. God had ordained that my husband and I were not to have children."

I caught the anguish in her tone as she said this, which took me by surprise – of course, having believed myself to be her son, I could never have known my parents were unable to have offspring themselves.

"You gave me love and peace and strength," she continued now, with a quiet, powerful emotion to her voice. "You were meant to be there for me to find you. You were my boy from the snow."

My eyebrows rose at that statement – the princess had called me that, when she had met me in the stables when we were children. But my mother had a different meaning – I was also the boy from the snow because that was where this good woman had found me, barely alive.

"Why did you keep me?" I protested. "Surely you knew that I had come from different parents. I was not yours to keep, Mother."

"Perhaps not," my mother agreed, a little sadly. "Your father had told me that day about what had happened in Klumeck – how King Cedric's wife and his sister and her husband were dead, and that you and Sarah were missing. Our first thought when we found you was to take you into the warm. Sarah recovered reasonably quickly, but you had a fever for twenty days," she continued. "By the time you recovered, we had heard that King Cedric was marching for Gaeson, and we were to head for the caves."

"King Cedric marched upon Gaeson because he was searching for me and Sarah," I replied impatiently. "If you had given me up, you could have prevented war."

"I didn't know!" my mother replied, her eyes beginning to well with tears. "King Reghan had already been telling us the most despicable tales about King Cedric's corruption and how evil he was. The rumours in Gaeson were that King Cedric had gone mad and killed his wife, his child, his sister and her husband himself. I could not be sure of your safety, Daniel. When you had recovered, the trauma of what you had gone through meant you had no memory of your true parents. You believed my husband and I where your parents, and with the war that had just begun, I had no way of getting you back to Klumeck."

"These are just excuses," I concluded, standing up and walking away a little, trying to control my anger. "You didn't have to separate Sarah and me," I stated, still facing the wall. Why did my voice seem to sound so feeble?

"We did not want to, but there was no other choice," my mother answered tightly. "My husband had already overheard that you and Sarah were missing," she explained. "Any neighbours or friends would have well suspected that suddenly I had two children of the right descriptions living in our homes. Bridget and I decided to separate you and pretend that you were the children of relatives, who had died in the recent battles."

I shook my head slowly.

"There was another reason, as well as being afraid for your safety. A reason altogether more selfish," my mother said.

I turned back to her, waiting.

"We loved you."

"The idea that King Cedric killed his own kin is preposterous," I muttered, and turned back to face them all. "That was by King Reghan's hand."

"What?" the captain asked loudly, in shock of my declaration. "How can you say such a thing?"

"That was another of the truths King Urien confirmed when I was in his presence," I explained. "King Reghan wanted to rule both kingdoms, so he sent his spies to murder the parents who had borne me, along with King Cedric's wife and his unborn child. The cousin that I will never know," I declared. "I have become convinced that King Reghan has long been driven mad by his thirst for power and greed. I would not be surprised if he would overthrow King Urien himself, if given the chance."

"How dare you!" the captain shouted, stepping forwards with his hand on the hilt of his sword, but John and Aife held him back.

"My lord, this is the Prince of Klumeck you consider striking," John stated, and the captain turned to him, his eyes raised. "His mother has confirmed it."

Presently we heard the sound of a child crying; the captain's shouts had woken one of the girls up.

"So it is true, then," the captain said, the anger suddenly gone from his voice. "But how do we know that you are a true prince of Rheged? How do we know that you are not trying to help your uncle simply gain power? Why should we obey your uncle, rather than the king we've served our whole lives?"

I turned to the captain. "I pray you know me enough to know that I would not be so false," I returned quickly. "If I were in league with King Cedric against Rheged, I would not have returned to warn you all, at risk of my own life," I finished. "Why else would I come back?"

At this, John crossed the room to me. "I believe you, Daniel, my brother," he told me, clasping my arm tightly.

I smiled, despite the pain to my bruised, bloody face, relieved to know I was counted as a friend once more.

"As do I," Aife declared, crossing the room also and putting her hand on my shoulder. "It was difficult indeed to think of you as a foe, brother," she told me now. "My heart is glad indeed to see you vindicated."

"Thank you." I smiled again, despite further pain to my mouth. I turned to the captain. "Even if I am the prince of Klumeck, I am still loyal to these people. This is still my home." I gestured. "That is why I had to come back, to warn you of what is soon to take place."

"Daniel… what are you talking about?" asked my mother. I turned back to her worried face.

"Never mind," the captain interrupted swiftly. I had half a mind to object to him being rude to my mother, but instinctively I held my tongue – he still might not trust me and he still had the power to slay me where I stood.

"You really think they would not kill us on sight, if we gave ourselves up?" the captain said now. "You might be King Cedric's heir, but King Urien will not simply welcome us with open arms, will he? Not when we have fought against her for so long." So even the captain seemed now persuaded, at least in part.

"We must try," I answered. "We have talked too long," I said suddenly, going to leave the room. "We must do something." I thought for a moment. "We must go to the princess."

The captain snorted, his sarcasm back. "She will not believe us. We are four soldiers against her father, against the whole kingdom. We would all be killed just for having this conversation."

"She knows me," I returned. "She knows how I risked my life in the forest. How I would not sleep at night so she could slumber in safety. How I sent myself to the bottom of that cliff to save her life. She knows I would still die now to protect her." She knows I love her, I added silently to myself. "Besides, that night on the balcony, she was more than willing to speak against her father. She may be our greatest ally in this fight. It would be doing something, rather than simply calling this an impossible task," I finished.

The captain searched my gaze. "Alright, then." He nodded abruptly. "We must move quickly, to get to her chambers before you are seen."

I nodded, and John, Aife and the captain made to leave the room. I lingered, stooping to speak to the woman who had risked so much to raise me, to love me, and to call me her own.

"You are my mother," I told her quickly. "I may not have come from your womb, but you clothed me and fed me and sheltered me from harm. You have done nothing but care for and love me since the day you found me, at the expense of your own health. I will always consider you and Father the only parents I have ever really known."

She smiled as a few tears slid down her face.

"Do not tell Sarah yet; I have not told her."

She nodded and wiped the tears away. I placed a chaste kiss to her forehead before departing the room.

I met Sarah downstairs. I yearned once more to tell her the truth, but there was no time. Besides, the captain and John were already waiting by the door, and I wanted to tell her the truth about us in private.

"Take care, Sarah," I told her urgently, knowing there was little time for conversation. "Be ready to head for the caves, for the war is not over. In fact, I fear it has only just begun."

Worry creased her face at this last warning, but she did not comment on it. "Go well, Daniel. Whatever has transpired, know that you, John and Aife are in my prayers."

I smiled at this comforting speech, despite the pain it caused my mouth. I took her hand, and swiftly bent my head to kiss it before departing my house to go to the princess. I prayed she would listen this time – for she was all that stood between hope and doom.

Chapter Eight

Though it was the middle of the night and the streets were deserted, I still put my helmet on lest I was detected. The captain and John led the way, with Aife and me walking behind them. As we walked I glanced at the sky; from its colouring and the position of the moon, I saw it was well into the middle of the night. In a few hours it would be dawn and all our fates would be decided. We spoke little, walking for the most part in silence. Although it felt good to simply be a soldier again, my mind was reeling. For now the claim I was King Cedric's long-lost heir – once a fantasy so ludicrous it credited no logical thought – had been confirmed, not only by King Urien himself but also by my mother. The truth about my past had been revealed, and I felt as though it was tearing the fabric of my being and twisting my life into some new, harsher reality. I suppressed these painful thoughts and forced myself to focus on the task at hand, but this proved even more distracting to ponder than the first subject; I wondered how my lady fared and what thought, if any, she might be giving me. It caused me distress indeed to consider how she must think me a traitor and despise me.

Soon we were back at the castle, and the four of us travelled with swift uniformity to Princess Evelyn's chambers. Two guards were stood at attention outside as per usual; the soldiers guarding the princess the night of her attempted kidnapping must have been slain before they could raise the alarm.

Having reached her chambers, the captain now strode forwards with strong confidence and purpose to the guards. "You look tired," he stated simply. "Go and rest; I will have one of these soldiers replace you. They are not so weary. You are relieved," he ordered.

"Yes, sire," the soldier replied gratefully, heading back to the regimental chambers without question. I was once more thankful that my captain was an ally – of sorts, as he still looked like he would slay me if I put a foot wrong.

The captain stepped to the door, raised his fist and knocked four times. A few moments later and the door opened.

"Yes, what is it? It is the middle of the night..." The princess broke off as she saw the captain. Through my helmet, I saw the princess with her gown around her, her hair tousled by her side. I looked away before her eyes met mine, wanting to remain in disguise for a moment – but never had I seen her so beautiful. "What has happened?"

"I apologise for disturbing you at this late hour, Your Highness, but I must speak with you. I bid entrance into your chambers."

The princess raised her eyebrows in surprise.

"I know it appears suspect," the captain continued, "but this is a matter of great importance. I assure you that you will come to no harm. These will be with me," he concluded.

She paused for a moment and then nodded. I wondered if she would have been so willing if she knew I was behind the helmet.

We were in her chambers now, and I saw they were grand, as I had expected. John remained by the door while the captain and I moved forwards.

"You!" she exclaimed as I removed my helmet, her voice hard and cold and fraught with anger.

"Your Highness, I beg you to listen..."

She darted backwards as I stepped forwards, back to a corner of the room where there was a thick, scarlet curtain. Here she put her hand behind it and when her hand emerged again, it was holding a sheathed sword.

"I assure you, my lady, I mean you no harm," I said, holding up my hands in what I hoped was a gesture of peace. Her eyes only seemed to harden further.

She drew the sword a little, exposing part of the blade. "Get back to the dungeons before I sound the horn and the whole castle awakes."

"Please just listen to him, Your Highness," the captain said in response. "We are convinced..." He paused and looked at me, and I saw in his face he was not fully convinced. "We fear Daniel just may be speaking the truth in what he says."

"Against my father? What traitors you are!" she hissed. "Leave now, before I change my mind." She drew the sword fully now, dropping the sheath to the floor. "I have the skill to slay you all where you stand. Do you dare doubt it?"

"I would not dare doubt it," I answered without hesitation. I stepped forwards, my hands still raised towards her. Her face contorted in further anger as she brandished her sword in front of her. "Your Highness, you have not heard the truth. You have only heard what your father has told you."

She drew her sword now, pointing it at me. "You dare speak those words?" she challenged me coldly. "Give me one good reason why I should not slay you where you stand."

"Because you know me, Your Highness," I told her earnestly. This was my one chance to prove my character, to prove my loyalty to her. "You know I am the boy from the snow, who helped you climb through that window." Out of the corner of my eye, I saw John and the captain frown in confusion, but I ignored them. "I vowed to protect you that day, to fight by your side always, whatever the cost. That I am still doing, Your Highness. That I will always do, even now when all things seem changed."

"How deep your deception runs," she almost snarled with scorn. "Even if you were to be right about my father not being allied to Rheged, no one would believe that an enemy soldier would be granted an audience of King Cedric, let alone King Urien himself. You would either be dead, or rotting in prison. That is how I know this is a lie," she concluded.

"You would be right, my lady," I answered cautiously, "if I had been recognised by them as a simple soldier from an enemy land. But," I added quickly, before she could reply, "King Cedric discovered something when he pulled me up from that cliff, and the surgeon lifted up my tunic to attend to my wounds. It was discovered... that I am his long-lost heir."

"No..." she whispered, drawing back further in shock. "This is pure folly!" she exclaimed, gesturing her sword at me. "How could this be true?"

"King Cedric recognised a scar on my side that I received as an infant." My heart suddenly burst to tell her how her father had sent his spies to murder my parents, my aunt and my unborn cousin – but I suppressed the rage inside me, knowing it was not helpful. "This was then confirmed by King Urien himself. I had dreams of my parents which also confirmed the truth – I am the Prince of Klumeck."

With this, I took my sword and drew it fully out of my sheath, raising it high. Princess Evelyn raised her sword to me, and at the same I sensed the captain, John and Aife automatically take a step towards me.

"I have many reasons now to see you as my enemy, Your Highness." Again, the rage against her father boiled inside me. With a swift movement I sank onto bended knee, holding the sword outstretched to her balanced on my palms. The captain, John and Aife followed suit, sinking to their knees behind me. "But I still consider myself in allegiance to you above all others. I would not care if I became as powerful as King Urien himself. I would die before I turned against you. That is why I came back," I added gently, still on my knees before her. "I rode here, against the wishes of the whole of Rheged, in order to warn you.

"They are coming, Your Highness," I continued. I could see from her eyes she was battling whether to believe me; I prayed she would, for the fate of her people rested upon her shoulders – her words would save or doom us all. "They are coming with the dawn, and surrendering is the only way our people have hope to survive this next morn."

"Our people?" Princess Evelyn asked. Her voice was still sceptical but, to my encouragement, was far less cold.

"Our people," I affirmed. "I have not betrayed or abandoned Gaeson, for it is still my home. This is why I have returned. I do not want this land destroyed any more than you do. We could have peace. There is no need for further death. Please," I begged her.

"You would have me betray my own father, the king of our lands? The throne which I am meant to inherit?" she challenged me again. "How are those not words of a traitor, boy from the snow?" She sneered her last words, but I held her gaze.

"I would have you do your duty, my lady. I would have you save your people against a needless war. I would have you spare the lands of Gaeson. Look at your kingdom," I added, nodding to the window behind her. She cast a furtive glance, still pointing her sword at me. "One day, Your Highness, this would all be yours, as you have rightly said. But all of this you see before you may not last if you do not speak to the king. Or, if you consider it like this," I continued, "if I am telling you the truth and you do nothing, then King Urien will arrive and sweep through this kingdom without showing mercy. But if you speak to your father and find out I am telling a lie, then no great harm will be done and I will be executed as planned."

She seemed to ponder this, with her sword still raised. Her eyes flickered as she thought quickly. "Captain of the Guard," she addressed him formally, turning to him. The captain stepped forwards and once again bowed low. "I saw how you nearly put this man to the sword earlier this evening, for daring to speak against the king. Are you so easily convinced now?"

The captain did not speak for a moment. I waited, still on the floor and bowing to the princess.

"I am convinced, at least in part, my lady," he responded to my great relief. "We have just come from conversing with his mother, who has confirmed that she adopted him as an infant, and that she knew he was the long-lost heir of Rheged. It seems she kept this secret from Gaeson and our lord the king for fear of his safety, should the truth be known. It seems wise to me, Your Highness, to assume Daniel is telling the truth – if it is true, then he has risked death both from King Urien and from Gaeson by returning to warn us."

"Why would I lie?" I asked her quietly, and her brazen eyes switched back to regard my countenance. "You have just heard it confirmed I am the long-lost heir of Klumeck. What reason would I have to escape the uncle and throne I have just discovered, to warn you of a phantom attack? If I truly was your enemy, my motive would surely be to simply let this attack go ahead. Why else would I return, knowing my life would be forfeit the moment I put foot upon Gaeson's hill? Search your heart, my lady," I murmured. "You must see the only logical conclusion is that I am telling the truth. Please," I begged, our gazes still holding. "You are the only one who stands before Gaeson's downfall."

She seemed to consider my plea for an eternity. "Very well," she murmured at length. "I shall speak to my father. It seems unwise to ignore this warning out of hand," she concluded. Relief swelled so vast in me I feared I would burst. "But be warned, Prince of Klumeck, if this is who you are," she cautioned me. As she spoke, her eyes flashed like the blade of a dagger glinting in the noonday sun. "If I discover you are deceitful in this matter, I will carry out the sentence of execution myself."

"I understand, Your Highness," I responded, bowing low – and feeling grateful that honesty was on my side. "If I might bid you make haste, Your Highness," I added, as she placed her sword in its sheath again and fixed it around her belt. "We do not have much of the night left."

"A moment," she muttered, and here went to her large oaken table. She opened a drawer and, after a few seconds of rifling through, pulled out a wad of parchment. "Captain, I entrust you with this; I will not make mockery out of you by asking you not to read it. For now you must conceal this – if I should have need of it, I will make it known."

The captain bowed in assent, proceeding to hide the unknown documents within his armour.

"I bid you leave. I shall dress quickly and join you outside. Daniel, put your helmet back on," she instructed me, by which point I had stood and replaced my sword. "I would rather not have you executed before it is absolutely necessary." There was a wry smile upon her face; it was good to see my love smile at a time such as this.

We trooped outside to wait, my helmet securely back on. The captain now nodded at John and Aife, and the three of them sank to their knees, bowing to me.

"My brothers and sister," I began at once, "you do not need to…"

"Yes, we do," the captain replied, whilst John and Aife remained silent, their faces bent and gazes fixed on the floor. It was the way we greeted royals, I realised – the way the captain

170

and I had greeted Princess Evelyn the night she had spoken to us on the balcony. "Your Highness," the captain said now. "I am sorry I ever doubted you. My sword is yours. We hereby pledge our allegiance to you, as will all of Gaeson."

"Rise, my friends, please," I told them quickly, for it was strange and unsettling to see them bow before me. They came to stand and I smiled at them, putting my hands on their shoulders. "My heart is glad to know you are with me, to know I can be trusted in your sight once more."

We turned, then, as we heard Princess Evelyn come out of her chamber.

"Onwards, then, captain," Princess Evelyn ordered. "Take me to see my father. He is in his hall; he informed me he had been so vexed by Daniel's betrayal he knew he would not slumber. Lead the way," she commanded, and he walked first, with John alongside him. Behind him was the princess, and then Aife and I behind her.

I was thankful that now I was to go to the king with these allies on my side – although I knew the captain and the princess would slay me if I gave them reason for it. I prayed my lady would have the courage to stand against her father in order to protect her people. I hated how I had been forced to turn Princess Evelyn against her own father, but if I wanted to save Gaeson I knew I had no choice. I prayed I would control my anger in the sight of the king; it was the thought of my lady that tempered my rage, for I knew what it was to be without a father and did not wish an ounce of it on her.

As we walked silently through the castle, and I marched through the corridors with her in front, the back of her head was continually in my view. I could not help but observe how her roughly braided hair gently swayed upon her shoulders. Oddly, the image of her before I fell from the cliff came to mind. What did she think of my declaration now? I asked myself. Would she have given my confession any thought? For although I had been wrestling with my identity and how the world around me had changed, she had never been far from my mind.

Soon we had arrived outside the palace hall, and I snapped myself out of my selfish ponderings – now was not the time to think about love, when all of Gaeson was at stake. The captain and John moved apart slightly as they stopped so that Princess Evelyn could simply stop in between them. My lady paused here, but gave no more instructions. Eventually she steeled her breath, raised her hand and knocked on the large oaken door. She was admitted at once by servants on the inside, and as the door opened, I could already see the king.

"Ah, my daughter. I am pleased you have come to greet me in these troubled times," he greeted her warmly as we walked through the door. The rest of us stayed at the back, as was usual for the princess' escort upon entering the palace hall. Princess Evelyn strode forwards and, upon reaching him, briefly touched his hand and kissed his ring with daughterly affection.

"I must speak with you, my lord the king," she spoke now. He raised an eyebrow but did not seem perturbed – and he had no reason to be, I told myself. There was nothing out of place yet. "I wondered, Father, why has it been so long since you last spoke with His Majesty King Urien, King of Rheged?" she asked calmly.

His eyes grew hard, and Princess Evelyn stood back from him. He frowned. "I am in frequent contact with him, dear Evelyn," he replied, his tone warm enough but with an undertone that chilled me. I wondered if the others sensed it also. A smile that seemed too casual now broke across his face – he had evidently decided to see her question as innocent enough. "But you should not let such matters trouble your mind. Why do you ask?" His question had a sharp edge to it.

"I have recently conversed with the captain," the princess replied. I saw the king turn to stare at the back of the room; evidently he had noticed the captain walk in. "He has just interrogated the soldier named Daniel."

"Do not speak his name here!" His loud voice, strong with rage, echoed round the halls. "I will not have it!" He banged his fist loudly on the arm of his throne. He then stood abruptly; walked a few feet and stopped. I clutched my hilt, fearful of what might happen. "Do not be troubled by him, my dear," he added, his voice softening – and for a moment I saw what appeared to be true concern soften his features. "He is nothing but a vile traitor, a liar. He will be executed at dawn for his crimes. He will have been fed poison since he woke up in Klumeck. It would have been better if he had simply fallen from the cliff," he spat.

"But that is what is so strange, Father," Princess Evelyn replied quietly, and her father glanced back at her. "He claims to have awoken in Caer Ligualid. What is more," she continued, her voice shaking a little but remaining steady, "he claims that King Cedric is allied with King Urien and that you, Father, are the rogue kingdom."

"What nonsense!" he exclaimed, and then breathed deeply, attempting to calm himself. "Treacherous lies, my dear. Do not worry yourself so; these matters are not worth your vexation." His words carried irony with them, as my king could hardly be more vexed.

"But, my lord the king, Daniel claims to have heard this from King Urien himself," Princess Evelyn said now. "He claims all this time you have been leading a farce. He claims that it is we who are at war with Rheged herself."

The king turned to face her, enraged. "What do you say, my dear?" he asked. His voice was soft as silk, yet the sharpness of it struck fear in me. "Who would you believe – him, or me? Would you rather believe the man who raised you, or a traitor you barely know?"

"I do not mean to speak against you, Father," she replied quietly. "Nor do I mean to choose between you. You know how I love you and all of Gaeson. Yet…"

The king turned from where he had walked, and I saw a dangerous flash of something in his eyes.

"Yet I am troubled by this man, who gave his life for me but three weeks ago. I am most troubled by the question it brings to mind."

"Oh?" he said, his tone almost daring. There was indeed a dangerous, deadly quality to his voice. I clutched the hilt of my blade still tighter. I prayed he would not have it in him to harm his own daughter, but I could not be sure after discovering how he had murdered my parents in their beds. "What question would that be, my daughter?" He pronounced the last word louder than the rest of his speech, and it was all the more sinister.

"If what he speaks is deceit, then why would he come back? If indeed he is now our enemy, Father, then why would he return? The only reason I can think of," she added with caution, "is that Daniel speaks the truth, and that he is going against the might of Rheged herself to warn us."

"Warn us of what?" he asked now. Did I imagine it, or was that a tremor of fear in his voice?

Her voice grew stronger still as she looked at him. "That the whole might of Rheged is coming here."

There was a pause. Then the king gave a hollow, bitter laugh and came towards her so their faces were inches apart.

"So, you believe him, then," King Reghan declared softly. "You would choose this simple soldier over your father?" he breathed, his voice barely audible from the back of the hall – yet I sensed the danger in it. My lady must have done also, for she now made to step back. As she did so, he leapt out of his throne and took her hand sharply. She gave a cry of pain, and instinctively I stepped forwards and heard my armour clink.

The king looked up. "You may leave us," he commanded.

Four of the soldiers left the chamber immediately. The captain, John, Aife and I remained where we were, but as he had turned back to his daughter we had not been noticed.

"So, you would betray me, then," the king stated. "The folly that you would believe Daniel over your own father," he whispered, slightly louder with a tone of incredulity to it. "As if he would be granted an audience with the supreme King of Rheged himself. Well, daughter, you will betray me no more," King Reghan snarled, and with his one hand still tightly gripping her arm, he raised his other hand to strike her.

"No!" I shouted, stepping forwards and drawing my sword. "You will not harm her, Your Majesty," I told him, moving forwards still.

The king froze for a moment, his hand still on her arm, as if held captive by surprise. His other hand remained poised and suspended, halfway to her check. "You would defy your king?" he growled at me.

"For the sake of Gaeson, I would," I replied. With that, I removed my helmet.

"You!" he shouted, in a flurry of shock of rage. He let go of the princess and she stumbled back. "Seize him, captain!" the king shouted, but the captain did not heed the king's order. "Seize this traitor now!" he roared.

"No, Your Majesty. I will not." The captain moved forwards, as did John and Aife.

"There is something you have not considered, Your Majesty," I began evenly. "You have not considered why I was granted an audience with King Cedric and His Supreme Majesty, King Urien himself."

King Reghan said nothing but raised his eyebrows high, daring me to continue. I saw his scorn and had to once more fight to suppress the intense rage I felt.

"I am King Cedric's long-lost heir," I declared to him.

"What?" King Reghan shouted, and then laughed loudly in disbelief. "What a ridiculous notion," he concluded. "What a delusion this fool has led you to believe."

"It was His Majesty King Cedric who told me," I responded. "He recognised a scar on my side that identified me as his kin. I then began to have visions of my parents and King Cedric's wife. When King Urien came back from his business, he confirmed that it was the truth. For what reason could this be a deceit?" I asked him now, stepping forwards. "Besides, you know I speak the truth, Your Majesty – because it was on your orders that my parents were murdered in their beds."

"Father!" Princess Evelyn exclaimed in shock, who had by now moved several steps away from him. As he turned to her, her countenance grew even more aghast. "I beg you to tell me that this accusation is false, my lord the king," she said, and I noted the desperation in her plea.

"Of course it is a lie," King Reghan snapped instantly. "This boy has no evidence to back up his claims other than his word. What stories he has led you to believe," he sneered.

"But he does have evidence, my lord the king." The captain spoke quietly, and King Reghan jerked his head to look at him. "That is why we believe him," the captain concluded.

"Oh?" King Reghan replied, his voice back to that low, soft whisper that somehow sounded far more dangerous than his outburst of rage. "What false evidence is that, captain, that you would defy me so easily? Nearly twenty-five years you have served me faithfully – you would now give that all up on one soldier with delusions of grandeur?"

The captain shifted slightly, and for a moment I wondered whether he would change his loyalties. "We have spoken with his mother, Your Majesty," he said, speaking louder. Even in the dangerous, desperate circumstances, his steady voice did not tremble once in his speech to the outraged king. "She told us that she knew he was the long-lost prince to Klumeck when she adopted him. She kept this silent, fearing his life and hers would be in danger if she revealed the truth."

"You murdered my parents." The declaration burst passionately out of my mouth – I could no longer suppress my anger. "While they were sleeping, you sent your spies to murder them in their beds. You murdered King Cedric's wife, too – while she was pregnant with their child. How could you?" My voice rose as I finished my speech hotly.

Princess Evelyn stepped back further. "I cannot believe what I am hearing, Father. Long have I suspected your greed and gain," she admitted now, and his enraged eyes turned towards her. "But I reasoned that was simply the ambition of power of being a king. I never would have believed you were capable of such atrocities."

The King glanced between his daughter and the rest of us and seemed to come to a resolution – abruptly he drew his sword, preparing to fight us.

"Put down your blade, Father. Father!" the princess implored him now. "It is over. You have lost. Give up now, before Gaeson is lost. I, your daughter, ask this."

"No!" King Reghan growled, like a wild animal. He lashed out, pushing the princess from him and onto the floor. I drew my sword and ran forwards, and she fell. His wild eyes locked onto mine and I saw the rage in them, the same hysterical anger currently rupturing through my own soul. He charged, his sword raised high.

For a fleeting moment I pondered the absurdity of it all – not long ago I would have gladly given my life for this man, and now here I was, fighting my own king. Then I had raised my own sword to parry him. He thrust his sword out again and I met it a second time, the metal of our blades clashing against each other. He started to circle me, and I followed him as he moved around. The captain, Aife and John had made their way forwards.

Suddenly, he roared and charged again, and as I darted out of the way, the captain and John leapt at him and he fell, tumbling to the ground. Aife kicked his fallen sword out of the way and pointed it at his neck; an instant later, John and the captain were there by his side also. I made my way over slightly and pointed my sword at the king's neck – a similar position to where the captain had rested his sword against my own flesh earlier this night. I had a sudden, intense urge to kill this man who had mercilessly murdered my kin and stolen my identity from me.

"Daniel?" It was my lady's voice, soft and sweet as always, sounding a little uncertain. I raised my head to look at her. One gaze upon her beautiful face and I lowered my sword. I had sworn, that day in the snow, to fight for her and keep her from harm as best I could. I knew then that the life I had been able to glimpse had truly gone; that nothing I did now could bring back the family I had known. It would only bring the one I loved pain – and she already felt enough distress, having discovered the truth about her father.

Princess Evelyn walked over to join us. "Thank you," she said to me quietly. "Captain, the papers," she ordered, her voice steadier.

The captain retrieved them out of his armour and handed them to her. I saw the shock in King Reghan's countenance as he recognised them, saw the blood drain from his face as he realised what it meant.

"I have some papers for you to sign, father," she told him. "I have kept these in my chambers the last few months, having observed you succumb to power and corruption. I believed you might repent at the last hour, that you might once again rule this land with justice... but I see now I was fooling myself," she finished scornfully.

"You cannot do this to me, daughter. I am your father and your king!" he shouted, beginning to writhe like an animal caught in a chamber. All were silent during his protest – he moaned and groaned as if fatally wounded, but we had not harmed him. It was simply due to his own anger and humiliation at his defeat.

Princess Evelyn was going through the papers undeterred, signing her name on the relevant pages. Finally she looked up, her face strong like steel. "Sign them, Father. Or my men will be forced to strike you and remove you from your throne with pain of death."

The king stopped moving and forced his gaze upon his daughter, his expression unbelieving.

"You think I would not do it, father?" she questioned him. "Death is the deserved sentence for your treachery. You led us all to believe we were allied with Rheged, when really you have been waging your secret battles against His Majesty King Urien. What is more, you have behaved despicably to King Cedric's heir. Had it not been for his kindness to me, Daniel may have struggled to not have had your head here and now," she declared, "which he could surely not be blamed for.

"I made a vow to protect and defend my people, to serve them loyally and consider their fate before my own. That was the promise you made too, my king, before corruption turned your heart and you became obsessed with power and greed. I will do what I must to restore this kingdom," she concluded in a louder voice, "even if it be your head. Sign them, Father, or force my hand in your refusal. Do you dare challenge me?" she added brazenly.

There were a few tense seconds while we waited. King Reghan and his daughter's gazes remained locked, and I saw it would be whose resolve would break first. Eventually – and without another word spoken – he bowed his head and took the quill she offered him. He signed his name on the pages of his document, signing away his kingship and rule. The princess – nay, the queen – took the document from him and handed it back to the captain before taking the crown from her father's head.

"It is done," she sighed. "I do this with a heavy heart, father. I do it to save Gaeson. I pray one day we can forgive one another from all our wrongs. Though I fear that day may not be for some time," she added, her features flashing with hurt and rage. But still, she reached out her hand and touched his matted, brown hair. Her father did not open his mouth, did not raise his head to look at her. He clearly thought this was the deepest form of betrayal, and in some sense he was right... but she had been forced to do this.

She stepped back from us and Aife, and I sank onto bended knee. John and the captain instead bowed low, their hands still restraining the former king.

"Long live the queen," the four of us uttered, our faces pointed towards her feet. Her father remained silent.

"Very well," she murmured. "Gaeson needs to know what has happened here," she declared at length. "John, sound the horn that summons them."

"Yes, Your Majesty," John replied. He immediately went to the corner of the room where a large horn was placed. He took the horn and went to the balcony to the west entrance of the hall, perpendicular to the throne. Certain members of Gaeson were charged with having the horn near them at night, at strategic positions so they could sound the horn to each other.

As the first rich notes entered our ears, I knew the whole castle would be awake soon. Some soldiers were also charged with riding through the town, checking that everyone had heard and was moved into courtyard. Except in cases of severe illness, or if there was a recent bereavement, everyone was forced to attend. My mother and Rachel could stay at home, but Sarah and the children would be present. Sarah... I still needed to tell her we were related.

This horn, however, was not to be confused with the one that spoke of war coming. When that horn sounded, all the soldiers would assemble in front of the castle, and all citizens would be required to go to the caves. If the horn then rang three times in a row, all those able to fight would go at once to the armoury and then to assist our forces in battle. No, the horn John was blowing sounded of mystery and suspense… and because of the late hour, Gaeson was bound to be anxious also.

"John and Aife," the queen ordered, as John finished this task. We turned and bowed again. "I bid you take my father to his chambers. Remain stationed there until someone relieves you. You are relieved from attending," she added. "Do not harm him in any way unless he attacks you."

"Yes, Your Majesty," John replied, and took the king's arm whilst Aife took the other. I fought not to show surprise – a minute ago such contact would have been inappropriate. But now, I reminded myself, the king was not the king any more. I knew not what to call him, but was distracted by the townspeople outside – the crowds were already beginning to gather.

"I will ensure no citizen of Gaeson brings you harm, Father," she told him. "But as for when the army of Rheged gets here… you will have to answer for the needless slaughter at your hand."

The former king flinched, drawing back with fear, but John and Aife still held him securely. I half expected him to fight back, but he allowed himself to be taken away without resisting. I watched my former king take his leave, his shoulders dropping and his head bent – it seemed as though the very life had gone out of him. Try as I might, however, I remained without any sympathy for him.

"Captain, Daniel." The queen spoke again, and we turned back to her. "I wish for you both to be present with me on the balcony. Captain, I will need you for your position in the army. Even if they are not sure of the monarchy, they will follow your command."

The captain bowed in assent.

"Daniel," she added, glancing at me now, "I must clear your name. My people need to know you are no traitor. I will also reveal to them that you are the Prince of Klumeck," she continued. "We will need you as an ally, Daniel. A mediator between ourselves and the might of Rheged." She looked between us. "Will you do this?"

"I will, Your Majesty," I replied at once, bowing to her once more. I straightened again. The clamouring of the crowd was growing louder, and I tensed as we walked to the corner of the hall to the balcony, where the royals made announcements and speeches. The queen had been a loyal princess here, standing by her father's side – an obedient heir to the throne. Now she would walk out there as queen. I tensed further as I imagined Gaeson's reaction when she would tell them all that had transpired here this night. She was telling her people the king had abdicated and was now imprisoned within his chambers. What would the people do when they discovered Klumeck was no longer their enemy, when their brothers and sons would have died in war with them? Would there be public outrage? The last thing we needed was a riot.

We had paused for a moment outside the balcony. The captain glanced at me, his face impassive. Queen Evelyn took a deep breath, and then drew back the large scarlet curtain and stepped out to face her people. It was still the night, but people had brought their oil lamps, and the captain and I now lit the large torches that had always been positioned here so that even in the darkest hour, one would always be able to see.

I could hear the crowd's anxious murmurings already. Where was the king? They must be wondering. Why are there soldiers next to the princess? Why is that traitor there? Was he not to be executed at dawn? I kept my face impassive and came to stand at attention. I was glad of my soldier's training now, or else my emotion would surely be visible for all to see. I did not want to imagine the confused expressions of Sarah, of Rachel and her children. I hid a frown, then – if I was to be recognised as a royal, surely Sarah should be standing here, ready to be declared as the other long-lost heir? But then, I had not found the time to tell my lady about Sarah, and Sarah herself did not know the truth yet.

"People of Gaeson," the queen addressed them. Her words pulled me from my wondering thoughts as the people went quiet. I was convinced at that point that you could have heard a stick snap, or a small cough throughout the whole kingdom. "Thank you for coming at this late hour," she began. "I know your little ones will be tired, and that this may affect your daily lives tomorrow. But I must speak with you, to tell you of what has happened this night." She paused here, and I could see the confusion on the people's faces.

"His Majesty, King Reghan has abdicated," she declared, and held out the papers. The silence was broken at once. People shouted out, out of pure shock. Fear and worry were on the faces of many, anger on the faces of some.

"My people!" she called, and at once people were reduced to silence again. "I am sorry to bring you such grave news, but I have taken over from my father to become your new queen. I did not do this lightly, my people, but with a broken heart." I felt the anger of the crowd lessen some as we all listened to the anguish and deep sadness in her tone. "You may find this news unwelcome, but this is the truth. What I am about to tell you," she continued, each syllable slow and clear, "comes from King Urien himself, the supreme Ruler of Rheged." Every ear was attentive to her majesty.

"My father King Reghan has been at war with Rheged herself," she announced. Noise broke out once more, but she waved them into silence with a simple gesture of her hand. I was full of admiration to see her power, but also filled with remorse for the dark circumstances that had forced her to take it. "We have long been told that Klumeck was an evil kingdom," she continued loudly, "with King Cedric as the tyrant who has been at war with Rheged herself. But I tell you tonight that Klumeck is indeed allied with Rheged, and that it is us ourselves who have been at war with the rest of our kingdom." You could see on the faces of many the question of where this information had been attained, and I knew I would have to step forwards.

"Daniel," she said, her voice low enough for only the captain and I to hear, her hand gesturing forwards. I came forwards to stand near the balcony rail, but was careful not to touch it. Here I surveyed all of the people of Gaeson – never before had I witnessed the view from this angle.

"You have been told that this man, the soldier Daniel son of Kellen, is a traitor to the throne, and has been sentenced to execution in the morning," the queen continued. "I now proclaim that the crime of treason he allegedly has committed is false. I tell you that Daniel, son of Kellen, is henceforth pardoned.

"The tradition of Gaeson," continued our queen, "has long said that only those with royal blood can touch the rail of the balcony. Daniel, touch the rail," she ordered.

I took another step forwards, feeling numb all of a sudden. I slowly extended my hand and felt it clasp the cold metal. It was surprisingly ordinary. More gasps were heard, along with a few outbursts of anger from those who were more daring, masked by anonymity of the crowd.

"My people!" she shouted again, and once more the people fell silent. "Most of you will have seen Daniel. He is one of our own – a loyal soldier who grew up in Gaeson with his father a soldier before him. Yet I tell you he is more than able to clutch the rail. Two weeks ago, this soldier nearly died saving my life. He did not die, however, but remained in a coma in Caer Ligualid itself. Two days ago, he woke and was met by King Cedric, who informed him of the truth. The truth that Daniel is the long-lost Prince of Klumeck," she proclaimed. The crowd's collective countenance turned to shock. "While in Caer Ligualid, Daniel also discovered that my father had been waging war against Rheged. He then heard all of this confirmed by his supreme majesty King Urien himself." More gasps arose from the crowd.

"Daniel, son of Kellen, is really Daniel son of Adair, and prince and heir to Klumeck," Queen Evelyn repeated. "As such, he is hereby entitled to touch the rail. Yet I tell you he is not our enemy. He is our ally, and I pray he will help restore peace between Klumeck and Gaeson once more. He returned, despite his new identity and the great risk to his own life, in order to warn us.

"King Urien and King Cedric's forces are marching towards us as we speak," she announced, and the people's surprise and confusion quickly turned to fear. "They will be here at dawn," she added, "but my prayer is that when King Urien, his eldest son Prince Owain, and King Cedric get here, there will be no need for war. If we surrender fully to them and assure them of our loyalty – loyalty to Rheged which we always thought we had – then we might yet have peace.

"Head to the caves nonetheless," she said now, her first royal order for her people. "I advise you go there immediately… they may yet arrive in the night, and it is nearing dawn. I apologise for the late hour; I realise this will be difficult for your little ones. Do not go back to your homes to collect your belongings. I am praying this town will remain safe. Soldiers, escort the people of Gaeson. That is all."

She gestured to the captain. It was the tradition of Gaeson for when the king or queen had finished speaking, they would simply look at the military representative standing near as an end of the speech.

"All hail to Evelyn, Queen of Gaeson!" the captain bellowed. I dropped to my knees also, to show my allegiance. All of Gaeson were bowed before her. The official coronation would take place later, but this was the sign of Gaeson accepting her as queen – her sovereign right given by God to rule over us.

I was immensely relieved the people had been so accepting; there had been a few cries of anger, but it could easily have been worse. We all stood once more and I thought that would be it, but the queen glanced at the captain once more and gestured to me. I tried to shake my head subtly, but I was either unnoticed or ignored.

"All hail to Daniel, Prince of Klumeck!" the captain shouted again. They all bowed in one motion – even the queen gave a small curtsey, which was acceptable to do for other royals. I stared at them all, knowing I would never have asked for this honour and unsure of what to do with it. It was too much… and the queen knew it. As soon as we came back from the balcony and she had dismissed the others, she spoke. I felt her dubious gaze upon me as we stepped away from the balcony and back into the palace hall.

"With your approval, I will instruct the soldiers to escort the people to the caves, Your Majesty," the captain said, breaking our eye contact. She nodded quickly, and he bowed swiftly before hurrying out of the palace hall and down the grand, stone steps.

Queen Evelyn's gaze roved back to mine. "You will have to develop your public appearances, Prince of Klumeck," she addressed me, a little sardonically. "I know you discovered your royal identity two days ago, whereas my whole life has been in preparation of the throne. However," she added, "you are now a royal of Rheged, as I am. The people will have detected your discomfort. They will want their future king to be powerful, strong. Bold and confident," she added.

I felt myself despairing at her speech, knowing there was a key detail in it she had forgotten. "But I am not their King, your majesty," I pointed out. "I am a prince of Rheged, but the throne I will inherit is Klumeck, not Gaeson. I never wanted this," I told her. Since I was now a prince, I reasoned I could be a little blunter with her. "I was always content to remain in the shadows. All I longed for was to be a soldier in Gaeson, defending our people. My greatest aim was to live a long enough life to settle down and know I had helped to keep her in peace and security."

"Noble aims," the queen agreed. "But that is not what our Lord has ordained. In time, you will adjust to your new life."

I bowed my head in assent.

"Daniel..." she began, and the almost fragile way she spoke my name cut right to my core. She was silent for another moment, and I heard the crowd's clamour as it moved to the caves, heard the captain still shouting orders to the soldiers. "I never thanked you for coming back," she continued quietly, "at such a great risk to yourself. You underwent torture, faced execution..." She was almost whispering. She crossed the room further to me and, suddenly, she raised her hand and it touched my torn, bruised face briefly. I had to keep further surprise from my features.

Her arm dropped back just as briefly, to now hang motionless by her side. A silence ensued, but I waited for her to speak. "You would face all this just for your people," she said, "Prince of Klumeck?"

"I would, and more besides, my lady," I told her firmly, my reply immediate. I paused now and swallowed. "I am sorry you have had reason to doubt me," I continued. "I am sorry I have had to betray your father and my king. I would do anything to fight for this land, Your Majesty, even to go against the man I have just learned is my uncle in order to warn you."

"I know." Her eyes flickered a little as we stared at one another, the meaning behind her countenance unreadable. "Thank you, also, for not killing my father," she continued in that same, quiet tone. "You would well have been within your rights – you showed him great mercy. I am so sorry," she told me poignantly, "for what he did to you."

"It is not for you to feel any blame, my lady," I murmured back to her. "Those actions were your father's doing, not yours."

She smiled here. "I know you spared him to not cause me any pain. You are still my boy from the snow," she declared quietly, and I smiled widely at her, despite the pain it caused me.

"Always, Your Majesty," I answered her quietly, "no matter who my uncle is."

A smile played at her lips further, and there was something in her eyes I could not put a name to. Neither of us moved away, and I felt my heartbeat quicken, feeling as strangely exposed as the time I had declared my feelings for her – the time I had cut the rope came to mind. I was aware of my mouth growing dry, palms becoming sweaty. I had been content to love and fight for this woman at a distance, but now I realised, since I was a prince, a union between us would not be impossible. Would it be possible? I opened my mouth and closed it again, searching for how to utter a little of what was in my heart.

The captain strode in then from the palace hall, and both of us instinctively took a step back and averted our gaze from one another. I felt an awkward tension, which the captain either did not notice or ignored as he came over to us.

"Captain," she said as he came near, her voice ready to give commands. "The soldiers are to line up in their ranks outside of the castle. I imagine they will come at first light of dawn. We will be ready to kneel to greet them as they come. Arm them, however," she added, "in case fighting does break out. We have been led astray by my father, but I will not let Gaeson be harmed when we have extended peace. We are not the only ones to have suffered losses."

My thoughts turned to Joshua as she spoke. It was true – there had been unwanted deaths on both sides. Gaeson had been in the depths of grief in war also; she had not been left untouched.

"That is all, for now," she added.

"Yes, Your Majesty," the captain replied, and promptly left.

"Daniel, I wish for you to be outside the castle with me, ready to greet King Urien and King Cedric," my queen told me. "I bid you go and aid the captain to ready the men."

This was a simple enough order, but as her eyes held mine again, I knew what she was asking of me. She knew she was asking me to be with Gaeson – to fight them potentially. She was asking me to stand with her, rather than with my uncle and the life and identity I had just found.

"Of course, Your Majesty," I replied, my mouth forming the words mechanically all of a sudden. I turned and left the hall alongside the captain, barely remembering the words Princess Evelyn had said to me, and how my heart had raced before the captain had re-entered the palace hall. Now was not the time to dwell upon my conflicting emotions; now was the time we all prayed there would be no war. For if there was, my loyalties would be torn in two. Not only would King Cedric be there, but also members of the kingdom I was now meant to inherit. Was I really meant to wield my blade against them, to fight the people I now belonged to as well as Gaeson? Could I bring myself to fight those I would one day rule?

Wrought with uncertainty, I did not go to the regimental towers where the captain would be, but instead left the castle, coming to stop in the town square. The people had dispersed, readying to leave their homes. I thought once more about my queen's order. She was asking me to stand by my men, to stand by her at the risk of fighting the people I would eventually lead. I might even have to stand against my uncle. What was I to do?

"Your Highness," the captain said; he had been waiting for me in the courtyard. As he spoke, he sank to bended knee in a bow.

"Please, my friend," I replied at once in surprise – he had already bowed to me earlier alongside John and Aife – and even that I had deemed unnecessary. "You do not need to…"

"But I do, my lord prince," the captain cut across me. "That is, my lord, I would bid you let me speak, if it pleases you," he added hastily.

I nodded at him.

"Sire, I wish to apologise for my rough treatment of you, for I can see where my blade cut you," he added, nodding to the point on my neck his blade had kissed. "I am sorry, Your Highness," he affirmed, "I am sorry I ever doubted you. You are a good man, and as fine a swordsman as your father, Kellen, ever was."

My eyes widened in surprise. "I did not know you knew my father so well," I murmured, and then crossed the few yards to him, placing my hand on his shoulder. "Rise, captain of the guard," I ordered, and he came to stand before me, his head still inclined in a bow. "You have committed no wrong, captain," I assured him. "You have only shown duty and honour to the man we both served as king, which only does you credit. I would have expected no less. Besides," I murmured, "you should have seen how I resisted the truth, while I recovered in Caer Ligualid."

I noticed a smirk cross his face here. "I thank you for your kindness, Your Highness," he said now. "Yes, I knew your father well; we served many years together through many battles. He was an excellent fighter and a good friend. I can remember the day, twenty-one years ago, when he said he was taking in his cousin's son from another village."

My head shot up at this. "You knew I was adopted? You never mentioned it, in all the years I served you," I added, feeling a slight resentment that he had known all this time.

"Forgive me, my lord," the captain answered, inclining his head quickly. "I had no reason to think you were one of Klumeck's heirs. He told me you were the child of his cousin, who had died in the recent battle – I had no reason not to believe him. When I saw he meant to raise you as his son, I knew it was not my place to tell you the truth, as often adoptive parents do not tell their children of their true heritage. I meant you no wrong, sire."

I pondered this as I stared out at the greying sky above the courtyard. "It was not you who did me wrong, Captain. It was King Reghan who tore me from my original family, not you." Then I smiled wanly. "It does seem strange to talk of King Reghan so freely, when, but an hour ago, one could have been killed for uttering such treason. Such is the way of things," I concluded. Then I glanced at him. "Is that why you believed my account so suddenly? I wondered what had convinced you."

"Yes, sire," the captain answered. "When you said how you had been kidnapped at the age of three, I remembered that was the age of the boy Kellen had adopted."

I nodded, and we both fell quiet again. I looked up and saw the sky was growing paler; the sun would soon rise.

"Can I ask you something, my lord?"

I glanced at him.

"What are you going to do? Would you really fight Klumeck?"

I sighed here, for his question articulated my heart well. "I do not know," I answered at length. "It is one thing to betray my uncle and King Urien by returning here to warn you; it is quite another to face him in battle. Can I stand against the man I now know is my kin?" I wondered aloud, articulating the conflict my heart felt. Could I oppose those who I would one day rule? Each person I would kill would be one of my potential subjects. "How could I be king over them, if I was to meet them in battle at the dawn?" I ventured.

"It is difficult indeed, my lord," the captain murmured, when I had not spoken again for a few moments.

Oh, never before had my duty and my heart been so at war within me! I was looking around the courtyard; the pillars of stone, the fountain in the middle. As I did, my heart affirmed once again that this was my home; these were my people. The thought of not fighting, the thought of looking on whilst Gaeson was attacked, was unbearable. All the ones I had fought alongside or wished to protect – Sarah, John, Aife, the captain, Rachel and her children – how could I not be beside them? As well as those I cared for deeply, I thought once again of my queen and what I had said to her in her chambers – that I would die rather than stand against her. I would fight for the one I loved

189

most; even at the cost of fighting the might of Rheged herself and standing against my uncle. I thought back to that day in the snow when, as a nine-year-old, I had vowed I would serve and obey the girl that captured my heart all those years ago. When I made that vow in the snow, after she had said goodbye to me and gone into the library, I had not known that I was really her distant cousin and that her father had murdered my parents – but still I knew even that would not release me from the oath I had made to protect her.

"I have lived here all my life," I told the captain, turning back to him with my decision made. "These people are my people; the queen is my queen. I will not allow harm to come to her. Let us ready the people for tomorrow," I ordered.

The captain smiled and inclined his head in assent; together, we walked back the way I had come out alone. I did not know if my chosen course of action was right or wrong. But I knew it was what I would do, as surely as I knew the next morn would rise. I would still protect these lands and my queen. I would not sit by and watch the worst happen. As she herself had said a few minutes ago, I was still her boy from the snow, and as I had affirmed to her, my loyalty would always be to protect her, no matter who my uncle was. With that, we headed for the regimental chambers to prepare for the dawn, when Rheged's might would come, and all our fates would be revealed.

Part Three

Chapter Nine

It was a chilly dawn and my eyes ached with tiredness. I stretched my still sore face, moved my mouth muscles. I wondered, not for the first time, how good I would be in a fight, for I was weak from my recent torture. I was also starving. I had managed to grab a cup of water and a couple of slices of bread whilst preparing the army, but that was the first food to pass my lips since I returned to Gaeson yesterday. That was without mentioning my fall from the cliff just over fortnight ago, and spending twelve of those days unconscious. Now I thought about it, it was a bit of a wonder how I was still able to sit straight upon my horse. But my thoughts never let me ponder my stomach for long – I was back to wondering what would happen once King Urien and King Cedric arrived. I was praying continually that all would be forgiven and peace would be restored, even if that scenario was rather unlikely. It was more likely they would react with rage and I would be seen as a traitor in their eyes, just as I had been seen as a traitor in Gaeson until the queen had pardoned me last night.

As if my thoughts had summoned them, suddenly I saw King Urien's army begin to emerge at the bottom of the hill. With him was his son, Prince Owain and also King Cedric, the man who I now knew was my uncle. I had never before seen Prince Owain; whilst I watched them approach, I took a moment to survey him. I saw King Urien's son was tall, well-built with broad shoulders. Minutes passed with great speed as the army continued to near us. I prayed once again that they would see our actions as a formal surrender to Rheged. As such, we had assembled outside the castle as per our lady's instructions, ready to bow before them.

By now, the army had stopped and King Urien, King Cedric and Prince Owain had broken out in front, almost the whole way up the hill now. I prayed that for once, peace might come from one of these negotiations. Whilst the captain stood in the front of the army, the queen and I broke into a gallop, riding a little way down the fields to meet them. It did not take much time, for King Urien, Prince Owain and King Cedric were still swiftly galloping. They slowed as they neared, and a few moments before they ceased, I looked back at our men and raised my hand. On my signal, the captain and the army sank to their knees in a bow. The queen and I dismounted.

"Hail, King Urien; hail, King Cedric; hail, Prince Owain," the queen greeted them as we bowed to the floor. It was more traditional for the queen to curtsey, but it was a more visible demonstration of her submission to the supreme King of Rheged.

"Greetings, Princess Evelyn," His Majesty King Urien greeted her, still atop his horse. "Prince Bryce – what a surprise to find you here," he stated sarcastically.

I heard the sharp note in his voice and looked up as he addressed me to see the anger in his eyes. Prince Owain's face looked just as angry. My uncle's face was hard and grim, with a hint of disappointment in his features. I felt remorse to have gone against my new found blood relative so quickly, but not regret.

"Tell me, where is your father? Will the coward not even come out to fight?" King Urien added in outrage, making a show of looking around.

"King Reghan has abdicated, Your Majesty." The queen looked up from her bow. I saw the surprise take their features. "I am now Queen of Gaeson," she continued. "We wholly surrender our army and lands to you. We beg a peaceful alliance with you, as we had always thought we had. Let us be brethren in arms; there is no need to fight this day."

"Oh?" King Urien challenged her, and my heart sank at his tone, still rife with sarcasm. "What about the people your father has slaughtered? What about the bereaved families of Klumeck, whose soldiers have been needlessly slaughtered by King Reghan? Should they not have a chance at vengeance?"

Queen Evelyn raised her head further still. "They are not the only families who have been bereaved, Your Majesty. It is my father who is to blame, but my men have not done wrong in defending our people. I beg for us not to fight this morning," she pleaded in earnest now. "There would be no glorious victory for families of the fallen, Your Majesty, on either side. No satisfaction of justice. There would simply be senseless killing, when we could be embracing as brothers and sisters, a united people once more. There would just be an increase in mourning and weeping, with grieving throughout your lands and mine."

"An inspiring speech." His tone still carried a hint of sarcasm, but much less than before.

I saw my queen's eyes harden slightly. "Has not enough blood been spilled on my father's account?" she asked now, a little more brazenly. "Do you think your men would want to fight us, knowing we have surrendered and wish to be kin to you?"

King Urien regarded her. I held my breath, tense. The men of Rheged would follow him, even to a senseless battle.

"We have surrendered, my lord the king," she said now. "Would you force your army into battle against people who have said they will be yours?"

King Urien stayed silent a moment longer and then nodded. "You are a woman of wisdom, Queen Evelyn of Gaeson. Already far wiser than your father. I agree with you that there is no sense in fighting. Enough blood has been spilled."

I let out the breath I had forgotten I was holding.

"Speaking of that traitor," he added, and his eyes flashed in rage, "where is he? At least justice can be done with him."

If my queen was upset at his speech, she did not show it. "He is imprisoned in his chambers," she replied grimly. "We will of course take you to him, Your Majesty. Your Majesty," she added, her eyes rising up to his. "I know my father has done many things, evil and despicable. I know he has betrayed not only his people, but also Your Majesty and the very might of Rheged herself. I know the kind of punishment that must be due him. But I beg you to have mercy," she added simply, "for he is my father."

King Urien regarded her again before nodding. "An inspiring speech," he repeated, but this time there was no sarcasm in his tone. "But I fear even such a noble plea cannot be granted. We have had a long night's journey," he added, changing the subject abruptly. "I ask for food and rest for my men."

"Of course, Your Majesty," the queen answered at once.

We both finally straightened, and I averted my gaze from King Cedric's hard gaze. Instead, I swung back onto Epos, following Queen Evelyn's suit as we rode back to the men and women standing under her command. I stole a glance at my queen as we rode. Her eyes were hard and determined as we reached the soldiers. I myself was almost dizzy, but with relief rather than my weakened state that my homelands would be spared. Even if King Urien still sentenced me to death for what I had done, I would accept the consequences gladly knowing Gaeson was spared, and no harm would come this day to those my heart loved most.

"There is to be no fighting this day," she declared. "I daresay we can hope for peace between our peoples."

The men and women cheered, and despite the unpleasant end my actions would surely bring me, I could not help but smile. My queen was a wonderful orator, giving each man and woman warmth and hope at the prospect of peace. I glanced back at all the men of Klumeck and the legion of King Urien's soldiers. There were many of them, larger than our own forces. Where were they to get rest?

"You are to go to the regimental chambers and clear them out of all belongings." I turned back to the queen as she began to order our people. "As many soldiers as possible from King Urien and King Cedric will remain there. Go," she ordered.

That was a good start, for the soldiers of Gaeson could simply go to their homes and stay with their families. But I calculated that there was three quarters of the army still to accommodate. I found I had to squash down feelings of indignation that we must open our walls to these men and women who had been ready to slay us – but we were at peace now, and after all that had been done in the name of Gaeson, this hospitality was the least we could do.

Two hours later and all were settled. The soldiers from Klumeck and Caer Ligualid were either resting in the soldiers' quarters or in the great dining hall, among the tables and chairs.

Mattresses had been brought in from other areas of the castle, like in the servants' halls or infirmary beds which were not used. The soldiers were fed with meals hastily prepared. The people had now also returned from the caves. As I walked through Gaeson, I well perceived the tense atmosphere; it was difficult for the people to have to house the men who had journeyed so far to war with them, whom we had been fighting with for so long.

I finished my current task of making one of the last beds in the regimental chambers and straightened, stiff and sore from the labour in my weakened state. The more minutes that passed, the more I was sure I would have been completely useless in the battle, had there been a need to fight. I left the last chamber and descended the spiral steps, only to come face to face with my uncle as I entered the large hall below.

"Your Majesty," I greeted him quickly, bowing low to him.

He did not say anything for a moment, merely surveyed me. I stayed silent, waiting for him to speak. Eventually King Cedric sighed a tired sigh and placed his hands on my shoulders.

"It is good to see you alive, my boy," he stated. His eyes had never looked wearier or heavier, betraying his years. "I feared you must be dead, that I had lost you all over again. Or perhaps worse," he added quietly, and a little anger entered his countenance now, "that you had decided to stand against me."

I swallowed, feeling shame and remorse that this was exactly what I had decided to do.

"I'm sorry, Uncle. Leaving you in Caer Ligualid... it was the most difficult decision I had ever faced," I emphasised. "But I had to try... I could not just let my people die. I grew up among them, have lived these last nine years a soldier, vowing to fight for my people and swearing an oath to protect them. I could not let them wage a war they did not understand, especially when I knew Queen Evelyn was not corrupted like her father. I simply prayed that there would be a peaceful resolution. I could not have watched them being slaughtered any more than you could turn on Klumeck," I told him, anxious for my uncle to understand. "It is for the best what I did," I stressed by nodding, "for now the whole of Rheged is united, when we would have had conflict and bloodshed."

King Cedric surveyed me. "That is all very well," he conceded. "It is fortunate that King Urien may have seen this point also. It looks likely he will spare your life."

My eyes widened in relief.

"You will not go against King Urien's orders ever again," my uncle told me. "He will not be lenient a second time. I will not lose you again, my boy, when I have just found you." King Cedric folded his arms. "I never meant to make you choose between your people, Daniel," he added sadly. "But you did make that choice today," he added as he met my gaze again – and the anger was back, even stronger this time. "You were standing with Gaeson. Would you have turned your sword against the people you would one day rule? Would you have even raised your blade against me?"

"No," I answered, immediately and honestly, "I would not have turned against you nor your people, for they are now my people also. My standing with Queen Evelyn was that I would be a mediator between you and Gaeson. If it had come to war…" I trailed off, unsure of what I would have done had battle broken out.

"You are meant to be my heir, Daniel," he finished with a sigh, his tone again sounding weary and beyond his years. "How are my army men going to trust and follow you, when you turn against them?"

I thought quickly; I had to admit my uncle had made a good point.

"Just your people, then. Just the men and women you're one day going to lead into battle. You are meant to be my heir, Daniel, the Prince of Klumeck," he snapped. "How are the soldiers going to trust to follow you, when you turn against them now?"

My uncle had made a good point. How was I meant to lead them, when at the coming of the dawn I had been facing them as if I would my enemies? Then an idea came to mind.

"Let me talk to them," I told him quickly. He raised an eyebrow sceptically. "Permit me to explain my actions to them,

Uncle." I knew I was not the best orator, and I felt anxiety grow in the pit of my stomach at the prospect of a speech – but I also knew I had to speak to them if I was to persuade them to follow me as their future king.

"Very well," King Cedric replied, and gave me a curt nod. I bowed swiftly in return, having noted his grim tone. Thus he parted my company, going to the other side of the room to give an order to one of his men. A Klumeck soldier blew his horn to summon King Cedric's army – the army I would one day inherit. Within moments I heard footsteps descending the spiral towers and forming their ranks at the room below where they gathered; standing perfectly at attention due to their years of regimental training. It was strange to see a different army marching down the stone tower the same way I had been doing for years. As I surveyed them, I had a moment of envy for the life I had known before, when all that had concerned me had been following the captain's orders and defending my king.

My simple life as a soldier, I chided myself now, was obviously not meant to be. This was my life now, and it was best I got used to it. Also, to wish to be a simple soldier meant wishing away the new identity I had discovered. It meant not knowing King Cedric was my uncle and that I had never dreamt of my biological mother with her warm laughter – things which, I realised now, I was not at all sure I wanted to part with. Plus, King Reghan in all of his corruption would still be on the throne – where would Gaeson be, if not facing King Urien's might still? At least this way we had peace.

"His Highness Prince Bryce has come to address you," the king said abruptly and nodded to me.

I swallowed, suddenly aware of the dryness of my mouth. "Good morning," I greeted them, continuing to gaze at them in turn. "As I look at you, I do not know whether we will have met. It's possible in my years as a soldier in Gaeson, before I knew my true identity as His Majesty King Cedric's nephew, I could have met many of you in battle. I may have even killed a friend or relative of yours." I paused here, but none of them had reacted – as per their military training. I pondered how many of them might secretly wish me dead, and cleared my throat.

"You may be wondering," I continued, attempting to make my voice a little stronger, "why, after discovering I was His Majesty's heir, and that one day I would rule Klumeck and lead you all, I stood against you today in battle. It is because I knew that had I done nothing; had I not warned Gaeson of the attack pending, many lives could have been lost. We can have peace between our peoples. I knew Her Majesty Queen Evelyn to still be good," I added, still watching their carefully impassive expressions, "even if King Reghan was revealed to be corrupted."

"You still chose to stand against us." It was a voice from the back, towards the left of the soldiers amassed before me – such was their ranks, the voice remained anonymous.

"What kind of king are you, to stand against the people you would rule?" another voice shouted.

King Cedric walked forwards immediately. "Who dares speak treason against their future king?" he bellowed, drawing his sword with great flourish. "Your lives will be forfeit!"

Nobody moved.

"Well?" he roared, and I understood the situation could quickly escalate.

"It is a fair question," I conceded loudly, before King Cedric could say anything further. He quickly shifted his gaze to me, but did not speak further. "In the light of King Reghan's corruption, I myself have learned that kings and rulers are mere men and not higher than ordinary mortals. I was asked by Queen Evelyn herself to be a mediator between our two peoples. I have a double citizenship, belonging to both kingdoms – and therefore I hoped I could speak peace.

"If it had come to war, though…" I hesitated. "I would not have fought against you – but neither could I have fought against Gaeson, those I still consider to be my brothers and sisters. I ask you what you would have done, were you in my position," I continued now, my voice slightly louder. "You are all soldiers, with the noble duty to defend your kingdom and your home. Imagine being told that you were actually a royal in Gaeson, and you had been ordered to attack your home, to the land you loved best.

"There is a bond formed between us fighting brothers and sisters," I expounded, "a bond all of us know, in the remnants of those who have fought and died together. Which of you could really wield a blade against the one standing next to you?" I challenged them. "Which of you could march upon your home, to ransack the house belonging to your mother, or raid the trade of your friends?

"I could not have raised a blade against those from Gaeson, but neither could I have raised a blade against any of you," I repeated. "Therefore I would have lowered my sword and prayed for a swift end, if that is what God had willed. But the Lord was gracious enough to spare us all. I swear that I will spend the rest of my life, for as long as God wills it, in your service. I will fight for you and lead you against the Bernicians. My heart is full of joy to know all of you have been spared and, as a result, all those of Klumeck currently prisoners of war here at Gaeson are hereby released. Those who have spoken against me today are hereby pardoned, for I know the reasons behind your speech. I pray that together we can have one united Rheged, with continued peace between Klumeck and Gaeson. I am Bryce, the Prince of Klumeck," I declared to them now. "I swear I will serve and protect our kingdom to the best of my ability for as long as God ordains it."

My speech concluded, I stepped back, praying I had won over their hearts. I glanced at King Cedric, who now had a hint of a smile spread across his face – this encouraged me greatly. A man stepped forwards now, his armour of a purer silver than the other soldiers; I reasoned he was the captain of Klumeck's army. The captain drew his sword and the army instantly followed suit, their metal clunking sounding across their ranks.

"Hail, Prince Bryce!" the captain of the guard shouted, raising his sword high, and at the same instant bending his knee to a bow.

"Hail, Prince Bryce!" the rest of the army responded, a fraction of a moment later than the captain, bending to bended knees also. I smiled in relief, silently thanking God that I had been able to explain my actions to them. I gave various nods of thanks to the ranks as King Cedric now stepped forwards.

"Prince Bryce has indeed been merciful, pardoning those who spoke out during his words," my uncle said, with the regal, assured tone of one who had spoken publicly for years. "I thank you for accepting him as prince and heir to the throne. Know that if any of you ever speak against my nephew again, you are speaking against your future king – and I will have your heads for it. As you were," he added. Abruptly, all of them bowed low and King Cedric and I nodded back.

We both left the circular chamber at the base of the tower to stand in the long corridor outside. We walked a few steps together and then he stopped; I turned back to see him stood with his arms folded, surveying me.

"You seem to have won them over," King Cedric stated. "For your first public address, that was not too bad. You put over your position quite eloquently and enabled them to have empathy with you. Not many of them would be able to wield a blade against their brother or sister – and therein lay your whole argument. I did not know you would have simply refused to take a blade against them," he added, his voice suddenly lower and softer.

"Neither did I," I admitted after a pause. "I realise now that had we fought, I could not have raised my blade against Klumeck any more than I could have raised it against Gaeson." I crossed the short distance in the corridor to him, searching his gaze. "I am sorry you have had to doubt me, Your Majesty. I am sorry I had to disobey you, so soon after learning you are my uncle and the truth about my parents. Know that my sword is yours, and I will do all I can to be worthy of Klumeck's noble lands."

King Cedric's smile broadened. "You are talking like a true royal," he told me, clapping a hand on my shoulder. "It will not be long before you are sitting at my right hand in Klumeck."

A moment of sadness flickered in me quickly, though I was careful not to show it. For as joyous as I was that there was indeed peace, I would leave Gaeson in sorrow.

"A happy ending for all, then," came an icy voice from the shadows, rife with sarcasm.

I turned on my bended knee at the sound of the voice, as I had done the night I had met Queen Evelyn on the balcony with the captain, long before she would have to force her father to abdicate and take the throne from him. The voice this time, however, belonged to King Urien. King Cedric had remained on his feet, long standing a royal as he was – but he had bowed his head low.

"It is well for you that it turned out this way, boy. Not many would be able to live after disobeying my orders. Usually they would be killed on sight for such reckless behaviour," King Urien ended sharply.

"I only wished to spare needless bloodshed and save the lives of both the peoples of Klumeck and Caer Ligualid, my lord the king," I replied quickly, "so as to unite both kingdoms under your rule. I meant no dishonour to you, Your Majesty; only to unite the land of Rheged once more." My eyes were fixed upon the floor as I spoke, so I could not know the king's expression, but I could well imagine those pale blue eyes piercing mine.

"Look at me," King Urien ordered; duly I raised his head to survey his countenance. The piercing quality of his eyes seemed to be even worse than my speculation of it; I felt as though he was staring into my very soul. "I suppose you may, after all, be suitable for the task ahead of you. A king you may be one day. But watch how you fare, boy," he added, the threat of his voice as palpable as his cold, cruel gaze. "If you disobey me again, you will not live another day, no matter who your uncle might be."

King Urien straightened now and turned to glance in King Cedric's direction. "There is a meeting tomorrow with King Ceric, Queen Evelyn and my son also in attendance. You are expected as well. I would have invited your sister, but I have heard she does not yet know you are related." Again how I perceived the sarcasm and scorn in his voice!

"That is correct, Your Majesty," I answered, bowing again, "I have not had chance to inform her yet. I thought perhaps this afternoon…"

"Or tomorrow morn, Your Majesty, after we have all had some rest," my uncle now cut in.

"Very well," King Urien agreed, before I could say another word. "You are to tell her. It will not do to carry on having royalty not even knowing it," he continued reprovingly, as if somehow I myself were to blame for not knowing the truth about my identity. "You will both be also required to attend," he added, looking between myself and King Cedric. "Princess Lynette will be welcome to join us, but she does not have to if she is only learning the truth tomorrow." With this he finished his speech abruptly and turned to leave.

"Your Majesty," we both chorused, and after he had quitted our company, we both straightened and King Cedric exhaled.

"You are fortunate to be alive, nephew, even if the day has turned out well. I would not tempt fate by ever disobeying him again, even if it were again to work in your favour. Regarding my niece," he added abruptly, "I am sure you are as anxious to explain things as I am to meet her, but you are barely able to stand."

This was true enough, but my pride had prevented me from admitting it.

"You should eat something and get some rest. Perhaps in the morn, you had better explain the truth of all these things. I will be here in the castle," he added. "Farewell, Bryce, for the present," he concluded with a nod, using my Klumeck name without thinking of it. He turned to leave, the swish of his deep red cloak following in his trail.

"That was the first time," I spoke after him, and in the middle of the corridor he turned back. "That, and when the men spoke it earlier."

"Spoke what?" my uncle questioned, his brow creasing slightly. A little unexpectedly, I found myself smiling – even though the action still hurt my mouth.

"That was the first time you called me Bryce and it did not seem strange," I explained. I watched then as King Cedric began to return my smile, saw affection take shape in his eyes. He nodded at me briefly and then continued on his way. I stood watching his departure, considering that each time I met with him, I found greater pleasure in being his nephew. I turned to see a guard waiting for me who bowed low.

"Queen Evelyn has asked me to show you your royal chambers, Your Highness."

I frowned; part of me had wished to simply return to my old house and see Sarah, but he was clearly expecting me to give my approval, and it would not do to appear ignorant of royal custom and traditions.

"Lead the way," I commanded, and the guard bowed again. He led me once more through the castle, and soon he was opening the door of the chamber and walking in. He remained standing at the door, and I realised he was awaiting my dismissal of him. "You may return to your other duties," I concluded regally.

"Very good, sire." He bowed low as he retreated, closing the door behind him softly.

I removed the sword from around my belt, having removed my armour earlier. As I did, I felt the adrenaline begin to subside. The turbulent events of the past twenty-four hours seemed to have caught up with me – I had not rested since leaving Caer Ligualid. I had enough sense to remove my boots and outer garments before I collapsed upon the bed, exhausted. My last conscious thought was of when I would see Sarah, and of how I would begin to explain things to her – but my mind was too heavy for such worries, and I instantly sank into a deep sleep.

***

My eyelids felt equally heavy when my eyes next opened – from this I speculated I had slept a while. I was a little cold, also, having not covered myself with the bedclothes the previous night. I rose from the bed and walked to the window, rubbing remnants of sleep from my eyes as I went. I then opened it and perceived it to be mid-morning, with the sun streaming through. I reasoned I had slept about a day. In the corner of the chamber there was a small bowl of water, and next to it was laid out fresh royal garments from Klumeck. I washed quickly in the cold water; it was refreshing against my sore face, which I now touched gingerly. During my slumber the swelling had gone down a lot, but it was still painful to touch.

As I dressed in the new clothes, I felt a gnaw of hunger – I had not eaten anything since that mouthful of bread yesterday morning – but I paid my stomach no heed, knowing I could delay telling Sarah the truth no longer. Abruptly, I departed my chamber and made my way out of the castle, finally on my way to tell my sister about the past.

Only a little later, I was nearing the end of the path between the castle and the town, hidden on the western slope of the hill. It was a relief indeed to walk through the streets knowing Gaeson was accepting me in their sights once more. The streets were empty; even though there had not been a battle, the air was tense with the same trepidation that always lingered when the people had returned from the caves. I reasoned this was because small bands of soldiers from Caer Ligualid continually filed past, and that my fair town was naturally suspicious of these warriors that had initially come to make war against Gaeson's walls.

Ere long I came to my old street, walking up to my old home for the second time – this time not as a traitor in the middle of the night, clinging to the hope that Gaeson might survive the dawn (and that for myself also, as I had been awaiting execution), but as a royal of Rheged, vindicated and pardoned, with a new monarch on the throne. I felt that though my house had not changed, I was a different person. I opened the door and crossed the threshold, hearing at once the footsteps of what was revealed to be Sarah hurrying down the stairs.

"Your Highness." She stopped abruptly and curtseyed, and then straightened but still had her head lowered, her gaze bent upon the floor.

"It's good to see you, Sarah." I smiled, elated to reflect once more on how this woman was my sister. "I wonder if we could talk."

"Of course, Your Highness." She stayed where she was whilst I walked further into the living room and sat down. Sarah still remained stood with her head slightly bent, and I realised she would stand there until I told her to join me. I had a sigh; at least before we could sit and relax with one another.

"Please sit, Sarah," I added, gesturing to the chair opposite me. "I'm still the same man, and I want you to relax and speak freely, as we always have done."

She sat and smiled, tucking as she did that stray strand of hair that always seemed to come loose.

"Thank you, my lord prince," she added, and smiled as she sat down. "I am so pleased to see you looking so well, Your Highness," she murmured, tucking a stray strand of hair behind her ear as she spoke.

"Sarah, I'm sorry I was never able to tell you about this personally. I had hoped to have the opportunity, but there was no time earlier. We had to act swiftly this night," I explained, "but I have much to tell you now."

"Of course, Your Highness, but you look so weak still," she added, that familiar little frown of concern upon her features. "Let me fetch you some tea."

I was about to tell her not to bother, but then my stomach gnawed at me and I remembered I had not consumed anything since dawn the previous day.

"Tea would be fine," I simply answered, reasoning that it would only delay the truth a couple of minutes longer. It transpired the tea had been recently made, for she came back in moments with a cup of hot water mixed with herbs and honey.

"Thank you," I said, and took a sip before speaking. I wished to tell her the truth right away, but I knew I owed her the whole account. Therefore I started from the beginning, explaining how I had been commanded to escort the queen – the princess as she then had been – to the Kingdom of Rheged. As I commenced telling her all that had happened these last two weeks, I supposed King Reghan must have always prayed the battle would never be as severe as for his men to take her there, where he would have known his daughter would not have been safe. I swallowed a knot of anger at the former king, pushing it further into my stomach as I continued my story of what had transpired, speaking presently of how I had cut the rope and then awakened in Caer Ligualid, and how King Cedric had recognised me as his long-lost heir after seeing the scar on my side.

"So you could actually remember being in Klumeck, Your Highness?" she asked me now. Her eyes had been wide during my whole account.

I swallowed as I thought back. "Yes, Sarah. I could remember a man and a woman smiling down at me. I know they were my parents. Sarah…" I knew I could not delay any longer. "My dear Sarah, there is something else. Before I woke up in Rheged and discovered my true identity, I had a conversation with the captain. He told me that King Cedric was looking for his heir… but there were two heirs. I have a sibling." I looked at her pointedly.

"A sibling?" Sarah questioned me. "Another heir, lost somewhere in Gaeson?"

I nodded slowly, but she still had not understood what I meant. "A sister, Sarah. I have a sister. A most beloved sister and oldest friend," I added, and smiled at her. Her eyes widened further, and I knew she understood.

"Me?" she asked in a whisper. "Your Highness… are you telling me we are related? We are brother and sister, of the same parents?"

"I am," I replied. I reached across and took her hands. "Sarah, you are my sister and niece of King Cedric. You are a princess," I informed her simply.

Her eyes were wide and she snatched her hands back, a bewildered smile upon her countenance. "No, my lord. I fear you are mistaken. My father was a baker," she replied. "It is logical for you to assume this connection, since we have known each other since infanthood, but you have the wrong person. That is all," she continued, a little too brightly.

"I do not have it wrong," I answered her patiently.

Sarah abruptly stood from the table, shaking her head and walking a few steps to the stand by the oven.

"I well understand your shock, since it is the same as I had when waking up in Caer Ligualid," I continued. "I could not believe my ears either, but nevertheless, it is the truth."

She said nothing more, just shook her head again, but only slightly this time.

"I remember you, Sarah," I replied hoarsely.

She turned back to me at this latest speech. Her frown was set hard, but she said nothing.

"As I have told you before," I began, "my oldest memory is of me wandering lost in the snow outside Rheged. My mother always told me that I had got lost in the snow and was trying to get back to her. In truth, that was the night our mothers found us. We were discovered on the outskirts of Gaeson, stumbling in the cold. You were crying," I added then, as I remembered more details – and then, suddenly, it was as if I was no longer in my old kitchen, but reliving it. Here in this house, I could almost feel the numbness of my toes and the utter despair at being separated from my parents and staggering in the blizzard. "Oh, Sarah, we were so cold," I murmured. "My fingers were without feeling. They took us in, Sarah. They clothed us and fed us."

"If what you are saying is the truth," Sarah at last said slowly, "then that would mean my mother was not the one who bore me. That would mean that both of my parents went to their graves knowing I believed the lie that I was their child." Her voice was so full of pain and bitterness that I longed to hold and comfort her – but I knew not whether such comfort would be well received.

"They lied to protect you, as they did me," I said quietly. "If the truth about us had been discovered, King Reghan may well have killed us and them. My father overheard a conversation he was never supposed to hear," I continued, "from two soldiers who had been to Klumeck the night before. They were speaking about how the Bernicians had raided Klumeck at night and murdered most of the royal family. King Cedric had survived the attack and the two remaining heirs – a boy and a girl – had gone missing. Except it was King Reghan, not Bernicia, who attacked. A few hours later that day, my mother and your mother were walking near the outskirts of Gaeson when they discovered us."

"But now you tell me they were neither your mother nor mine," she responded, wrapping her arms around herself as though she were cold. "What happened?" Sarah asked now. "Who died that night?"

I hesitated a moment, drinking more of my tea before answering.

"Who, Daniel?" Sarah asked directly as she stood up straighter. "I need to know."

"It was both of our parents," I said at last, "King Cedric's wife and..." I paused. "And their unborn child. Our aunt was pregnant when she was killed," I finished.

Sarah's countenance changed from shock to sadness at this reply, her hand upon her mouth. I felt a similar stab of sadness as I thought once more of the cousin I would never know.

"King Cedric had given us an escort to take us to Caer Ligualid, but something must have gone wrong in the journey for us to arrive in Gaeson instead."

"Why did our parents never tell us?" Her voice was as quiet as a whisper, but every syllable was clearly audible. "I do not understand why we were not adopted into the same family. Surely that would have been much kinder, not to separate us."

"It was a risk they could not take," I replied. "If they raised us together; it would have been too obvious. Two children adopted by family relatives who had died... that was believable. Our mothers did not want us to die, nor did they not want us to be enemies of Gaeson. So they took us in," I finished.

Sarah was looking at the table, and I saw her hands were shaking. "My parents..." she murmured, raising her head so her eyes met mine. "My mother and father... they went to the grave, not telling me who I really was," she repeated.

"They did not want to risk you harm," I murmured. "They thought if the truth came out, King Reghan would have killed us both." I paused here and saw her shoulders beginning to shake, saw a whole range of emotions displayed in her countenance. "I know this is difficult," I muttered. "I had a day or two in Caer Ligualid to adjust myself to the news. King Cedric had wondered if you might wish to meet him, but I quite understand if you are not ready." I paused again, but she said nothing further. "Perhaps I will leave you a while," I stated, and stood. "Farewell, then," I bade her, when she still did not speak.

"Wait," she said, stepping forwards. I turned back, and her eyes were full of unshed tears. "You are my brother," she stated.

"Yes." I nodded.

Without another word, she came forwards and I embraced her. Her head came to rest on my shoulder.

"I am sorry this truth has such a bitter sting," I murmured, "but I must tell you it brings me great joy to know you are my sister. We oft pretended we were kin, playing as children, and now we know the bond is real."

She stepped back from me, nodding as she sniffed and wiped at her eyes.

"In a way, we did grow up together, Sarah – all those times from our childhood we can recall. If we had known we were related then, I doubt we would have been much closer."

"Our parents... can you remember them? What were they like?" she asked me as she took her place again at the table.

"I remember them only a little." I sat down at the table again and took another drink of tea. "A few images have come to me since discovering the truth," I added. I closed my eyes for a moment, attempting to remember them from my dream and conjure them anew in my mind's eye. "Our mother's hair was much the colouring of yours, and your eyes are from her also. My hair and eyes come from our father," I added now – even as I spoke, more memories were coming to the forefront of my mind. "I remember a room with lush, red carpets... and toys," I finished. I tried to remember more but it was in vain. "That's all I can remember. It's like trying to remember a dream... the harder you try to remember, the more it disappears and eludes you."

"I cannot remember them at all," Sarah murmured, with sadness. "I know why my parents never told me, but... it still causes me pain they went to their graves, never saying a word."

I sat up now, taking her hand. "Perhaps they were trying to tell you," I told her now. "Our parents must have named you from the Scriptures." Sarah had been the wife of Abraham, to whom God made the sacred promises. "Sarah means 'princess'," I reminded her. "Maybe your name was given to you so that you might one day know your true origins."

Sarah nodded, but her face still showed dismay.

"You may not have come from your mother's womb, Sarah, but I know they loved you." I sought to reassure her. "I could see how much they loved you. Besides, Sarah, we have a lifetime of memories from our childhood. Even though we did not know the truth, our mothers ensured we still grew up together. If we had known we were related, we would not have been much closer."

Her hands were shaking. Tentatively, I reached across and took one of them in my own hands again. She gazed up at me. "I know what you say is true, dear brother… and my heart is filled with joy to know we are kin," she sighed, "but I feel like my identity has been lost."

I nodded – I knew this feeling well.

"I feel my parents have been taken away from me and there are strangers in their place. I have never known them; I have no memories of them to speak of as you do. Did they even love me?"

"Of course they did. Think of our uncle, how long he searched. They called you Lynette," I informed her now. "You know what that name means." It was a sweet name to be given to a cherished daughter, meaning "beloved" or "darling". "They would not give you such a name if they did not love you," I continued. "I do not remember much, but I can remember how they loved. I remember enough to know they loved both of us dearly. That is why our uncle sought so long for us."

She looked up at me now, fresh tears forming in her eyes – but she did not weep. I thought Lynette fit her perfectly, as well as the name Sarah suited her. Thinking upon her name, I had a new, sudden memory, sharp and fresh.

"I remember," I told her after a few moments. "I remember how dearly they loved you. They used to call you 'my little Lynette'." I had closed my eyes in memory, for I saw my mother form these words on her lips as she spoke them. They used to say she was their little Lynette, a gift from God.

"Forgive me," she murmured, taking the first mouthful of her own tea. "This is a lot to hear at once."

"There is nothing to forgive, dear sister," I told her quietly. "You took this truth with much more calmness than I did."

Sarah gave a small smile but said nothing further, and so we simply sat there, the two of us, whilst we drank our cooling tea. Then, abruptly, she looked up.

"This means Enid also knew the truth, all those years. That is the reason why you wished to see her the night before last, is it not?" There was a sudden sharpness to her tone. "The captain wanted her to confirm the account you just told me."

"Aye," I admitted. "Your perception does you credit."

Sarah shook her head a little, her countenance suddenly full of anger. "We have always had such a close bond, her and I," she stated now, "even before I took the position of caring for her." She stood now and crossed the kitchen to pour the dregs of her cold tea into the sink. "Yet after all this time of living under the same roof, I find that she has deceived me every day I have been here."

"I well understand your feelings," I said, standing and folding my arms as I answered. "I too was vexed at how she had deceived me. But she thought she was doing it for our good, to protect us."

Sarah now turned her head in the direction of the stairs, as if looking right up to my mother's bedroom, while she pondered this. "Very well," she said eventually, although she still looked like she wished to have rather strong words with my mother. "I can see why the deception stayed, even if I object to it." She turned back to me. "You said earlier that King Cedric wished to meet me."

I nodded, placing the empty cup on the kitchen table.

"Then let us depart, for I shall meet him," she declared, a small smile upon her features.

"Our uncle will be delighted," I returned as we left the kitchen. "Where are Rachel and the children?" I asked her now, suddenly realising I had not heard them once since entering the house.

"They are at the village a little south of here," Sarah answered, her smile growing as she locked the house, "at a nearby trade fair."

"Rachel has recovered, then," I said, pleasantly surprised. "I am pleased their business has restarted so quickly," I added as we began the walk back to the castle.

"I have been helping them a little," Sarah admitted, and I smiled, having thought as much. "I still cannot take this in," she

213

stated as we journeyed through the town. "The day before last I was grieving with your mother," she murmured quietly, "for we both believed you dead. Then to hear you had come back alive, but sentenced to death..." She shook her head again, and then smiled. "Then it was a turn of events, to see you pardoned and declared as prince! Now to know I am your kin and a royal..." She ended her speech, lost in thought.

"I am sorry for causing you both pain," I told her meaningfully as we walked; we were now almost at the top of the hill. Though there was still an air of tension and fragility about the place, I could not help pondering what the state of Gaeson might be had I not returned. "I wanted to come back to you and my mother as soon as I returned... but I was met by the captain and escorted to the palace. It is my only regret that I could not see either of you first to tell you I was well," I concluded.

"The fault is not yours, brother," she responded – and I was overjoyed that she used the term so naturally. "I am only delighted at this outcome, that all of us have peace because of you."

I returned her smile – fortunately the pain in my mouth had dulled, for I had performed this action many times this afternoon. My sister spoke little more, and I did not speak either.

Presently we came to the courtyard, and as we did, my thoughts flashed briefly to King Reghan. I wondered if he was still alive, whether I would ever meet him again. A seed of rage sprouted in my heart, unbidden, and I clenched my fists to suppress it – for as much as I hated what he had done, I knew the Lord would not want me to hate another, tempting though it was. I pushed the stab of anger aside as we came to the corridor in between the courtyard and the palace hall to find the Klumeck soldier dressed in silver armour – the man I had guessed to be Klumeck's captain.

"Your Royal Highnesses," the guard said; I noted he had assumed correctly that Sarah was my sister and therefore the other heir. "I am Klumeck's captain of the guard, my lord prince, at your service." He bowed a third time. "Sire, King Cedric asked me to escort you both to his chamber."

"Very good," I responded simply.

He turned and at once departed for my uncle's chambers. We followed him down the corridor, and as we proceeded in his footsteps I began to wonder, before I could prevent it, whether I had faced this man in battle. I shook my head mentally, and instead took in the familiar surroundings as the corridor opened up into another indoor courtyard, with smooth paved stone and large pillars. A lot of the royal advisers spent their day here, discussing various strategies. They were here now as we walked past them, huddled quietly together. I did not have to guess at the reason for their discomfort – their king had just been revealed as corrupt and been forced to abdicate. No doubt the queen would wish to ascertain the exact nature of their advice and whether they had been all too aware of their king's deceit.

As we came to the base of the large white staircase leading to the royal chambers, I suddenly saw Taliesin also sat in the courtyard, an ink quill behind his ear, swinging his legs in much the same way as when we had last met. He began to smirk a little as he saw me in that mocking way of his. No doubt he thought that since he was King Urien's personal bard, he was beyond reprove. His countenance was beginning to vex me, thus I ignored him and fixed my eyes ahead of me as we reached the top of the staircase.

After heading down yet another long corridor, we came to my uncle's door. I nodded at the guard to dismiss him and raised my hand to knock, knowing that this would be the first time in twenty-one years that my uncle would see his niece.

Chapter Ten

King Cedric opened the door in almost the same instant I knocked, and I saw his eyes move to Sarah and stay there, his gaze already transfixed on her.

"Your Majesty," I greeted him, and bowed; Sarah also curtseyed low. "Uncle, may I present to you Sarah, my sister."

"Your Majesty." Sarah repeated my greeting from her low curtsey, and at once I knew such a formal introduction had been unnecessary. I spoke no further, allowing them the silence appropriate for their reunion. King Cedric did not speak for few moments, and I perceived his whole countenance to be mesmerised; he looked almost at the point of weeping.

"My little Lynette," he murmured at length, taking a step forwards. "But your name is Sarah, of course," he corrected himself, and took her hands briefly. "You may think this is impossible, my dear," he continued, "but I recognise you. Even though when I last held you, you could barely walk. You look so like your mother, my dear niece," he stated now. "You have her eyes, just as Daniel has the looks of his father." His smile faded slightly and his expression became heavy and weary. "I am so sorry," he said now. "I am sorry of all that has befallen both of you. What a beautiful woman you have become. I am so glad to meet you."

"I am glad to meet you, sire," she responded quietly.

"My heart is full to see both of you at last. I feared I would never see either of you again," he smiled. "Please sit. I have had a servant prepare us some food. We will have the coronation feast also in your honour, of course," he added, "but we shall also celebrate now." He gestured to a table laid with the makings of an excellent meal, with goblets of mead to accompany it. The three of us sat down, and I had to go against every instinct of simply tipping the whole lot of food into my mouth. My gaze upon the food must have given me away, for King Cedric laughed.

"Please eat," he encouraged me – and so with urgency in my movements, I began to pile up my plate. "I assume Daniel has informed you of everything," he added to Sarah. As he spoke, a shadow crossed his face – a shadow, I realised, which seemed to appear every time he spoke of the past and that awful night when we were taken from him.

"Yes, Your Majesty," Sarah replied, and I saw a similar sadness befall her own features. "I am so sorry, sire, for all that transpired," she murmured.

King Cedric gave her a small smile in thanks.

"Daniel was kind enough to give me an account of our parents," Sarah continued, glancing at me briefly, "though it is still strange to call them my parents."

"Of course – it will all have been a sharp revelation to you," my uncle responded. "Though from what Daniel has told me, the people who adopted you sound fine indeed."

"Yes," Sarah said, nodding. "They must have risked so much in order to keep us safe, at great danger to themselves. "They must have even faked our birth deeds," she added, clutching my wrist in sudden realisation.

"Of course," I murmured – I had not even thought about the legal process they must have manipulated in order to keep us hidden from King Reghan's searches. "They risked their lives for us," I said now. "Once the search was over, all my parents needed to do was move so we could grow up together. They must have rejoiced at us making friends so quickly."

Sarah nodded.

"Yes," our uncle replied at length. "My heart is full of thankfulness that our God has kept you safe and given you such a loving upbringing, even allowing the two of you to know each other. All those years I searched with anxiety and despair… you were well tended." King Cedric did not continue and there was a pause in the conversation while we continued to eat; we had nearly come to the end of our meal. I poured Sarah some more mead, thinking it was probably a good remedy for her shock at recent truths abruptly coming to light.

"I have begun to remember our parents a little more," I said now, as I refilled the other two goblets on my table, and King

Cedric looked my way. "Little fragments, here and there, in dreams sometimes or if I concentrate my mind," I explained, in between swigs of the mead. "My initial discovery of them seems to have triggered other memories."

"More memories will surely come to the surface once we return to Klumeck," the king responded with a smile. I saw Sarah's eyes widen slightly in surprise; I had hoped this day was far off yet. Something hardened, almost imperceptibly, in his countenance. "You must know I intend to return soon, Daniel. I cannot rule my kingdom from afar for long. You promised me allegiance, as you did my army."

"Of course, Your Majesty," I answered quickly. He raised an eyebrow as if he was not quite convinced, and then stood from the table. Sarah had said nothing further and I cursed silently – another thing I had not told her about.

"How is the woman and her two children?" he questioned Sarah now, changing the subject abruptly. "Daniel told me what happened to the poor boy that died."

I blinked – I had almost forgotten I had mentioned it to him. So many hundreds must die in each battle, and yet this mighty king had remembered someone not even from his own kingdom.

"They are faring well, I think, Your Majesty," Sarah replied, recovering quickly. "They seem to have grown accustomed to their new surroundings. Indeed, they are away trading in a nearby village, trying to restart their business." My uncle nodded in approval and gathered his royal cloak around himself.

"I regret to leave, but I must prepare myself for the meeting with King Urien. You are welcome to come, niece," King Cedric added, "but we quite understand if you would like to take a day or two to adjust to the news. The coronation of the queen will be in three days, including today," he clarified. "That is also when the two of you will be officially recognised as royals of Rheged and heirs to my throne."

"In three days? So soon?" I questioned him automatically. Sarah's face had turned to surprise yet again. "I think Sarah may need more time…"

"The timing is unfortunate, I agree," King Cedric replied evenly, "but it is the wish of King Urien himself. We need to return to our kingdoms in haste, Daniel – the supreme king does not desire to stay in Gaeson any longer than needed."

"That is kind of you, Your Majesty, to give me these few days," Sarah managed – I perceived she might well be distressed, as I had been at hearing I would have to leave fair Gaeson. We bade goodbye to our uncle and he then departed with the now familiar swish of his cloak. I turned to Sarah but her gaze was fixed on the floor, with a hand poised on the back of her chair.

"Folly of me," Sarah began after a pause, finally looking up at me, "but I had not realised we would have to leave Gaeson so soon."

I felt for my sister; in much less time than I, she had discovered not only her true identity but that she would have to leave our fair city.

"I am so sorry I did not tell you," I told her earnestly.

She now moved her other hand, shaking it lightly. "Do not concern yourself about that – you have been rather occupied since your return," she replied brightly.

"I am sorry also that the coronation is so soon," I added. "I had thought there would be more time to prepare. I am sure you will do very well."

"Thank you," she said with a smile. "But do not stay talking with me – you must prepare yourself for this meeting; I shall return home. I need no accompanying," she added, as she made her way out of the room. "I insist," she said, before I could tell her it was no bother. "From what I can gather, King Urien is still not best pleased with you. It would not do to make him wait."

From this, I sensed she wished to be alone, which I could well understand. "Very well." I nodded with a smile which she returned, and we clasped hands warmly. "I shall see you soon," I told her with another nod, and with a swift nod of her own, I watched her go.

I ran a hand through my hair, rebuking myself again for not telling her. As far as I could tell, Sarah had always seemed so content in her life – now I was to wrench her from everything she knew, as the truth had done me. For a moment I pondered whether it would have been kinder to leave her in ignorance, to still believe the parents who had raised her in Gaeson were her true parents – but surely the truth always won over deception. With a sigh, I swigged back the rest of the mead in my goblet and headed for the meeting.

I ensured I would arrive at the meeting early, having taken heed of the warnings to be punctual. As I entered the small room with its large, rectangular table adorned with decorations of white, red and gold, I saw the only other person present was Queen Evelyn.

"My lady." I bowed as I entered the chamber.

She looked up and smiled as she saw me, which encouraged me greatly – surely this attested to my character being restored. "Prince Daniel," she greeted me, inclining her head. I waited, too accustomed to following her orders. "Sit if you wish," she added, having noticed my predicament, "for you are no longer my soldier but a fellow monarch. You need not wait for my permission. I met King Cedric a few minutes ago," Queen Evelyn continued, while I took my seat across from her. "He told me that he has met your sister. It is a joy indeed that he has been reunited with you both once more."

I smiled.

"Indeed, Your Majesty. I thank you for my chamber at the castle," I added, "although my house…"

"As fine as your house is, you are obliged to stay in the castle," Queen Evelyn interrupted. "Your sister will also be obliged to move here – at least, for the few days whilst you remain at Gaeson."

My eyes met hers again at this statement. Would she feel sorrow when I left?

"King Cedric also informed me of your promise to your soldiers to release all Klumeck soldiers," Queen Evelyn said briskly, changing the subject rather abruptly. "It is a good idea," she reflected, "but it might have been prudent to consult me first," she added, a slight rebuke in her tone.

"I apologise, my lady," I answered quickly. "It was an unprepared speech, and I thought it would be a good way to convince them of my trustworthiness. I wondered if I might have them released after this meeting," I added. "I also wonder if we might relieve the interrogator of his post," I ventured. "He is a sadistic man, too in love with violence. When I was in his keeping, he did not ask me a single question."

"Very well," Queen Evelyn agreed. "You have my permission for both requests. It will take some paperwork to prepare, but it will be easily done." She paused for a moment. "I assume it will not be long before you leave for Klumeck," she stated lightly, returning to her earlier subject.

My eyes roved to meet hers again, but her expression was unreadable. "Yes my lady," I answered, my own reply as impassive as hers. For how could I truly say anything, knowing that to leave Gaeson was to leave the service of this woman? She seemed to be waiting for me to speak further. "I expect it will be soon after your coronation," was all I could think of to say.

"Yes," she replied faintly. There was a pause, but I could not think what else to say to her. As we held each other's gazes, my mind took me back further to when I cut the rope and fell from the cliff, of what I had told her in those final moments. Did she think that in all that had happened, my heart had changed also?

She opened her mouth to say something else, but just then the large doors to the chamber opened and King Cedric and Prince Owain walked in. I stood immediately, swallowing a knot of resentment that my conversation with the queen had been cut short. We both inclined our heads; King Cedric took the seat next to me and Prince Owain took a seat next to the queen. We sat down again, and Prince Owain watched me with a sullen, almost bored expression. A moment later, the doors opened and King Urien entered the room.

We all stood in unison as he entered; Queen Evelyn gave a curtsey while the rest of us bowed low. He walked with all royal dignity to his chair at the head of the table. The others paid their respects again as he sat; swiftly I copied them and bowed low, and then we too sat around the table. The supreme king said nothing for a moment, but his icy blue eyes roved around the table. His gaze came to me last and stayed for a moment. I noted that though the gaze he bore upon me was harsh, it was filled with much less anger and dislike.

"I assume Princess Lynette is not joining us," he stated drily.

"She is not, Your Majesty," I replied, inclining my head as I spoke, "but we have informed her of the truth and she has now met King Cedric. She is very grateful, sire, for the time you have given her to adjust to the truth," I added quickly.

"Very well," he replied, his steely gaze lingering on me a moment longer. "We shall have to proceed in her absence. This is the first meeting we have had in twenty-two years with representatives of Gaeson, Klumeck and Caer Ligualid," he declared.

A year before peace was fractured, I calculated swiftly. A year before King Reghan invaded Klumeck. The year before my natural mother and father were killed and I was forced to flee in the snow with Sarah. The year before I came to Gaeson, with no knowledge of what I was leaving behind. As King Urien began his speech, I dragged my thoughts from my own past to focus on the matters at hand.

The meeting was long but productive. We ironed out the treaty between Gaeson and Klumeck, and the documents formally realigning ourselves to King Urien, which we all signed. I was silent, for the most part – I was still trying to let the fact I was a monarch sink in. Nothing happened of great consequence; I was not able to understand most of it. Would I really be sat here one day, a king?

"The meeting with King Rhydderch, King Gwollag and King Morgant has gone well. They have agreed to assist us in our war against Bernicia." King Urien had spoken in a concluding, almost bored tone – but my head jerked up at his speech. These men were the foremost kings from some of our neighbouring kingdoms, beyond the borders of Rheged. All three were kings from Strathclyde, a kingdom to the far north. King Gwollag was well-known to Rheged, being His Majesty King Urien's cousin. King Rhydderch had also long been a friend of Rheged. King Rhydderch was known as a good and righteous king; the people of Strathclyde often called him "Rhydderch the generous". However, I was unsure about the other king's trustworthiness.

"Are we sure we can truly rely upon His Majesty King Morgant?" asked King Cedric, showing he had had the same doubts as me.

King Urien's hard eyes turned towards him, but he said nothing.

"He is known for his power and greed, sire," King Cedric added hastily, and King Urien's eyes hardened – I saw he was severe even with the kings he was fond of.

"If we are to survive the Bernician scourge, then we must seek assistance," King Urien answered sternly. "We simply do not have enough men. We have spent far too many on the petty feud between you and Reghan; I thank God your arguing has come to an end." His point was clear – if Gaeson had not been at war with Klumeck, there would be more men to fight Bernicia.

King Cedric's gaze hardened, but he said nothing. A silence both awkward and uncomfortable ensued.

"Do you have a hidden supply of men we do not know about?" King Urien asked my uncle with scorn.

"No, my lord the king. I would simply advise…"

"Then we have no other choice," King Urien declared, cutting across him. "Unless anyone has any other matter to bring up, I suggest we conclude the meeting here," he added abruptly. He waited but a moment before he rose from the table, leaving with the swish of his cloak following behind him. Swiftly Prince Owain also stood and departed from the chamber, following closely his father's footsteps.

"I am sorry my father has caused such pain among our peoples," Queen Evelyn said, as we all stood from the table.

"Your father's action is not your doing, my dear," my uncle replied with a sad smile. "Your recent actions have spoken of bravery, wisdom, honour and sacrifice. I pray your father will see the error of his ways and take pride in you once more."

Queen Evelyn curtseyed to him in thanks for his kind speech. She and her royal escort then also left the room, leaving only King Cedric and myself.

"What tragedy has inspired," my uncle sighed. "I do not trust King Morgant," he continued.

"Neither do I, sire. I was as surprised as you," I replied quietly, folding my arms. "How long will it be until Bernicia is ready to attack?"

"The rumours state we still have some time left," King Cedric answered, raising a hand to scratch his vast auburn beard in thought. "She is still preparing her people for war, but it will not be long. But that is enough heavy talk for one day," he added with a sudden smile. "Now is the time of celebrating the peace between our peoples. Alas, the business of a king keeps me moving. Farewell, nephew, until later."

"Farewell, Uncle." I gave him a short bow and then departed the meeting chamber at once to aid in the proceedings of releasing the Klumeck prisoners. The paperwork for all the prisoners took a good hour or two to prepare and then I, along with Klumeck's captain, went to the cells in order to release them.

"Prince Bryce," the chief interrogator greeted me – the same interrogator who, around forty hours ago, had beaten me until I was unconscious. "Looks like the royal prince was telling the truth," he sneered.

"You dare talk to His Highness like that?" the Klumeck captain shouted, drawing his sword from his sheath a little.

"Another word out of you and I'll have your head," I reprimanded the interrogator. "We are here to release all Klumeck prisoners – I have the papers. I also have the order for the relief of your post," I added to him, trying not to feel a sense of satisfaction. "I suggest you pack your things."

The interrogator's anger was obvious. "Very good, Your Highness," he muttered through clenched teeth. "If you'll come this way," he added, and led the way to the dungeon where the Klumeck prisoners were held.

"Well, this is a strange event."

I had almost finished letting the prisoners go and I turned at the voice. There was one prisoner left of Klumeck to release; he was concealed in the shadows. I stepped further, holding up the candle to better see – and I instantly recognised him as the soldier I had spared twice, whose brother had fallen from the castle wall.

"My brother's killer becomes my future king." His voice was deadpan with a hint of sarcasm.

"It was not what I would have foreseen, either," I replied evenly. "All Klumeck soldiers are being released, as a symbol of the peace and unity between the two kingdoms. That includes you," I pointed out, stepping forwards further.

"You would trust me not to attempt to slay you, as soon as you free me?"

I paused, watching his face flicker in the light of the lamp I held out.

"You are a soldier; you are obliged to follow your king," I responded. He inclined his head in agreement, but I was not convinced he would do such a thing. "What is your name?"

"I am Conall."

I nodded.

"My brother's name was Glyn," he told me now, and I heard the pained resentment in his tone. "Or did you wish the man you killed to remain nameless? Tell me," he went on, before I could reply. "How do your people feel, knowing you faced them so many times in battle? That you would have fought them yesterday, had peace not been restored? How many would give their lives to follow you?" he finished quietly, a hint of menace in his tone now.

I swallowed, moving the lamp a little closer. "I know not what is in their hearts," I answered, "but I would pray they would follow their king and his heir. I asked the men yesterday to put themselves in my position," I told him. "To imagine that they had been taken from the life they had known and told to turn on their brothers and sisters in war. You are right to say I would not have fought against Gaeson had battle commenced," I continued, "but nor would I have fought against Klumeck."

"So, what action therefore?" Conall smirked. "You would have simply stood there, waiting to be killed in battle?" He continued his scorn until he saw that I was serious.

"Yes," I answered plainly. "Our two peoples were one day at peace," I stated. "It is only due to one man's corruption that war has broken out. The war with Bernicia is coming soon, and we could do with a fine warrior like you at our side. Glyn fell from the castle wall, and I am sorry," I told him. "Blood is always spilled in war – but we could be on the same side, you and I, both fighting for the Kingdom of Rheged together. I will do all in my power to be the king your people deserve," I swore to him.

He regarded me for a moment and then ere long he gave one nod. "Very well," Conall assented. "I cannot promise to serve you, but I can promise not to slay you once I am freed."

It was my turn to nod and I drew my sword then to cut his bonds. "That will do for the present," I told him.

Conall did not reply for a moment as he rubbed his wrists where the ropes had been. Then with a final nod, he departed my company. I replaced my sword and left the now empty cell.

I stood for a moment in the dank dungeon, the exit on the left, before I turned deliberately in the other direction. I was to pay Reghan, the former king of Gaeson, a visit. I knew this course of action was perhaps not the wisest, but the sensation of a knife twisting in my stomach had grown too strong to ignore. I wondered how my uncle could resist not going into his cell and slaying Reghan himself, but perhaps a lifetime of waging war had diluted his thirst for rage and revenge, whereas I could feel the emotion, strong as it could be as a man, surging through me like a poison.

"I wondered when you would ordain to see me." There was a triumphant smirk across his face, as if my coming had already made him the victor. Why had I come armed? I asked myself. The temptation to strike his neck was too strong – it was only the thought of his daughter which stayed my blade.

"You murdered my parents." It was a statement, not a question. Reghan's smirk faded, and now his countenance was impossible to read. "Also my aunt and my cousin," I continued hotly, stepping closer to where he was restrained. Strange, how not that many days ago I had been ready to give my life for him, and now it was all I could do not to kill him.

"Of that I am aware," he replied drily. How could he stare at me so coldly and reply so? I wondered. He must have seen my expression, for now his eyes narrowed. "You are expecting remorse? Regret? You are still a child, boy." He snarled almost like a monster, and then his sadistic smile was back. "So naïve to the acquisition of power. How many men and women of your own kind have you killed, in service of me? What a wonderful irony that is. Do you not think they would have been someone's child, someone's parent, someone's friend?" He posed the question with a dangerous softness, as he had done when his daughter had confronted him the night he had abdicated.

"Actions in war are different from murder. I do not assassinate royalty whilst they sleep innocent in their beds," I replied calmly.

His eyes widened and he smiled. "Is that so?" he questioned me, eyebrows raised slightly. "How blessed you are to have such an unshakable moral code. Are you sure, it was all that different? All kings need power and to secure their position. It was my order to kill those of Cedric's family, but not my hand. That was carried out by decent men, soldiers in my service, no doubt friends with your father," Reghan continued. "What if you were one of those soldiers, still loyal to me as you once were?" His voice had lowered again. "What if I had told you that Cedric was planning to attack Gaeson, and to assassinate him was the only chance of Gaeson's survival? Would your unswerving loyalty have been questioned, or would you have carried out my word?"

"My uncle is a king, Reghan," I retorted, knowing I was not answering his question which was turning my insides. "You will pay him all due respect."

"Look how the prince taunts his captor!" Reghan gave a hollow laugh. "What would you have done, though?" he persisted. "If you believed in the goodness of your king and you knew it would bring peace, would you not have obeyed me?"

"I will not listen to this," I declared, already regretting the folly of coming here – but I wanted to look this man in the eyes, to hold him accountable for what he had done. Yet he had simply tried to justify his actions. "No argument you give can justify what you have done. You did not do it other than for your own selfish greed."

"Is that not the actions of every king? You think your precious uncle has never shed dirty blood? All kings are corrupt, man. Or queens," he sneered, as I began to walk away. My heart stilled as I twirled back at him. "You think my daughter so innocent and good? War would drive her to unspeakable things, Daniel. She might yet murder royals in their beds."

"How dare you!" My hand had left my side and struck him hard before I even realised it. My fist had come into contact with his nose, and as blood spilled forth he gave a howl – but it was of laughter, not pain. There was enough slack in his restraints for him to take a hand to his nose and hold it to stem the bleeding, but he continued laughing as his blood trickled into his mouth. From his prolonged hysteria, we both knew who had won our exchange. Alas, the rage surged in me too strong, and presently I drew my sword, holding it up against his neck as I had done the night of his abdication – but this time there was no one here to stop me.

"Go on," Reghan goaded me with a sneer. "I can feel the hatred, it is quite understandable. Kill your former king."

The temptation was so strong; the desire to puncture his neck with my blade and watch as the blood drained out of him, this man who murdered my parents that I could barely remember and the cousin I would never know.

"Go on," he repeated in a murmur, his eyes filled with such a frenzy I wondered if he were mad. I shifted my sword an inch upward, unsure of what I would do. Suddenly, in the midst of my rage, I sensed somewhere within his eyes a resemblance to Queen Evelyn. The thought came to me that I was not just taking revenge on the man who had murdered most of my family – I would be killing the father of the woman I loved.

This notion caused my anger to lessen greatly, though it did not altogether dissipate. Slowly, I lowered my sword and replaced it with a heavy clunk before there was no turning back. Through the blood coming from his nose, I saw Reghan looked almost disappointed.

"You are wrong," I said flatly. "Being a king does not mean that you simply live as you see fit. There is a higher king, who sees all – and all that we do should be at his governing. He tells us to love our enemies," I ended, and Reghan gave another loud laugh.

"You really still believe there is an almighty being who watches over us?"

I paused a moment to pluck a spare cloth from my tunic and handed it to him; he promptly put it to his nose to better stop the blood.

"I do," I replied heavily, and he began to chuckle with scorn again. "Farewell," I told him shortly, and departed before he could poison me any further. I did not stop moving, even though in my peripheral vision I saw the interrogator – even as I saw the glint in his eye and the smirk upon his face that told me he had witnessed it all and would soon tell the queen – for my priority was to leave before my anger any further got the better of me.

I soon left the castle behind, swiftly travelling until I reached the castle stables, not far beyond the square. I paced inside to find two hired hands at work.

"Leave," I ordered abruptly to them, as they hastily stopped work and bowed. "You may return to your duties later." They bowed again a little clumsily and at once departed.

Now alone, I closed my eyes briefly and breathed in deeply the scent that was so familiar to me. A few tears of rage and nigh despair at what I had done rolled down my cheeks; I bowed my head to the stable floor and prayed for forgiveness for what had just transpired.

Gradually, my irate breathing eased and I became calmer. I opened my eyes again and mechanically brought myself to my feet. I began to walk, at a much slower pace, down through the cubicles. I did this until I met Epos, who shook her head and neighed softly as her ears twitched in recognition.

"Hello, old girl," I greeted her softly, raising a hand to her head and stroking her there. "Are you happy to be home?" I reached into a packet of oats and fed her some, and she snorted happily in response. I found I envied her contentment. I stayed in the stables for some time, chiding myself for my folly and awaiting the consequences of my actions.

"So, Prince Bryce." News travels at speed, I thought grimly, as I turned to face Queen Evelyn. I did not need speculate as to the reason for this sudden visit. She greeted me so formally; it was the first time she had used my Klumeck name.

"Your Majesty," I responded gravely with a bow. I folded over the bag of oats and put it back down; as I did so, I noted absently the guard who accompanied her; the same guard who had shown me to my chambers the previous day.

"Leave us," she ordered the guard who had escorted her, who bowed low and retreated. I noted absently it was the same guard who had shown me to my chambers the previous day. "I just spoke with the prison interrogator. Daniel, please tell me what he has said is not true."

Shame prickled me and I could hold my eyes no longer; I lowered my gaze to the floor.

"Well?" she prompted me, and I raised my head back up. My lady's gaze was difficult to read, but I sensed anger behind it, lurking so far unseen. I gleaned also how much she desired me to deny the interrogator's claims.

"What did he tell you?" It was a brief evasion, nothing more.

Queen Evelyn's eyes hardened; we both knew I was avoiding the question – but then she seemed to allow it. "He told me that you went to my father," she answered in a measured tone, "that you nigh broke his nose, and put your blade to his throat and nearly killed him."

I rubbed my hands, letting the remaining oats on my fingers drop softly to the floor. What had I done?

"Then what he has said is true," I replied wearily. I saw her harden in anger, saw the disappointment in her features. "Though I wish it was not and am sorry that it is the truth," I was quick to point out. "No doubt you have had that interrogator's version of events."

"No version of what you have done could be considered noble or justified!" Queen Evelyn retorted, her anger coming to the surface now. "You attacked my father," she stated bitterly. "He may not be the king, but I am his daughter and the queen. Far lesser things have been considered treason!" she shouted, with full rage in her voice.

"I know, my lady," I replied wearily, for what else could I say? I was in possession of all the facts. I knew my life could well be forfeit again – as many times as in many days, it seemed. "But you do not understand the whole of the event."

"Little more needs to be explained; it is all too clear what you have done," she said, glaring. "I shall have to consider this," she continued angrily. "You best pray I am in a more merciful mood." She turned to leave.

"Would you really have me condemned to death?" I questioned, perhaps against my better judgement, "when King Cedric has sought for his heir for so long? If you had me slain, you could provoke war when we have just made peace."

"Oh, but you are a naïve boy!" Queen Evelyn unleashed her fury, much to my shock. "You take advantage of your new position," she snarled, "but you do not realise how your actions of folly could provoke war regardless?"

I frowned in confusion.

"Yes, you are indeed ignorant," she confirmed, nodding. "How weak does it make me appear if I allow a Klumeck royal to attack my father and I do nothing?"

My eyes widened.

"You have not thought of this other than your own selfishness." She finished her speech and my shoulders sagged, defeated. She turned and headed out of the stables; I followed her in haste.

"Perhaps no one yet knows," I called out urgently. "It is possible that my folly could remain unknown," I ventured.

She turned back to me. "Well, of course," she snapped. "I had the foresight to swear him to silence after he had informed me of his claims. No doubt he wants me to charge me with treason, especially now we have dismissed him. Either way, I do not trust that snake." She turned back to me, anger still her prevalent emotion. "How could you betray me like this?"

"How?" I shouted, anger welling in me before I could prevent it, at the sheer disbelief at her audacity to ask such a question. "Have you forgotten what your father is, or what he has done? He as good as murdered my parents!"

There was a moment of silence after this outburst, and we regarded each other across the field. I realised she stood almost exactly where she had done when we had first met.

"He murdered my parents, my aunt and my unborn cousin," I stated. "Your father did this," I repeated slowly, seeming to realise anew that Queen Evelyn was her father's daughter. It was an obvious statement, but it was the first time Reghan's actions had had any impact on the way I thought of her. For the first time since I was a boy, standing in the snow and making the vow to serve her, I felt as though my love for her had become complicated.

"I am sorry for what he has done," Queen Evelyn returned now, the pause over, "but that does not justify your own actions. King Cedric has not attempted such vengeance – and it was his own wife and child!"

"He has had years to have his rage grow stale," I said, my voice calmer now. "He might well have killed your father had he the chance. Or perhaps he is just a better man than I am," I conceded. "At any rate, it was not just self notions, like vengeance or anger, that motivated my actions," I continued, a little more hotly. "I also did it for your honour."

"What?" Queen Evelyn's voice rose, indignant. "What possible reason could attacking my father be for my honour?"

"Because he claimed that you would one day be just as corrupt as he was," I replied. My lady's eyes widened slightly. "That you, like your father, could order the assassination of innocents, just for your own power and greed. I could not bear to have your character so slandered. The idea that someone as good as you could fall to evil… it was unthinkable."

She said nothing for a moment, and we simply regarded each other.

"I am not above evil and corruption, Daniel," she murmured, her voice becoming a little softer, "but thank you for your faith in me. It does not make what you did right, however," she rebuked me, her voice becoming sterner again. "You could have put him to the sword. What stopped you? You had enough anger," she commented.

"It was the thought of you," I told her honestly, and her eyes widened. "The thought of the harm it would do you was what stayed my hand."

Queen Evelyn frowned. "Three days ago when I visited you in the cell," she said now wearily, "you told me that you would never cause me harm – that, in fact, you would die first." Her meaning was clear – in my actions, I had caused her pain and therefore had broken my word.

"That was, is and always will be my desire, my lady," I affirmed. "But my limitations as a human man means I may not be able to keep that promise. As you yourself said – all of us are capable of falling."

Queen Evelyn regarded me a moment longer and then nodded. From a distance across the field, I could see the guard coming back.

"I am truly sorry, Your Majesty, for the pain my actions have caused you, and for the difficult position this has put you in," I told her in the few moments we had before the guard returned. "If I can do anything to help rectify my folly, I will do so."

She nodded a final time and opened her mouth – but closed it again as the guard drew near.

"Your Majesty," he stated as he bowed. "I apologise for disrupting your meeting with His Royal Highness, but there is a matter in court of a rather urgent nature."

"Very well," she said to the guard, and then glanced once more my way. "I shall see you at the coronation tomorrow," she stated. "Farewell, Prince Bryce, for the present," she concluded formally.

"Farewell, Your Majesty," I responded, and bowed low. I watched her retreat back towards the castle, and then headed back inside the stables, heading distractedly back to Epos' cubicle.

"This day could have gone better," I said to Epos, who neighed loudly as if in agreement. It had only been a few hours since King Urien's meeting, and in the space of one afternoon I had given the queen enough cause to end my life. I prayed in time she would forgive me.

I stayed in the stables another few minutes before leaving, walking the solitary road of one who knows he has done wrong and knows not how to rectify it. I returned to the castle but headed into Gaeson town, knowing Sarah would have been told by now to move to the castle. I returned to the street of my old home to see John and Aife loading boxes of what I presumed to be Sarah's belongings onto a cart.

"Your Highness," they greeted me with a bow as they saw me, before Aife lifted another box.

"With the royal guard fully occupied, the captain asked us to aid Princess Lynette in the move," John explained. "Is that all, Your Highness?" he added to Sarah as she came outside, another box in her hands.

"Yes, I think so. I am thankful I do not have many possessions. My lord," Sarah abruptly greeted me as she spotted me. "John, Aife, would you check I have nothing left in the house?"

The two of them gave a short bow in assent and went back inside my home.

"I did not realise I would have to leave home so soon," Sarah confided.

"I know. I am sorry," I replied. "Queen Evelyn said earlier it was our royal obligation to reside in the castle for as long as we remain in Gaeson."

"But that will not be for long," Sarah replied with a frown. "It hardly seems logical to move just for a few days."

"It is what Her Majesty has said," I replied, a little wearily, as I was still rather animated from my heated conversation with the queen.

Sarah must have perceived my tone, for she raised her eyebrows. "Is everything well with you, brother?"

"Of course," I replied airily – but my change in tone was a little too obvious. "I am a little tired; that is all," I added quickly.

"Well, that is no surprise," Sarah agreed, but the slight frown on her countenance told me she did not believe that was all it was.

"I believe that is all, my lady," Aife said, as she and John came back out of the house, "if you are ready to depart for the castle."

"I think so," Sarah answered with a little sigh as she looked at our old home. "Do not worry about Enid," she added to me, as John and Aife ensured all her belongings were secure on the cart. "We can employ another to take care of your mother, and I assume Rachel will be staying in the house." I noted a sadness in her tone; dealing with the affairs of my house and caring for my mother had become her employment for several years.

"I will find it difficult to find anyone to perform those duties quite as well as you," I murmured to her.

Sarah smiled in thanks.

"Come, sister," I added, putting a hand on her shoulder. "Let us go to the castle."

***

"John, Aife," I greeted my comrades as they entered my chamber, and they bowed as they saw me. It was a few hours later, and I had sent a message for them to join me; I needed their company after today's events. Sarah had declined the offer to come; she said she wished to get used to her new identity, which I well understood.

"Please sit." I gestured to the table and opened a bottle of mead. "No more bows tonight," I informed them both. "Consider that an order. It is not 'Your Highness' either, or 'sire'."

Aife smiled widely. "Had enough of royalty, my lord? You said nothing of that term," she grinned, and John chuckled. I feigned annoyance, but I was glad I could banter with my friends once more.

"I am Daniel, just as I always have been," I said, and I smiled back. I poured us each a generous measure. "Yes, I am tired of royalty," I admitted. "I am used to following orders, not giving them." I took a gulp of mead. "Sarah found out the truth today," I confided. "She seems to be taking it well. It has been a shock, of course – I have had several days to get used to my new identity, whereas Sarah has only had these few days. She only has this night left before she is forced into the public sphere."

"Sarah is strong," Aife reassured me. "I am sure she will handle it well." She paused here. "Is there something else on your mind?" she asked me, and I gave a small smile at this, for these two had always been able to tell when something was troubling me.

"Nothing," I lied, though I could tell they were not convinced by my attempts to be an impassive soldier.

"Something happened today and it was not good," I admitted, my thoughts instantly taking me back to my encounter with King Reghan. "I do not wish to discuss it, though," I added. "More mead?" I refilled their glasses before they could speak further. Aife and John said nothing further, though I knew they would wish to discuss it more.

As we talked about other things, already I was distracted by the awful events that had happened this day. I hoped I would be able to speak to my queen tomorrow, and that she would forgive me for the wrong I had done her. Most of all, I prayed that it would not adversely affect me being in her service – but only time would tell.

Chapter Eleven

It was now the day of the coronation and I went over to the palace hall at just before noon. I still had not spoken to Queen Evelyn since our encounter the previous day, and I knew not what she would think of me now. I gave a short bow in greeting to them all.

"Prince Bryce," Queen Evelyn said formally, but I saw a little more coldness in her eyes than usual, and I swallowed.

"Your Majesty," I replied. "I hope the day finds you well." She gave me a brief nod, and then as the captain walked in she immediately turned to speak to him. I went and stood next to Sarah on the other side of the room.

"Daniel, brother," Sarah greeted me and walked over, a frown upon her face. "Is everything well with you?" she asked quietly. She was also looking at Queen Evelyn, but I chose not to indulge her curiosity.

"Of course," I muttered back. "How are you feeling about the coronation?" I asked quickly, before she could comment further on my lady's slightly colder than normal response.

Her eyes narrowed slightly, but then she seemed to allow the change in subject. "A little anxious," Sarah admitted, "but I suppose as a royal now I need to get used to the public sphere."

"You will do fine," I replied with a smile as genuine as I could make it, still pondering as I was the queen's current regard for me.

The double doors opened, and King Urien swept into the room with all the regal finery he had displayed when entering the meeting chambers yesterday. Queen Evelyn and Sarah gave a low curtsey each, whilst the rest of us bowed.

"Princess Lynette, I presume." King Urien strode over to her, immediately surveying her under his stern gaze. "Finally, both the heirs have been restored to Klumeck's kingdom and all six royals are together. The only one missing is your fool of a father," he suddenly added to Queen Evelyn. "Do not forget, I have not yet decided his fate. No doubt his time in the dungeons is doing the rat some good."

Queen Evelyn said nothing, simply inclined her head at him. At the mention of her father, I could not help but risk a glance in her direction; she met my gaze, but her expression was unreadable, as it had often been of late.

"It is an honour to meet you, Your Majesty," Sarah replied quietly.

King Urien gave her a nod and then proceeded to move on to converse with his son, Prince Owain. I saw also that King Cedric began speaking to Sarah, and so seized the chance to speak to Queen Evelyn.

"Your Majesty," I greeted her quietly after walking over, determined to reconcile before the coronation started, "if I might speak to you regarding our conversation yesterday..."

"It was a little more than a conversation, Daniel," Queen Evelyn interrupted stonily, "but this is hardly the time or the place."

"I know, my lady... but my conscience cannot bear it any longer unless I apologise once more for yesterday's events – and wholeheartedly beg your forgiveness," I said hastily. She glanced at me then, seeming to ponder my request, and then finally nodded.

"Very well, then, you have it," she replied, and at once my heart soared with gratitude and relief, even with her voice still a little colder than usual. "I can well understand your rage and desire for vengeance," my lady continued. "If most of my family had been murdered, and I could have a few moments alone with the killer, I might well have attempted the same. Think of the anger I had yesterday at you making his nose bleed," she reflected, with some irony in her tone. "The interrogator knows he speaks at forfeit of his life; he knows that any word of it would be traced back to him. Therefore you need not fear any consequences for your actions."

"I thank you unreservedly, my lady," I murmured, bowing my head in thanks. "Your grace and mercy is more than I deserve."

"I fear you may have too high an opinion of me," she replied wryly. "I know also your actions were because of my honour, and it was on my account that you stayed your blade," she continued, her voice slightly softer. "Though I disagreed with your actions, I knew you had heart behind them." She paused, and I lingered over her choice of words. Did she really know the full contents of my heart? Did she know, even though it was complicated because of who her father was, how much I still loved her? Our gazes held and I searched for any hidden meaning, but found none.

"Are we ready to begin?" King Urien asked loudly. Queen Evelyn and I broke our eye contact immediately and turned towards him. As King Urien began to explain the procedure of the ceremony. In my peripheral vision, I saw Sarah glancing my way with a frown upon her face, but refused to turn and look at her, instead concentrating on King Urien to hide my embarrassment. Privately I wondered how long Sarah had been looking at us; even though I had not said anything that would reveal my heart, I still felt somehow my sister's gaze had intruded onto something. Another set of double doors opened – the ones that would lead through the great hall and out onto the square – and I put all these thoughts aside, for it was nearly time for the coronation to commence.

The town square was crowded with people, and it was even busier with the armies of Klumeck and Caer Ligualid joining us. The palace hall had as many people as could physically fit. With true grace and elegance, Queen Evelyn ascended the few steps to her throne at the back of the palace hall. King Urien too walked up to stand beside her; he was the official and so would place the crown upon her head. The rest of the monarchs stood perpendicular to the throne. At the front of the audience were John, Aife, and the captains of Gaeson and of Klumeck.

The ceremony began, and King Urien conducted the service with ease and splendour. After the queen received her coronation, King Urien looked to Sarah and me and gave a simple yet ornate gesture of his hand. There were two smaller, simpler crowns near him. My mouth had gone dry, but I ignored this as Sarah and I walked forwards. I was pleased again for my regimental training, for I was able to feign a confidence that I did not feel.

"Kneel," King Urien ordered directly.

Sarah and I obeyed, coming to kneel before him.

He gave a few ceremonial words and suddenly it was over, with a crown that didn't quite fit upon my head. "Hail, His Royal Highness Prince Bryce of Klumeck and hail, Her Royal Highness Princess Lynette of Klumeck," King Urien declared.

I smiled; the name was less and less strange to me each time it was used. I wondered briefly if my parents were standing in heaven gathered with the rest of the saints, whether they would be looking down with pride at us finally being recognised as their children.

King Urien now offered his arm to Queen Evelyn, and the two of them walked to the side of the hall to ascend the steps leading to the balcony. My uncle and Prince Owain next, walking with the ease of ones who were used to public walks and speeches, of royal custom and duty. Sarah and I fell into line behind them and I offered her my arm, and as I did so I was suddenly anxious she would ask something about the conversation she had witnessed between myself and Queen Evelyn. Sarah merely smiled, however – an easy smile that made me speculate she had been most nervous about the formality that had just passed. Indeed, I shared some of that ease; the only thing now left for the day would be listening to Queen Evelyn's formal speech on the balcony, smiling and waving at the crowds, enjoying the feast, and dancing in the evening. Plus, I was still feeling the elation of being forgiven for my actions yesterday.

We had now come to a stop on the balcony above the square – the same one we had been standing on when I had been officially pardoned and ordered by my queen to touch the rail only those of royal blood were allowed to touch. As Queen Evelyn began her speech, speaking words of true wisdom, I found myself thinking of her father. My rage and thirst for vengeance had diluted somewhat since my encounter with him, though some anger still remained. I had observed that any mention of Reghan had been avoided with precise care. Rather we were celebrating a new monarch and peace across Rheged.

Queen Evelyn's speech was brief; she spoke of a new, unified Rheged with peace between Gaeson and Klumeck. After the speech there was a royal parade, where we rode through the city in carriages – King Urien and Prince Owain in the first carriage, Queen Evelyn and King Cedric in the next, and finally Sarah and I in a third carriage. The people were cheering and waving flags, bearing the seals of Gaeson, Klumeck and Caer Ligualid. We waved and smiled until my mouth was sore – my face had recovered a lot from its injuries, but it was still stiff.

The day continued into the feast with around two hundred people sat in the great hall, with the best food I had ever tasted. The plates were eventually cleared away and servants hurriedly pushed the tables back. More wine and mead was poured, and soon everyone was singing and dancing, but I felt restless. I found I could not join in the merriment when I knew soon I would leave all this behind – and it was almost jarring to go from my anger and sadness yesterday to such joy today; much of it seemed forced. Eventually, I left the hall to enter one of the palace gardens, seeking a few moments of quiet. I saw my sister already there, standing underneath a large oak tree.

"Hello," I greeted her with a smile, and handed her a glass of mead. "It is not often royalty can escape such an occasion, princess," I told her in good humour.

"Aye, I managed to slip out in between dances. There is a slur on your tongue, brother; you should not have much more."

I smiled further, knowing she was right, but almost in spite of such wisdom I then took another mouthful.

"It is a magnificent feast, is it not?"

"It is," I agreed. I came to lean against the tree, the two of us standing together under the canopy of the stars. "Though all I can think of is how we are soon to leave this place." I looked up towards the sky. "Will the stars be much different in Klumeck, do you think?"

"I know not," Sarah replied quietly. "I shall miss Enid, despite learning the truth. I meant to tell you, I told her I knew the truth. I nearly didn't," she added, "but they were words that needed to be said. She said she was sorry to have kept such deception, told me that Bridget had been one of her closest friends and how much she had grieved her. We were both shedding a few tears by the end."

"Of course," I agreed easily. "I shall miss John and Aife, also. I am so glad you are coming with me," I told her after another drink of mead. "You would be one of the people I would miss most."

"I share that sentiment," she returned with a smile. "If leaving Gaeson is the price to pay for having you as a brother, then I shall gladly pay it." She brought the mead to her mouth again and we stood there a moment, the two of us together.

"I shall miss Rachel and the children, also," she ventured airily. "I can think of lots of friends I would miss," she continued casually, and suddenly, far too late, I saw the trap she was verbally planning for me. "Is there someone in particular you shall miss?" There was something almost knowing, almost mocking, in her tone.

"No one immediately comes to mind," I replied neutrally, carefully. Could she know? I wondered quickly. "Except perhaps the captain," I added casually, attempting humour. Sarah merely nodded and smiled, and I felt relief that the subject was dropped.

Suddenly, she sighed. "It will indeed be sad to leave here," she added, and her sorrow resonated with me.

It was my turn to nod, my throat at once tight at the thought of our departure. I thought of the landscape of Gaeson now, from the stables to the town and the forest beyond. Behind us, of course, at the other end of the castle, was the view of the lake, which I could presently imagine sparkling and glimmering in the moonlight. Were we really to leave this place behind? The place I had given my whole life defending? As a simple soldier, I had known I would probably die in battle. Either way, I had believed to have been born in Gaeson, and I had believed I would die in Gaeson, or in a battlefield defending her. Was I now to leave?

"Let us go back inside, sister," I told her, feeling flat, for I could not help her. She nodded. I held out my arm and she linked hers around it, and we walked through the double doors back into the banquet hall.

I lifted my arm to taste more mead, but it stopped halfway to my mouth. King Cedric was talking to Queen Evelyn, and he seemed very urgent in his manner.

"Something is wrong," I murmured to Sarah. Indeed, I had hardly expressed this sentiment when John suddenly appeared next to us.

"Your Highnesses," he said swiftly, and bowed. "I was sent to relay to you an important message from the captain. He sent a group to apprehend some spies from Bernicia. A small group of the spies were captured, sire."

My eyes widened. "The spies who attempted to kidnap the queen? The spies who caused our watchmen to slumber when Klumeck attacked?" How strange it was to think back to that night, when my uncle was still my mortal foe.

John inclined his head in a nod.

"At last," I murmured. "Have they said anything?"

"Aye, sire," John responded. "Under duress from our interrogators, the spies revealed to us what the Bernicians are planning to do next. According to the spies," he continued, "they plan to attack Klumeck. King Cedric is readying your people now."

"Klumeck," I echoed in a harsh gasp. I glanced over; King Cedric was still intently conversing with Queen Evelyn – and now the captain was present there also.

Without another word, the three of us hastily made our way over to the three of them. By this point I detected a change in the feast's atmosphere – people had begun to notice something was wrong – soldiers were reporting for duty, and nobles and officials were returning to their homes.

"Prince Bryce; Princess Lynette," Queen Evelyn said directly as we ran over. "The captain has just told me he can ready half our people to journey with you through the night."

"Thank you for this most generous offer, Your Majesty," King Cedric replied. "If there was any doubt remaining of your allegiance to Rheged, it has now been cast aside. Perhaps King Urien can also give us some of us his men…"

"Alas, I cannot do that," King Urien cut in gravely, in his usual steely tone. We all bowed. "This is indeed a tragedy," he stated, "but remember it is only one battle that is probably already won. We need to start preparing for the bigger war – I cannot spare any of my men to salvage something that will no doubt be already half destroyed."

"With respect, sire," King Cedric retorted hotly, "this is my home and my kingdom! I have just spent twenty-one years searching for my heirs; am I only to find them now my lands are about to be destroyed?"

"Many kings have lost their kingdoms in this war," King Urien replied quietly. "Most of your people will have already fled to Caer Ligualid," he added. "Prince Owain and I will travel back to aid them. I bid you good speed," he said, and with a swish of his cloak he had gone.

King Cedric cursed under his breath. "Well, it's not going to help our people just standing here," he remarked angrily. "Make haste!"

The soldiers began to run out of the room to get ready.

"Farewell, sister," I murmured, touching Sarah's arm briefly – and then she left my sight as I ran in the direction of the armoury.

Within half an hour we were off, people from Gaeson and Klumeck united as never before. I only regretted the cause of such unity. Riding along with me in the front line was King Cedric, the two captains of the guard from both kingdoms, and John and Aife. It was only a little less distance from Gaeson to Klumeck as Gaeson was to Caer Ligualid – both were roughly a day's journey away if we rode hard and true. As we rode, I tried to sort the confused emotions of my heart – three weeks ago I could have been riding to Klumeck for battle, and now I was riding to aid her. Three weeks ago Klumeck was my enemy, and now I was next in line to the throne, a throne I wasn't at all sure I wanted, but was my duty by blood.

As we journeyed on, I realised how unfortunate it was that the news had come just after the coronation feast; most of us were still half drunk on mead and wine. It was probably designed as such by the Bernicians – these spies might well have known it was tonight we planned the celebrations, so that if we found out their plan, we would be coming to Klumeck's aid

244

intoxicated. The compensation to this was that there was nothing like riding through the cold night in order to sober oneself up. I pondered, rather selfishly for a moment, whether I would ever return to a normal sleeping pattern – my slumber routine had been off ever since I had woken up in Caer Ligualid. Now was not the time, however, to worry about sleep – I shook these thoughts from my head.

"Come on, girl, that's it," I murmured to Epos, tapping her neck for encouragement. We had been riding for roughly twelve hours; as we travelled I had noted distractedly the sky's changing from midnight blue to grey as the dawn paled. The morn came cloudy and soon the rain began to fall – the first rain I had seen in some weeks, although I supposed it could have rained whilst I had been unconscious.

The incline began to grow steeper as we headed towards the tall hills where Klumeck was based. Klumeck was a fortress just before the hills began, with a large wall carved into the steep landscape. It was originally chosen by King Cedric's ancestor to be the last line of defence, as on the other side of the hills lay the Kingdom of Bernicia.

The first thing we saw as the fortress of Klumeck finally came into view was the smoke. Vast, big pillars of it, stretching wide and far into the sky. We spurred our horses faster, in fear of what we would find. As we galloped closer, we began to see the flames – vicious flames that licked up the ground, blazing everything it touched.

"There are people alive down there, sire," Aife commented, her sharp eyes spotting the survivors first. We spurred our horses on faster, though they were weary to the point of exhaustion. It was verging almost on cruel as she whined, but I had no choice if we were going to spare any lives this day. As we neared the fortress I saw a man, an ordinary villager, trying to defend himself with a thick slab of wood against a soldier. I kept Epos going until the last possible moment before drawing my sword and thrusting it into my foe's side.

Our presence had now been detected and the rest of the Bernician force turned as I leapt from Epos, not wanting to cause her further harm. I landed on the wet grass, my boots sinking a little in the sodden ground. Aife and John were on either side of me now, and together the three of us ran forwards to meet the enemy line. Soon the other warriors from Klumeck and Gaeson had followed suit and we crashed into the Bernician scourge with considerable force. Our swords clanged and parried in the grey rain; out of my peripheral vision, I saw more villagers leave their homes.

Even from the outset, I knew we had the advantage. Our enemies had relied on us not knowing of their plan and this meant they had not come with enough reinforcements; in short they were severely outnumbered. The battle did not last long; such was my passion for these people that I put to the sword any that came in my way. Soon, the Bernicians began to flee and I considered giving them chase, but even before I could voice it, King Cedric raised his hand and we looked towards him.

"Let them run," he instructed hotly as he put away his sword. "The people are our first priority. Do all you can to help them," he ordered simply.

I put my own sword away and helped another soldier to his feet, looking about whilst the others searched the area for those in need of aid. I saw now that Klumeck's castle was far smaller than I had anticipated, and so was its town – if it could be called a town, as it was more like a village. Most houses had been burnt down and pillaged. I estimated perhaps one thousand people had lived here, whereas the people in Gaeson would be around five times that number. Now even as people began to put out the fires, it would be clear the place had been destroyed. The castle itself was now in ruins.

I glanced again at my uncle, who had not spoken any further but was simply staring into the fire that had been his kingdom – even I could tell that though we had beaten them, this small enemy battalion had still won; we had simply come too late.

"Uncle..." I murmured, and he glanced towards me, his countenance hard like any king's would be. I swallowed as any words of consolation I could think of became stuck in my throat. The kingdom I had been due to inherit was burnt to the ground and still burning; from this distance, though we were safe, we could feel the intense flames on the ground. All was smouldering fire and ash. Bodies lay charred and strewn about. "I'm sorry," I said, feeling foolish and useless.

"We thought we had more time before this horror was unleashed upon us," King Cedric replied gravely. "The spies would have known I was not present. I never should have left them," he finished bitterly.

"This was not your doing, Uncle. It was the Bernicians, as you said. You would have appointed a good steward in your place. There are not too many dead," I added, scanning the ground. "Most of them will have escaped."

"Let us pray you are right." It was not my uncle who had spoken these words, but it was a voice I well knew. I swiftly turned to see a soldier put their sword away. The soldier lifted up their helmet, but I already knew who it was.

"Sarah," I greeted, a little harsher than I meant as I strode the few steps to her. "What are you I doing here?"

"I wanted to help," she replied earnestly. "I did not think you would let me come, if you knew my intentions. I may not have been in the army, brother," Sarah continued before I could voice my protest, "but I've known how to handle a sword almost as long as you have. I needed to come, Daniel. I needed to see this place, to see, where we were both born and where our true parents lived. I knew well the risks," she concluded.

"It does ease my heart a little to see you both here," King Cedric said now, "even in these dark times. Come, let us see if there is anything we can salvage." My uncle dismounted his horse and we walked towards the flames.

There were some soldiers who had survived the onslaught. They were gathered in a corner. Some were weeping for all they had lost; others were grimly staring around. A short talk with them allowed us to glean an account. The steward of Klumeck had done right by ordering the village to evacuate, and had fought bravely whilst the villagers had escaped. Fortunately, according to the soldiers, it seemed the Bernicians had had enough mercy not to hunt them all down, but allowed most of the people to escape. However, the bodies of dead Klumeck citizens were scattered all around. Most of them were soldiers who would have died fighting for their land and their people –

but a few looked as though they had simply been caught up in the flames, trapped in the fires they could not control.

After a moment I curled my fist, beat it against my chest and then raised it out in front of me – the sign used in Gaeson to honour the dead. Out of the corner of my eye I saw John, Sarah, the captain, and the other Gaeson soldiers perform the same symbol. After a moment, the Klumeck soldiers did the same gesture. My heart lightened a little to know that they were united with me in this. It was like an affirmation that we truly were brothers and sisters now, lamenting together what we had lost.

Sarah and I began to walk among the ruins of Klumeck in silence, my soul devastated by the blood that had been spilt. A large number of the soldiers were attempting to put the fire out, and as the flames slowly receded we could begin to see the extent of the damage; the fortress was in ruins and it broke my heart. For although my heart would have been saddened to leave Gaeson, I had grown used to the idea of coming here, to the place where my parents had lived and died. It was with a heavy sadness I now knew I would never be able to see Klumeck as it had once been.

Soon the fires were out and we could see an area of the fortress that had not been touched by the flames – it looked structurally sound still. In truth, I felt a desperate kind of yearning to identify myself with this place, to connect somehow with this life I could no longer remember. Though now in ashes, I knew this kingdom was still part of who I was. I glanced at Sarah and wondered if that desire to see Klumeck was even stronger in her; at least I had some glimpsing memories of our parents, whereas Sarah would have been too young to remember anything.

We entered into the castle fortress through a side gate that had escaped the fire. We found ourselves in long, thin corridors that triggered no immediate memory. There was little that had not been in the fire, and soon we had been in almost every room we could.

"Do you remember anything?" Sarah asked quietly, her voice vaguely hopeful.

I shook my head, trying to squash a stab of disappointment.

"Perhaps we lived in another area of the castle," she said, by way of encouragement.

"Perhaps," I agreed flatly. "Come, let us see if we can be more useful," I said decisively, and we both turned – but then, out of the corner of my eye, I caught sight of a door we had not yet opened. The door seemed ordinary enough, but as I stared at it I felt more compelled to open this room than any other chamber we had seen.

"Brother?" Sarah questioned me, her voice barely above a whisper.

My breathing tense, I made my way slowly to the chamber, walking the last few yards in trepidation, and then I was there, putting my hand on the door knob. I glanced at my sister.

"I wonder," I murmured, and tried the handle. The door was unlocked but heavy, and as I pressed my weight against it, inch by inch it opened.

As soon as I saw the chamber, recognition filled me. It was such a strange experience – I had no memory of this place and yet I knew it. There were lush, red carpets across the floor with golden tassels at either end. Abruptly I saw myself, as a three-year-old boy, running around the carpet, enjoying the soft feel beneath my feet.

"What do you remember?" Sarah asked, but I was transfixed. For, rather abruptly, I could suddenly see my mother in my mind's eye. She was walking around the room, in her arms carrying a baby.

"Daniel?" she prompted, her voice slightly louder.

"I see our mother," I answered her ere long. As I studied her – the woman who had borne me – I suddenly felt like I had always been dreaming of her face, but had immediately forgotten her upon waking and found the images disappearing the more I tried to clutch them within my grasp. "She is holding you," I added, hearing the rough emotion of my own voice. I saw her now, in my mind's eye, lower herself and Sarah carefully to the floor as my toddler self clambered onto her.

"Hello there, darling." Such love; such warmth in her voice! The vivid auburn of her long cascading hair; the smile upon her face. I felt the simple security in her voice. "Little Lynette has just awoken from her slumber."

"Lynny." My toddler self smiled as I took hold of her outstretched fingers, a happy smile on my infant sister's face. It was such a powerful image – my mother holding my sister and me in her arms – that I had a sudden pang of loneliness and longing for her comfort that it almost made me want to weep. Though I knew I had been well loved by Enid, the woman who had raised me in Gaeson, I felt severe pain at being separated from the one who had given birth to me. The one who had known me and loved me first.

"I am sorry for all that was taken from us," Sarah muttered, seeming to sense my emotions. She took a step closer to me and reached down and put her hand in mine. I turned to her and managed to give her a weak smile.

"You remember this chamber." We turned to see King Cedric in the doorway, his eyes fixed on me. "You loved this room. You used to crawl all over the red rugs on the floor." He pointed to the thick fleeces covering the floor, now old but fresh and clean. "This was where you used to sleep and play, and your mother would tell you stories, whilst your father was employed at court."

He stepped into the room now, the thickness of his beard less visible in this dim light. "You were hiding in this chamber, the night you were taken from me," he murmured. "When your mother screamed upon her death," he began heavily, "the castle maid who used to help care for you hid you in there." He pointed to the corner of the room, and we saw in that direction a large, furnished wardrobe.

"It was not until I heard Imogen scream that I knew of the danger," he continued. "I ran in haste to your parents' chamber, and was then told by a guard that they were both dead, murdered in their sleep. I ordered the guard to follow me and hurried to this room. By the time we arrived, the Gaeson soldiers had entered the room and the wardrobe door was about to be opened, but we caught them just in time."

As my uncle spoke, I began to remember it – hidden in the wardrobe holding Sarah, holding her tightly.

"Father will come and rescue us. Mother will look after us," my toddler self told her. I placed my hands hurriedly upon her ears as I heard the sounds of fighting. I was afraid, so afraid. Sarah had begun crying and I had known not how to stop her, so I had pressed my hand against her mouth to prevent her sobs being heard lest we were found.

"We cut them all down and you were safe, thank God. I took hold of you in my arms," King Cedric continued, and I suddenly became aware of the present once again.

"You promised us you would see us again soon," I said softly. "You bundled us in our cloaks and we went to the side entrance, you holding Sarah while I was running alongside. You placed us in the horse and carriage and told us you would collect us in a few days, when home had been made safe again." I could hear my uncle's urgent whisper in my head, telling me to be brave and to look after my sister.

"I saw they had meant to kill you," our uncle murmured softly. "I touched your cheek one last time... had I known it would be the last time I saw you for over twenty years, it would have been a full embrace. But there was no time; you had to go." He broke off for a second, lost in reliving what must have been such a nightmare.

"Excuse me for interrupting, Your Majesty." It was Klumeck's captain who bowed to him. "Your Highnesses," he said to us, and bowed again. "Sire, we have done our initial search of the area. We count thirty-three dead and another twenty-eight survivors, sire." This was both a relief and a tragedy – a relief that most of the people had been able to evacuate and the deaths were relatively low, but a tragedy that any had perished at all.

"Very well," King Cedric replied evenly, nodding at the captain. The captain bowed to us and then departed the chamber; he turned back to us from the threshold. "We must soon depart for Caer Ligualid to aid our people there," he said gravely. "We must leave this place; these ruins have nothing for us now." He left, and Sarah moved to follow him, but I reached out and touched her arm.

"Brother?" she questioned me, as she came to standstill.

251

I met her gaze and felt tears well in my eyes. "It has been twenty-one years since we were last in this room," I said hoarsely. "Now we have finally come here, knowing who we are. This should be home, but this is probably the last time we will ever stand here, in this chamber." I turned on the spot slowly, taking a final glance at the room; as I did I could almost see our mother's face, could almost hear her voice. "She is almost here with us; my memory is so vivid. I could almost reach out and touch it..." I outstretched my arm, but my fingers grasped at nothing.

"You can remember her, Daniel," Sarah told me quietly, and I turned back to her. "That is a prize worth more than all the gold in the world. What I wouldn't give to see her from the past, as you do," she added, as a tear fell down her face.

"I'm sorry," I muttered, taking her into an embrace. "One day, sister, you shall meet her," I assured her, taking a step back. "She trusted in God and is now rejoicing with Him, and one day we will be there also."

She nodded and smiled, wiping away the evidence of her weeping.

"Let us leave," I suggested, and we both walked together to the doorway. As we left, I turned and lingered, taking in the chamber of my childhood one last time before closing the door gently shut.

We found King Cedric outside, staring at his kingdom. Now the flames were out, the extent of the damage was visible, and it was clear Klumeck now lay in ruins. I realised now the wall behind the fortress was still intact, to my surprise. As I stared looking at it I sensed someone watching me, and as I turned I saw the Klumeck soldier, Conall. The man whose brother had fallen from the balcony wall, the one who I had spared twice in battle and released from prison in Gaeson before my encounter with King Reghan. Upon seeing me notice him, he did not do anything but continue to watch me.

"My heart is full of sorrow," I said to him eventually, "to see this place in ruins. It is strange," I continued, taking a few steps over to him, "that I feel this so strongly, given not so long ago King Cedric was still my enemy. I used to think that if I came to this fortress, it would be to attack it myself. Then I was trying to process the fact that I was King Cedric's heir and due to inherit this… that this place was about to become my home."

"This place always has been my home," Conall said now thickly, and I nodded; I could not imagine how much more devastating it would be for him. "I did not find my mother or sister among the dead," he continued now, "I pray that they have made it to Caer Ligualid safely."

"Aye," I agreed quietly. "I could remember my true parents in there," I told him, nodding at the fortress. "I now know this was my true home before I came to Gaeson. We will make them pay, Conall," I promised, turning to see him in the midst of such ruins and ashes. "This will not go unanswered."

Conall seemed to watch me for another moment before he nodded. "Yes, sire," he murmured.

I gave him another nod and began to walk back to where the Gaeson army was beginning to form their ranks, and saw Sarah and King Cedric were already there.

"Every time our foes came over the tall hills, we defeated them," King Cedric was saying to my sister. "Those group of spies must have found a longer, more dangerous way around that, avoided the wall, and opened the way for the rest of them," he added. "I am sorry, both of you, that our kingdom lies in ruins. I'm sorry you will not get your throne after all, Bryce," he added to me.

I stared once more about the destroyed fortress that would have been my home as I pondered this. It was a strange thought; ever since waking up from my fall from the cliff, I had been struggling to accept my new identity as a future king… and now my kingdom had been taken away from me just as quickly.

"Those left at Klumeck are going to Caer Ligualid, to help our people. I will try to persuade his majesty to prepare our armies for attack. I vow we will make Bernicia pay," he declared, and nodded at Klumeck's captain. I saw all his soldiers were ready to go.

"Shall I go with you, uncle?" It was the moment of truth, of whether I was to go to Gaeson or Caer Ligualid from here.

"No," King Cedric replied after a moment. "Nephew, I bid you take the men of Gaeson back. Tell Queen Evelyn all that has befallen," he instructed.

"If that is what you wish," I replied, "but could not Gaeson's captain do that? Is not my place with Klumeck?" I questioned him. Part of me could not believe my speech – I was opposing the decision to return to my home – but I was convinced that even if I no longer had a kingdom to rule, I was still the prince of these people, and I wanted to do right by them.

"Not for the time being, Bryce," King Cedric returned. "Do not forget that only a few days ago, Caer Ligualid and Klumeck marched against Gaeson, planning to put it to the sword. Reghan himself left a strong impression that he would not march against Bernicia," he continued. "If you go back with Gaeson, it is a symbol of our unity and will deter anyone thinking that Gaeson will not assist us."

"I understand," I replied, for if I returned to Gaeson, it would remind all in Caer Ligualid that Gaeson was no longer corrupt. "I will do all I can to maintain the unity of Rheged," I told him.

"Good," my uncle said simply. "May God be with both of you. I pray we will see each other soon," he stated, reaching out to put one hand on my shoulder and the other on Sarah's.

"I am sure of it," I told him earnestly. "May he also be with you, sire."

King Cedric gave a small smile then as he looked between us. A moment later and he had turned and swung up on his horse.

"Lynette," he said now, holding out his hand. She stepped forwards and took it, and another half-smile crossed his face. "It has been so good to find you at last, my dear. I am only sorry to have to depart from your company, having just found it. Your mother and father would be so proud of both of you," he continued, his eyes flickering to me briefly.

Sarah smiled and inclined her head to kiss his hand softly. "I pray you have a safe return to Caer Ligualid, uncle," she said now.

King Cedric nodded as he gathered his reins. "You best hurry, Bryce," my uncle instructed now. "We did defeat the small band here, but we let any that escaped go." He was speaking quickly, urgently. "They may be gathering reinforcements as we speak. It is not safe here. Farewell, both of you," he added, before I could reply. He raised his voice. "We march!"

The soldiers who had ridden here had given up their horses for the refugees that were left, who had already been helped onto horseback. I watched them for a moment as they headed off into the distance, in the direction of Klumeck. The line of horses soon disappeared, bearing both soldiers and the Klumeck citizens. I turned to see the men and women of Gaeson standing at attention, and it took me a moment to realise they were waiting for my command. In the space of a month, I had gone from a humble soldier to a royal prince. I was now in charge of these men and women.

"Prepare to march," I ordered. "We go back to Gaeson." The captain at once shouted out instructions, and the men who were riding saw to their horses. I was thankful to have the captain, John and Aife by my side, as well as Sarah. I turned to scan the route we would be taking and had an idea.

"Aife!" I called as I spotted her pass, and immediately she turned and came over. As she did, not for the first time I noticed how she was swift without appearing to hurry; even when she was in haste, she kept a kind of serenity about her movements.

"Your Highnesses," she bowed to us. "What are your orders, my lord prince?" she asked. I glanced once more at the route we would be taking.

"You have the best eyes of any archer I know," I stated. "I want you to take a route up to the high ground and keep your face to the horizon behind us. The Bernicians may be following us."

"Sire," she assented, and immediately ran in the direction of her horse. I watched as she swung up onto her saddle and set off immediately for the higher ground.

I went in haste to Epos, who was standing drinking water. I reached into the sack next to the saddle, retrieved some oats, and fed them to her. Despite the hour or two of rest she'd had, she still looked exhausted.

"Easy does it, girl," I soothed her, stroking her neck. "We'll be much slower on the way back." I quickly made Epos ready, and had just completed the task when Sarah walked over.

"I told the captain I'd ride with you to spare my horse," she said, and I nodded in agreement as I finished adjusting the reins.

"That should be fine. We'll just have to take it slow; she's tired enough as it is." I readied Epos for another rider and saw John out of the corner of my eye speaking to two other soldiers. "A moment, John," I called, and he immediately dismissed the men, came over and bowed to us. It was still strange to be giving orders to my old friend.

"Brother, I want you to be at the back of the lines, ensuring the injured soldiers have all the help they need. Every time I stop or I call you, I want you to come and tell me how they're doing," I instructed him.

"Very good, sire," he said simply, and left.

I swung up on Epos, and Sarah did the same behind me. It had begun to rain again; a slow drizzle seemed to incessantly pour from the sky like sleet. The captain was now also on horseback and trotted his horse over to me.

"The soldiers and villagers are all prepared, Your Highnesses. Awaiting your orders, sire," he stated.

I swallowed; it seemed more foreign still to be giving orders to the captain, the man I had been obeying since first signing up in the army. "We're to take our time, captain, stopping every hour or two. The injured cannot move for much at a time. I have placed Aife up on top of the hills to give us warning if she sees the enemy," I concluded.

"Very good, my lord," the captain replied, inclining his head. I glanced behind our lines a final time to see my people ready, either on horseback or the line of soldiers behind the villagers who had to walk.

"Permission granted," I agreed. I then nodded at him and we draw our swords together, raised them high and then pointed them forwards. "We march!" I shouted, and we set off at a walk. I glanced up at the hills to where I could just see Aife and raised a hand to her; she raised a hand back. She had a horn with her in case she did detect our foes, but I prayed that if the Bernicians were to return to Klumeck, we would be long gone.

"You are doing well in this prince role, brother," I heard Sarah mutter behind me, and despite what had happened to Klumeck today, her gently teasing words caused me to smile.

It was difficult to judge the time when the day was so gloomy and dark, but approximately every hour or two we stopped for the injured among us to rest. The wind got so blustery and the rain so dense that I sent two soldiers to go up and escort Aife back down the hills – in the adverse weather it was no longer safe for anyone to be put there, and she would not have been able to see the enemy coming anyway. I prayed that since any Bernicians would be invisible, we would be invisible to them also.

Despite our outer cloaks and the fact that most of us wore armour, we were all soon soaked to the skin and achingly cold. Every time we stopped, John came and told me how the injured soldiers were doing – mercifully all were still alive. Gradually the day wore on and the sky turned an even darker grey, but even then the rain did not relent.

Eventually I held up my hand to signal the captain that we were going off the road to make camp, for even the ones who were uninjured were exhausted, not to mention the horses who had been forced to gallop for so long who desperately needed rest. We came to a stretch of field that was open but hidden from view by a low cliff that curved into the landscape. The tents and other materials for the night had been transported in a wooden carriage that had thankfully stayed dry, for the most part.

It so happened that just as the soldiers prepared to make camp, the rain eased and finally stopped. I sensed the relief among the camp and morale seemed to improve instantly; they hurried in their movements, lest the rain began again and they were stuck out in it. I helped prepare the main medical tent where the injured soldiers would be able to rest, and watched for a while as the surgeon began his work, but it was clear there was little else I could do. I came out of the tent to see the rest of camp set up, including my own tent. I entered and could finally discard my armour and change into clothes which were only slightly damp, compared to being completely sodden. I had just re-buckled my belt when there came a soft knock on the flap of the tent.

"Come in," I invited the caller. "Captain. How are the soldiers doing?" I asked him quickly, before giving him a chance to bow; he had to contend with merely bending his head.

"They are doing well, Your Highness. The injured seem to be recovering well and did not suffer too much with the day's journey. I have also sent a group of soldiers to be on watch for the night now the rain seems to have passed; they doused their beacons just before they reached the top of the cliff, and are to blow the horn if they see anything."

"Aife said that for the half of the day that was clear, she could see nothing. Hopefully even if the Bernicians are following us, they are at a great distance. I cannot see them wanting to travel in this weather," I added, as there came another knock on the flap of the tent. "Come in," I repeated, to see Sarah walk in holding bowls of stew.

"Your Highness," the captain greeted her, standing. "Well, sire, that was all I had to report," he added with a nod.

"Stay, captain; I brought you some food." She handed a bowl to him and a second one to me. "I know a servant could do it, but I'm too used to doing it myself," she added wryly as she sat.

"You're very kind, my lady," the captain responded, and we began to eat. The beef stew tasted good, and I felt its heat warm my bones; I was impressed at our people's resourcefulness that they had managed to make a fire in such wet conditions.

"May I ask you a personal question, sire?" he asked me.

I raised my eyebrows, but I had a mouthful of stew so I just nodded.

"What will you do, now you are not to inherit Klumeck's throne?"

"I don't know," I answered after swallowing. It was the question I had thought about oft today as we travelled away from my birthplace, which now lay in ruins. "I do know that we will make the Bernicians pay," I told them both in earnest. "Our counter attack must be the next priority. We will not stand by and let this attack go unpunished. We will hold them to account," I vowed.

"Well said, sire," the captain replied, but I noted Sarah simply looked down at her bowl. The captain said nothing further, and we ate the rest of our meal in relative silence.

When finished the captain stood and took our bowls. "Thank you, Your Highnesses. I wish you both a goodnight." He bent his head again before departing the tent.

"I expect we should get some rest," Sarah murmured, getting to her feet also. I stood also as she walked across the tent floor.

"Wait," I ordered, and she turned back. "You did not agree with what I said to the captain." It was a statement rather than a question, but she did not deny it. I frowned in confusion. "I do not understand. Is it not your kingdom that has been destroyed, as well as mine? Do you not want justice to be done? Are you not angry at what has transpired?"

"Aye, I am angry," Sarah replied, folding her shawl more closely about herself against the chill. "I do want them to be held accountable for their actions. I just want you to take care, Daniel," she reprimanded me gently. "Vengeance, if it overcomes you, can be like a poison." Her speech instantly made me think of how I had nearly slain Reghan in my anger, of my heated conversation with Queen Evelyn afterwards.

"Very well. I shall watch over the emotion," I responded. We then bade each other goodnight, and she left the tent also.

I took off my boots and sat down on the bed, lost in thought. I wondered whether I did get too hot-headed about things. My future throne had been dissolved, and I had confronted the man who had ordered the death of my family... but did that excuse my actions? I knew not. I climbed into bed, and before I succumbed to sleep, I wondered how King Cedric, his army and the villagers were doing. I prayed they would all survive the journey, and that God would lead us all safely home.

Chapter Twelve

It took us a few hours after setting off the next day to reach Gaeson. To my relief, though riding was tense, the Bernicians had not seemed to follow us at any point. The day had dawned far brighter with clouds much lighter than the day previous; Aife had once again been positioned in the hills, and her sharp eyes saw nothing of our foes. The sky had broken patches of blue, and at one point we even caught a few glimpses of the sun. The journey back took much longer than the one there; my people were weary from battle and so the pace was slow. We arrived back at Gaeson by mid-afternoon, and though my heart was full of sorrow at what had passed, it was a relief to be home.

My first destination was to go straight to the castle with the captain and report to the Queen as ordered. My only stop was to guide my tired horse into the stables and hastily drink a skin of water. I then sped as quickly as my armour would allow to the palace hall and was admitted at once.

"Your Majesty," I greeted her, striding into the room and coming to a halt before her where I sank into bended knee, my gaze fixed upon the ground. I knew that being a fellow monarch, I need not bow like this – but I continued it out of habit more than anything else.

"Arise, Prince Bryce," she returned formally. I stood, and as I did so met her gaze. Her countenance was concerned, urgent. "What news from Klumeck?" she asked swiftly.

"We were too late, my lady," I answered, and I saw sorrow flicker over her features. "Most of the people had been able to flee, but thirty-three bodies were found. We managed to put to the sword those of our enemy who remained, but Klumeck had been set on fire. We could not salvage her." A vivid image of the ruins of Klumeck filled my mind, preventing my speech for a moment. I swallowed and cleared my throat. "I fear Klumeck now lies in Bernicia's domain. King Cedric left with the refugees and his soldiers to Caer Ligualid; he instructed me to return here with the rest of your people, Your Majesty, to report all of this to you. He also wished me to return, so that we might better present Gaeson as united to Rheged in the war against Bernicia. King Cedric strongly advises a counter attack, my lady, as do I," I concluded, a little passionately.

"Indeed," Queen Evelyn replied, and stood. "I am grieved to hear all that you say," she continued. "We will certainly prepare for war. Captain, inform our army," she instructed.

The captain stepped forwards and bowed again. "Your Majesty," he greeted me, clasping his arm to his chest; he then stood and swiftly left the palace hall.

I was greatly relieved to hear we would indeed be fighting Bernicia, though I was mindful of Sarah's counsel to me last night. I had not been dismissed, and so I remained where I was; presently my lady descended the palace steps and walked up to me.

"It is because of my father, is it not?" she asked, quietly so that the other guards did not hear. Her voice had hardened slightly. At the mention of her father, I wondered instantly whether her regard for me had indeed changed, after she had professed to forgive me. "Because my father was corrupt, if you went back to Caer Ligualid then they might believe Gaeson was once more attempting to follow their selfish desires." She folded her arms. "It was not that long ago that they themselves came here to make war; they may forget the peace we have now and think ill of us. You are here to prevent that. Isn't that so?" There was a challenge to her voice now; as though she was challenging me to disagree with her.

"Yes, my lady," I said simply, because we both knew this was the reason why I had been sent back. "King Cedric only advised it because of what a few citizens would say who had not travelled here, who had not seen your bravery and goodness in standing up to your father and honouring King Urien," I sought to assure her. "No insult was meant. The problem lies within their own hearts to accept the peace, rather than a questioning of Gaeson's loyalties."

She stared at me for a moment before her lips curved into a slight smile. "Spoken again as a true orator of wisdom," she murmured wryly. "That I well know." Presently she gave a short sigh, but said nothing further. For a moment we simply held each other's gazes; my queen looked as though there was something further she wished to convey, but without words I could not tell what it was.

"I am truly sorry for all that has befallen Klumeck, Daniel," she said now, her voice so quiet and soft that I almost missed it, "but I am glad to see you alive and well." A small smile now graced her beautiful features. "Make sure you rest. It has been a long journey for you all."

Thus being dismissed, I bowed.

"My lady," I said and I straightened as I left her presence and walked back through the castle. The fact that she had been glad to see me alive and the sincerity of her words had almost made me sing, but my thoughts were darkened with the pain of Klumeck in ruins and the difficult task ahead to prepare for war. The next battle hung in the air so close we could almost touch and taste it – a battle that was different like no other. Most of my battles as a soldier was us simply defending our own kingdom and people; here we marched to attack them. Whether we won or lost would alter greatly the shape of the war as a whole against those who came across the sea.

So it was that we began preparing for this battle which had such finality to it; I sensed everyone else also had this trepidation. Over the next few days we attempted to make ourselves ready. We ensured the injured soldiers were recovered as soon as possible and sent them to their homes – most of them were in no shape for war. Instead, we recruited new soldiers from Gaeson and the surrounding towns of trade, and spent much time training them. It seemed so cruel to thrust newly formed warriors into battle so quickly, but we needed every man and woman who could hold a blade if we were to win this fight.

As I helped train the warriors I knew that we could not take every fighting man and woman with us, thus leaving Gaeson utterly defenceless. If the Bernicians won the war and we had sent up all our people, then there would be nobody to protect the people if the enemies marched directly to here. Therefore I grew all the more anxious about who would be fighting in the war and those who would remain to fight here.

I knew that Queen Evelyn was currently deciding whether or not to go to war; so far her role had been to be the leader of those who were in the caves, ready to fight the enemy should they be breached. I could not help but pray for Queen Evelyn that she would decide not to go into battle. It was pure selfishness, but I did not want to see the woman I loved harmed. Besides, if anything happened to Queen Evelyn, it was likely that Gaeson's throne would fall to me – and I was not ready to become a king, even if it was of the people I had spent my whole life knowing and living alongside.

I was equally anxious about Sarah. With every other battle I had faced, Sarah had chosen to remain at the caves to care for my mother and, in the worst situation, to defend the caves while the rest of the citizens fled. I hoped in earnest this would be her continued decision, but to my horror, as I entered the armoury one morning, I found her taking off her sword and shield. In the brief time before she saw me I noticed the determination upon her countenance; she was a woman preparing for war. A moment later, however, I saw her tucking a strand of hair behind her ear in the way she had done since childhood, and I knew I could keep silent no longer.

"Do not go," I said as she sheathed her sword.

Sarah turned abruptly and I saw her bristle; her face already indignant.

"Please do not go," I repeated.

"You say that to me, after what Bernicia did to Klumeck?" Anger was evident in her tone. "They are my people too, brother! Do you still doubt my ability?"

"It is not a question of your ability, Sarah. That I have never doubted. It would be my ability that would be in question," I told her honestly, taking her aback. "You are my oldest friend, Sarah. I have loved you as a sister long before I knew we were kin by blood. If you went out to battle, then I would constantly fear for your safety, thus my ability in battle would be impaired."

"That would be your own affair and no doing of mine," she replied defensively, and then frowned. "You feel a similar sense of affection for John and Aife, yet you do not mind that they go into battle."

"I am used to thinking of them in the battlefield. Besides, think of our uncle. He is expecting me to fight," I continued, "but think of his anguish if he knew you were fighting, sister. I saw the anxiety on his face when you removed your helmet in Klumeck. He has only just found you! Imagine if I die but he survives – he would wish for your counsel. There is another reason," I added, before she could further object. "I was hoping you would watch over my mother, the way you always have. Rachel and the children may also be depending upon you to protect them in the way I cannot. I need you here," I concluded, "Not because I do not think you can fight, but because I need you to fight here and protect them. I need you to do this, Sarah. Please," I pleaded.

My sister remained stationary for a long moment, and then gave a tired sigh. "Very well," she relented. "I will do all I can to defend our people here, and to protect Enid, Rachel and the children from harm."

I was so relieved at her speech that I at once strode across the room and embraced her. "You have my thanks," I muttered. "I am your older brother, and I could not bear if anything were to happen to you," I explained tenderly, as our embrace ended. Sarah now gave a little smile, which I returned.

"That is one of the reasons why I wished to fight, Daniel," she told me now, "because I knew you and our uncle will be fighting. Who will I have, if you both die in this war and only I survive?"

"I know," I murmured, "and that is why you must stay. If you are the only one who survives, then my mother will be under your charge. You may well also be needed in Caer Ligualid, as you would be the next heir to the Klumeck throne. They may not have a kingdom, but they will still want their rightful ruler there."

"I understand," Sarah told me in a little above a whisper. We smiled at each other once more before she turned and placed on her helmet. "I may no longer be going to war," she told me, "but if I am to defend the caves, I must train also." She squeezed my hand before departing the armoury. I left also, my heart nigh flooded with relief. It had been painful enough to watch so many, both men and women, prepare for war without the sister I had just found doing the same.

***

It was a piercing cry that suddenly awakened me to the darkness. For a moment I wondered where I was; I had not yet grown used to sleeping in royal chambers. A moment later, the bell that raised the alarm echoed through the castle. I jumped out of bed as the cry came again – my heart lurched as I realised the voice was Queen Evelyn's. I raced out of the room, grabbing my sword along the way. The castle was now fully awake – people were heading to the nearest staircase. Then my sister's door opened and I saw her running out, sword in hand.

"The queen," she stated simply, and I nodded; she fell into step beside me as we sprinted down the corridor, bustling through the people coming through to the staircase. We rounded a corner, and I saw at once that Her Majesty's door was open and unattended. I drew my own sword as we darted inside.

My eyes widened as we beheld the scene; Queen Evelyn knelt upon the ground, her sword abandoned by her side, covered in blood. That same blood was also on her hands. In those hands rested the head of her father; Reghan lay flat on his back, coughing heavily with a little pool of blood forming at the corner of his mouth. It was then I saw a second man lying elsewhere in the room, dead. Looking at the man, I saw it was one of the Bernician spies. Had he escaped, or had someone set him free? I knew not.

"I have called for the surgeon." Queen Evelyn spoke quietly, her voice cracked with emotion. My eyes locked with hers for a moment, and the pain in them took my breath away. Then a moment later she bowed her head to look at her father. "He will be here soon," she told him reassuringly.

"I told you not to bother, my dear. My time is long past," he groaned brokenly. I stole a glance at Sarah; her face was transfixed, staring at Reghan. I reasoned it was the first time she had seen him since she had discovered the truth – that my sister and I were related, and the man she was staring at was the man who had murdered most of our family. As if he was aware of my thoughts, he suddenly moved.

265

"Stay still, Father," she murmured, trying to keep her hand on the part of his neck which had been pierced.

Reghan turned towards us, raising his head a little to meet my eyes. "Daniel," he said and then coughed, causing the whole of his head to shake and more blood to flow out of his mouth; he then wiped the blood from his mouth and breathed heavily. He turned his head to face Sarah. "You must be the other heir," he rasped, and then swallowed. "I suppose I deserved an end like this," he mused, and then coughed again.

"Do not speak that way; you may yet recover," my lady said, but even as she said it I knew it was impossible. He was still bleeding heavily from his neck and the cloth that Her Majesty held to where he was pierced was soaked through with bright crimson. As I stared at this poor, feeble man, sputtering blood and dying in such a painful manner, I felt something stirring inside of me akin to mercy and sensed my heart changing. Almost outside of my own will, I strode forwards towards him and sank in front of him on bended knee.

"You murdered most of my family and forced me to flee to a land that was not my own," I began quietly. "You separated me from my sister and allowed me to fight alongside my people in Gaeson against those who were also my kin. But," I added swiftly, for I saw out of the corner of my eye my queen was about to protest at my words, "I want you to know something, before you die here," I continued. I stared at him for a moment longer, and as I did, I was reminded of the other time I had faced him, the time when I had almost killed him in cold blood.

"You were right to say that none of us are free from corruption," I muttered. "When I think of how I almost murdered you in prison… I know my heart is surely as full of evil as yours is. I want you to know that it is not too late for you, Reghan. Turn to God," I beseeched him. "Ask him for forgiveness and you shall receive it."

He gave a loud breath but I could not tell whether his emotion was relief or scorn.

My hand clasped his. "I forgive you," I declared. "I forgive you the great wrong you have done me."

Reghan held my eyes, but before he could speak, a coughing fit overcame him again and I knew he had precious seconds left. I stooped back as Reghan glanced up at his daughter.

"I am sorry for all the pain I caused you," Reghan breathed, moving his blood stained hand to cup her cheek. "May you be a better ruler than I was," he murmured.

"Father, please…" my lady stated, but then the former king suddenly convulsed and a moment later he became still – he was dead. My love began to shake with quiet sobs, her arms entwined around his head still. I swallowed and stood, wiping my bloodied hands on my shoulders and turned towards the door to see the captain standing there.

"The people are in the caves and our army in the usual positions, Your Highness," the captain stated gravely.

I nodded. "Go to the soldiers and tell them that Reghan, King of Gaeson, has been assassinated and the culprit is dead. Then take them to search the whole of the castle in case there are any more spies in hiding. Also send four soldiers to here – two to protect Her Majesty and two to remove the body," I added, lowering my voice still further.

"I bid you take my sister with you," I added in a normal tone. "Sarah." I glanced at her. "Go with the captain and then head to the caves. Tell all those there what has happened and do a search there, for any foes posing as ordinary citizens. Arrest anyone who seems suspicious," I added.

"The dungeon interrogator," Queen Evelyn now stated, and we all looked at her. "Take him into custody also."

"Your Majesty." The captain bowed in obedience, and then he and Sarah departed.

I looked towards my lady. "I will stay here until the soldiers come," I told her, but I doubt she heard me. I took a step towards her, but before I could do or say anything else there came a knock at the door. "Enter," I ordered, drawing my sword in case it was a trap.

"You sent for us, Your Highness. Your Majesty." The guards bowed, but my lady did not acknowledge them. They glanced to me and I nodded at them; they came forwards to take the body.

267

"Stay back!" Her Majesty abruptly shouted, anger suddenly prevalent in her features. The guards looked to me again, and I held up a hand to stop them. I then came forwards and knelt in front of her, where she still firmly held onto his body.

"I bid you let them take him, Your Majesty," I murmured, and her eyes rose to meet mine. "There is nothing you can do for him now. Let him rest," I implored her.

Her eyes held mine, wrought with uncertainty. How I longed to comfort her! Gently I reached out and disengaged her arms from her father's corpse; her hands shook, but she did not object.

"Guards," I called. They walked quietly over and picked up the body of Reghan, former King of Gaeson. They placed him on a stretcher and began to carry him out. I looked up at them from where I still sat on the floor. "He is to be given a king's funeral," I instructed them now.

"Sire," they obeyed. "Your Majesty." They bowed to my queen in addition, whilst still carrying the stretcher between them, before they left the room.

"My lady," I said, walking down and holding out a hand, "perhaps you would like a different chamber?"

Her eyes met mine as she nodded and she took my hand; I felt the moisture of Reghan's blood smear between our joined fingers. I pulled her up and then turned to pick up a blanket and drape it round her shoulders in case she was cold.

"You two, lead the way," I ordered.

"My lord prince," they replied and began walking. I walked behind them, parallel to my queen. Her Majesty's face was cold and hard, as her bloodstained hands held the blanket tightly round her shoulders. We walked for no more than a few minutes before we arrived at one of the guest rooms in the castle that would be appropriate for her.

"It should be safe in here, Your Majesty," I told her quietly.

She nodded and walked into the room.

I glanced at the two guards. "Go and assist in the search. I will remain outside and keep watch."

"Sire," they chorused, as Queen Evelyn shut the door behind her.

Alone in the corridor, I noticed my hands were still covered in Reghan's blood and distractedly tried to wipe my hands on my trousers. The castle was as still and as dark as it had been a few minutes ago, before any of his hell had happened. My mind was alert with questions; namely how boththe former King of Gaeson and the Bernician spy had come to be in Her Majesty's chambers. My heart, too, was trying to process all that had happened, but I forced my emotions to become calm. I was already relieved I had chosen to forgive Reghan – I knew if I had clung to my rage and vengeance, I would have always regretted it. I also knew that my sudden desire to forgive him had come not just from myself; I would not have been able to do it simply out of my own human strength.

I stood in the corridor for about an hour, my ears strained to hear the slightest possible movement – but there was nothing. I had never known the castle to be so quiet – not since the night when I had come to speak to the captain, the night when I had escaped with my lady into the forest. Was that so long ago? The night after Joshua died, before I fell from the cliff and discovered who I really was.

Before long, I heard noise outside again. I heard footsteps approaching and drew my sword part of the way; John rounded the corner and I relaxed, placing my sword in its sheath once more and tried to give him a smile; I perceived his mood to be as sombre as my own.

"My lord prince," John bowed quickly. "The captain sent me to report to you – all of the castle and the caves have now been searched. Most of the city has also been inspected and soldiers are accompanying the people back to their homes in case any more of the spies should be hiding." John paused here and raised a hand to scratch his chin. "There is something else. It seems the interrogator has fled Gaeson."

"What?" I protested loudly, for this proved his guilt if nothing else. "Damn him," I cursed, my hand lashing out to punch a nearby wall. I then dropped my arm back by my side, ignoring the throbbing ache in my knuckles. "Is there anything else you have to report, John?" I asked him wearily.

"No, sire," John replied. "I have sent some of the men to search for him beyond our borders, but it is likely that with the cover of darkness he will elude us."

I nodded but did not say more; for a moment we simply stood together in silence in the corridor.

"I was about to enquire after the queen," John said presently, "but that seems a foolish question."

"I am sure she appreciates her people's concern," I stated dully. "Thank you for telling me, brother. I bid you go aid the captain in whatever is needed," I added. "I will report to Her Majesty myself."

"Your Highness," he replied, and left just as quickly as he had entered, leaving me once again alone in the corridor.

I turned to the door and knocked.

"Enter," the call came. I entered the chamber to see her sat in her chair. Though there were remnants of tears in her face, her eyes appeared hard and dry. I saw she was wearing fresh clothes, and her hands were now clean and free from blood. I also noticed she had a goblet of wine in her hands; she now took another drink of it. "I assume you have come to tell me that nobody else has been found." Her tone was cold yet precise.

"Aye, Your Majesty," I replied. "It seems the danger has passed. However... it seems the interrogator has escaped the kingdom."

At this her mouth pressed into a tight line, but she said nothing.

"Already some of the men are searching for him..."

"He will be nigh impossible to track, with it being night," Queen Evelyn interrupted, reiterating what John had stated earlier. "So that is why you shouted," she muttered, and I cringed inwardly that she had heard me.

"I apologise, my lady," I said quickly, but she said nothing else. I stayed where I was for a moment, wondering whether I should take my leave.

Then, abruptly, my queen stood and walked to the table in the far side of the chamber and poured another goblet of wine. "Here," she said, almost as if it was a command.

I opened my mouth to object, but then changed my mind and accepted the goblet. "Thank you, my lady."

She gestured another seat in the chamber and I sat. I raised the goblet to my mouth and took a long drink.

"You will want to know what happened," she murmured, after taking another sip of the ruby liquid. "There is no reason to delay," she continued before I could say that it could wait. "My father is dead, Daniel," she told me bitterly, looking down at the goblet she held in her hands. "As you said, there is nothing more you can do for him now."

I said nothing; I longed to know all that had transpired, but I knew it would be impertinent to ask now. I simply wished to comfort her. "There was a sharp knock on my door," she began the account, "that woke me from my slumber. I assumed it was one of the guards that are usually outside, but when I opened my door I saw my father standing there.

"He came into my chamber before I could protest," Her Majesty continued after taking another drink of wine; I had another gulp of my own while she spoke. "He told me the interrogator had let him escape; that he had come to see me on an urgent matter. He came in here and..." She paused now and swiped angrily at a tear that had fallen from her face. "He said nothing of great consequence," my lady resumed, "and indeed I could hardly understand him. He only said that all of us were in very real danger. The next I knew, the spy was barging through the door and my father shouted me to grab my sword. But by the time I retrieved it..." She trailed off, looking at her wine again.

"Your father was already pierced," I finished quietly.

She nodded as another tear sped down her cheek.

I paused here. "So you know not why your father came up here, or how either of them escaped the dungeon."

Queen Evelyn now shook her head, seeming to be simply staring into the middle of the room.

"You believe the interrogator to have a part in this," I said now, posing it as a statement rather than a question.

"Long have I distrusted him," Her Majesty returned. "When you were his captive, he did not even seem to ask you any questions. Then when you saw my father last..."

I lowered my gaze now, cringing inwardly once again – for I knew all too well what she was referring to.

"He was only too zealous to tell the whole of Gaeson about that incident, no matter what the consequences might be for me," she continued stonily. "This is all before stating the simple truth that he has the only key in the dungeon, being the chief one in charge of the other prisoners – so how else did both of them escape?" She inhaled deeply now. I saw more tears were welled in her eyes and I perceived her to be attempting to fight them.

"There is no shame in your grief, my lady," I murmured to her. She managed a swift nod and I stood. "Perhaps you would prefer to be alone now…"

"No," she replied abruptly, "actually I would not." She stood quickly. Our eyes met and held. "Oh, Daniel," she murmured, as the hold on her grief broke again. In the next moment, she had crossed the room to me and placed her head on my shoulder. Never before had I seen this woman so in pain, and it only made me love her more. It was our first embrace, but the circumstances of it were so dreadful I felt nothing but a longing to comfort her.

"I am so sorry, my lady," I muttered, as her tears fell thick and fast, feeling my words were so contrite and foolish. She did not respond, merely bowed her head still further into my shoulder as she wept, so that I felt her tears moisten the edge of my tunic. We stood there like that, the two of us, until my queen suddenly moved back and wiped her eyes. I saw her composure and formality come upon her as though a window were closing. For this last little while, it had seemed as though her defences had been broken and I had been allowed a brief glimpse into the very heart of her – but now her defences were rebuilding themselves. I had nothing but admiration for her courage and steadfastness in such dark circumstances.

"I think I shall rest now," she murmured, her tone flat and resolute. I nodded and stepped back also, mildly aware of the damp patch on my shoulder where she had wept.

"Of course, Your Majesty," I bowed and went to the door; at the threshold I turned back. "I bid you let me know, my lady, if I can aid you in any way."

At this, a glimpse of a smile graced her features. "I know, Daniel. Thank you," she added quietly. "Thank you for honouring my father with a royal funeral and for forgiving him. I cannot imagine what strength that took, knowing what he did to you." As she spoke, once again my earlier encounter with Reghan came to mind – how I had nearly slain him in his chains. She now reached out and took my hand. "Thank you for being here to comfort me."

"Always, my lady," I replied hoarsely, squeezing her hand for a moment before my arm dropped listlessly by my side.

Her smile grew a little more, but I could perceive the makings of more tears in her eyes.

"Your Majesty." I bowed. She gave me a swift nod and closed the door, leaving me alone once again in the corridor.

Most of Gaeson had now returned to their homes or rooms inside of the castle – the nightmare of Reghan's death had ended as swiftly as it had begun, leaving the whole city shaken in its wake. Like I had been the night I had returned to Gaeson to be sentenced to death, numbness and emptiness were my primary emotions. Indeed, my legs felt like lead as I turned a corner to be back on my own corridor – presently I saw the captain was waiting for me.

"Your Highness," the captain addressed me and saluted – I raised my own weary hand in response, at once noticing it was still stained with Reghan's blood. "I did not wish to disturb Her Majesty, in case she was asleep, so I presumed to report here."

I made no comment, but simply gave a nod to signal he should go on.

"Sire, the city has now been searched, including every building. There is still no sign of the interrogator, but we will continue the search," he concluded. "Are there any further orders, my lord?" he asked now.

"Just ensure the queen is well guarded at all times," I instructed him. At this, he bowed and saluted again before taking his leave.

With a heavy sigh, I retired to my chamber. Once inside, I again saw the state of my hands and went to the bowl of water to immediately begin washing them. The water was still shockingly cold in its temperature so I wanted to be swift; however, each time I took them out of the bowl again my imagination told me they were still crimson red. In the end, I rubbed them so much until the flesh of my hands was pink and I barely had any feeling in my fingers. After this, I removed my belt and heard the clunk of my sword hitting the floor.

The king was dead – that fact kept swirling around my brain until the logic of it seemed impossible. Even though the man had abdicated his throne to his daughter, in his heart he had still been a king. Presently I sank to my knees before my bed and prayed that if it had been in God's will, Reghan had indeed asked God for forgiveness. I prayed also that God would give the one my heart loved and the rest of Gaeson the strength to face tomorrow. It was strange – only a few days ago, the desire to kill Reghan had been so strong that it was only the thought of my lady that had stopped me. Now, however, I would do anything to bring the man back to life, if only that Queen Evelyn would not face any further pain.

The day of Reghan's funeral three days later dawned miserable and dark, as if the weather had rendered itself more appropriate to such an event. The soldiers and the townspeople stood silent in the square – the last time they had gathered like this was when Her Majesty had been forced to take the throne. We had sent messages to Caer Ligualid, but both my uncle and King Urien declined attendance, as we expected. I speculated that even during peace time they would not have attended the funeral of the man they considered a traitor and responsible for so much bloodshed – and that was without the threat of imminent war.

Queen Evelyn, Sarah, myself and the captain were on the royal balcony during the event, as was tradition. With King Urien not being present, it was Queen Evelyn herself who spoke about the life of her father. This was indeed the most logical, as she knew him the best, even despite his secret atrocities that had recently come to light. She spoke of him as the king we knew best, saying that his secret war against King Urien and my uncle were due to him being driven mad by the acquisition of power. Once again I was struck by my queen's wisdom and oration –

she was able to remind us elegantly of the man we had all been proud to serve, without ignoring the pain he had caused by recent actions.

It was usual for a royal funeral of this kind to be followed by a feast, but Queen Evelyn had already declined this – we had not long since had the coronation feast and another one could not be so quickly arranged on the brink of war. Besides, I knew most of Gaeson, though they would have respected the queen's speech, it would have jarred with them to celebrate the life of the one who had committed such awful deeds at the end of the life.

The occasion seemed to end as soon as the speech was finished. The people dispersed in an ever-grim mood; we all knew that war would be coming soon. In many ways the death of Reghan was tragic, but the funeral just before the soldiers departed would surely cause low morale among the army. The four of us presently left the balcony.

"Leave us," she called to the soldiers who remained in the palace hall. "Prince Bryce, I bid you remain behind," she added, as I made to leave along with Sarah and the captain. I turned at once and gave her a swift bow. "I have new orders for you."

"Your Majesty," I replied, bowing in obedience as she descended the steps from the balcony to where I stood; presently my queen and I were alone in the palace hall.

"I can well sense the fear of our people," Queen Evelyn began, folding her arms. "They need someone to lead them and protect them should we not win the battle. In the days since I took the throne," she continued in a lowered voice, though we were alone, "I have begun to fear that my counsel cannot be trusted. They seem to speak wisdom, but I have no way of knowing whether they were in league with my father." At the mention of Reghan her voice had stiffened slightly.

"From the time I was of fighting age, I have seen my role has been to protect the people here who take refuge in the caves," she continued. "Since I know not of a suitable steward…" She paused here, and I wondered if she was to ask me whether I would lead the people in her stead. Though this decision made sense – I was now royalty, I knew the workings of Gaeson well – but objections rose to the forefront. I wished to be in this war, to see Bernicia brought to justice for the wrongs they had done Klumeck. Also, if she went to war and I did not, I had no way of fighting for her, from ensuring the one I loved most was kept from harm. I hoped I would be able to do her bidding, whatever she would require of me; we both knew I would assent to anything she asked.

"I see no shame in continuing my role of fighting for my people here," Queen Evelyn stated now, her speech taking me by surprise. My eyes widened in surprise and my heart threatened to explode with relief. "You thought I was to ask you to be my steward," she speculated. "I did think of this reasoning," she said before I could reply, "but I have never been in a full battle as you have. I believe I am experienced to serve here, as you are better experienced to serve there. I am asking you to lead the people in my place," she concluded.

"I accept this honourable task, my lady," I replied immediately with a bow. Though the idea filled me with dread – I had gone from a humble soldier following the captain to leading the whole army – it was sheer joy I was having to keep from my voice – sheer joy that she was to be kept from harm, at least for the time being. "By God's grace, I will do all I can to lead your people well," I vowed.

"I am sure you will serve me well, Daniel; you always have." She paused. "You are pleased I am not going to war."

My head jerked back up to hers, knowing my relief had been made plain despite my best intentions. It seemed I could keep to my old routine of having an impassive countenance, except when speaking with her; my heart was too full to hide. She had a single eyebrow raised.

"Yes," I admitted – when had my voice grown so hoarse and thick? "Yes, my lady," I repeated, yet more fervently as my eyes held hers. "I am indeed relieved that you are not going to battle. It has been my selfish plea to God every day since we decided to march," I added, hearing my voice go softer now as I lowered my eyes out of embarrassment.

"This is the third time that I know of where you have risked your life to save mine." Her voice so quiet and soft that I almost missed it. "The first was when you cut the rope and fell from the cliff."

My eyes jerked back to hers; it was the closest she had ever come to mentioning my love for her.

"The second," she continued, "was when you risked your life to return here, against the might of Rheged, to warn us of King Urien's attack... and now you lead the people in my place. It is quite a debt I owe you, Prince of Klumeck."

"No debt is owed. I would do so a thousand more times," I declared passionately, hating myself for such foolish talk. "I want you to know, my lady," I added, for I knew not when I would next converse with the queen alone, "that even with my change in identity, even with all that happened with your father..." I saw her stiffen and chided myself instantly for mentioning him. In earnestness, I now reached out and touched her hand. Her eyes flickered down to my hand and back to my face, but there was no objection in her countenance. Her skin was soft beneath my own rough, war-hardened hands.

"I have no less regard for you," I told her simply. It was the closest I had come to telling her again how much I loved her, but she did not respond. I dropped her hand just as swiftly as I had taken it. "I will serve you just as I always have," I added quickly, so that my earlier statement could be more ambiguous. I now could feasibly just be talking about my loyalty to her father despite his actions – but we both knew I had not just been talking about loyalty.

"I know," she responded at last, her voice barely above a whisper. Then she stood back and cleared her throat. "I pray your love for your people will win us victory and keep us from harm, Prince Bryce," she stated formally, as though our almost intimate conversation had never happened. "Prepare to march," she commanded.

"Your Majesty," I replied, and bowed, my voice sounding foreign to my ears.

I turned and departed from the throne room with mixed emotions – joy, fear, embarrassment, sadness – rolling around in my head until they seemed one and indistinguishable. Joy because she would not be going to war; embarrassment to how I had nigh confessed my feelings for her and fear for the army I was now to lead into battle. My fear was due to the arduous task set before me to lead my people to war. The sadness, however, was because I knew that if I were to die in battle, then I would never see the woman I loved again.

The next day or so passed by with an encroaching swiftness and simultaneously an aching slowness. The day dawned like any other, and in the few moments after I woke, I prayed to God that he would deliver us from our foes and that, if He was willing, I would see Gaeson and my lady once more. We had spent the second week further training up the men and women and readying provisions for the journey, as it would be a long journey to the small island where the Bernicians were based and would take many days. When I had finished praying, I took a quick bath that had been prepared for me and dressed mechanically.

It was still an hour or two before we departed for Bernician lands, and so I took one last walk from the town square to Gaeson. The townspeople were just starting their businesses for the day, and in my peripheral vision I saw them stop and look in my direction, but I paid them no heed. I turned onto the steep side street of my house, came to the door and opened it.

"Your Highness," Rachel greeted me, and bowed from where I saw she was putting a shawl around the younger daughter's shoulders; the other daughter was eating breakfast, and though this place was still in my possession, I felt intrusive onto this family scene. "Please come in if you wish, my lord prince," she said, gesturing.

"Thank you." I walked into the house and looked around at the old living chamber. For a moment, I had forgotten Sarah no longer lived here and I found her absence strange. I glanced at Rachel. "It is good to see you looking so well, Rachel."

"Thank you, sire," Rachel replied quietly. Through her smile I saw the anxiety and sadness in her face. "I wish you every safety and victory," she told me now.

I smiled in response. "I came to speak to my mother, but also to talk to you," I told her. I pulled some papers out of the satchel I had been carrying and held them out to her. I saw her frown as she took them from me. "These are the deeds to this house," I informed her quietly as she glanced at them. I saw her face jolt back up to meet mine, confusion on her features. "I'm giving the house to you," I supplied.

"My lord, surely not," she replied, surprise turning to shock as she stared down at them. "Sire, such generosity..."

"I have no further need of it," I interrupted her gently. "If I survive this war, then I shall reside at the castle. I have many memories of this place from my childhood," I added, glancing around the living room. "I hope that you and your daughters may make many more happy memories here. My only condition is that my mother continues to live here," I continued, "unless she has a change of situation."

"Of course, Your Highness," Rachel replied quickly. Abruptly, she reached out and took both my hands in hers. "You have shown us such great kindness, sire. First taking us in after... Joshua..." I saw the pain flash across her face as she spoke his name. "But now to give us your house..."

"I have no need for it," I repeated. "I would rather it be a home than standing here empty. I have had all the relevant documents signed," I told her presently, pointing again at the papers in her hand. "All you need to do is sign your name at the bottom and the house is yours. If you will excuse me, Rachel," I added abruptly, "I must now speak with my mother."

"Of course," she repeated, as I began to move through the house. "My lord," she said again, and I turned back. "Thank you."

I merely gave her another smile before heading up the stairs. I came to my mother's door and knocked.

"Come in," came my mother's voice, and I entered. I saw her smile at me as she saw me, but I noticed the tear marks on her face and knew she had recently wept. I walked over to her and placed my hands in hers. "It is good to see you, my boy," she managed.

"It is good to see you, mother," I replied – for though I knew I had been borne to another, and I had even begun to remember her in Klumeck, this woman was still my mother at heart. "How do you fare?"

"I am well, my son," she replied. She paused, and her teeth grazed her bottom lip a little anxiously. "I fear today is the day you march," she said eventually.

"Aye," I answered her quietly, "in a little under an hour." I held her hands tightly as the realisation began to sink in that I may never see my mother again. "I have given the house deeds to Rachel," I informed her, "but she has agreed upon your continued living here."

My mother smiled and nodded. "I reasoned you would do this, as you will live in the castle when you return." I glanced up at her and she smiled, almost too brightly. "I am certain you will come back, Daniel. I can feel it."

"Mother, you must prepare yourself..."

She shushed me now, and placed her finger on my lips to silence me, but I took her hand and gently took it from my mouth.

"You must prepare yourself for the possibility," I warned her quietly, "that I may not be."

She closed her eyes and bowed her head. Was it too cruel to tell her the truth? I could not promise my return and she needed to see this.

"Sarah will remain in Gaeson," I said presently. "She will be ready to defend the caves, should the worst happen. She will take care of you." That was something I could promise her, for I knew as long as she drew breath Sarah would defend our people and my mother.

My mother's eyes met mine now and tears fell from her face as she nodded. My heart broke as I watched her pain, and I pulled her into my arms as a few tears fell silently from my own cheeks. We held each other for a minute or two before the embrace ended.

"I have nothing but the greatest pride for you, my son," my mother spoke now, "more than any woman could have for her son. I am sure you will lead our people with great strength and courage. Go in wisdom and honour, Daniel," she told me. "Go knowing that I love you and will not stop praying until the moment you return."

"I love you, Mother," I told her passionately. I stood and kissed her on her forehead before letting go of her hands. "Farewell."

My mother reached up and her hand rested on my cheek briefly. "Farewell, my son."

I looked at her for a moment longer before leaving the room. As I shut the door behind me, I could hear her begin to weep, but forced myself to not go back into her chamber. I took a moment to wipe my eyes before heading back down the stairs to see Rachel standing in the kitchen. I managed a small smile.

"I must go," was all I said. Rachel nodded, and I walked away, her footsteps telling me she was following me. I came to the front door and opened it, but glanced back before I stepped through. "Goodbye," was all I said.

"Farewell, Your Highness," she returned. A moment later and I closed the door behind me gently, knowing that I may never again enter my old house and see the woman who had raised me. I paused to take a breath and gather my composure before heading up the side street back towards the castle.

As I walked, I attempted to reign in any further emotions and sentimentality, though this was difficult, and instead fix my eyes on the task ahead. It would be a day or two before we met and joined with the army from Caer Ligualid, including those from Klumeck and my uncle; I prayed I would be able to lead Gaeson's army until then and be as good a leader as they deserved. I was ever thankful for the captain, John and Aife who would be my wise counsel.

Having already been to the armoury, I headed straight to the square. Many of the soldiers were already assembled and I saw Queen Evelyn was also there. There were townspeople also gathered all around in order to see us depart. I saw Sarah was standing next to Epos and I walked over to her. She did not speak for a moment, but we smiled at one another.

"Epos is well rested," Sarah said at last, reaching out to stroke my mare's neck. "I am sure she will serve you well."

"She always has, haven't you, girl?" Epos darted her head to the right and to the left, this way and that. My eyes roved to meet Sarah's. "Thank you again for staying," I told her in earnest. "You have as much right as me to fight in this war."

"No, brother, you were right about me being needed here. Besides, I only wanted to go out of revenge; that is no good motive to go to war. I was the one who warned you that vengeance is a poison."

The captain called out suddenly; the army began to form their ranks, and those that were riding mounted their horses.

"It is time to depart," I told her quietly, and she nodded; I saw tears glisten in her eyes but they did not fall. "I pray this is not goodbye for us, and that we shall see each other again soon."

Sarah nodded again. "If it is farewell, Daniel," she replied, her voice no louder than my own, "I want you to know that even though it means my parents deceived me… I will always be glad that we discovered the truth. You are my oldest and dearest friend," she muttered fiercely, batting away the tears that were still in her eyes with her eyelashes.

"You are mine, dear sister," I returned, and we embraced quickly. I felt the pain of our parting keenly; I suddenly felt that I was in the snow once more, being torn away from my kin, for Queen Evelyn was not the only woman to be in my heart. Our embrace ended, and she stepped back a little whilst I turned and mounted Epos. Then I turned Epos around and saw her, and we exchanged another small smile before she stepped further back into the crowd, a hand busy swiping at her tears.

Then I began to walk Epos to the front of the line, and as I reached it I saw Queen Evelyn. She turned; our eyes met and she began walking towards me. I felt time slowing, and yet my heart beat faster and faster. I used the last few seconds before she reached me to study her features – the pale cream of her skin, the curls of her hair. Her countenance was unreadable as usual, fully composed in all formality. Then, abruptly, she was standing in front of me, and I knew the time had come to say farewell.

"I wish you well, Prince Bryce. May you lead my people wisely and grant them victory from their enemies," she said, too loudly for her words to just be for my hearing.

"Your Majesty," I replied as evenly as possible, bowing my head in assent.

Queen Evelyn stroked Epos' neck almost absently, and then her head rose. I noticed in her face such sadness that she never showed another that it almost made me gasp. How I longed to enquire after her heart, to know whether she could possibly return a fraction of what I felt for her.

I felt my own impassiveness drop from my features, until I knew I was looking at her with the open intensity I had done when I had fallen from the cliff. I perceived my love to be almost at the point of weeping – how I yearned to comfort her.

"You best return to me, boy from the snow," she murmured now, her voice thick with emotion.

I could bear it no longer; I reached down and gripped her hands tightly, uncaring to all who would be witnessing it. "I swear, my lady, I will do all I can to come back to you," I whispered roughly.

My queen did not let her tears fall; she blinked and they receded. In the less formal tradition that monarchs could greet and bid each other farewell, I lifted her hand to my mouth and kissed it. How rough my mouth felt against the smoothness of her skin. Surely this would not be the last time I held her!

"Farewell," I whispered.

"Farewell, Daniel," she whispered back. She stepped back as Sarah had done, and I noted how, almost instantly, the emotion disappeared from her face.

I was forced to relinquish her hand. My own hand fell to my side, clumsy and lacking her sweet touch. I dropped the barriers onto my own emotions and gathered Epos' reins in my hands. I gazed at her for one lingering moment, for if this was the last time I beheld her beautiful features I would not be robbed from it. Then I turned swiftly, tearing my eyes away.

"Forwards!" I shouted, and set Epos off at a quick walk. I heard the clinking of armour and knew the others were behind me; I heard women begin to weep as their husbands left them for war.

We were exiting the square to the north, just to the left of the palace hall – the road that led to the portcullis. Then, all too abruptly, we were marching down the hill, away from Gaeson, away from all that I knew and loved and cherished.

Part Four

Chapter Thirteen

We rode for eight hours straight, alternating between walking and cantering, and stopping only as the last of day disappeared. We set about making camp, and some of my brothers and sisters made a fire. As I reflected upon the day, I acknowledged that we had made good riding; if we made good time, I prayed we would reach our destination with enough time to rest. Tomorrow we would travel further north, and halfway through the morning we would join forces with King Urien and my uncle. Indeed, I knew it would bring us much comfort to be joined with so many other warriors, for currently our army felt almost insignificant in size compared with the foes we faced.

Once we joined with the armies of Klumeck and Caer Ligualid, we would head further to the east, across the width of Briton until we reached the Bernician army. We had learnt the location of the Bernician stronghold from the Bernician spies we had recently acquired (the small good that the chief interrogator had done before he was revealed as the traitor he really was); the Bernicians made camp at a fortress on an island called Ynys Metcaut, off the northeast coast of Briton. From what I could glean from the captain, it lay far beyond the borders of Rheged, across the vast hills that bordered the former Kingdom of Klumeck. At this point we would also join with the confederation kings, whose aid King Urien had requested.

After several hours of marching, we came to a stop in a solitary field and made camp. We had travelled directly north; tomorrow we could change to sojourn more to the east. I spoke to some of the soldiers in the hope of encouraging them and assessing their morale; I then headed into the solace of my own tent. I stripped off most of my armour, feeling more human with each bit of metal I removed. A bowl of clean water had been procured from somewhere and now sat on a small table for my convenience; this, I supposed, was the benefit to being a monarch at war. I had not even been obliged to set up the tent myself – this had already been done whilst I had been talking with my people. Presently I changed my clothes, washed my hands and face, and then at last allowed myself to sit upon my makeshift bed and rest.

I now reached inside the breast pocket of the tunic I had discarded and pulled out the cloth my lady had given me all those years ago. It was probably to my own folly, but I still carried it with me everywhere. I turned the cloth over in my hands; the embroidery was much faded but still legible. As I stared at it, my mind wandered to the past and the day we had met. I felt I was not in a camp in a forest on the way to war but nine years old, crying in the snow for my favourite foal who had died in the night from fever.

"Your Highness?" There came a soft knock on the door of my tent and I looked up, abruptly and almost cruelly jerked back to the present.

"Come in, John," I replied, already knowing it was him. As I spoke I swiftly put the cloth back into my inside pocket.

John entered, bearing a bowl of stew.

"Thank you," I said, crossing the tent to take it from him. As I reached out to take the bowl, the cloth slipped from the pocket underneath my tunic; clearly in my haste I had not properly secured it, and since I had previously loosened my clothing from my belt, the cloth fell free to the floor.

"Sire, you dropped something…" He stooped to pick it up before I could stop him. He paused a moment, his thumb tracing over its finery. For some reason, I tensed as he held it, as if this was a precious memory that belonged to me. I held out my hand. He handed it back to me. "Might I ask what it is, Your Highness? The symbol embroidered on it, it almost looked like…"

"It's the royal seal, yes," I replied. "Join me, brother, but if you do, you must give the formal titles a rest." I gestured a vacant seat in the tent.

"Very well," John replied, and came to sit down opposite me. He said nothing else, but I could tell he was wondering about the cloth, and suddenly I found I wanted to tell him.

"Her Majesty gave it to me when we were children," I confided to him ere long and John's eyebrows rose.

"I did not know that you knew her when you were children. That is, you never mentioned it," he added. "Is that why she called you the boy from the snow?" he asked presently. "I wondered about that when I heard her use the term."

"Yes," I replied simply, tasting the stew again. "Her Majesty gave it to me when we were children. I was doing my morning work in the stables," I began the account, "when I heard her run inside. She had been playing with the guard and saw me there. I had been crying because of my favourite foal dying during the previous night from fever," I explained. "The queen – or princess, as she would have been then – gave me the cloth to wipe my eyes. When I went to give it back to her, she told me to keep it."

"You've kept it with you all this time since then?" John questioned me, and I nodded. "I see," was all he said. As he bent to eat more of his meal, I wondered how much he did see, whether he could sense my regard for the queen and all that I truly felt for her.

"Carrying it with me reminds me why I am fighting," I told him; suddenly it seemed imperative that one of my oldest friends should understand. "That day, after the queen had gone back inside the castle, I vowed I would serve and fight for her to the best of my ability. The cloth helps me keep that oath."

"Your dedication is to your credit," John replied as he put his empty bowl down. I used a crust of bread to mop up the rest of the stew from my bowl. "Since we are talking more informally," John murmured now, and I glanced up at him, "you should be encouraged that you have led the people well today, Daniel. Your father would be proud of you. That is, the man who raised you in Gaeson," he clarified, "though I am sure your Klumeck parents would take great pride in you also."

"Thank you, brother; your words are a comfort," I said, and smiled. We talked with one another for a few more minutes, until I saw his eyelids start to drop and began to sense my own fatigue. "You should get some rest, John," I directed to my friend presently, "it is still a long journey to war."

"Sire," John responded with a bow of his head and came to collect my bowl. "You too, brother," he muttered, quietly and a smirk crossed my face in return before he departed my tent.

The tiredness was strong in me now, and I hastily prepared for bed. Indeed, my head was barely able to touch my pillow before slumber found me. The last thoughts before I fell asleep were, as usual, of Sarah and the queen – hoping and praying that they were well.

***

We rose at dawn the next morning, and after taking down our tents, we continued our journey higher, all of us knowing that with each mile that passed, we grew closer to war. Despite this, the mood among the men and women under my command remained calm, if not grim. I was pleased that after six straight hours of marching, we had reached a place of encouragement – we were at the designated place to unite with the armies of Klumeck and Caer Ligualid. Presently I signalled that the army should stop and gave the captain the order for them to begin making camp.

I saw them at once to begin once more to put up their tents, and noted with almost surprise at how relaxed they seemed to be. I then dismounted Epos and patted her neck briefly before taking her to where the other horses were. Whilst I gave her some water to drink and a few oats to eat, I glanced up to the slightly higher ground to the group of archers Aife was leading in order to keep watch over us. I had instructed them to stay on the higher ground for a while before they were relieved for the night – this meant both the archers and those down here could have a little respite before traipsing across the hill to replace each other.

Soon camp was made; as we had stopped earlier in our travels than yesterday, we had the distinct advantage of being able to put up all the tents before the sun went down and it became dark. The soldiers then were able to rest, and though some took shelter, many others were content to stay outside, sat upon the grass despite the cold. Although the air was bitter, the warriors were content with the spectacular view of the sunset the high altitude had given us. The sky was a vivid orange, with soft lilac and coral hues in the background. As I took in the scenery and those who were enjoying it, our situation suddenly seemed ridiculous – things seemed almost peaceful, despite so obviously being prepared for war, bloodshed and disaster.

Indeed, as sky turned to twilight and we shared our evening meal together, I was sure it was some form of illusion that kept us serene whilst knowing the terrible times that surely awaited us. This veneer seemed strong and yet fragile, so that it resonated with us deeply but was ever on the cusp of being broken if it was too strongly acknowledged. So it was the men and women spoke in hushed tones – not only because the enemy could be present, but also, I suspected, in fear that the tranquillity would be lost. The spell of calm remained steadfast however, even after night came and we had retired to bed.

Everyone seemed to fall asleep within moments that second night – whereas unlike the night before, I found myself unable to slumber. I tossed and turned, but the more I sought sleep the more it appeared to elude me. I wondered if I had found the outward peace of the army unsettling – it did not seem to fit such sombre circumstances of war. In the end, I gave up on the idea of sleep and stood. I ran a hand through my hair and reached for my sword before heading out of the tent and into the still night air.

The sky was as clear as it had been during sunset and twilight, and I perceived the sky to be alight with a thousand stars. As I walked through the camp, I was reminded I had seen the stars like this, when I had escaped with my lady away from Gaeson and into the forest. I came now to a rock, and promptly sat on it. I looked out at the camp, dimly lit by the moon and stars. How many men and women would survive this? I wondered. How could they sit and laugh, so relaxed with one another, all the time knowing the fate that could be theirs? I sighed inwardly, and as I rubbed my hands over my face, I sensed I was not alone and looked up to see the captain.

"I saw you leaving your tent, Your Highness," he stated after bowing. "You could not sleep?" he guessed, and I shook my head.

"Come and join me, if you wish," I suggested, and he moved to sit down on the rock beside me. "It was a strange thing tonight," I said to him now, and in the near darkness I saw him frown. "The mood of the soldiers," I expounded. "It almost looked peaceful."

Here the captain gave a wry smile. "Aye, my lord. I have seen it many times when heading out to war. Not when the enemy is at our gates," he specified, "for then the threat is immediately at our gates, and therefore all they feel is fear. But for now, the danger is still far away, for the most part. The men are relieved they are still alive, sire," the captain concluded with a small shrug. "When we get closer to Bernicia, their mood will change."

I nodded at this answer, grateful for the captain's wisdom. "I pray they keep the courage they have now," I murmured. "It would be easy for fear to take hold of them; all our lives we've heard stories about Bernicia. The giants that will hail from the east." I smiled ruefully. "I do not know if we will win this fight," I told him honestly, "but we must fight all the same."

"Aye," the captain agreed. "I always find it a comfort to know that our God knows the battle and its outcome, even if we do not. Not a sparrow will find a worm, or a hair from our heads will fall without his sovereign will and good approval. We must encourage them to stand firm and not forget the God who watches over us."

"Thank you, brother," I smiled, finding his speech greatly encouraging. "I needed reminding of those truths just as much as our people." The captain nodded, and here I paused. "It is a beautiful night," I remarked presently. "It was like this when we spoke to Queen Evelyn on the balcony."

"I remember, sire," he mused, and I saw the wry smile had returned to his features. "That was right before I was struck in the chest."

"When I left with Her Majesty, I did not know whether you had survived," I murmured. "Do you find it strange, having to address me formally and follow my orders?" I asked him presently. "I wondered whether you found it as strange as me having to give you orders, rather than follow them," I added, and he now gave a low chuckle.

"Aye, I admit it was not the situation I foresaw," he muttered. "Although you have become a fine leader – I am regretting not giving you more leadership roles earlier."

I smiled at his encouragement. "I was always more content to follow orders than give them," I agreed.

He nodded but said nothing more, and we sat silent for a few moments. I looked out once more towards the camp where my men and women dwelt.

"I wonder if I might ask you a personal question, captain."

"Anything you want, sire," the captain answered, and I looked at him; it was something I had wanted to know ever since I enlisted in the army nine years ago.

"What is your name?"

The captain chuckled once more; he had always chosen to keep his name a secret – a common custom of our peoples. It was thought that if our commander's name was revealed, we could think of him too personally or forget our place. Of course, the army had known his name before he became captain, but it was no longer spoken of in public. Then, over the years a captain had served – as this captain had served almost fifteen in his position – the older soldiers would retire, and generations of new recruits would join until those who knew his true name were a small number indeed.

"My name is Bredon," he replied at length.

I smiled – the name meant "defender", or "warrior". It fitted the captain of the guard well.

"My father was captain of the guard before me," he replied. I raised my eyebrows, surprised. "He chose it deliberately, so I would follow in his footsteps. It seemed I was always destined to be captain of the guard."

I nodded at this. "I think I can sleep now, for a while," I stated now, and stood. The captain also did the same. "Thank you, brother, for your wisdom."

The captain smiled and nodded. "I'm sure you will continue to lead us well, Daniel," he told me, and I smiled at his use of my first name. "Goodnight, Your Highness," he added upon bowing.

"Goodnight," I replied as he straightened, and then I watched as he departed my company for a few minutes before I headed back to my tent. As I did, I looked once more towards the night sky and prayed that if it was in God's will, as many of us as possible would survive the days to come.

I found myself able to sleep a few hours that night, but when I woke I was only a little rested. I dressed quickly and put my armour on before leaving my tent again; when I did, the sky told me it was about an hour or so after dawn. We still had some time before we were expecting King Urien and my uncle, so we did not need to take down our camp so early. The weather was not quite as cold, but it was cloudy rather than clear; I hoped this would not hinder those who had already travelled to the high ground keep watch.

After a breakfast of boiled wheat, we began taking the camp down and tending to the horses. We had not long finished the task when a horn sounded; the men and women were standing and sitting upon the frosted grass and talking with one another. I glanced up to the higher ground to those who were keeping watch, my hand already on the hilt of my sword.

"Your Highness," John greeted me, already beside me, but my eyes were still fixed upon the hillside as the archers signalled to me that King Urien and King Cedric were only minutes away. I nodded at the group and turned to my friend.

"Tell them to form ranks," I instructed, "for I'm not sure His Majesty King Urien would approve of their relaxed moods."

"Aye, sire," John obeyed with a wry smile. Within moments, he had relayed my order to the captain and the soldiers got to their feet, placed their helmets back on their heads, and reformed their lines. I, too, swung back onto Epos and walked her to the very front. By the time King Urien and King Cedric came into view, we looked as though we had been standing ready for orders since we had first stopped. I perceived Prince Owain to also be riding with them. The combined army of Caer Ligualid and Klumeck were marching and riding behind them. As soon as they appeared I raised my hand, and the riders bowed as low as they could on horseback, whilst the marchers all sank as one onto bended knee.

"Your Supreme Majesty King Urien, Your Majesty King Cedric, Your Highness Prince Owain," the captain, John and I chorused.

"Prince Bryce," King Urien replied dryly, and did not acknowledge anybody else. "I take it Queen Evelyn is not present," he said in his usual gravelly tones.

"I am leading the army of Gaeson in her place, my lord the king," I answered quickly. "Her Majesty the queen was unsure of who to leave as steward in her place," I went on, feeling the need suddenly to defend my lady's actions. "She felt that since I am more familiar with marching out to battle, we could use our skills the best in this way."

"Very well," King Urien replied simply after a moment. "My men will require a brief rest," he added shortly, and with the usual swish of his cloak, he rode on, Prince Owain following close behind.

King Cedric at once began to dismount from his horse; I did the same, and we walked forwards towards each other.

"Your Majesty," I greeted him, and then smiled. "It is good to see you, uncle," I added as he came forwards further still and we clasped each other's arms. "I hope you fare well."

"As well as can be expected in war," he returned. "I was unsure of whether to expect you or Queen Evelyn; I had reasoned one of you would stay behind in light of recent events." He ended his speech quietly, and I was abruptly curious of what he truly felt about Reghan dying – though of course I would never ask about it.

"Part of me had hoped to not see you here, nephew; that you might escape the bloodshed," King Ceric continued now, "though I am sure you are pleased you are here in her place."

"Of course," I replied, a little too quickly. "My whole life I have served Gaeson as a soldier," I expounded, "so I was relieved to be able to keep her out of the greatest danger, so that she be kept from possible harm."

King Cedric raised an eyebrow but said nothing; suddenly, I wondered whether he might know about my feelings for her.

"Sarah is also not here," I continued quickly, lest my uncle say anything more about Queen Evelyn. "I persuaded her not to come here."

I saw him smile and the relief take form in his eyes. "I had hoped you would do so, Bryce. I am pleased to hear she is out of danger; I would not want her to come to harm, not after I have just found her." King Cedric now looked beyond me to where King Urien was busy ordering his army. "We shall depart soon. How are your men doing?"

"They were relieved to reach here last night, my lord," I replied. "We arrived at the appointed time, so they had opportunity to rest. I fear they will grow more anxious, now we are on the road to war again."

My uncle nodded. "We have only been travelling in the hour or two since daybreak," he said presently, "so it will not be long until we are on the road again." At this point, King Urien turned to King Cedric and gestured him over. "I'll see you shortly," King Cedric stated, patting me briefly on the shoulder as he passed by me.

"Your Majesty," I said quietly, and watched him walk over to King Urien. The Supreme King of Rheged began to speak to him in a very animated tone; alas, they were at such a distance that I could not hear anything. I noticed my uncle began to look angry, and as I observed my scene, I felt apprehension begin to fill me. Though my heart was gladdened to see my uncle and to have so many soldiers joining us, I was unsettled by King Urien's demeanour and whatever he was saying to King Cedric that I could not hear.

The feeling of unease stayed with me even after we had begun marching. We had set off, our three ranks formed together with the army of Klumeck on the left, Caer Ligualid on the right, and Gaeson forming in the middle. I was riding on Epos at the very front of the lines, along with King Cedric, King Urien, Prince Owain, and the three captains of the guard from our respective armies. Even though it gave me a little joy to see how all of Rheged was finally united, there was still something about our supreme king that I was unsure of.

Soon, though, any misgivings I had about King Urien were replaced by the routine of the journey to war. As we rode and marched together, I perceived the path we were on to be even, which made it far easier to travel. We continued across the tall hills placed along the length of Briton; after two days we had left these peaks behind and were heading further east. At this point we were deep within Bernician territory, but strangely the lands were deserted, and we had no resistance from our foes.

As we neared our journey's end, presently I saw King Urien turn to his captain and begin speaking to him in hushed tones that I could not hear. It was not long after dawn on the seventh day since I had left Gaeson with Queen Evelyn's army; we had been travelling across Briton for six days now, so I knew our meeting point with the other confederation kings had to be near. I glanced around me and instinctively tightened my hands slightly on Epos' reins; this was the beginning of the third day of being out in open plains like this, and I sensed we all felt very much exposed.

It seemed King Urien sensed this also, for presently he ordered that we should take cover in a nearby forest. We all marched into the trees, and I noticed all of our armies were anxious that they not be caught. I sensed Epos was aware of this also; over the last day she had grown increasingly agitated. I tried to reassure her as much as I could, but it seemed she had ever-growing knowledge that we were heading to war.

As we all waited in the forest, I turned my attention to King Urien, who was again speaking secretly with his captain. It was clear he was angry at something, which was no new experience – but then from the way King Urien was looking around whilst he was walking, I suddenly realised what the problem was – he was clearly no longer sure where the meeting point was. In other words, we might well be lost. I sighed inwardly at this, but then, as I glanced around the forest, an idea abruptly formed in my mind.

"I'll see you soon, my girl," I murmured as I dismounted her, stooping to stroke her mane softly. Then I abruptly began to remove my armour.

"Prince Bryce," King Cedric said formally as he walked over, "what are you doing?"

"We need to see what is beyond the plains, Your Majesty," I said, removing my breastplate, "as we have lost the advantage of high ground. Aife," I called, and she immediately ran over. "Climb that tree," I instructed, pointing to a wide oak; I had already picked out a similar tree for myself.

"My lord," she replied in obedience with a smile; it seemed she knew exactly what I meant. She at once began to remove the heavier parts of her own clothing as I walked up to the tree. As I did, King Cedric came much closer to me.

"Are you sure about this, nephew?" King Cedric hissed in my ear. "What if you fall?"

I glanced at him and smiled. "Do not fear, Uncle; I have been climbing trees since my youth." I nodded to Aife and she began to clamber up; I fixed my eyes ahead of me and I myself began climbing rapidly. The skill I had learned in my childhood alongside Sarah easily came back to me, and soon I was lost in the enjoyment of jumping between branches, that I could tell were easily strong enough to support my weight.

As I climbed yet higher, I began to remember afternoons with Sarah having races to see who would reach the top first, our mothers calling at us with worry until they realised there was little chance we would ever fall. The skill of climbing trees was also the requirement of any archer, which was why I had, as always, full confidence that Aife would complete her task.

I now gave myself one final push up to poke my head above the canopy of foliage that covered the forest, and immediately the open sky was once again around us.

"My lord," Aife called; she had already reached the top and was pointing to the northeast of us. I had to smile at her speed – I thought I had scaled the tree quickly, but it seems I had not been able to keep up with her. My smile faded as I now followed where she pointed – I saw that not too far away from us the ground began to descend, and then, in the afternoon light, I began to make out the island of Ynys Metcaut and the Bernician stronghold that awaited us. Beyond that was the pure vastness of the sea; I had never before seen the ocean in all its fullness.

"I see it," I called back presently. I carefully stepped my feet further along the branch, but all I could make out between here and there was large open ground, perfect for the Bernicians to suddenly attack us. My eyes continued to scan the landscape, and then I saw a landmark I recognised.

"That dead tree," I said now, pointing, "that is where we are to unite with the confederation kings. It looks only half a mile away."

It was Aife's turn to follow my gaze.

"Aye, sire," she agreed, and then frowned. "We will still be on slightly higher ground compared to the island – we should be safe from view there if we remain parallel to the forest. We need to stay on the left, my lord."

"Let us return to the others," I ordered now, and swiftly climbed back down to the tree. I jumped the last few metres clean to the forest floor where King Urien stood.

"Well, what did you see?" he asked immediately, folding his arms with some impatience. Aife and I immediately sank onto bended knee before I responded.

"The meeting point is but half a mile away, Your Majesty, to the northeast," I answered him. "There is a danger of being seen, my lord the king, but not if we keep to the left of the fields. I recommend we run in several groups; the archers can remain in the trees to signal to us."

"Very well. Get the men into positions," he added to his captain, who quickly bowed and ran to assemble the Caer Ligualid soldiers. "A clever plan, young prince," the supreme king said with a smirk, as I straightened once more.

"Thank you, Your Majesty," I said, keeping my surprise silent that he seemed to have said this without any sarcasm. King Urien regarded me for a moment longer before heading off to ready his soldiers.

My uncle stepped forwards now, a smile upon his face. "I'll never doubt your resourcefulness again, my boy," he chuckled, clapping his arm around me.

I returned the smile before I turned to Aife. "Aife, I bid you choose a group of archers and position yourself in the trees," I instructed her quickly. "Give us a signal each time a group has made it across safely – and give us a signal if you see any danger. Also," I added, "make sure you also come safely across to us."

"Sire," she responded with a smile, and at once began climbing the tree again.

Presently I turned to see our three armies splitting into around fifty different parties – as we were around five thousand fighting men and women in total, there were about a hundred in each. We assembled as such in the entrance of the forest and waited for the signal from Aife.

Almost immediately, Aife gave a low shout and the first group were off, riding on their horses across the plains that separated us from where we would meet with the other confederation kings. I waited atop Epos calmly, who was neighing distractedly again.

"Hush, girl," I murmured, and reached for some oats to calm her. A few tense minutes passed, and then another archer shouted again. I exhaled in relief, for if the first party had made it across unscathed then it gave hope for us all. The ones who were sprinting off into the distance presently had both King Cedric and his captain; my party contained King Urien, Prince Owain and Captain Bredon. I knew I was next, and I found myself aware of each pressing moment, my ears straining to hear the shout from the archers.

Then, abruptly, the call came, and in the next moment we were galloping across the field. The grass below us was blurred with our movements, and the cold breeze whistled through my ears. We curved across a field, and soon I could see the dead tree in the distance, and I knew that in the next few seconds we would arrive…

Suddenly, an arrow shot past near King Urien's head and landed in the ground; rapidly I pulled up Epos' reins, jerking her to a stop. Immediately, I recognised the arrow and glanced towards Aife – from this distance I could only just make out her signals.

"Take cover!" King Urien shouted, coming to a stop beside me. "We have been detected, prepare to fight," he instructed us sharply.

"No, my lord the king," I protested urgently, before he gave away our position, turning to the king. His eyes grew wide in confusion and rage that I should dare undermine him. "That is, Your Majesty," I said, modifying my response quickly, "the arrow was not fired from our enemies; it bears Gaeson's seal."

"What folly is this? We have a traitor in our midst," he snarled, looking around him as if he could summon the means to kill Aife from our current position.

"If they had wanted to shoot us, we would be dead, sire," I replied hastily, lowering my voice in the hope that he would too. "I have just seen Aife in the forest; she has just signalled me to say there is a patrol heading in our direction and we should remain here." I glanced towards the forest again, but she was now no longer looking in our direction. "If we had carried on, my lord the king," I continued, "then we would have been detected. They simply acted in urgency to preserve our lives."

"You had better be right, boy," King Urien hissed, "otherwise that archer's life will be forfeit."

I sighed inwardly at this but said nothing; at least his voice had become quiet.

"Be ready, men," the king then ordered to the others, as he walked his horse to the others in our party.

I walked Epos on a foot or two and bent down to retrieve the arrow. Upon closer inspection, I perceived there to be a thin mark along the length of the arrow. I sensed movement now and as I looked up, I saw the captain had ridden over to me.

"My lord?" the captain whispered and frowned. "That is Aife's arrow," he stated in a low voice.

I nodded and quickly placed it in my quiver. "Best not tell King Urien," I returned quickly, "lest he wishes to carry out his threat of death."

The captain nodded in agreement.

I then glanced up towards the forest to see Aife signalling; I watched her for a few moments and then nodded. "It is clear to move on, Your Majesty," I called to King Urien.

King Urien's features hardened at this as he rode his horse to the front of the line once more. "Be on your guard, men," he ordered, clearly no longer trusting my word. "March!" he shouted, and we set off into a swift gallop again. Only a minute or two later, we had traversed the plains that were the most exposed to the island and were in the shelter of the field with the hollow tree. As we arrived, I realised that the soldiers who had gone before us were already in the process of making camp.

"Good girl," I murmured to Epos, as I dismounted her. As I did, I caught sight of King Urien marching towards his tent and could tell he was still in a rage about Aife's arrow. Indeed, so prevalent was his anger that I reflected upon whether, if we all returned home alive, our supreme ruler would hold an enquiry to investigate who had fired the arrow. As I pondered this, I saw my uncle coming over to greet me.

"What happened, Bryce?" King Cedric greeted me quickly with a frown upon his features. "We were worried to see your delay."

"The archers signalled for us to stop," I explained. "There was a patrol heading straight for us. The archers had to fire an arrow to get our attention," I added, "which landed not far from King Urien."

"Ah, that explains it," King Cedric murmured wryly, as we saw our supreme ruler shouting orders at one of his soldiers. The sight of his anger was almost comical, if it were not the case that he had the power to slay any one of the people standing near him. I made a mental note to try to avoid his path, as I could still remember when he had threatened he would have my head if I ever disobeyed him again.

Over the next hour, the groups continued to reach our meeting point, with my heart lightening considerably with each troop of soldiers that entered our camp. Then at last I perceived all of our force to have made it across without harm, and concern for Aife and the other archers grew – they now had the most difficult task of making it back without anyone providing watch; they would be running across the open fields without any oversight.

"She is a formidable warrior; I'm sure we will see her at any moment," I said to John, who was standing beside me.

"Sire," was all he answered, and I had to begin fighting the fear that threatened to creep into my heart – because we both knew that we couldn't be sure that she was still alive. Then my fear turned to joy as we saw her leading the rest of the archers in the final sprint and came to a stop a few yards in front of us.

"Ah, finally." King Urien strode across to us, arms folded and with pure indignation in his countenance, as we sank into a swift bow. "So, which archer was it that almost hit me?" he roared.

"With all due respect, my lord the king," I began, raising my gaze off the floor to look at him, "what the archers did were on my orders. I beg Your Majesty to see that if the archers had not stopped us, we would certainly have been detected, and this war could have been over before it began," I pointed out.

I noticed King Urien's eyes narrow, and his mouth drew into a thin line.

"I fear you speak your mind too much, Prince Bryce. That arrow nearly had my head, and you will find out who did it, or I will have all of yours," he ended violently, and then, with a swish of his cloak, he swiftly marched off back towards his tent.

Presently, I turned to face Aife and the other archers; they were all were looking at me expectantly. "It is good to see you all alive," I told them, "for I know what you risked in travelling here without watch. You have all served the Kingdom of Rheged today; I bid you go and rest, for tomorrow we fight."

"My lord," Aife began at once, "it was me who fired the arrow. I do not wish all of these to die upon my account; I beg you tell him the truth."

I gave a wry smile as I regarded her, and then I put one hand behind my back to take her arrow from my quiver. "I know. I recognised this was yours." I held it out to her and she took it. "King Urien will be too preoccupied with war to act on his words. Then, by tomorrow, if we are still alive, we will all be relieved and mourning those we have lost. His angry speech will be all but forgotten. Get some sleep, my friend," I added, and she now returned my wry smile as she placed her arrow back in her quiver.

"Sire." She bowed her head and made to move past me. "You too, brother," she murmured, and I smiled as she walked to the tent she was sharing with some other archers. I had positioned new archers onto the top of the field where the castle could just be seen, in order for them to keep watch.

Presently, I straightened and walked through the camp in the sunshine; it was indeed strange to be going to sleep while it was afternoon, but we were planning to attack that night, and we had been up marching since daybreak as well as the run from the forest to here, so I knew sleep would come easily to the soldiers simply due to exhaustion. Like the other night, though, I found it difficult to sleep –I felt like I had remained awake the rest of the day, but I knew some slumber must have found me because when I opened my eyes again, all was quiet and still, so I knew most of the camp must still be asleep.

"My lord," the captain greeted me, "I was just coming to wake you; the confederation kings will be here soon."

I nodded and rubbed my face. "Very good," I murmured, and then he vanished from the tent flap as quickly as he had appeared.

I stood and stretched; quickly assessing my physical state. It was almost five weeks now since I had fallen from the cliff, and most of my wounds had healed. My arm had also now fully recovered from when I had been pierced in the battle when Joshua had died. I hurriedly dressed and placed on my armour, praying swiftly now we were on the cusp of battle for the strength to lead the men and women in my command. Finally, I slid my sword into my sheath and picked up my helmet and shield; in the moment before I left the tent, I spared a thought for those in Gaeson, hoping that all were well and safe.

The day was now almost over, and I stood leaning against the trunk of the dead tree that looked almost gold in the evening sun. We had all slept for most of the day, and now the last of the camp was being taken down. The soldiers had been on rotation between resting and readying the ladders and catapults we had brought with us to use in besieging Bernicia; these now looked complete. As I glanced around the camp, I caught sight of King Urien in another part of the field, and to my relief it looked as though he had calmed down somewhat; I prayed that if we would survive this day, the archers' lives would be spared from his tyranny. As I stood there, I sensed my King Cedric coming to stand beside me.

"Do not judge him by his anger, Bryce." I turned to him, and my uncle smiled grimly. "He is our supreme king, and he was almost killed by one of our own archers. I know Aife would never have missed," he added, as he saw me open my mouth in protest. "King Urien probably knows that too. But he has to appear strong, my boy – and this is how he does it. Kings have different approaches to ruling their people; his is to rule it by instilling fear into the hearts of his subjects."

I frowned now, folding my arms. "Do you choose to rule this way, sire?" I asked him. "Do you choose to rule through fear?"

My uncle tilted his head a little as he reflected. "Sometimes, it is necessary," King Cedric conceded. "I could well imagine myself reacting in the same way, if I were in his position. Not you, though," he added now, and I glimpsed a small smile in his features. "I can see that if you ever were to lead a kingdom, people would not fear you the way they do King Urien. You were one of them, Daniel," he explained, seeing me frown further. "You have fought beside your men and even risked the wrath of Rheged herself to save Gaeson – your people would follow you anywhere. Even Klumeck seem aligned to you," he stated with almost surprise in his voice, as we stood there waiting for the other kings to arrive.

"There's something I've been wondering, uncle," I remarked quickly, conscious that the confederation kings would be here shortly and so I had little time. "What was King Urien talking to you about so urgently, after he first arrived?"

"Oh," King Cedric replied, "that." His countenance had hardened a little. "He was talking to me about you," he explained quietly, and my eyes widened. "He wanted to know whether I had full confidence in your abilities; that's why I told you to be on your guard. I think your skill in climbing the trees impressed him, but then…"

"An arrow flew past his head and I told him it was under my command," I sighed. "Thank you, Your Majesty; I shall remember his distrust of me."

"Don't fear, nephew – if we survive this, then I'm sure he will have full confidence in you."

I made no reply at first, for I myself did not know if this was true – and I wasn't sure my uncle was so certain either, or if merely he sought to comfort me.

"I pray you're right, Uncle," was all I said. Then, presently, I heard the sound of marching; both of us looked towards the end of the field where the confederation kings would be arriving, and I could just make out the light of beacons.

"They're here," my uncle murmured. He nodded to me and quickly ran to his horse as I did the same, hurriedly climbing atop Epos and riding her to the front of the lines as the armies formed their ranks. Together, the other commanders and captains called for ranks to be formed and as this was done, I looked towards the beacons again.

As I did, I was strangely reminded of the night, almost six weeks ago now, when I had woken in the night due to my thirst, when I had seen King Cedric's army as a sea of beacons. How strange to think it was just a short time ago, when I still regarded King Cedric as a tyrant who was my enemy. Presently, I mounted Epos and walked her to the front of the line to wait for the confederation kings. When they arrived with their armies, there would be a short time of respite and a meeting of the commanders to discuss strategy. No matter how long we talked, however, the end would be imminent. We all knew that the bloodshed was about to begin.

Chapter Fourteen

The confederation kings entered our field as twilight began to sweep over the sky, erasing any impression of the sun. They marched over to us and I almost gasped at the size of them – there were almost nine thousand of them in their four different armies conjoined together. The first king I could see was King Rhydderch (having recognised his seal and standard the soldier next to him was carrying). He was the one they called "the Courageous". He had thick sandy hair atop his head, and I saw his face was shaven with his cheeks red and full. I could not make out his countenance... his eyes looked bold as he stared straight ahead, and I realised his eyes were bold with a hint of what could be triumph in his gaze. I realised it was the face of a king who desired most strongly to be in the war already.

Then the second king came into view, and I instantly speculated him to be King Gwollag, King Urien's cousin; so similar were they in likeness. Even from standing far off, I could detect the same piercing eyes, the same narrow mouth, and the same sharp nose. Behind him was the third king – I reasoned this was King Morgant, the king I had heard my uncle say could not be trusted. This man had full dark hair and a beard, and his eyes looked almost black in the darkening sky; I had a feeling of unease just watching him.

Almost immediately after their arrival, there was a meeting of the army commanders and their respective captains; I myself was in attendance as one of the seven monarchs. The discussion was brief; it was merely a confirmation of a strategy we already knew – we were to approach Ynys Metcaut under the cover of darkness and besiege the stronghold. It would be strange to be initiating a huge attack like this onto the stronghold; it was the first time I was attacking a castle rather than defending it in Gaeson.

Neither the commanders nor their captains said anything new at the meeting, which I had suspected. Our strategy was that the majority of the army would march to Ynys Metcaut, whilst we would divert off to our own position to ready our arrows. I myself had been given the task of leading the archers – we were to provide cover for the main attack. My band of archers would be the signal to charge, and then the first wave of soldiers would charge.

The discussion ended rather abruptly and we walked to our ranks, ready to get into our positions. Soldiers with their respective seals upon their armour filed past me as I went with the other riders to where the horses had been stationed. As I neared Epos, I saw a man heading in my direction to join the other marchers and I stopped still as I recognised him; he then lifted his head and saw me.

"Your Highness," he greeted me quietly, giving a small bend of his head after regarding me for a moment.

"Conall," I returned, nodding at him. I had been wondering whether I would see the Klumeck soldier here, but since Gaeson's army had joined with Klumeck and Caer Ligualid I had not spotted him until now. "It is good to have you with us in this fight."

"Thank you, sire," he replied. We stood still for a moment while soldiers filed past us, and I wondered what this man thought of me – the man who was his royal prince, who was also indirectly responsible for his brother's death. I hoped that us joining together to fight a common enemy – answering the threat of the Bernicians – would heal the rift between us.

"Your Highness," Conall abruptly said with another small bow of his head – he was suddenly gone. My eyes widened slightly as I looked around for him, but there was no sign – he was already lost in the midst of soldiers forming their lines. I, too, turned now and walked the last few steps towards Epos.

"Hello, old girl," I greeted her softly. She pawed the ground distractedly, and I knew she could sense the tension in the air and that something was wrong. Tonight would be the first time I would ride Epos to attack such a vast army; before now I had only ever ridden her in relatively small battles. I gave her some water and oats before swinging up onto the saddle and guiding her to the enemy lines to wait for the order to march.

As I sat upon Epos in the lines awaiting King Urien's command, I began thinking of Sarah. She had been on my mind especially since climbing the tree yesterday, as climbing the trees had been one of our favourite activities, when we were not practising swordplay with wooden sticks or simply running in fields. A different memory of our childhood now surged through me, and I could almost smell the sweetness of the hay from the days when she used to help me and my father (that is, the man who raised me in Gaeson) in the stables.

Presently, I could see in my mind's eye the few times we had journeyed to the great lake and fished, without much success. Indeed, Sarah had always been interested in walking barefoot in the water, picking small stones that glimmered and shone, whilst I teased that it was her movements that chased all the fish away. I smiled to myself at the memories, which was a rare thing before a battle. I was truly thankful that even though we didn't know it, we had indeed been brought up together. We had not been separated cruelly – when I had discovered the truth about who I was, I could have found myself with complete strangers. No, it was far better that due to the kind women who had raised us, we had already had such a close bond.

"Something amusing, Your Highness?" came a voice to my right, and I turned to see John on my other side. It was a great comfort to see both of them, but I knew our time together would be brief; John was not an archer, and therefore he would be in the charge, along with the rest of our armies.

"I was thinking of Sarah," I smiled, "about when we used to climb trees. Climbing that tree yesterday reminded me."

A wry smile crossed his face as he nodded; John himself had often joined in with our playing after we had formed our friendship.

"I came to give my farewell," John explained, and I felt the smile fade from my face as more soldiers formed their ranks. I glanced between him and Aife, who was still beside me.

"May God be with you both," I muttered, having to fight my emotions that this could be the last time that all three of us were together in this way.

"Your people are ready to follow you anywhere, sire," Aife murmured, as she extended her arm so that it was in front of me. Instantly, I reached out and touched it. "As are we, Daniel," she added in a whisper.

I glanced at John, who now put his hand on top of mine. "Thank you, both of you," I murmured, managing somehow to keep my voice even, despite the sadness so prevalent in me. "I know I would have died a hundred times without you here beside me. I pray you both survive this night," I concluded quietly.

Our hands now fell to our sides and my emotions grew stronger, knowing that I would be with Aife a little longer, but I might not ever see John again, and I reached for his arm.

"I pray we see each other again, brother," John murmured. In the near total darkness, I could just make out the sadness of his smile.

"As do I, old friend," I murmured back.

In the next moment, he had given us a nod and was riding quickly to his position. I pushed back the sadness of my emotions as we awaited King Urien's command to move, to surround Ynys Metcaut. In the few seconds before the order came, I occupied my time by curling and uncurling my fingers – the cold surged right through my thin gloves, and so I was warding off numbness. The last thing I wanted was for me not to be able to hold my sword or bow properly.

Then, King Urien drew his sword. "We march," he commanded in a low voice, and we and the other commanders set off on our horses at a walk, heading over the field, where the slight incline had protected us against Bernicia. The going was slow; we were not carrying beacons, lest we should be detected. Epos began turning her head to the left and to the right; immediately I placed my hand on her neck to assure her.

"Keep going, girl," I murmured. I raised my head to look at the sky, but could see nothing – the weather had changed from this morning's sunshine, and now clouds helped to hide us from detection, which was an answer to prayer. The castle, however, was lit brightly – we could see the watchmen walking on the roof, beacons accompanying them.

As with any battle, I had the feeling that my whole life had been preparing me for this moment. God's grace had kept me alive thus far, but I wondered whether tonight would be the night He would call me home. If not, I was glad I finally was content again; I felt here and now, with the other six monarchs leading the lines on their horses, that I was used to my new identity. Indeed, I was glad Gaeson and Klumeck were standing together this night, finally allies. If nothing else, this battle would bond us and our kingdoms – however long God granted us to remain – we would be strong brothers and sisters, men and women of Rheged together, rather than needless enemies. These thoughts brought me to Reghan, and I had to deliberately occupy my mind with other thoughts – thinking of him now was complicated. He was the man who had ordered the deaths of most of my family and caused my separation from my sister; but he had also been the father of the woman I loved.

"Archers, with me," I instructed in a low voice, as we neared our position. We broke off from the general army, and as I did I caught sight of King Cedric, and we exchanged a sad smile – I prayed that if it was in God's will, it would not be the last time I saw my uncle's face.

We came to a stop about half a mile from the castle whilst the rest of the army travelled on. I was unsure how close the rest of the army could get before they were seen, but by each footstep and horse hoof they moved forwards. Eventually, though, about two hundred metres from the castle, we pulled to a stop. We waited with bated breath, but we appeared as yet unseen. Even from our distance, I heard the loud moving of heavy metal and knew that those on foot now pulled the heavy catapults into position, and I knew all was ready.

The moving of the catapults had caught the attention of the watchmen; I saw them peer into the darkness in confusion. Immediately, we readied our bows and selected our targets, and I forced myself to keep breathing; otherwise in such suspense surely I would forget to draw in more air. It was always in these moments that the world never seemed more quiet or still – there were thousands here and yet I was sure it would be heard if one stepped on a dry twig.

"May God be with us all," I whispered. As my queen now came to mind, I reached into my armour, into my tunic pocket for one last time before we stepped over the threshold. Gingerly, I touched the corner of the cloth between my forefinger and thumb. I was glad that my final thoughts before the battle were of her – of her long curls, her warm eyes, and beautiful smile. She symbolised everything I loved, everything that was home. I prayed that whatever happened to us this night, she and all of Gaeson would be safe.

"Fire!" I ordered in a low voice. As soon as the word sounded from my lips, I released my arrow into the night and I saw the man, lighted by his beacon, fall as he was pierced. "Fire at will!" I shouted as swiftly I placed another arrow onto the string of my bow.

"Charge!" came the bellowing shout of King Urien, and with that, the first wave of our confederation army galloped forwards, marchers sprinting as they held on to the ladders, brave souls who had to run without their arms because of what they were carrying.

"Fire the catapults!" King Urien cried, and seconds later the huge stones were hurled into the stronghold wall as I fired another shot. By now, the marchers who had run with the ladders had arrived at the walls and were beginning to raise them up against the castle.

"Cover the ladders!" I shouted, as we concentrated our arrows onto the stronghold walls where enemy archers were attempting to pierce those climbing up. It had only been a couple of minutes since the battle had begun, and already the Bernicians seemed to be swarming upon us. Soon, we continued to pick off our targets; the first few marchers were over the top, and it became incredibly difficult to aim once the close combat began.

We continued to fire our arrows until at last I reached into my quiver to discover it was my last arrow. A quick glance at Aife told me her quiver was empty also. I nodded at her; it was time for us to march also. I estimated there were about thirty of us archers, selected from the armies of Gaeson, Klumeck and Caer Ligualid. I suspected we were nigh insignificant to the vast armies, but I prayed we would make an impact.

"Fire your last arrows and prepare to march!" I shouted, replacing my bow upon my back and gathering Epos' reins in my hands. It was a tense few seconds whilst the other archers prepared for battle; I steeled my breath and drew my sword.

"Charge!" I shouted, and we set off on a gallop. I had one hand on the reins, and the other held my sword ready. Then, suddenly, I was in the thick of the battle, with enemy soldiers and their blades bearing down at me from all sides. I rode through them with my horse, piercing them as I passed, until a soldier struck Epos and I fell. I used a brief second to assess her state; she was not pierced too badly. I then was forced to duck as a foe advanced upon me and, as I twirled, I raised up my shield to batter his head.

In the next moment, I lifted my shield and bashed it against Epos' hindquarters, shouting for her to go as I did. At once my horse set off at a gallop and was gone from my sight; I hoped if she survived, I would see her again. An instant later I sensed movement to my right, and I launched myself through the ground as a mace cut heavily through the air. I rolled forwards and turned to face the attacker as I jumped to my feet. The man with the mace came forwards again, and I darted backwards to avoid another blow. As I did so, I realised I had no more space to evade my foe; soldiers were fighting all around me. He seemed to realise this, for presently he curved his face into a manic smile as he elevated his cruel weapon to bring it down upon me again.

I instantly lifted my shield to block it, that being the only option I had left. The force of impact launched me into the air, and I fell back several feet before crashing into another enemy soldier. My shield then battered my face so that splinters flew off and sharply embedded themselves into my skin. I swiftly rolled away from the enemy soldier I had landed on, and pierced his neck with my sword before I then saw the man with the mace was back. As he tried a third time to hit me with his mace, I leapt to the side, and as it swung through the air I sliced my sword across his knees and he fell down with a grunt, the mace landing with a heavy clunk beside him. He curled up on the ground, and

I then hit him hard in his right temple, rendering him unconscious.

I was vaguely aware my face was bleeding from the splinters, but I had no time to remove them as I became embroiled in the next fight. After I had cut down the next soldier I heard a roaring cry, and I looked up to see the large door of the stronghold opening and the swarm of Bernician soldiers spilling out onto the field. This filled me with dismay, but then I saw that another wave of the confederation armies were running forwards to meet them, and then the noise of battle cries, the screams of the wounded, and metal hitting metal were almost deafening.

On and on we fought, with cries and gasps and horror continuing to fill the air that had been so still. How could battle be so loud and so quiet all at once? I pushed on, dancing my blade with others, seeing their glimmering steel in the moonlight before their wielders brought them down towards me. I had learnt the steps of the dance long ago, learned how to weave and evade, how to slice my opponents as if I was cutting into fresh bread. But the horror of what my blade caused had never left me, not since my first battle and the first cry came out of the first man I had ever put to the sword.

I soon lost count of how many I had killed, how many confrontations I had won. I was vaguely aware that time and space were passing; the clouds had cleared somewhat and the moon was full, which helped friend and foe alike see each other better. As I continued to wield my blade against the enemy, I struggled to remember a world existed where those around me were not being torn apart. I did not even know whether John, Aife, Captain Bredon or my uncle were still alive.

Presently, I dived to the floor to avoid a blow to the head; as I rolled across the slick mixture of mud and sand, I sliced my blade through the air to cut my enemy down. I took a moment to assess my physical state – I still had no major injuries apart from my splintered and cut face, the blood of which had by now hardened. I gave thanks to God, for I knew it was only due to him that I had survived this far. In the brief respite I had been given before my next fight, I glanced around and surveyed the battle; though we had moved forwards, we still fought only on the outside of Ynys Metcaut. The door to the stronghold had still not been opened, though we had made a strong battering ram made from many logs and thick ropes which hammered against the door again and again.

I noticed, however, there were still soldiers swiftly climbing the ladders that we had mounted against the castle walls; presently, I decided to try to scale the stronghold to aid the battle. I began to move forwards rapidly, wishing at this point I had Epos for even greater speed – though I was glad she was removed from battle, and prayed that my horse was still alive. Again and again I weaved around my foes, darting to the left and to the right. For a moment I wasn't sure if I would make the journey, but seconds later I arrived at the ladder, and I immediately sheathed my blade and began to climb.

The few moments climbing the ladder seemed to last for an eternity, but then I had leapt onto the wall and drew my sword upon landing to cut the first enemy down. I defeated my next three foes and then I acknowledged the problem – there were too many Bernicians who were effectively halting our advance. A few more of the Briton army presently jumped onto the castle wall, and I saw our only chance was to run right at them and force them off the narrow steps descending from the castle wall.

"Britons, with me!" I shouted, and abruptly rushed at them, quickly evading the first man's blade. I raised my shield so it made contact with his head and he fell down, either unconscious or dead. A Briton had by now reached my side and was also beginning to push back our enemies; in my peripheral vision I saw it was John, and I smiled at him briefly, thanking God that of all the soldiers that could have been my side, I had been granted to see my friend alive at least once more.

"Forwards for Rheged!" I roared, and those under my command and I, still holding my shield in front of me, began to descend the stone steps of the fortress. As we buffeted them away we came to the small hall, and my eyes widened to see how many soldiers were there – a whole legion of them – simply waiting to strike whoever came in their way.

"My Lord!" John shouted, as I alone reached the bottom of the steps and plunged into the fierce Bernician warriors. I knocked three of them to the floor as I landed, and whilst my blade blocked a sword to my right I felt the man beneath me beginning to get up. Rapidly, I incapacitated him with a sharp kick to his forehead and jumped clear, bashing into another enemy soldier. For a few terrifying seconds I realised I was surrounded, but then ten more Briton soldiers leapt into the fray and chaos, and John ran over to me.

"Daniel, are you alright? he asked quickly.

I nodded as I straightened, and our conversation was paused whilst we both turned to slaughter another enemy.

"With respect, you either have incredible courage or incredible folly," he called to me.

"Those ideas are not entirely separate," I shouted back, as I slit another man's throat with my blade. "Behind you!" I shouted, and the two of us swiftly clasped hands and pulled each other forwards so we went in opposite directions to slay each other's foes. "Come, we need to get that door open," I said urgently.

"Your Highness," John agreed, and the two of us made our way through the enemy forces. This seemed such an insurmountable task, but it encouraged me greatly that with each step I took, more and more Britons were joining in the fight. I suspected another wave from our armies had been called forth, but I had not been able to hear it over the roars of battle and the cries from the wounded as they fell. Presently, we neared the door.

"Sire, give me your hand," John stated, and I saw at once he meant me to raise his feet up. I held out my hands and he stepped into them; I gritted my teeth as I lifted him up, for he was heavy with the weight of his armour. John drew his sword and began hacking away at the wooden bars that had been so effective in blocking the door.

"Join him!" I commanded to another couple of Briton soldiers fighting nearby; they finished their battles and began climbing up to the door also. "Cover them!" I shouted, and we tried to hold our ground as John and the other soldiers continued to break the wood covering the door. "Hurry! We can't hold them for long!" I shouted up to them, as more Bernicians advanced. At last the wooden barriers were cut, and John and the others jumped clear as the battering ram finally broke down the door. There appeared a legion of soldiers who ran in, and we now had a clear advantage; as we put the Bernicians to the sword, they began to retreat.

"On their heels!" I ordered with a shout, and we chased them through the stronghold, which seemed eerily familiar to Klumeck. I hurried forwards to join the other Britons in the taking of the stronghold; this task took up a long section of the night, and the fighting indeed seemed endless. Eventually, we cleared it, and the remaining Bernicians either surrendered or fled.

Presently, I ascended a set of steps that took me out to another area of the castle wall which faced the battle, where a Briton was fighting a Bernician; I rushed headlong at him and the force of the impact threw him off the castle wall. Upon closer inspection, I saw it was a soldier from Caer Ligualid I did not know.

"Thank you, Your Highness. I shall join the others," she stated quickly, and I nodded briefly. She turned and ran back down the steps, and I paused there on the balcony for a moment to survey the battle scene; by now I heard the horn blowing, and the final wave of the confederation armies was unleashed into the fading night. As I watched them sweep through more of the enemy lines, I found myself more and more grateful that King Urien had made the decision to align himself with the other confederation kings.

I was about to leave the balcony when I saw something strange that caught my eye. As I took a better look, I noticed King Morgant was not fighting, but had moved a little way from the battle and was speaking in earnest to one of his soldiers. They then happened to move so they were out of sight, but I had a worrying suspicion lurking within me, for King Morgant was the confederation king that many had distrusted. I was beginning to think that perhaps my earlier gratefulness had been felt too soon.

Swiftly, I made the decision to discover what King Morgant was doing, and so I raced back down the castle steps to the main hall of the stronghold. Some Bernician soldiers were there fighting the Britons, having realised that their small castle had been breached and had retreated to retake it. All were so embroiled in their own fighting, however, that I was able to run through undetected.

Soon I exited from the castle, and tried to evade the Bernician soldiers as I neared King Morgant. The king was still talking animatedly to his soldier, but now the king raised his hand and pointed at the battle. I followed King Morgant's gaze to see he was pointing to King Urien, who was fighting nearby. I frowned, for there was something deeply suspicious in King Morgant's countenance. Then I saw the soldier nod, and his hand went to the hilt of his sword; all too suddenly I understood.

"Your Majesty!" I shouted, but nobody could hear me above the sounds of war. I moved as fast as my body and the enemy would allow; King Morgant's soldier also had to keep stopping to fight off Bernicians. I continued to make my way forwards, but I could already see that I was too far away; I would not get there in time. King Urien was about to die, and I seemed helpless to prevent it.

Just then I caught a glimpse of Aife's hay-like hair flying loose as she expertly twirled her spear and thrust it into an enemy soldier.

"Aife!" I shouted, and miraculously she heard me and looked up. "Stop him!" I said, and pointed. "He's about to kill King Urien!"

Aife glanced where I had pointed, and she obviously realised who I had indicated – another miracle since there were so many nearby – and immediately she ran forwards, her hand grasping her spear tightly.

I continued to press forwards as Aife neared King Morgant's soldier. I saw she had reached him now, but I cursed as I saw the soldier turn at the last moment and block her spear with his sword. She lunged forwards at him, but he deftly evaded it and leapt towards her with his blade, which she jumped backwards to avoid. The two of them held their weapons high, continuing to circle each other as I ran forwards. They crashed their weapons again and again, metal hitting metal. I perceived them to be evenly matched; I had almost reached them when another

318

Bernician soldier began his attack. I spent a few frustrating seconds evading and battling the soldier before he was knocked down. I looked towards them again and saw they were still battling each other. Even though I well knew the scope of Aife's skill and ability, I began to get a horrible feeling in my stomach.

"Hold on, Aife!" I shouted. To my relief, as I leapt away from another enemy I saw I had a clear path and began sprinting down towards Aife and King Morgant's soldier. I was but twenty yards away when a Bernician soldier suddenly began fighting with Aife – she twirled and quickly brought him to his knees and then used her spear to pierce his heart.

"Aife!" I shouted, for King Morgant's soldier had advanced upon her whilst she was embroiled in another fight. In an instant, I saw the soldier we were pursuing would not fight cleanly; he would easily strike her when her back was turned. I was proven right, as the soldier now lunged forwards and pierced her side with his sword.

"No!" I shouted, my heart filled with despair as I sprinted towards her. A moment later I was there, and I dropped down to my knees beside her. "Aife, can you hear me?" I asked desperately, my hand reaching out to cover hers.

"Daniel…" she murmured in halted breath, her whole countenance rife with pain. "Stop him…" she rasped.

I glanced up to see King Morgant's soldier standing there watching us, his sword in his hand. As our eyes met the soldier smiled, and suddenly he spun around and began to run forwards.

I gave Aife's hand a final squeeze before I leapt up and pursued him, my blade in my hand ready to cut him down. Running across the battlefield further was not what I had expected to do, but I knew he had to be stopped. I willed myself to go faster, and prayed as I chased the soldier that I would stop him before he got to King Urien, who was now coming into view. I had almost neared him… abruptly, I felt a sharp stab to my left leg, and the pain of it caused me to fall and roll over; somebody had tripped me up with their sword, and my leg was now bleeding. I jumped up, but already I knew I could not run as fast; still I struggled forwards as fast as my injury would allow.

Time seemed to slow as the man reached King Urien; I reached behind me to retrieve my quiver and grasped thin air; I had forgotten I had already used all of my arrows. King Morgant's soldier was now cutting a Bernician soldier. As the distance between us shortened, I saw that hope was not all lost; he was only yards away, and then the yards became inches. I raised my sword, but he had already reached King Urien's soldier. Just before I brought my sword down upon him, the man had sliced his own blade across King Urien's throat.

"No!" I roared again, as I immediately dropped my sword and outstretched my arms in order to catch him. Together, we both fell clumsily to the ground. "Your Majesty!" I shouted, but it was no use. Blood still warm from his body had poured out of his neck, and his eyes were wide in horror; the great king was already dead. I lowered his lifeless form to the ground, and as I lifted my head I found myself face to face with the enemy soldier, a smirk upon his features.

Rage exploded within me, and I darted my eyes to the right, where I knew my sword was. The soldier had guessed where I was looking, and as I leapt forwards, so did he. Both of us lunged towards my blade whilst he wielded his. I knew if I did not reach it first, I would be dead.

A moment later, as I hit the ground, my hand grasped the handle of my blade firmly. I turned over, and as his sword came down upon me, I blocked it. As he prepared to strike me again, I swiftly kicked his legs from under him.

As the man hit the ground and rolled away, I scrambled to my feet. In the next moment he had jumped up too, and we began to circle each other, readying ourselves for this ancient dance of metal and blood. I could hear the blood pounding in my ears and tried to concentrate on the task at hand – for even if it were to cost my life itself, I would kill this man. He had betrayed us all – an ally who had slaughtered King Urien and Aife as well, most probably.

Aife came to mind now – the image of her lying half dead on the battle floor coming sharply to mind and I lost my patience. I charged forwards at him, but he blocked me easily. We twirled together, the two of us, bringing our blades on each other again and again. He was an extremely skilled fighter, and it was difficult to avoid his blows. Our swords clashed again, and this brought our faces close together – I saw the smirk had gone from his countenance, and in its place was pure hatred – a hatred which I was sure was present in my own features.

We broke off for a moment and circled again; instinctively, I knew this would be my toughest battle yet. As he smirked once more, I saw that his coldness and arrogance was his weakness. Unbidden, the image of the father who had raised me in Gaeson suddenly came to my mind. He was the one who had first taught me how to hold a sword, and had always told me to remain calm, and so I forced myself to become still. I breathed deeply, exercising all the patience I could muster as this time I waited for him to charge.

Just then, he charged forwards, and as I blocked him, I saw my opportunity – a predictability in his pattern of fighting that I could manipulate. As he came forwards to strike me again, instead of blocking it I darted to my left. His sword sliced through the air beside me, and in that instant I brought my blade down upon his arm and then slid it across his chest. He began to stagger, and as he did I raised my sword, and in one swift movement I cut his head clean from his shoulders.

"Bryce," I heard to my left, and as King Cedric approached and I looked up from where the severed head lay at my feet. My heart eased slightly to see my uncle was still alive. "You're injured," he remarked, seeing the splinters and hardened blood on my face, and the blood running from the cut on my leg. "What happened here? That man is King Morgant's!" he declared now, confusion and some anger evident in his features.

"Aye," I replied heavily. "This man has just killed King Urien, on King Morgant's orders," I explained now.

"What?" King Cedric shouted loudly. Then I saw his eyes rove to where, a few yards away, King Urien's body still lay. "How did this happen?" But I paid this question no heed.

"Aife was struck also," I told him quickly. "I must find her."

My uncle began to say something else, but I had already started running as fast as my injured limb would allow, and could no longer hear him. As I ran I looked around wildly, but I could already see we had won; the majority of the Bernicians had either surrendered or were dead. I also could see it was nearly dawn, having fought most of the night.

I retraced my steps swiftly to the spot where Aife had fallen, but she was nowhere in sight. I knew I was in the right place, for I saw her blood on the ground and recognised the place where she had fallen. I looked around to see the last of the Bernicians surrendering. We had indeed won, but at a great cost. As I straightened, I saw John and Captain Bredon speaking with each other, and my heart eased a little to see them both alive. I walked over to them slowly, for the pain in my leg had further increased.

"Your Highness," the captain greeted me with a smile as soon as he saw me. John had been facing the other way and he now turned, and I saw the relief on his face to see me alive.

"Brother," was all I said; he came forwards and we embraced. Next I reached out for the captain, and we clasped arms tightly. "It is good to see you both alive. Have you seen Aife?" I added, my worry at once returning. "She was struck down…"

"Aye, sire, she has been put on a carriage with others that are wounded. She is still alive," John confirmed, and I felt at once almost dizzy with relief. "The surgeon is preparing them now for the return to Gaeson. She is currently conscious, but I…" He swallowed. "The surgeon does not know whether she will survive," he added heavily.

"You are injured, yourself, Your Highness," Bredon commented now, whilst I digested the difficult news about Aife. At least she was still alive, for the moment. "Here, sire, I bid you sit upon this rock," he advised.

"I am in better condition than most," I replied, though I sat down out of pure exhaustion. Gingerly, I had removed all of the splinters that had been embedded in my skin from where the mace had battered my shield, and now I was just bruised and sore.

"There is your leg, also, sire; allow me," John said, and knelt to bandage the wound with some spare cloth. It seemed he was always the one to bind up my wounds after a battle.

"Captain, I bid you report," I insisted, whilst John attended my leg. "How do the rest of Gaeson's army fare?"

"We have five hundred and fifty strong enough to walk, sire," the captain replied now. "Two hundred are critically injured, with another three hundred dead."

I sighed in dismay as I took in these numbers; we had come with just over a thousand, and now at least half were either injured or dead. Six hundred had been our own army, and the other four hundred had been recruited from the nearby villages and towns.

"Gaeson is safe." I was reminding myself as much as Bredon or John. This was our true aim – home had not been harmed physically, but I knew Gaeson would be forever changed. How many children would have to grow up without a father? Or a mother, in the case of our female warriors? No wonder our fighting people had been so afraid.

"Yes, sire," the captain affirmed, and then he paused a moment. "You knew this was where Aife fell, my lord prince," the captain said presently, as John finished bandaging the wound and stood. "Did you see what happened to her?"

"Yes," I replied at length, moving my gaze away from the spot where she had fallen to look at both of them. "She was pierced by one of King Morgant's men," I supplied now, realising they probably did not know about King Urien. Both of them widened their eyes in shock. "King Morgant had ordered one of his men to assassinate King Urien," I explained.

"What treachery," the captain declared loudly. "So Aife was trying to prevent King Urien's death," he reasoned, and I nodded.

"He was a snake of a man, for he did not strike her cleanly," I told them. "He struck her whilst she was fighting another foe and her back was turned. I went over to her, but she told me to catch him and so… I left her there," I admitted, feeling suddenly ashamed.

"You did right, sire," John assured me. "Our great king's life was in danger. What happened?" he added quickly. "Did you stop him?"

"I pursued and killed him," I replied quietly, "but not before he pierced King Urien's throat. His Majesty is dead," I concluded heavily, and their countenances turned immediately to further shock and anger.

"The king is dead," the captain repeated slowly, his face aghast. "King Morgant's army have already left," he added now.

"So soon?" I responded angrily; I had hoped that the rest of the monarchs would confront him about what had happened. "What about his wounded?"

"They are travelling with King Rhydderch, sire," John explained presently. "King Morgant said he had urgent business that could not be delayed any further."

"That coward simply wishes to flee," said King Cedric from a distance; I glanced up at him, and John and the captain bowed. "Did you find Aife?" my uncle asked me as he walked over.

"Aye, sire," I answered, "she is in a carriage with the others wounded from Gaeson. The surgeon is unsure whether she will survive the journey home."

"I am sorry to hear that, but she may still live," King Cedric replied. "I have rarely seen a warrior with such courage and skill."

I gave a small smile at this as I nodded.

"I pray you are right, uncle," I returned. "Does Prince… King Owain," I said, correcting myself, "know of his father's death?"

"Yes, I have heard."

We turned around at the voice, and the three of us at once bowed to Owain, now King of Rheged. He was a brunt of a man, with his father's hardened eyes, but his chin far softer. The grime and blood spattered his face, and his jaw was locked in grief.

"All hail, King Owain," the four of us chorused, immediately sinking to our knees in a bow. There we remained, waiting for a moment, waiting for the new King of Rheged to speak.

"We shall not pursue King Morgant," His Majesty declared now. "Too much blood has been spilled. Besides, his forces far outnumber our men. It would be suicide."

"It might be that King Rhydderch or King Gwollag will bring Morgant to justice, Your Majesty," King Cedric replied, but even as he said it I considered this unlikely. It would be far wiser for the other confederation kings to ignore Morgant's actions and keep him as an ally, rather than to confront him and risk further war.

"We are greatly sorry for your loss, Your Majesty," I told him.

He simply nodded roughly, whilst kicking loose stones from the ground with his left foot. We waited for him to speak, but he said nothing more. He now strode into the distance to speak with his own military advisors. It was usual for him to say nothing more in the best of times, let alone when he had just lost his father – in my brief time of knowing him, I had never heard him speak much.

"How do the soldiers from Klumeck fare?" I asked King Cedric now.

"Many are dead," my uncle replied, and I saw a shadow cross his face – the same shadow that appeared whenever he spoke of my parents or his late wife. Presently, he stepped towards me and put a hand on my shoulder. "My heart does rejoice to see you, Bryce, my boy," he sighed, "but…"

"My heart grieves also," I replied, "not only for those in Gaeson. I may not have been raised in Klumeck, but they are my people too. I am sure they fought bravely and with real courage."

My uncle smiled slightly, my speech about my identity seeming to comfort him. "I believe they did," he murmured in agreement. "Come," he added abruptly, taking his hand off my shoulder again. "We have much to do before we can leave this place."

"Uncle," I agreed, giving a small bow of my head in assent. He then left, heading to the survivors of Klumeck's army.

I knew my own orders from Queen Evelyn were to return to Gaeson and report to her, and though the thought that I would see her again filled my heart with gladness and thankfulness, not for the first time, I felt a wrongness that I was not going to Caer Ligualid with him. I supposed it was the tension of being a citizen of two peoples, of belonging to two different kingdoms.

It took two hours before we were ready to move out. I knew this timing was swift, long though it had felt. I tried to ensure most of them were able to rest a little before leaving, but most of them had already begun moving those who were wounded or dead. I saw King Urien being carried out on a stretcher. The citizens of Rheged knew we would not be able to carry back their dead, and so we had no choice but to gather them into a pile and then burn them. The only exception to this was the great king, currently being placed on a carriage. His body would be taken back to Caer Ligualid, where he would be given a royal burial.

After we had finished piling the bodies up, I walked back through the battlefield, intending to visit Aife and the rest of the wounded. Fairly near to the fortress, I spotted something in the grass which was indeed bittersweet – one of Aife's arrows lay discarded upon the ground. I perceived there to be blood on it, and I reasoned that an enemy soldier had been pierced but then had removed it. I retrieved it and cleaned it as best I could, ready to give it back to her. As I held it between my bloodstained fingers, I prayed she was still living.

Soon I had neared the long, black carriages where the wounded had been placed, each holding at least ten injured. Gaeson had twenty such carriages in its possession; they formed two parallel lines. I found myself perversely glad that we had brought so many with us to war, since we had not underestimated the number we had needed. I braced myself for the agony I might well perceive among the injured, and then went into each carriage, greeting the wounded and encouraging them we were about to leave this place. I was relieved that most looked like they would survive with medical assistance, though this sadly was not the case for every scarred individual.

Aife was in the last carriage, and as I entered it I perceived her to be in one of the worst states. Her countenance was grim and pained, but I saw the same determination in her eyes. This caused a glimmer of a smile to pass my features, for I knew then that she would not simply die without a fight.

"Sire," she rasped as she saw me. I walked over to her and placed my hand over hers. "I heard we won," she said, a hint of a smirk across her strained face. Now I was closer, I could see her hay-like hair lay tousled about her, matted with sweat and dirt.

"That we did," I encouraged her. There was a small wooden chest next to her thin, ragged bed, which I now sat on. "We will be departing imminently," I informed her. "I would ask how you are, but…" I trailed off and swallowed, unsure of how to comfort her.

"I heard His Majesty still died," Aife muttered now, blinking rapidly.

I looked at her for a moment before nodding. "I managed to slay him," I replied, running a hand through my hair, "but not before he pierced King Urien's throat. I am enraged that he did not fight you cleanly," I told her now, "for you certainly would have slain him if he had engaged you with decency."

"I'm glad you killed him, my lord," Aife stated. "It was John and the captain who found me," she told me, and I nodded. "The surgeon said…" She halted her breath and swallowed; I realised speech was becoming more difficult for her. "I asked him to be honest with me. He said I might not survive…"

"Save your strength," I murmured, my heart full of sadness to see her like this, as her condition cut off her breathing again. "The surgeon said there is still a chance," I reminded her. "You are the one of the strongest warriors I know; I am sure you will outlive us all."

"But you are not sure, sire," she murmured back. "I want you to know that if I am to die in your service, I die well. You led your people well, Daniel. You will make a fine king indeed, even if you do not rule a kingdom."

"Thank you," I managed, though I knew not how to speak evenly with the emotions rising within me at the thought of this strong, courageous woman dying. "Try to rest," I encouraged her. I glanced around me, but no one was looking our way, so hastily I bent to kiss her forehead. She managed to give a pained smile before I left her company and made my way quickly out of the carriage.

I stood outside breathing in the fresh air for a few moments, attempting to gather my composure. I rubbed my face, momentarily forgetting about the splinter marks, causing me pain anew. I began to walk past the carriages and the place where the horses were gathered when I heard a soft neighing I instantly recognised.

"Epos," I said as I walked over to my horse, relieved to see my old friend still alive. "It's good to see you, girl," I murmured, stroking her mane, feeling a little ashamed for almost forgetting about her injury with everything that had happened this day. I glanced down at where her leg had been cut; it had now been hastily bandaged.

"The wound is not too bad, Your Highness," said a young soldier beside me, who was tending to the horses. "She will be placed in one of the carriages prepared for the injured horses."

I nodded at him. "Very good," I agreed, and then patted Epos' neck once more. "I'll see you back in Gaeson," I murmured to her.

Then I turned and saw that the dead had now all been gathered. I watched as a couple of the soldiers set the bodies ablaze, and soon the stench of burning flesh reached all of us. I thought of Aife again, and my already prevalent emotions won as I stared at the fire, causing me to weep a little, though I attempted to tell myself it was simply the smoke in my eyes. I looked past the flames now, and in the distance I watched King Owain and King Cedric give their farewells to King Rhydderch and King Gwollag, the other two confederation kings.

King Cedric then came, a frown upon his face. "Both of them expressed their sympathies well to King Owain," he stated. "They both said they would confront King Morgant and bring him to justice." As he spoke, I heard the scepticism in his voice. "They even know who the soldier was," King Cedric continued. "A man called Llofan Llaf Difo."

I nodded, taking in the man's name with interest, as I had wanted to know who it was that I had defeated – the one who had killed King Urien and pierced Aife so mercilessly.

"Do you think they really will hold King Morgant accountable for his actions?" I asked my uncle now.

"I do not know," King Cedric replied, as together we watched the two confederation kings leave with their respective armies. "I believe King Rhydderch is a righteous man, and King

Gwollag will not want to leave the death of his cousin unanswered... so perhaps. What I am sure of is that King Urien was right," my uncle added now, and I glanced at him. "We would never have defeated the Bernicians without their aid, even if one of them was treacherous."

"Perhaps King Urien even knew King Morgant could not be trusted," I speculated now, as I listened to the gentle roar of the ocean nearby. "Maybe he invited King Morgant knowing his character, even knowing that his own life might be sacrificed for it."

King Cedric nodded now. It was strange to think of such a brutal man being so selfless – but maybe, I wondered, his character had been better than I had presumed. It was possible that King Urien, knowing that King Morgant would betray him, had asked for his aid despite this. It showed him a fine king who fought for his kingdom, even if his life was forfeit.

"Let us depart," he said now, and I nodded. The two of us walked back to the front of the lines, where by now all of the soldiers had gathered and were ready to leave. There was King Cedric's horse waiting for him, and another horse I did not know. I mounted this new, pale horse and gathered the reins – though it was strange to not be atop Epos, he seemed to handle well. Before we left, the three of us looked back to the pile of the dead bodies with its fire still burning.

Without a word, King Owain clenched his fist to his heart and stretched it outward. My uncle and I quickly followed, along with all others belonging to Rheged – whether they be from Gaeson, Klumeck or Caer Ligualid. Never before had I felt so united to all three kingdoms, which brought me great encouragement. With that, I turned to face the bleak, empty skies – the day had darkened considerably since dawn.

"March!" King Owain ordered in a loud, clear voice – and with that, the long lines of our three armies set off.

Presently, I prayed for Queen Evelyn and all of Gaeson; hoping that they would be safe and that we had prevented war from coming to her gates. I hoped the idea of home would bring comfort to those who had survived this onslaught, and I prayed for us all, that we would journey safely and arrive home together.

Chapter Fifteen

I kicked my horse gently, and with that the long line of our three armies set off. It was folly, but I found the air easier to breathe with each step my horse took. The travelling was indeed slow going, however; we rode and marched at a sluggish pace with regular intervals. Every time we stopped, I sent John to report to me how the wounded were doing. By the time evening fell, four more had died from Gaeson's army. This news was hard to receive, but I was ever more relieved Aife was still alive. It was with heavy hearts that we set up camp that night – we had stopped to make camp earlier than usual, what with the number of wounded and the sheer exhaustion of those who were not.

I gave the order that not all the soldiers should be busy with preparations for camp – I sent several to go to the nearby stream to collect water, not only for cooking with but also for washing, as I knew how desperately the warriors would desire a bath after today's battle. After this, John and I visited Aife and the other wounded, but there was no improvement. On the contrary, she seemed that night to be even worse – barely conscious, turning and writhing in her bed with her face covered in sweat.

"She has a fever, Your Highness," the surgeon said, mopping Aife's brow with a damp cloth. "It shows the wound is infected. I cleaned the wound thoroughly and bound it, but… the damage may have been done upon impact." He was busy now preparing a poultice, and I watched in confusion as he placed wood and other substances in it.

"Oak wood will draw out the infection, my lord," the surgeon stated. "I have mixed it with honey, which also is known to fight the poison that may be in her body. I bid you excuse me, sire; I have to change the bandage and apply the poultice," the doctor added. "I am sorry to prevent it, but I bid you to leave visiting Aife until the morning. She is currently vulnerable to attack from illnesses."

"Of course," I answered. "May God's wisdom be with you. Will she live?" I added, the words coming rapidly out of my mouth almost before I could help it.

"I fear this night will be her last, Your Highness," the physician replied ere long. "If she lives through till the morning, then she might well survive the journey back to Gaeson."

"Such a change in her condition," John murmured as we left the wounded carriages. "Aife is so strong; it is a sin to see her so weak."

"Indeed," I muttered in agreement. We were walking through the camp, which by now had mostly been made. I perceived the morale to be low; this was understandable after such a great battle. The war seemed to have been won, but not without great cost. The soldiers might have felt relief at still being alive, but mostly they would be worrying about their comrades who were still alive, and mourning the brothers and sisters they would have lost. I saw that many of the soldiers were stood in their undergarments washing in the cold of the night; I was only sorry the water could not be heated.

"Aife will survive this, Daniel," John replied, fierce determination upon his countenance.

Presently, we arrived at my tent. I did not have the resolve myself to make such a guarantee, so I merely nodded. Looking closer at his features, I saw there could also be desperation.

"Try to get some rest, John," I told him instead. "We still have a long march ahead of us."

He bowed his head swiftly and there departed my company.

I entered my tent and was surprised to see a large basin in the corner of the tent, with clean towels beside it. When I touched the water, I discovered it was warm. Never before had I so appreciated the luxuries that went with being royal, but I also felt guilty that my brothers and sisters had to do with washing in their undergarments in the cold. It was with weary relief that I removed my boots, armour and clothes. I checked in the inside pocket of my tunic and saw that the cloth from Queen Evelyn was damp, but thankfully clean.

Before I did anything else, I knelt down and washed my face and hair. My auburn hair had grown longer recently, and presently it was matted with sweat, dirt and blood. It was a difficult task, but at last it seemed to be soft and relatively clean. I then stepped into the already dirty water and washed the same filthy concoction from my body, whilst ensuring that the bandage on my leg remained dry.

As I lay in the water, the images of the battle came to mind, and as with other times, I did not hold them back. I thought of the enemy who had nearly killed me with his mace, and that treacherous Briton who had killed King Urien and had brought Aife to within an inch of her life. Presently, I prayed for my friend; never before had I seen her in such distress and agony. It was with great sadness that I now remembered keenly all those who had given their lives for Rheged and the rest of Briton. Though the captain, John and I were attempting to keep up the morale as best we could by reminding them that we were homebound, and that because of their sacrifices Gaeson was safe. I knew, however, we would not change their mood, nor would I wish to. In many ways I was still a simple soldier; I could well understand their pain.

Presently, I got out of the bath and dressed in clean clothes, which also felt in itself a luxury. A soldier brought me a simple meal, and it was not until I saw the food that I realised how ravenous I was. I wolfed it down, wondering whether John might join me, but I did not see him again for the rest of the night. I knew how sad he had been about Aife. So close was their friendship that, not for the first time over the years, I wondered whether he might have feelings for her – but then I knew their close bond could simply be the deep friendship of being a brother and sister in arms. After all, I myself loved Aife dearly, though it was not love in that way.

As I climbed into the narrow, hard bed on the tent floor, my thoughts now ran to the one my heart loved the most, and I turned the cloth over in my hands. I had survived the battle, and my hopes ran high at the thought of seeing her again. I could just about make out the imprint of her initials, but in my mind they were as fresh as on the day she had given it to me.

"God be with you, my lady. I pray that you are safe," I whispered aloud, before placing it back in the inside pocket, and

I prayed for Aife quickly; it was awful in a way, but despite her peril due to the hardship of battle, I could barely keep my eyes open. Indeed, no sooner had I whispered the word "amen" when I fell at once into a deep, dreamless sleep.

***

I awoke just after dawn, having sensed that someone was nearby. My first thought was of Aife, and I leapt out of bed and began to dress just as there came a soft knock on the door of my tent.

"Your Highness?" I recognised it as John, and as I threw on a clean tunic I told him to come in. "Sorry, I do not mean to rush you…"

"I am ready," I cut him off, pulling on my boots. "Let's go and see her."

John gave a swift bow and we both left my tent.

"Did you manage any sleep, brother?"

"Aye, my lord," John answered, "though I feel guilty resting when we do not know if she still lives," he added, and I heard the bitterness in his tone.

"I know well what you speak, John," I replied as we walked to the wounded carriage, "for I am sure we all feel it keenly. There is no shame in resting, however, after yesterday," I assured him.

John nodded but said nothing more as we entered the carriage where Aife was. At once I noticed a large curtain had been drawn around her bed, separating her from the rest of the wounded – I speculated this was to prevent further infection.

"Your Highness; John," the surgeon greeted us from behind; we turned to him to see him washing his hands in a small bowl. The physician dried his hands on a towel and smiled at us. His cheerful countenance at once told me it was good news, and I sensed both John and I relaxing in relief. "She has improved greatly," the surgeon told us as he drew back the curtain. It encouraged me greatly to see Aife was no longer turning and tossing but sleeping peacefully. The sheen of sweat had also gone from her forehead.

The doctor assured us Aife should continue to improve, and that there would be no immediate danger to her health to have another day of marching, which was a great relief to hear. He then added some news which was rather more sobering – that the conditions of three others had become critical during the night, and one of those had died. Therefore when I departed the carriage with John, Aife's recovery gave me great encouragement, but the news of the soldier's death had left me in some sadness.

The veil of sorrow continued to fall across our armies over the next three days, as we travelled to the point where we had joined with Caer Ligualid and Klumeck. I perceived the lands to be mostly empty; even though we were travelling in Bernician territory, we had met no resistance. On the contrary, the fact that Bernicia had previously been part of Briton (indeed, it had been ruled by that traitor King Morgant) meant that any people we encountered seemed full of thankfulness that the occupying forces had fled. Indeed, the more the news of our victory began to spread across the lands, the more people came out to greet us. They gave us food, clothing and more bandages for the wounded, all of which were gratefully received.

By the third day of our marching and riding, we had traversed the tall hills of Briton and had reached our first destination. Like on the way here, we had reached this point when the sun was set low in the sky, and so we were able to make camp whilst it was still daylight. Our armies were able to rest further from the battle and the days of riding and marching, but the mood of the warriors was still sombre the next morning, and I myself awoke with mixed emotions. I was relieved that we were now so close to home; but I knew this day would mean my uncle going to Caer Ligualid, and once again I partly felt a sense of wrong that I was not returning with him.

Once again, I went with John to visit the wounded; it was a great relief to see Aife further improved, but the surgeon again told me the hard news that another soldier had died during the night. He was doing his best, but marching with the wounded – despite them being secured as much as possible in the carriages – was a battle in itself. This latest casualty brought the total to eight dead since we had left Bernicia. Aife was slumbering when we went to visit, and so we did not speak with her. I was also relieved to see Epos doing so well, having checked her early this morning. Her leg was nearly recovered, but she still was not ready to be ridden.

"Come," I said to John as we left the wounded once more. "The time is nearing for us to march." The soldiers were busy forming their lines. "My uncle has told me Klumeck's wounded are not doing much better," I told John in a low voice. "I fear King Owain's people are in a similar situation."

"I am sorry to hear it, sire," John replied. "The weather does not help much," he added, and I nodded in agreement and looked towards the clouds as we walked to the front. It had been another bleak, dark day. It was not currently raining, and the rain so far had been soft; however, I expected that a storm was well on the way.

"Your Highness; John," the captain greeted us presently, as we joined the front of the lines, our camp having been fully dismantled.

"Captain," I returned, as I noticed the horse that had served me well so far on the journey home was waiting for me. I then turned to see King Owain and my uncle approaching. "Your Majesties," I greeted them with a bow.

"Prince Bryce," King Cedric replied. King Owain merely nodded at me as he mounted his horse. "It should encourage our people that we are all over halfway home," King Cedric commented as he stretched. "I am glad of it, for I am not as able in the saddle as I used to be," he said with a smirk, and I smiled. "We are about to depart," he said, and I stepped forwards.

"I hope to see you soon, uncle."

We clasped each other's arms in a tight embrace. How strange I should feel such affection for this man who not long ago had been my enemy – but that now felt like a different life, a different world.

"I too, Bryce. Take care; write often."

I nodded as he mounted his horse.

"Remember, if ever you wish to join me at Caer Ligualid, you are more than welcome. Give my love to your sister," he added.

"I will, sire. Farewell," I said. "I pray you reach home safely, Your Majesty," I added, with another bow to King Owain. The new king of Rheged merely nodded.

John and I stepped back as he gave the order to march, and I watched as he and King Cedric led their lines forwards. As their armies moved out behind them, the warriors bent their heads in a bow to me. I then suddenly spotted Conall, and I nodded to him as our eyes met.

"Your orders, Your Highness?" the captain asked me, but I did not answer for a moment, for suddenly I had spotted Conall in the crowd, and I nodded to him as our eyes met. "Sire?" the captain prompted.

"We march," I stated as I turned to him. I then swiftly mounted my horse; John and the captain followed suit. "March!" I shouted, and we began this last part of the journey.

***

My heart sang when, two days later, I at last glimpsed the castle of Gaeson atop the hill; never before had the kingdom seemed so full of beauty, despite the rain that pounded down on us and filled my eyes so I could hardly see it. My people who had survived the awful battle began to traipse up the hill behind me – hearts full of relief to know that they were almost home, to know that they had survived. All in all, it was two weeks since they had last been in Gaeson, and this day had not come soon enough.

As we neared the top of the hill, I saw that there was movement outside the castle – joy abounded to see Sarah standing there, a large cloak partly covering her royal garments to protect her from the adverse weather. We marched closer, and now I could see some of the soldiers who had stayed behind mounting their horses and readying themselves for travelling – suddenly I detected something was wrong.

"Prince Bryce," Sarah greeted me, as we finally stopped in front of her and dismounted. I wasn't able to say anything before she had run forwards and embraced me.

"Sister," I said warmly, almost overwhelmed at the emotion of seeing her again. "But what are you doing out here? What is happening?" I added, nodding at the soldiers.

Sarah swallowed, and in her hesitation I instinctively knew something of what had caused this.

"It is Her Majesty," Sarah answered quickly, confirming my worst suspicions. "She has been kidnapped." she told me, and my eyes widened in shock and rage as my body turned numb. "She was taken from here only a few minutes ago. It was the Bernician spies," she added rapidly. "The ones the captain captured are still secure, so it must have been the others who had escaped that day. We tried to stop it..."

"Stay here," I cut across her, somehow managing to find my voice. "I need your horse," I added to a soldier. "Mine is weary from battle."

"Your Highness," he replied at once, jumping down. I instantly mounted the horse and turned back to the others, gathering my reins quickly.

"John; doctor," I added, "I know you must be tired..."

"We will accompany you, sire," John answered, before I could finish. He gestured to another two soldiers, who immediately also dismounted.

"Captain, I bid you take the army inside; they must rest," I ordered, as John and the doctor swung up onto their own horses. Keep an eye on the wounded," I added. "We will bring Her Majesty back," I called, gave a swift nod to Sarah, and kicked my hose into a gallop.

The rain poured thick and fast as we rode, like huge sheets covering the earth. It ran into the ground, making the grass squelch under the hooves of our horses. Everything was submerged by water, so we could well have been walking in a river. The rain battered my helmet again and again, making my way under my armour so it soaked me to the skin. I could not feel my toes, swishing about in a mixture of mud, water and sweat within my boots.

Where was she? How my heart yearned to see her. I had to keep blinking to get the rain from my eyes, but even when I had clear vision, all I saw was a blanket of grey beyond my brothers marching in front of me. I felt a keen pang of concern for them – at least I had my horse. I reached out to pat the steed reassuringly, and my hand grew slick with water and horse hair.

I returned my hands to the reins, clutching them with my fingers numbly. I scanned the horizon once again, but it was to no avail. Would I ever find her?

"I am sure she will be well, sire." John's voice somehow reached me beyond the scourge. I glanced at him, riding alongside me. "I am sure we will find Her Majesty before too long."

"Of course," I returned. How perceptive my friend was – but then he had known me for so long, and he could imagine what I must be feeling. My mind went back again to the last time I had seen her, when my hand had held hers until the last moment when I was torn away. Because of duty and responsibility and the protection of my people, I had been taken from all I loved, away from the one I loved the most. I had beheld her face with her creamy skin and her thick curls, knowing it might well have been the last time I ever saw her features and kind countenance. I had accepted I might die in battle, then to find that I had survived and had then dared to hope to see her again. I had believed then I might well never see her again. I had then returned all the way to Gaeson, longing to see her once more – but to discover her capture on arrival seemed so cruel and unjust. Indeed, I was so full of angst I could hardly bear it.

John had spoken with such confidence and hope, the way he had spoken when he had said so certainly that Aife would survive. I pushed the dreaded sensation of doubt further into my stomach and tried to glean as much optimism of finding her alive as I could. I knew the Bernician spies had only left minutes beforehand, and I could only hope that they were returning on the same, weary horses that they had used to come to Gaeson – whereas we were using horses that were far more refreshed.

I could hardly believe it was this same group of Bernician spies – the spies that had threatened to destroy Gaeson so many times. It was this same group of spies who had caused the watchman to fall asleep that first battle, when it was only my thirst that had given us any warning. It was the spies who had then attempted to kidnap her, the time I had been ordered to escape with my lady into the forest to take her to Caer Ligualid. The last time we had seen them, however, was the night King

Reghan died in my queen's chamber. I suddenly remembered that the treacherous interrogator had been involved in that dreadful episode – I wondered if he was involved now.

I imagined her with this assailment, lost in the storm. How I longed to find her. The knot in my stomach tightened further, and further I pushed it down, clinging to hope.

"To the northeast, sire!" John suddenly shouted from beside me, and I strained my eyes – suddenly I could make the spies out.

"A good spot, brother," I called back, immensely relieved to have found them. "Surround them!" I shouted. "Keep going," I murmured to my horse, prodding my boots into his side to increase his speed. Soon we had encircled them, and I drew my sword. "Stop, on pain of death!" I roared.

The spies saw their route was cut off and slowed, but then they drew their swords and pointed them at us.

That was when I saw my queen. She was holding onto a spy in front of her, with her mouth gagged and on closer inspection. Now that the spies had stopped, however, she suddenly jumped free.

"Your Majesty!" I shouted, as the man that had been on the same horse suddenly jumped down and grabbed her, and before I could prevent it, the man had fiercely hit her cheek. "Is this how you would treat a queen?" I roared in anger as I leapt to the ground. In the next moment, I had the point of my blade kissing the skin of the one who had struck her.

"You think we come alone, boy? The one who would call himself the Prince of Rheged?"

The air had lifted slightly, and I could see about ten men, all also on horseback. My eyes roved around them until I spotted the man I had expected to see; it was the interrogator.

"You," I said, knowing I had spat the word like poison from my lips. "I knew I would find you here, you coward."

"Coward, am I?" the interrogator replied as he jumped down and, I noticed he was standing dangerously close to Queen Evelyn. "At least I know who I truly am. You are a sorry excuse for the heir of Klumeck and a traitor to His Majesty King Reghan," he declared.

"You are outnumbered and your king has lost," I continued evenly, as my soldiers continued to form ranks around me. "Surrender now and we will spare your lives, but if you move to strike her again I will kill you." I spoke loudly, for I wanted each syllable to be punctuated above the storm. I knew he had heard me, for he only grinned louder.

"Lose, did we? Yes, we may have lost… but the great King Urien, how is he faring? Your greatest king is dead, and we will kill his son as we have killed his father before him. You may have won the battle, but we will have this victory. Charge!" In the next moment, the interrogator had drawn his blade across Queen Evelyn's shoulder.

"No!" I hollered, as my warriors advanced forwards. My anger was as rife as it ever could be, and I sliced the neck of the man who had given the order. I had the desire – so strong it scared me – to strike them all down again and again, to cause unimaginable pain for how they had hurt her. I reached the interrogator now, and within moments I had pierced his stomach with my blade. I approached my queen now and sank to my knees beside her.

"My lady," I rasped, "can you hear me?"

Her eyes were filled with fear as blood spurted from her wound. Abruptly, it had stopped raining; there was now nothing to wash away the blood that was pooling out of her body. I grabbed some cloth from my cloak and ripped it, rapidly trying to wrap it round her neck, placing pressure on it in attempt to stem the bleeding.

"Bring the doctor!" I shouted.

All was eerily silent now; my people had defeated those who had tried to kidnap my queen. The surgeon who had accompanied us fell to his knees beside me and helped to stem the bleeding, but the blood did not seem to stop. It poured forth, covering our hands and dripping from our wrists onto the floor.

Dimly, I became aware of a sound thoroughly objectionable to my ears. Someone was laughing. I raised my head up slowly to see it was the interrogator, the one who had struck her. I had pierced him, but somehow he was still alive. He was laughing hysterically, his eyes wide with what looked to be joy.

In an instant I had moved towards him, raised my sword and struck it down upon his chest. He stopped laughing instantly, his mouth filled with blood. Now I had impaled him, I twisted the blade. He began to howl in pain but I cared not; I would show him no mercy. Rather than relent, I twisted the blade again. Blood spurted out from him, splashing my face and clothes and armour, but I cared not. Such rage had never filled me before, filled me with such a fire I felt my very blood was boiling inside me. He coughed, and spluttered blood from his mouth, his arm outstretched. His eyes were in agony, begging me to stop, but I paid him no heed. I wanted to hurt him as much as I possibly could, as much as this man had hurt me in all the time I had known him. I made to twist my blade further.

"Sire." It was John, his voice unreadable. I glanced up at him, my face still contorted in rage. "We have to get Queen Evelyn back to Gaeson."

I made no reply. Didn't he think I knew that? I glanced back at the interrogator and he was dead. To my shame, I had a burning desire that he would be still alive, just so I could kill him all over again. I half wanted to put him to the sword again now, despite his clear demise.

"Sire?" John questioned me.

"We must make haste," I answered at length. Was that my voice, so strange and foreign in my ears, so filled with hatred? Never before had I felt such an emotion; it was so strong that as I mounted my horse, I could barely even breathe.

Within the half-hour we had returned to Gaeson, but Queen Evelyn had slipped into a coma. She was immediately taken to the medical chambers of the castle, and I paced the corridor outside it, wishing the doctor would work more swiftly – but then the process of sealing and stitching such a wound must be a precise operation.

Finally, after what seemed an age, the doctor emerged, sweat upon his brow. "I have stopped the bleeding, Your Highness, but our queen is very weak," he said at last, as he removed his gloves. "Only time will tell. If she perseveres through this night, then she will live. There is nothing more I can do; we can only wait," he concluded, stooping to wash his hands.

"But you are injured, sire," he added, taking in my bloodied appearance.

I shook my head, irritated – he should be focusing on the queen, not me. "This blood is not my own," I answered. "Go – tend to your other patients, if there is truly nothing else you can do," I added, failing to keep the irritation and spite from my tone.

"Her condition is stable, for the moment, sire," was all the doctor said. "You can enter the chambers now, if you wish. Your speaking comfort to her might help," he added. The doctor then inclined his head in a bow and departed from me.

I felt tears of rage form, but I blinked them away as I entered the chamber. None of the other wounded were in sight; I presumed they were in other parts of the chambers. I sank into a chair and took in the sight of the pale, weak form of my beloved.

The doctor had also had the nurses wash her. and now the blood was wiped away I had never seen my fair beauty look so pale. I reached out, took her hand, and saw how the blood and dirt from my own fingers stained her once more. Distractedly, I took a spare cloth, but that only made the cloth dirty. In haste I rubbed my fingers, but the blood and grime would not desist. I threw the cloth behind me in my frustration.

"You must get rest, sire." It was John again. I looked up at him, and his face was once more unreadable. How was it he could always sense what I was feeling, and yet he could remain so elusive?

I swallowed a ball of despair forming in my throat. "I will not leave her, John." I spoke the words simply, and yet with great force; my voice sounded like a stranger in my ears.

"You heard the diagnosis. There is nothing more we can do for her now."

I ignored him, my filthy hand still holding Queen Evelyn's.

John stepped forwards, placing his hand on my shoulder. "Daniel…"

"Leave me," I answered hotly, far sharper than I intended.

John drew back, his face still unreadable. "Of course, Your Highness." With that, he left the chamber. Immediately I regretted my harsh tone.

I sat back and, as I did, I became aware of how heavy my armour was. With numb, lifeless hands I began to remove it. I took a bowl of water and washed my face and hands, tried to remove most of the grime and the blood. I left the bowl of now dirty water next to my abandoned armour and, with nothing else to distract me, I sat back down.

"Please wake up, my lady," I whispered to her. Knowing we were alone, I dared to reach out and remove a stray piece of hair that lay across her left eyelid, folding it gently back to join the others. I wished I had been bold enough in the past to enquire after her heart, but the timing had never seemed appropriate. No sooner had I found my true identity, I had raced to Klumeck in the attempt of saving my uncle's kingdom – and it seemed only moments later that her father had died – and then war had occupied almost all of our thoughts.

"My lady, you must wake up," I whispered again, but there was no flickering of her eyes, no movement of her bones. I had never felt despair such as this – the only depth like it was when I was in that dungeon, when no one believed my words, when my beloved had seen me as the enemy. Even that emotion, though, deep as it had been, seemed nothing compared with the despair I felt now.

"My dear brother." I looked up to see Sarah in the doorway, a bundle in her arms. "Don't get up," she added as I made to stand, so I sat back down in my seat. She ran over, placed the bundle on the floor, and embraced me before I could object on account of my filthy clothes. "I am sorry to see you in such distress, but my heart rejoices that you are alive."

I somehow managed to smile at this, despite my private thoughts that I would much rather myself be dead and Queen Evelyn alive.

"All of Gaeson is praying for her to be well," she added.

"She will be well," I replied – but I felt I spoke more to myself, in an adamant whisper that would defy anyone who offered a contrary opinion. "She must be well," I continued, for I did not know if God would grant me the strength to carry on should she die. I reached forwards and removed the cloth from my lady's forehead, dipped it in the cool water, and placed it once more on her forehead.

"I can see she is in good hands," Sarah told me now as she brought over the bundle. I saw she had packed fresh clothes, and wrapped in paper was some bread, cold beef, and a small bottle of wine. "I have told Rachel to tell your mother you are back safe," she added, whilst she pressed the damp cloth to my lady's forehead. "Your mother is currently ill," Sarah told me, and my eyes widened slightly in alarm as I glanced at her. "It is nothing serious," she continued, "but that is why I did not tell her myself. I did not want to risk making anyone at the hospital more unwell. I'm sure she will be herself again in a few days."

"Aye, that seems most wise," I replied, smiling at her for her kindness – but then my smile faded as I glanced at my pale queen once more.

"I shall leave you to tend her," Sarah murmured, placing a comforting hand upon my shoulder. "If you require anything, you need only send a guard to fetch me."

"Of course, sister. Thank you."

Sarah squeezed my shoulder briefly before leaving the chamber. Now I was alone once more, I quickly went into the small cupboard at the end of the ward. There I changed my clothes, careful to take the cloth out of my tunic pocket. I sped back to Evelyn's side, but there was no change in her. I reached into the pocket of my fresh tunic and pulled out the cloth Evelyn had given me, so many moons ago now. In another time, when the lands were white with snow. It was a time before my father died, long before I would ever glimpse my true destiny as a Prince of Rheged. Long before this dreadful day, and long before I would ever imagine I might lose her. Even though that time had been in the depths of winter and it was now spring, nothing could be as cold as today.

"Can you hear me, Your Majesty?" There was no acknowledgement that she could hear me, but I remembered the doctor's instruction that talking to her might help. "You told me to come back to you," I told her in earnest now, leaning forwards, as if somehow she would hear me better. "I have come back to you, just as you requested. But I never imagined that you would not be here. I had hoped…" I heard my voice wavering as I spoke now, and I tried to swallow my emotions down. "I had hoped that with me going to war in your place, I might keep you from harm – that danger would not come to you unless we lost the war. We won, my lady," I murmured now, my frustration rising at the pure nonsense of it. "We won, so how could this have happened to you? That damn interrogator!" I cursed loudly, and then I grew silent for a moment.

"Please come back," I whispered after a time. I longed to trust God, longed to put the life of my love into his strong hands – but dread and despair was ever rife within me. I was so wearied with the battle, the travelling, and this fierce despair that tears began to form. "You must come back," I whispered. "I cannot rule Gaeson; I could never lead as you do. I beg you; do not leave me here alone." Never before had I felt so helpless, so useless. So without ability to do any good. "Please awaken," I muttered, as my tiredness and emotions defeated my pride, and the tears began to fall. I was too exhausted to even wipe them away.

"Evelyn," I whispered desperately, abandoning her title.

There was no answer. Never was silence so cruel and cold, so without mercy or pity. I sank to my knees in prayer beside her bed. As I knelt there, I had not the rational capacity to even form a sentence to God – but I knew He heard what I would want to say.

"Please, God." I opened my eyes, but I could hardly bear to look at her in this state. "I love you," I whispered desperately. I dreaded to think of what the future might hold – with all the strength my exhausted body had, I prayed that she would be well. I began to weep truly and, in my shame, sobs began to form, and I buried my head on the bed. Thus I remained in the space between her frail form and the end of the mattress – and there I wept loudly, as I had not done since a child, until there was nothing more left in me.

I did not know how long I stayed like that – I believe I slept at some point, for I found myself lying on the floor, having laid down as I fell into a slumber. I stood quickly, and my muscles complained, as did the wound in my leg. I paid them no heed, however, as I quickly checked Queen Evelyn's state. There was no change in her, but at least she was still alive. I sat back into my chair; I noticed the plate of beef and bread Sarah had brought still sat on the table near me. I ate the meal and drank the wine, for though I was not hungry I knew I needed to eat. When finished, I leaned back into the chair and took her hand. Thus positioned, I slumbered once more.

I woke to feel soft fingers stretching across the back of my hand. I dared not open my eyes yet – for I knew whose touch that was, but I feared so that I was dreaming. After a few moments, I dared to open my eyes and my heart rejoiced – lo, my queen was awake!

"Your Majesty," I rasped, jerking forwards, taking in her appearance. She still looked weak and pale, yet not so much; a little more colour was in her cheeks. I could tell from the light in the chamber that a new day had dawned; she had lived through.

"Daniel," she whispered now, and I almost wept with relief at hearing her speak, at the sound of my name from her lips. "You came back to me," she murmured with a smile. "That means Briton won," she stated, and I nodded. She then tried to move and instantly winced.

"Careful, my lady; you are injured," I said – a little foolishly, for her condition must be obvious to her. "What do you remember?"

"I…" she frowned with concentration. "I was kidnapped," she said, while I changed the cloth on her forehead. I sought to calm my heart; it was beating frantically with the joy of seeing her alive and awake. "It was the spies," she muttered. "You found me… what happened?"

"You jumped down from the horse, away from your captor – but he then struck you," I supplied, still feeling weak with relief. "The interrogator leapt from his own horse, and he then pierced your shoulder with his blade. We were unsure…" I paused. "We were unsure whether you would survive, my lady. The doctor informed us that if you lived through the night, you would be well."

She nodded, and the action caused her to wince.

"Your wound has been stitched, Your Majesty, I bid you try not to move," I told her. "My heart is so glad to see you alive," I said, full of elation and stupidity all at once. I realised I still had hold of her hand, and swiftly I lifted it to my mouth and kissed it. This made me feel even more like a fool, but she intertwined my hand with hers and gave a small smile.

"Rest, my lady," I murmured.

She rested the back of her head against the pillows in agreement, her hand still holding mine. She blinked once more before she closed her eyes fully, but then her eyes widened in surprise. "But that is mine," she muttered.

I frowned and followed her gaze to see she was looking at the cloth that bore her seal, the one she had given me when we were children. Before I could do anything, she had reached out her hand and taken it.

"It is old; I can barely read my seal," she stated, and I fought not to blush.

"My lady," I said quietly, as her eyes roved to meet mine. In that moment, I knew she understood. She held it out to me and I took it from her.

"This is the one I gave you, that day in the snow," she said slowly.

I averted my gaze, feeling more of a fool than ever.

"Daniel?" She prompted and I knew it required explanation.

"Yes," I answered ere long, raising my head to meet her gaze once more. "I take it with me everywhere, for it is the most treasured possession I own."

She held my eyes a moment longer, a small smile on her face, before they finally closed and she gave in to sleep. Moments after this, the surgeon entered the chamber.

"Doctor," I muttered, "she woke."

The surgeon walked straight over, the sound of his footsteps echoing in the otherwise empty ward.

"She looks a great deal less pale, does she not?" I asked him hopefully.

"Yes, Your Highness," the doctor replied with a smile. "Her Majesty is strong; she will survive."

I exhaled breath I didn't realise I was holding.

"She is much improved from a few hours ago," the surgeon said. "I looked in on her a few times during the night."

I looked up at him, trying to hide my embarrassment, for he obviously knew I had been beside her all night.

"As your physician also, I insist you rest now. I will attend to her with the greatest care."

"I know, doctor," I returned, managing a small smile. "Thank you."

I then left the ward and entered the corridor outside. I took a moment to open a window, and breathed in the fresh air deeply. I saw that it had dawned a fine day, in sharp contrast to the stormy gales in which we had discovered the queen.

I walked a little down the corridor now – the surgeon had instructed me to rest, but I would not do so until I had visited the remaining wounded. Presently, I therefore entered the main hospital ward, which still had many wounded men and women residing in it. Even though the doctors and nurses had done well in attending to them, many were still recovering, and pain was all too clear in their expressions. I made my way through them, trying to speak to each person and encourage them as best I could.

Many had heard about the kidnapping of Queen Evelyn, it having been talked about so much in the castle; all were relieved to hear she had survived the night. I enquired of the doctors, and it comforted me greatly to know that since we had arrived at Gaeson, none of the other wounded soldiers had died. It encouraged me even further, as I neared the end of the ward, to see Aife sitting up and talking to John.

"Your Highness," John greeted me, and both of them inclined their heads in a bow. John had spoken perfectly normally, but abruptly I remembered the harsh way I had spoken to him yesterday and was filled with shame. "I hear Her Majesty is recovering," he said now.

"Aye, she seems much improved. The doctors are confident she will soon be well," I answered. "How do you fare, Aife?"

"I am also much improved, sire," Aife replied, and I smiled. "If I am honest, I am growing a little tired of my confinement," she added, and my smile grew further.

"That is surely a good sign," I pointed out, "though I am sure I would find it just as frustrating to not leave my bed," I admitted with another smile.

"She still must rest, Your Highness," said a nearby physician, as he put his hand on her forehead to examine her. "In fact I am sorry to inconvenience you, my lord prince, but I need to change her bandages."

"Of course, doctor," I returned. "I shall see you soon," I added, touching Aife's hand briefly. John also bid his farewell and the two of us left the medical chambers together.

"John," I said presently, seizing the opportunity to apologise, "about my manner to you yesterday…"

"I am your servant, my lord," John replied swiftly. "It is for me to apologise for my manner to you. Perhaps I was too familiar," he continued.

I stopped my walk down the corridor to look at him; he followed suit and halted beside me.

"You know that is not true," I told him earnestly. "You are my friend and brother, John, whether I am a prince or not," I went on in a low voice, lest we were overheard. "Seeing Her Majesty like that was difficult, but I should not have spoken to you in that way."

"These are indeed difficult times, sire," John replied. "It would be grievous for any subject to see their queen thus. She is indeed loved by all," he added.

"You know you can speak freely," I commented, for I perceived him to have more to say – and, in truth, I wanted his counsel.

"I had only reflected…" He seemed to hesitate, and I folded my arms and leant against a closed window nearby whilst I waited. "I cannot imagine the pain it caused you, Daniel," John began eventually, "since I know not of anyone who could love her more."

My eyes widened in surprise at his speech – though in hindsight I was not shocked very much that my friend knew.

"I am sorry if I have spoken out of turn," he added quickly.

"You have not," I murmured in reply. "I suppose you have always known," I ventured now, and after a moment John nodded.

"I began to suspect over the years," John admitted, "but I did not know for sure until the road to Bernicia. It was when I saw the cloth, when you told me that you had met as children, and that you had kept it safe till this very day. You stayed by her side all night," he said now, after my friend seemed to pause again.

I nodded, even though I knew it was not a question.

"You do know, Daniel, that your change in identity makes you quite the suitor," John added presently. "In fact it even makes sense, as it would further unite Gaeson with Klumeck. It would be well celebrated among both peoples."

"Aye," I answered, though again I knew it was a statement. "I had always thought that I would simply love her as a soldier," I continued, as I rubbed hands over my tired face, which was still a little sore from the splinter marks. "But then these last few weeks... discovering who I really was, and then finding out what her father had done... it became complicated, though my feelings for her have not wavered.

"She knows how I feel," I added, "but with everything that happened with Klumeck, her father and this war, we had not the chance to talk about it. When I saw her last night, John," I said now, "my biggest regret was that I had not enquired after her heart. The way we parted company when I left... made me think perhaps..."

"I advise you to speak her," John responded, "for even if she does not feel as you do, you would know."

I nodded, for I knew his advice spoke sense. "Thank you, John. The captain will be wondering where you are," I added now. "You best give him your report of the wounded. Thank you, brother," I repeated, and he smiled.

"My lord," he returned. "Get some sleep; you must be exhausted."

I gave a single nod in agreement, and a small smile crossed my face as he left my company. He had left me deep in thought as I walked through the castle with the intention of visiting my mother, as I had not seen her since getting back to Gaeson yesterday. I continued to walk with the resolve to speak to my lady at the next opportunity. I knew I had to talk to her soon, though as she was in her injured state I knew not when that would be. For I knew my brother was right – if I spoke to her and she did not return my feelings, then not much would have changed. If she did love me, as well, however, then that fact would change everything.

Chapter Sixteen

"Are you sure you do not wish for our escort, your majesty?" the guard asked cautiously. It was eight days since Queen Evelyn had been kidnapped, and I had spent that night at her bedside. It was the first day that she had felt strong enough to walk; we were going to take a short stroll through the palace gardens, as spring had finally arrived during the last week. To my encouragement, many of the wounded had recovered much since my conversation with John, and Aife had by now been allowed to leave the medical chambers.

"I assure you I will be perfectly fine in Prince Bryce's company," Queen Evelyn presently replied. "Take a patrol around the garden," she added as a compromise, as this would enable the guards to remain nearby should anything happen.

"Very good, Your Majesty." The guard bowed and they dispersed.

My lady and I walked along a way together among the blossoming flowers. Rarely had I seen a finer day as this. The sky was a pure blue, the clouds crisp, white and idyllic, and the sun shone strong and warmed everything it touched. Such a day provided a great contrast to the nightmare we had all recently endured. We had received a message to say King Owain and King Cedric had arrived back at Caer Ligualid safely – indeed, the letter informed us that His Majesty's coronation would be in three days time. Queen Evelyn had been deemed able to travel, but she would be transported in a carriage, rather than riding herself.

"We have peace, for now," she said at length, as we walked through the path. I looked up her – after giving her a day or two to rest, the captain and I had given Queen Evelyn a full report of the war, and my lady had expressed deep sympathy at how many we had lost, as well as sorrow for the death of King Urien.

"Let us pray that the next time they strike, it will be many years into the future," I agreed. For though everything seemed at peace, I knew the threat from Bernicia still existed, though for now it had withdrawn. Gaeson was still deep in mourning for her dead. Queen Evelyn had already decreed that as soon as she was well enough, we would hold a funeral to honour those who had given their lives. It was strange to think that it was now almost three weeks since we had battled and King Urien had died. It was stranger still to consider that today marked two months since I had woken in the soldiers' chambers due to my thirst.

So much had happened in eight short weeks! In that time I had fought in several battles, and discovered my true identity as King Cedric's heir. I had discovered the truth about King Reghan, and risked death to tell my people that it was he who fought against Rheged and not my uncle. Queen Evelyn had been forced to take the throne after the abdication of her father.

It was also the first time Queen Evelyn and I had been alone since that day in the hospital chambers, as her care had been attentive from the moment she had first woken. We walked slowly down the length of one of the gardens, and by the time we had reached the corner of the path, my lady's breathing was slightly heavier. As we turned it, we passed a rose bush, and I paused to pick one and hold it out to her. It was a foolish, whimsical gesture, but it caused her to smile. She took it from me, being careful that the thorns did not prick her nimble fingers. I watched as she brought the rose to her nostrils and breathed in its fresh, delicate scent.

As we continued to walk, her breathing grew heavier still and I deduced her independence might make her reluctant to say she had become tired.

"The grass appears soft, my lady," I suggested. "Shall we sit awhile?"

"Yes, thank you," she replied, and so we sat. The grass was indeed soft, dry and warm. Ever since the day I had left the medical chambers, this glorious spring weather had continued and the sun had long dried out the grass after the storm of last week. Currently, it was about the sixth hour of the day, so the ground had long been heated by the sun. It was difficult to believe such a change had only occurred in the last few days. Queen Evelyn appeared to be content, despite being in some pain from her shoulder wound.

Presently, my queen trailed her hand through the small, green blades, idly picking daisies and tossing them into the breeze. Never had I seen the grass such a vibrant green. I glanced at my queen, who looked more beautiful than ever.

"My heart rejoices to see you looking so well today, my lady," I commented.

My queen smiled as she twirled the rose in her other hand without lifting her hand too high from the ground – she still could not move that arm much. "I was in good hands," she replied, and glanced at me. "I am not referring to the doctors and nurses, wonderful though their care was," she continued. "The surgeon told me that the first night, you did not leave my side."

"That is true, Your Majesty," I answered quietly. I felt embarrassed that she knew this, as if it betrayed some weakness – but it only caused her to smile wider. I saw it was that smile, the smile I had first seen when she had said goodbye to me at the window in the snow, all those years ago. The smile that had first caused me to love her. What a contrast it was from the pale face I had seen a week ago! So starkly different when she lay on that bed in the hospital chambers. I was reminded of my despair that night, when she had been lying at death's door. Never before had I felt such hopelessness, that I might not ever again see her warm, beautiful eyes, or the smile she was now displaying so vividly.

"What are you thinking of?" she asked presently, concern in her features.

I realised my thoughts must have shown on my features. I opened my mouth to tell her it was nothing, but then I hesitated. My instincts told me this was the time to enquire after her heart.

"I was thinking of that night, when we found you," I answered. "The doctor said you might not survive through the night... it caused me sadness to think you might not live." I broke away, turned my head to gaze upon the grass.

"I remember," she said suddenly and I looked up at her swiftly. She tilted her head and blinked, like one attempting to remember a dream upon waking. "All was grey fog... but I remember. Yes, I could hear you," she told me, nodding earnestly now. "You said I had to wake up. You were weeping."

I looked away again, my embarrassment prevalent.

"You told me you…" She paused, and I glanced up at her again as the unsaid words hung in the air. I knew well it was my declaration of my heart she could remember me saying. I surveyed her carefully, but I could not make out her countenance.

"It was because of you I endured through the fog," she murmured now. "I heard your speech and your tears, and it was like a beacon. I could have disappeared through the fog forever, but your voice gave me strength and hope. You saved my life yet again. You were watching over me, my boy from the snow," she murmured. She laid a hand on top of my left hand now, slowly, for it was the side where her shoulder had been injured.

My eyes were locked into hers; my breath kept catching in my throat. I joined my other hand with hers, so that her hand rested in between my fingers.

"You had my cloth," she whispered at last, and though I felt shame that she would remember this foolish moment, my mind was latching on to every word she spoke. "You told me you took it everywhere with you, that it was your most prized possession."

I said nothing to this.

"I do not think I have ever had a loyal guardian as you, or one who should weep so over me," she continued, and then paused, looking at me intently. "You watched over me all night, didn't you?"

"Of course I did." I spoke rapidly again. "How could I have been anywhere else?"

My lady gave a small smile in response, but again I could not make out her full expression. Neither of us said anything for a moment, and it felt as if everything had been turned to stillness. Our conversation could have easily become ordinary again, but she did not look away and neither did I. Now that my heart was vulnerable and she knew of my emotions, I reminded myself again that now was the time, finally, at last, to ask after her heart. I willed myself not to blink, to keep this moment going, for surely if I looked away the moment could be lost. Still gazing upon her face, I reached out and took her hand and bent to kiss it. Not as formal tradition, but out of affection. She did not object; rather, her thumb now grazed over my palm softly.

"Evelyn," I whispered, using her name for the first time. There was no sign of objection in her face, on the contrary, she smiled again. "Ever have I loved you," I told her earnestly now. The words sounded rushed and as folly to my ears, but I needed to speak while I could; at any moment her royal guards could come and the opportunity would be over. "I have loved you ever since I saw you in the snow that day. That day in the snow, I vowed I would always love you and serve you to the best of my ability." I hesitated now, but only for a moment. "If I might be so bold... I wish to enquire after your heart," I concluded.

"Daniel," Evelyn murmured quietly, and then she seemed to wait before saying anything further. She had her head bowed and did not speak for a moment. During the pause in our speech, all was eerily quiet; the gentle swishing of the breeze was the only noise. Then she looked up at me, and I saw a single tear journey down her cheek.

"Of course I love you," she murmured at last. "What caused such a long delay in you asking?"

Joy, unabated, had filled me, however, and for a moment I was quite unable to answer her question. Indeed, I had never known happiness like it – I felt I could barely even speak. Her smile was now as wide as I had ever seen it.

"The timing never seemed right," was all I could think of to say. "It seemed as soon as I became a prince, war threatened to destroy us. It is folly of me, I know," I continued, "but you are a great queen! I never imagined I would ever meet you again, or that I would ever know you, let alone that you would feel something for me..."

"You are a prince of Rheged now. Our match is quite appropriate – I have heard rumours about a union between us across all of Gaeson."

My eyes widened – I had not heard this.

"Besides," she continued, "even if you had remained a soldier all your days, I would have broken tradition and loved you anyway." Her words made my heart sing. "No one has protected me and loved me such as you. My boy from the snow."

My love spoke this last sentence with true warmth and affection. I felt my smile grew wider, my heart glad and full. I heard voices in the distance, and my boldness drew me to impulse.

"I hope this is not too bold, but if you truly do feel the same way…" I lifted myself onto one knee and took her hand. "Evelyn, Queen of Gaeson," I said, hardly daring to believe my own words. "Will you marry me?"

"Yes," she breathed, her reply immediate.

Happiness exploded within me, threatening to possess my soul forever. At once I took her hand again and swiftly kissed it, her palm so soft beneath my mouth. My heart was so full I thought it would burst. Before my courage gave out, I leant forwards. She did also, and our mouths met halfway.

The moment we kissed, my heart threatened to explode out of sheer joy. I had long marvelled at Evelyn's beauty from a distance, content to know I would never hold her. But now, my mouth was on hers, my hands were holding hers. Kissing her was like tasting the best wine, or the purest honey; in truth, it was like the sweetest foods I had ever eaten. Her skin was like the fragrant scent of warm spring, of berries ripening in the sunshine. Kissing her felt like coming home, as if all the questions and struggles about my identity suddenly came into place. Prevalent though these questions were, they seemed to melt away into nothing in comparison to this. It was as if whether I was a poor soldier or a royal prince, it didn't matter. In her arms, whatever else I was, I was hers.

A moment later and our kiss was over. How many feelings, sensations, tastes – and in but a second!

"My heart rejoiced so to see you," she told me now in earnest, her voice as soft as her skin. "Even though I was captured and feared death. Not just because I hoped you would free me. I had felt such despair at the thought of not seeing my boy from the snow again. The thought of not seeing you again…" She trailed off for a moment. "The only other despair I have felt like it was the day you fell from that cliff," she told me now, and my eyes widened.

"When you cut that rope, it cut my heart," she continued. "We returned to Gaeson, and as soon as I was alone in my chambers, I wept for you. We all believed you dead, of course. Then when I saw you walk into the hall... I knew beyond doubt my heart. I knew I loved you," she told me now in hurried breath; the voices were ever near now, but it was safe for the moment, for they had paused again in their journey back. "That moment when I saw you there, in the palace hall in front of my father..." Pain crossed her face at his mention, but she continued regardless. "I felt such relief that you were safe. That's when I knew I loved you, though it seemed such a ridiculous notion – I had known you but a few days! But as soon as I knew you were the boy from the snow, I felt safe with you, more so than with any guard. I felt no harm could come to me, because my boy from the snow was watching over me.

"Then," she continued now, speaking even more swiftly, "when I heard you were a traitor to the crown and to our people, it was as if someone had taken my blade and stabbed me with it, such was the pain I felt. Then the relief to know you truly were for Gaeson and you had not betrayed us..."

"I could never betray Gaeson," I informed her quietly. "I could never betray you. It caused me great pain when you thought I was a traitor."

"I know," she answered. Our eyes were lingering again, and then I leant forwards and our mouths met once more briefly.

We sat with each other for a few minutes more, both of us smiling rather than talking, before we heard footsteps approaching, and looked up to see the guard had returned.

"Your Majesty," the guard greeted her with a bow, and then bowed at me. "Your Highness."

I turned to nod back at him, hiding my foolish grin.

"Alas, a queen cannot sit all day in the grass," she told me with a smile. I got to my feet and took hold of her hand, helping her up. "Farewell, Prince Bryce, for the present."

"Aye, Your Majesty. Farewell, for the present." As I bowed, our hands touched briefly when the guard was not looking. Then I watched as my love went into the castle, the guard by her side.

Scarcely had the guard turned his back when my grin of folly came back.

I felt almost lightheaded as I departed from the gardens and travelled through the castle; truly I thought I perhaps was in some wonderful dream, though my senses told me I was awake. As I was about to ascend the stone steps that would take me to my chamber, I passed a soldier heading my way, and ordered that the soldier to send the message to Aife and John to meet me in my chamber in half an hour.

Before they arrived, I went to Sarah's door, wishing to tell her before I spoke of it to anyone else. She opened the door almost as soon as I had knocked on it.

"Daniel, do come in," she invited airily, with her usual bright countenance. "I heard you were walking with Queen Evelyn. How does she fare?"

"Well," I replied quietly, but my sister did not seem to have noticed the strange, surreal mood I had been in since I had become betrothed. "I have something to tell you, Sarah," I added, and this made her look up. "I bid you come to my chambers. John and Aife are meeting us there soon."

"Very well," Sarah responded, with what seemed to be both a smile and a frown, "though this seems a little strange."

I did not reply to this as we crossed the hall from her chamber into mine, and I closed the door behind us.

"Does this concern Her Majesty?" Sarah asked, perceptive as she was.

"Aye," I answered her, "I have just come from speaking to her in the palace gardens. I asked for her hand in marriage, sister," I declared at last, and I saw shock take her features. "She has accepted me," I added.

"Brother," Sarah said, responding instantly by coming forwards and embracing me, "this is wonderful news. I thought you would never ask her," she added as we came apart again, and then it was my turn to be shocked. "I have long known," she continued, whilst her hand still held mine. "I only discovered it because a few times over the years, when I looked after Enid and your house, I saw that you had an inside pocket in your tunics when it came to washing clothes. For years I thought this was just for some practical reason, but one day I was checking a tunic when I found the cloth inside. I recognised the seal and inscription on it, and began to suspect that you might have some extraordinary devotion to her. I'm truly happy for you," she concluded.

"I see," I answered – her method of discovery seemed so obvious, but I had not thought of it. "It is a little early, but I could do with some mead," I then said.

"Indeed," she replied.

As I went to pour it, I glanced across at Sarah – she was still smiling, but then I saw a shadow had crossed her face. I then saw her attempt to rearrange her features, to pretend there was nothing wrong – but I sensed there was something troubling her.

"Please tell me," I bid her. "If you see a fault with the match, then please tell me. I would wish to know if something upsets you." I handed her some mead as I spoke.

"Very well," she conceded after a moment, and she looked up at me. "I love our queen, as do the rest of our people. In almost every respect, I could not be more delighted. It is only that…" She paused. "In doing this, you are joining us to the family of the one that murdered ours," she said. "I know he is dead, but you are making us son and daughter by marriage to the man who murdered our parents. It will just be difficult, at first, to get used to that fact."

"Of course," I said in realisation, understanding at once. "Forgive me, I've been such a fool," I added, but she shook her head at this. "I have been selfish, not considering things from your perspective."

"No, you have not. She is a good woman and a wise ruler, and there is no shame in your love of her. Besides, Her Majesty is certainly not accountable for any of her father's actions. In fact, you marrying her will be of great help in reconciling our two peoples," Sarah added as an afterthought, and paused here to drink some mead.

I opened my mouth to say more when there came a knock on the door.

"They are early. I am sorry," I said.

Sarah merely gave me a small shake of her head, which I took to mean that it did not matter.

"Come in," was all I said, as I opened the door to them.

"Your Highness," Aife and John chorused as I opened the door.

"We received your message to come here," John added. "I am sorry we have come before our time, but the message sounded rather urgent."

"I am so pleased to see you looking so well, sister," Sarah told Aife earnestly, as she walked right up to her and took her hands in her own.

"I thank you kindly, my lady," Aife replied. "I too am pleased to have recovered."

I looked up from where I had been pouring the mead for us all. "You can both cease to address us formally," I informed them presently. "It is Daniel and Sarah, as it has always been."

I saw both of them smile slightly in agreement. "In that case, I must say that it seems a little early for mead," Aife replied with her usual wit. "It does beg me to wonder at our mysterious summons. Will you tell us what is going on?"

I did not speak for a moment as I set the bottle of mead down.

"You have spoken to her, haven't you?"

I looked up and caught John's eye as he spoke; we exchanged a knowing glance.

"Well, Daniel?" John prompted.

"I have just spoken with Her Majesty," I began. "After a conversation… I asked Her Majesty for her hand in marriage." I saw Aife's countenance in shock. "She said yes," I added hoarsely, for I still felt as though I could not truly believe it.

"I have been waiting to hear such news," Aife replied, as she grinned and came forwards to clasp arms with me briefly.

"Does the whole kingdom know?" I asked bewilderedly, as John laughingly came and embraced me also.

"Only those closest to you, I'm sure," Sarah answered breezily. "Though the news will come as a great shock to Gaeson. It is logical," she continued at my frown, "since you are both unmarried royals of the same age. It is also a strategic match, as it would bind Klumeck and Gaeson together formally."

I hid a frown as she said this, for that was very similar to what she had said to me earlier – but Sarah's countenance was cheerful, betraying nothing of her previous confidence to me about my marriage.

"That is what John said," I agreed at length, when I saw Sarah would not say anything more. Sarah and Aife glanced at him in surprise. "I spoke with him, the day after we brought Queen Evelyn back to Gaeson," I explained. "He had seen my despair at seeing her barely alive. He told me that if she recovered, I should tell her how I felt."

I spent a pleasant hour or two in their company, whilst Sarah looked every bit as jovial as John and Aife – but I could not get her words out of my mind. When I had first discovered what King Reghan had done and had nearly slain him for it, it was then I realised my love for Queen Evelyn was complicated. It was the war with Bernicia, however, that seemed to overshadow her father's recent actions, as Klumeck and Gaeson had fought side by side. Then once I had returned from the war, I was too overwhelmed by desperation that she could die, and then the sweet relief to see she would live.

"You are deep in thought, brother," John commented presently, taking me away from my difficult questions. "Perhaps we should leave you in peace."

"When you told me to ask after her heart, John, that was good advice," I returned, pausing to take another drink of mead. "I am so joyous about the marriage in so many ways. However," I added, and I saw John frown, "I wonder now whether it is for the best, given the kind of man her father was, and what that will mean for Klumeck."

"Is this my doing?" Sarah asked, before John could say anything else. "Daniel, I mean for you to marry her, certainly," she continued quickly. "I only mean that it might be difficult… but that does not mean it would be wrong to do it."

"But I had not considered it from our family's perspective," I explained. "I love Evelyn dearly, but should I marry the daughter of the man who murdered our parents? Should I expect our uncle to be content?"

"Tell him, then," Aife advised. "You are both going to King Owain's coronation tomorrow. You can speak to him of your intentions there. I do not know King Cedric's character well, but I suspect he will not object. He knows Her Majesty is not accountable to her father's actions; she bears no guilt of the crimes he committed. If King Cedric is against it... then you can address that if the time comes."

"I am pleased to have such counsel in you both," I reflected. "Now as much as I would have you stay with me for the rest of the day,'" I added, glancing out in the sky, "the sun is set very low, and the captain will be wondering where you are."

"We had a special message to report to Our Royal Highnesses," John smirked, "such are the privileges of being friends with royalty," he commented, as he quickly finished his mead.

"Careful, John," Sarah warned him. "You have not had much mead, but do not let the captain smell it on your breath."

John only smiled as Aife also finished hers. They then left the chamber and I poured us both another mead.

"The same goes for you as well, brother," she admonished me with a small smile.

"Only a little more," I protested. "Besides, the captain is hardly about to rebuke his prince." I clinked my glass with hers and had another drink. "Sarah, what you said before," I said, and she glanced up at me. "I'm sorry I did not consider it from that perspective. I used to think my love for her had become complicated, but then seeing her almost die and then recover... I almost forgot who her father was," I finished quietly.

"I quite understand," Sarah answered. "Really, I do," she emphasised, for a little scepticism must have shown in my face. "I bid you follow Aife's advice, brother – tell our uncle about all this when you see him next, for he is my greatest concern. If he blesses the match and is as happy for you as I am, then I will be quite content," she concluded.

"Are you sure?" I questioned her, and she nodded and smiled. "Very well," I murmured in assent, thankful that I had such a caring, selfless woman as my sibling.

A little later and I was walking through the streets of Gaeson, this time going to my old house. It was strange to be on that same side street, knowing that my house no longer belonged to me, for I had given it to Rachel and her daughters before embarking for war. It did give me comfort, however, knowing that the house was being well used.

"Your Highness," Rachel greeted me with a smile, bowing low as I opened the door. "I bid you please come in."

"It is wonderful to see you so well, Rachel," I returned as I walked in. I noticed already the rooms were different; on the other side of the door it now looked like a place of trade, where dresses and skirts lay. The eldest was sitting, brow furrowed in concentration while she sewed. "I see you have changed things a little," I commented.

"Aye, my lord prince," Rachel replied. "We turned a chamber upstairs into the living chamber, so that this house combines as home and where we make trade," she explained. "We left Enid's chamber as it is, of course. Your chamber might house a lodger in the future. I hope you do not mind," she added, a frown of concern now upon her countenance.

"Of course not," I answered quickly. "This house is yours now; you are free to do with it whatever you wish. I am pleased to see your trade is doing so well," I added.

"Aye, sire, we seem to be making profit. Part of me felt wrong, attending to the business – we changed things around on the day you left for Bernicia. I knew it was a risk, that if you did not win the war, Gaeson would be in danger. All the other trades had remained open," she continued now, "and my children have to eat."

I saw a shadow cross her face and reasoned she must be thinking of Joshua. Shame burnt my heart that in all that had happened, he had almost been forgotten from my memory – but sometimes the toll of the dead was so high that the individuality of them faded.

"You have acted wisely. I'm sure Joshua would be very proud of what you have achieved," I told her quietly.

Rachel managed to smile, but I saw her eyes well a little.

"I shall visit my mother," I added with a quick nod, desiring to leave her in some peace.

"My lord," she said as I began up the stairs; I turned and looked back. "Thank you," she said, smiling a little. "I fear I will never be able to pay back your great kindness."

"You do not owe me anything," I told her, before going up to my mother's chamber. I saw her eyes alight with gladness as she saw me. I went to her and kissed her forehead gently.

"I have some news for you," I told her, my hand holding hers, "but you must promise to tell no one." I paused but she only nodded, her eyebrows raised expectantly. "Queen Evelyn and I are to be married."

"Oh!" she exclaimed rather loudly, seemingly forgetting my instruction for her to keep quiet about the news. "Sorry," she apologised in a whisper, when I motioned her to lower her voice. "My boy married to a princess! I am so happy for you," she stated, and then she frowned. "What does Sarah think? Might it be a little awkward given your history with King Reghan?"

"You are very perceptive," I replied after a moment. "Sarah seems happy enough for me – she only wishes for me to speak to King Cedric about it. As you know, we are leaving for Caer Ligualid tomorrow, to attend King Owain's coronation. I will speak to my uncle then, and hopefully we can announce the betrothal publicly."

"That seems wise," my mother agreed.

We spoke a little more on that subject and others before I realised it was night and I headed back to the castle. Part of me wanted to speak to Evelyn, but I saw there was the usual guard outside her chamber door, and so I did not wish to risk any of the castle staff guessing today's events.

So it was that three days later, after travelling once more, Evelyn, Sarah and I arrived in Caer Ligualid. It was pleasing indeed to return to the splendid kingdom; I had not been back since I had woken here from falling from the cliff, believing myself to be in Klumeck at the hand of my enemy. It was here when my whole identity and life had changed; on this visit I knew my life could now change again.

The coronation of King Owain was much similar to the ceremony that had marked Evelyn becoming Queen of Gaeson. There were royal duties of greeting the people after the coronation, so I did not manage to speak to my uncle until the banquet. My lady had agreed that we keep our betrothal a secret until I could confide in him; she well understood the need to tell him, lest the marriage would cause him distress.

Presently, I saw my uncle, standing talking to an official who seemed well nourished by mead and wine. It seemed a long conversation, and it was difficult to stand nearby without being persuaded by another to move around the hall and be involved in talk myself.

"Sire," I said at last, coming to stand with him after he had finished speaking with yet another official, and I had escaped a session of introductions to wealthy noble people.

He turned to me and, as always, there was a genuine affection in his countenance. "My boy," he said warmly, clasping my shoulder, his countenance marked with genuine affection and a little merriment caused by the mead he had no doubt drunk. "Are you enjoying the feast? Where is Lynette?"

"We are, Uncle; Sarah is currently with Her Majesty. I wonder if I might speak with you, alone," I added, and I saw him frown in surprise. "I'm sorry if this disturbs you, but I have been waiting to tell you about something. This is the first opportunity I've had."

"How very mysterious. Very well, Bryce – but I detect that we might require more mead for this conversation." He refilled both our goblets before we headed outside.

"Well, what is this about?" he asked, as we stood in one of the little gardens outside the hall.

"I wanted you to know, in case you objected. I care a great deal for Sarah's happiness and yours, and I do not want to cause you distress."

My uncle frowned, but said nothing more as he waited for me to go on.

"I have asked for Queen Evelyn's hand in marriage, Uncle," I told him ere long. "We are betrothed."

King Cedric did not speak for a few moments; he was standing in near darkness, so I could not make out his countenance.

"I see," he said quietly. I saw his shadow turn away slightly as he now raised his glass and took a long drink of his mead. "I had suspected this," he continued. "The way you spoke of her even weeks ago, when you were so sure Queen Evelyn would not follow in her father's footsteps and betray King Urien… I perceived even then the loyalty you had towards her to be far more than that of any ordinary soldier." He said nothing more for a moment.

"What do you say of it?" I asked him presently, unable to bear the silence any longer. "I have always loved her, Uncle," I told him, "long before I knew her father's true character." At the mention of King Reghan, I noticed his posture stiffened. "It would truly unite Gaeson and Klumeck," I pressed on. "It would help our two peoples to develop their peace towards one another. If I simply used reason," I continued, "then my mind would tell me it would be ridiculous to marry the daughter of the man who murdered my parents. That it would be too foolish for words to become related by marriage to her, when her father killed most of our family and separated me and Sarah from you. But I love her," I declared.

"Aye," he murmured, taking another drink of his mead. "Tell me one thing, nephew," my uncle asked presently. He stepped forwards to where his features were illuminated by the light of the palace hall. His features were sad, but I saw nothing else that could reveal his thoughts. "Does she feel the same about you?"

"Yes," I replied immediately – and the thought of her love for me caused me to smile, unbidden, despite the severity of the talk with my uncle.

"Then you have my blessing, if that is what you wish for," King Cedric told me. My eyes roved up to his and he smiled. "The match is well suited, and you are right in the advantage it would bring both our kingdoms. I imagine half of our kingdoms will expect it already. More than that, though," he added, stepping closer to me so I could make out the intensity of his expression, "she is a strong, kind woman with both great wisdom and great heart. I admire her, in fact, that she was raised by such a tyrant, but that her own character is marked by such beauty and good. Evelyn of Gaeson is not her father," he concluded, "so though I despise what her father did whilst he was on the earth, I could only hold that against her as much as I can blame the clouds for the rain."

"Uncle," I responded after a moment, "thank you."

He gave me a swift nod, stretched out his arm and clasped it with mine. Relief coursed my soul as we stood there outside the palace hall, and I knew instinctively that my uncle would be the finest king and the finest man I would ever know.

***

As soon as we were back but two days later, Evelyn and I announced the betrothal and began to prepare our wedding. All the citizens of Gaeson were thrilled. I realised Sarah and my uncle had been correct – none of them seemed particularly surprised. Time continued to speed by until suddenly it was the morning of the wedding. It was twenty-seven days since I had arrived back from Gaeson; it being a month since I proposed, both of us having wanted a short engagement. It was now three months since I had awoken with thirst, when King Cedric had marched his army, long before I knew he was my uncle.

Evelyn and I had said farewell to one another the eve before; I would now not see her until we were about to be wed. It surprised me slightly that the day had dawned like any other. I had expected the world to feel slightly different, for my life was so soon about to change – but nothing appeared out of place.

"Stop pacing, brother." John grinned at me, turning around to look at me. "All will be well. We shall be going in soon."

I nodded, attempting a smile, which may have turned out as more of a grimace. He merely laughed and clapped a hand on my shoulder. We were standing in the wooden church building placed halfway up the hill between the castle and the town. He turned back around to his position. He was standing in front of me as my chosen groomsman, bearing my ancestral sword. I would give the sword to Evelyn during the ceremony, as was the custom of our people.

Suddenly, the knock came on the door, signalling we could go into the main room of the church building. I took a deep breath as John opened the door and we walked through.

As I had expected, the first person I saw, in my direct line of sight but across on the other side of the room, was Evelyn. She had walked in with groomsmen behind her. The sight of her took my breath away. Although she always looked beautiful, somehow today she appeared more so than ever. Her lovely, dark hair hung loose, apart from a rope of her hair that was braided round the front of her head; this was intertwined with small, white flowers. She wore white beads around her wrist and neck, and all this matched her dress, which was long, white silk. She was altogether radiant, and my heart beat so loud I was sure John could hear it.

We walked forwards towards each other, as was tradition – me with John in front of me, and Evelyn with the groomsman. John carried my sword in front of him, and Evelyn's groomsman bore a cup of mead that I would drink during the ceremony.

I walked with halted breath as Evelyn walked the same time as me, until we came to a stop a foot apart. The priest, who would lead the ceremony, stood in front of us. The church building was full of people from Gaeson, Klumeck, and Caer Ligualid. At the front, not so far from us, stood the royals who were witnessing our marriage – Sarah, King Cedric, and King Owain. People were waving flags from all three kingdoms, and it brought such comfort to see all of Rheged united in this way.

The ceremony began with the priest saying a few words about the seriousness and the sacredness of the sacrament we were about to undertake. After the priest had prayed for us both, we then began to say our vows to each other.

"I, Bryce, Prince of Klumeck and royal of Rheged, do take you, Evelyn, Queen of Gaeson and royal of Rheged, to be my beloved wife," I declared to her in the presence of all the people. "I pledge my love to you and everything that I own. I promise you the first bite of my meat and the first sip of my cup," I continued, thankfully remembering all the words I had trained myself to remember. "I promise I will honour your name above others, and that our love is never-ending." I paused here and smiled at her; she returned my smile. "This is my wedding vow to you; my prayer is that I will keep it and forever cherish it, all the days of my life, so help me God," I concluded.

"I, Evelyn, Queen of Gaeson," Evelyn began in turn, "receive you, Bryce, Prince of Klumeck and royal of Rheged, to be my beloved husband." Her voice was clear and strong. "I promise you the first bite of my meat and the first sip of my cup. I promise I will honour your name above others, and that our love is never-ending." She smiled here as I had; I returned the gesture as she had done. "This is my wedding vow to you; my prayer is that I will keep it and forever cherish it, all the days of my life, so help me God," she finished.

"May we have the rings?" the priest asked now. John handed me the ring to place on Evelyn's finger. The ceremony seemed incredibly fast, but I was glad of this.

"Evelyn, I take you my heart, by the rising of the moon and the setting of the stars, to which God alone ordains. I give you this ring in His name as a sign of the covenant we have promised each other in His presence, and to love and to honour you through all that may come." I slid the ring onto her finger, which to my relief fitted without a struggle. She then held out the ring she would give to me.

"Bryce, I take you my heart, by the rising of the moon and the setting of the stars, to which God alone ordains. I give you this ring in His name as a sign of the covenant we have promised each other in His presence, and to love and to honour you through all that may come." Mine, too, fitted with ease.

John then stepped forwards and placed the ancestral sword in my hand; once I was holding it, I stretched the hilt out to her.

"Evelyn, Queen of Gaeson and royal of Rheged, I give you this sword to save for our sons to have and use," I promised her.

Evelyn took my sword and placed it in front of her with both hands on the handle, so that the blade touched the floor lightly. She then gave it to the groomsmen, while he passed her the cup of mead that she would give to me.

"I name you, Bryce, Prince of Klumeck and royal of Rheged, that you shall be my husband from this day forth. I bid you, then, husband, do take a drink of this cup," she said.

Smiling, I took it from her and drank. John took back the bowl and we glanced once more at the priest; it was now time for the handfasting, and he now picked up a long piece of white cloth from the table as Evelyn and I joined hands.

"We bear witness today to this union under God, of Her Majesty Queen Evelyn of Gaeson, royal of Rheged and His Royal Highness Prince Bryce of Klumeck and royal of Rheged," he stated. As he spoke, he wrapped the cloth round our joined hands, but I almost paid it no heed, for I was looking intently at Evelyn. The priest began to make a loop out of the cloth, in order to tie a knot. Once he had this ready, he laid his other hand on top of ours.

"I declare to you, in the sight of these witnesses and in the sight of God, that you are husband and wife," the priest said. He then pulled the cloth so it tightened the knot around our wrists. "Let what He has joined together, no man break apart," he concluded.

"Amen," Evelyn and I murmured together. My heart was overflowing with joy; I could hardly believe I was married to the one I had loved for so long.

"Your Highness," he added, in a less formal tone, "you may greet your bride."

Full of joy and elation, I leaned forwards and kissed Evelyn.

As our mouths met and we kissed briefly, there was an explosion of noise, so much I thought it could have been thunder – but the day was fine, finer than I ever could have imagined. When I opened my eyes again I saw it was the people who had made such noise, giving loud applause, and the church building amplifying the volume. The ceremony was now over, and the priest quickly untied our hands. I held out my arm and Evelyn took it. The two of us now left, down the middle of the church building, in contrast to where we had walked in through the separate doors. This symbolised our new union; we had entered the building separate and now we were leaving together as husband and wife.

We left the church building and stepped out onto the street, where it seemed the whole of Gaeson and Klumeck had gathered to meet us, minus those amassed in the church. There was applause, cheers – I could even hear a few screams. We smiled and waved before turning to the carriage that would take us around Gaeson before we arrived back at the palace hall to stand in the royal balcony for the first time together as man and wife.

The carriage was white and ornately decorated; not since King Owain's coronation had I travelled in anything so fine. It pleased me greatly to see Epos as one of the horses in front; I paused to greet her briefly. I then stepped into the carriage first and then held out my hand to my new wife, who smiled and took it as she followed me into the carriage. We sat down together, and as the carriage started to ride off, Evelyn turned to me.

"So," she commented, "I was to marry my boy from the snow." She held up her hand now, and it came to rest on my cheek; instinctively I turned my face towards her touch, my lips brushing the palm of her hand briefly. "Husband," she greeted me, her beautiful eyes sparkling with affection.

My mouth stretched into a large smile. "Wife," I returned in kind, utterly delighted to be able to call her that. The windows of the carriage were open, and I presently turned to look out of them; the crowds were following us, cheering and waving as we rode through the streets. In the carriage behind us sat King Owain, and in the carriage before that was my uncle and Sarah, thus making the royal procession. Both of us now lifted our hands to wave at the people.

Once we entered the castle itself, the noise lessened – at one point it had almost been deafening. We dismounted the carriages and she grinned at me in elation and relief – the same emotions I was feeling. We went right to the end of the palace hall, and I perceived there to be another chair next to Evelyn's throne, made of the same scarlet furnishings and ever so slightly smaller.

"That chair has been locked away since the day my mother died," Evelyn told me presently. "It is the chair for the husband or wife of the ruler of Gaeson. My father never married again, so no doubt they will have cleaned it well since they heard of our betrothal. It is good to see it in its proper place once more," she commented.

"I agree," I murmured.

We turned and saw the palace hall was now crowded and the noise had escalated once more. As I surveyed them all, my eyes suddenly widened in delight as I caught sight of my mother, leaning heavily on Rachel's arm, sitting on a chair that had been provided for her. It brought me further delight to see her there, on my wedding day.

The din quietened considerably now as King Owain now entered the room, followed by King Cedric and Sarah. Evelyn and I then bowed low to King Owain, to show our obedience to him as the supreme ruler of Rheged. King Owain bent his head to us briefly, and then walked over to the steps to the balcony. We repeated this with King Cedric and Sarah before Evelyn walked up to her throne and sat upon it. Before I joined her, I turned to her and sank into a bow before her; she was now my wife, but she was also still my queen. Evelyn bent her head, and I then straightened, went to my own throne and sat down upon it, reaching for my wife's hand as I did so.

The crowd gave way to cheers again to see us sat as husband and wife together with our joined hands. I glanced meaningfully across at King Cedric and Sarah, wondering if they truly were without objection to our marriage, but happiness was the only thing I could see in their countenances, and I hoped their expressions reflected their hearts.

Still holding Evelyn's hand, I stood, and we walked together to the steps by the balcony. We ascended them first, followed by King Owain, King Cedric and Sarah. The crowd outside was vast, filling every inch of the square, and the five of us waved and greeted them. Then, after a moment, I turned to Evelyn and kissed her, and the crowd shouted all the more. My eyes settled on hers, and it sank in again that here was my wife. She had married me, her boy from the snow.

Suddenly, the crowd seemed to melt away, loud as they were. All I knew was Evelyn – that I was hers and she was mine. In these last three months, in the battles and the change in my identity, I had felt adrift. As I looked at her, though, I realised God had always intended I marry her. I knew that in her arms, the boy from the snow had come home at last.